SECOND SIGHT

BY

PAULA NEWCOMBE

SECOND SIGHT

First printing August 2008

Copyright © Paula Newcombe 2008

SECOND SIGHT

ISBN-10: 0-9552315-4-X
ISBN-13: 978-0-9552315-4-4

All rights reserved, including the right to reproduce this book, or any portions thereof, in any form.

All characters in this book are fictitious. Any resemblance to actual persons, living or dead, is purely coincidental.

Printed and bound by
IPS Print Management
59 Winchester Road, Countesthorpe, Leicester, LE8 5PN

NEW WRITERS UK BOOKS

Published and Distributed by DSC Publications
20 Wreake Drive, Rearsby, Leicester, LE7 4YZ, England

SECOND SIGHT

I would like to thank, Dragonstail Designs, Jo Field and Helen Hollick for their hard work and advice in making this book happen.

SECOND SIGHT

SECOND SIGHT

CHAPTER ONE

Sarah heard a distant voice. It sounded familiar. She was trembling violently; her whole body shaking. She could feel the cold, hard bathroom floor tiles beneath her. The voice came nearer and the door was flung open. She whimpered, cringed, her eyes tight shut, afraid to look.

"Baby, are you alright?"

Weak with relief she recognised the voice as her husband's. In two strides he had reached her and was kneeling beside her petite frame. "Adam," she murmured, clinging to him tightly, finding the courage to open her eyes.

"Hush baby, I'm here. It's ok, everything's alright now." But his expression said it was far from alright. He was eyeing her intently looking for signs of injury. She was lying next to their bath, her T-shirt was wet through and she could not stop sobbing. Tears streamed down her face, but there was no blood, no bruising.

"Tell me," he said, holding her as if he dared not let her go until her sobs had subsided and she had calmed down. "Tell me what's wrong. Has someone hurt you? Has something happened? Please tell me," he coaxed again. He scanned the bathroom, but Sarah knew there was nothing to see. Would he think she was just being hysterical – put it down to the time of the month? They had not been married long, had only moved into this house yesterday.

"It was awful," she whispered, still clinging to him as if to let go she would drown. "The bath was full of blood!" Her voice rose almost to a scream, the words falling out of her mouth in a rush, her face taut with fear.

Adam's expression cleared. He unwound her arms from his neck, looked down at her and smiled. She could see him thinking, *so that's what it's all about - a bad dream*. Was that it? Had she fallen asleep, had a nightmare and sleepwalked into the bathroom?

"You've had a bad dream, darling," he smiled, echoing her thoughts. "Look, there's nothing in the bath. It's all nice and clean."

Sarah risked a nervous glance. The bath was white and shining. Clean. Empty. She could smell the bleach. The bathroom was now extremely warm, everywhere bright in the hot afternoon sun. It had not been like that before. The house had been cold, so very cold and the bath had been full of water. Sarah looked up at the mirror on the wall; it had been steamed up. She remembered that she had gone to it, wiped away the condensation and… and…

She buried her face in Adam's shoulder seeing it all again in her mind's eye; her face staring back at her, and someone else – the back of someone's head, someone with jet black hair behind her own blonde mane. Sarah gasped as the memory flooded back. And the bath! The water had been red, red with blood; red with the blood of the severed limbs floating on the surface!

Sarah felt the gorge rising in her throat, wanted to be sick; wanted to say: *Adam! There was ice cold air blowing from somewhere, and someone else was in here; here in the bathroom*, but even as the words hovered on her lips, she realised there had to be a rational explanation. Adam must be right. It had to be a dream; nothing more than a bad dream. She shook her head in an effort to clear the images still so vividly imprinted on her brain.

Adam smiled and squeezed her hand, reassuringly. "The house looks great. You must have been working hard all day."

She felt silly now, embarrassed. "Perhaps I did overdo it a little. I expect that's why I passed out."

"You gave me a real shock when I saw you lying on the floor," Adam grinned sheepishly. "I thought you'd had a heart attack or something."

Sarah returned his smile as he helped her to her feet and with his arm firmly round her waist guided her downstairs, through their living room and out of the French doors onto the patio, which was bathed in sunshine.

"You sit here," he said, "I'll make a pot of tea and put the rest of the pictures up later, you just relax."

Sarah did as she was bid and closed her eyes. Out here in the sun, already she was beginning to relax, the ghastly memory fading. She pictured instead her husband's easy smile. Tall and muscular, he had a rugged, handsome face and square jaw, yet was a gentle, well-mannered man who had always made an effort to get on well with her friends and family. No wonder she loved him so.

The house, Sarah decided the next afternoon, could wait to be tidied, the sun was too glorious to miss and the garden in too much need of attention. She wanted to cut the lawns; the grass both back and front was ankle high; the roses ready for deadheading and several beds were sprouting weeds.

After almost three hours of hard work Sarah smiled with satisfaction; not quite *Homes & Gardens*, but looking very much better. Maybe, now this was done, she and Adam could go to the pictures tonight and make the most of their evening together. She sat and rested for a while on the ornate bench that had been one of their wedding gifts, feeling lucky, happy with her new husband, new home; new life. She closed her eyes and settled down contentedly to work on her suntan. The air was heavy, very still and quiet. Most of the neighbours were out – at work or on holiday, she presumed. She had not met them all yet – aside from Sophie across the road, who seemed a bit of a livewire, but very nice.

Disturbed by a wasp buzzing around her head, Sarah irritably brushed it away. As she looked up at the house, a movement caught her attention. A figure stood at her bedroom window – stood there for a few seconds and then disappeared.

Sarah froze, memories of yesterday's horrific nightmare suddenly flooding back. The front door was locked and so was the gate that led to the back garden. No one would be able to get in - except Adam. Of course; Adam! Air puffed from her cheeks. Here she was being silly again. He'd said he would be home early.

Shielding her eyes from the sun, Sarah pushed herself off the bench and peered up at the window as she strolled towards the house, letting herself in by the back door. That was odd, it was still locked. "Ad?" she called. "Adam? Is that you?"

As she walked into the utility room she heard footsteps crossing the landing. She grinned, felt foolish again. Her husband sounded like an elephant – she had told him so, many times. She checked her face in the mirror, her cheeks were bright red and peppered with freckles. She had forgotten to put on any sun lotion. She wiped the smears of mud off her nose and smiled at her reflection, her blue, almond-shaped eyes were clear, her skin was glowing, devoid of any makeup; her lips were full, teeth very white and straight. She did not look too bad considering how hard she had been working in the garden.

In the kitchen, she put the kettle on, called out to Adam; did he want tea or coffee? He obviously had not heard her. She picked up a pile of ironing and took it upstairs. At least her new husband could not accuse her of being lazy. She shivered; it felt cold after the warmth of the garden. "Where are you, Ad? Rather take a shower than say 'Hi' to your lovely wife, eh?" Laughing, Sarah pushed open their bedroom door.

She stopped dead; dropped the ironing; stifled a scream.

A tall man with jet black hair stood at the bay window, his back to her.

Frozen to the spot, Sarah tried desperately to think of a weapon she could use to defend herself. Where was her mobile? She remembered it was in her handbag downstairs. Slowly, she backed away. The man continued to stare out of the window as if unaware of her presence.

Who was he? And what the hell was he doing in her bedroom? Anger suddenly overcame her fear. Disregarding her safety, she cried out, "Who are you? What are you doing here? I'm going to call the police right now!" She went towards him, intending to do what? She did not know; grab his arm? Make him leave? She was beyond rational thought, shaking with indignation.

He swung round and for the first time she saw his face. She stopped in surprise. He was younger than she had first thought, maybe in his early twenties, good looking with piercing blue eyes, the black hair long and swept back from his face. His fists were clenched and she could see that he was angry.

Suddenly, without warning he rushed towards her. Sarah gasped, raised her hands to shield herself; waited for the attack. Felt nothing but a rush of cold air. She spun round, but he was gone. She shuddered. It was as if he had passed right through her and vanished. There was no one there; nothing. She rushed to the door. There was no one on the landing, no one on the stairs. She turned back to the window and looked down into the garden, but there was nothing to see.

Sarah stumbled onto the bed and for a few moments sat on the edge shaking, her mind and body numb. Had she imagined it? Was she still sleepwalking? Something terrible was happening to her. Was she going mad?

She started to shiver uncontrollably, tears spilling onto her cheeks. Had she seen a ghost? Was it possible? He had looked strangely old-fashioned. His suit was a bit like one her Dad used to wear and the tie – was that what they called a kipper tie? Sarah shook her head, wiped her tears away with the back of her hand. It wasn't right. She couldn't have seen a ghost. Their house was too modern. Ghosts only appeared in really old houses didn't they? And besides, he had not *looked* as she imagined a ghost would look: he had been solid; *real*. Sarah knew she was wide awake. She had not been dreaming; she knew she had just seen this man.

Slowly, cautiously, she went downstairs. No ghosts. Sarah took some deep breaths and tried to pull herself together. Everything looked normal. She switched the kettle back on, watched it boil; made a cup of tea. She never had sugar in her tea as a rule, but deciding she needed the sweetness for the shock, she ladled in a heaped teaspoon and stirred it vigorously. Sitting on a stool at the breakfast bar, she sipped the hot, sweet liquid and tried to convince herself that she had been hallucinating, but the more she tried, the more she was convinced that it had actually happened. She thought back to the bathroom nightmare. Had that been real too? She was certain it was the same man she had seen in the bathroom mirror. Was their house haunted after all? Who was he? If he was a ghost he must have died at some point. How did it happen? Was it a tragic accident? Was that why he had seemed so angry?

Trying to think rationally, Sarah took a grip on her emotions, concluded that she would have to do some research on the house. Try to find out if any awful traumas had happened here. Finishing her tea, she glanced at the clock. Adam would be home soon. What was she going to tell him? She sat for a long while, her arms wrapped around herself, gently rocking to and fro. Should she tell Adam what she'd seen? Could she? Tell him she had seen a ghost? That their new house was haunted?

She gave a hollow laugh. What? And make him think she was insane?

CHAPTER TWO

Sarah returned to work after the weekend and found her morning schedule was busy enough for most of the time to keep her mind off the terrible visions she had seen – that is, until she went to make her first coffee of the day. As she waited for the kettle to boil her mind wandered to the young, dark-haired man in her bedroom, convinced now that she had seen a ghost. She had never experienced anything like it before. He had seemed so angry and so real. Sarah shuddered as she recalled his face; the way he had charged towards her with a look of pure hatred, as though he had wanted to kill her. Yet she did not recognise him; had never seen him before. What had she done to upset him so much? Sarah's hand shook as she picked up her coffee mug. She had not been able to eat or sleep properly since it happened and knew she had dark circles round her eyes. She was frightened, unable to get him out of her mind; her biggest fear was that he – it – would return.

Sarah's team was involved in many new I.T. projects and these, together with chairing meetings for various local government departments, were making her working days longer and longer. It was after six, a few evenings after she had seen the ghost, when Sarah decided to call it a day. She was just in the process of saving her work and closing down the computer when Susan, her friend from the accountancy section, strolled into her office.

"Hi Sarah – how's it going?"

Susan was the only person Sarah had told about the ghost and the nightmare in the bathroom: she'd *had* to tell someone. She was regretting it now; not that it mattered if Susan thought she was a mental case, but she was not in the right frame of mind to be teased.

"Not too bad," Sarah gave an exaggerated sigh. "I do so wish other departments would let us know in the beginning what they actually *want* from a Financial Management System, not wait until the Implementation's already taken place."

Susan smiled sympathetically. "I know what you mean. People always moan when it's too late. Still, I heard you might be in line for the Service Manager's job so you must have impressed somebody."

"Well I'm not counting my chickens. The interview process will be very tough and Steve from Financial Planning is a very strong candidate." Sarah shrugged, attempting to sound nonchalant. She had tried not to think about the job. There were a few other people equally qualified and with more managerial experience than she who would surely apply for it.

Susan looked thoughtful for a few moments, twirling her auburn curls around her fingers. Then, giving her friend a big grin, she slumped onto the chair beside Sarah's desk.

"What?" Sarah said, wondering what was coming.

"I've been thinking. How do you fancy coming to see a medium with me? I've heard this woman's very good. My cousin Sally recommended her to me - you remember Sally? She went on a few girlie nights out with us?"

'How could I forget?' Sarah shot Susan a wry smile. No one could forget Sally; she was a slip of a girl, barely five-foot-two, yet she had drunk everyone under the table.

"Well, she went to see this medium six months ago," Susan continued, "and everything the woman said came true!"

Conjuring up an image of a wizened, shawl-clad gypsy reading tea leaves, Sarah, who was more than a little sceptical about such things, raised her eyebrows in disbelief.

'No, really," Susan said. "Lola – that's the medium's name - told Sally she would come into some money, get the job of her dreams and meet someone special before this year ended, and that's exactly what has happened."

"It could all just be coincidence."

"Yes, it could, but Lola was so accurate with details of Sally's past, her personality, likes and dislikes, even her star sign."

Sarah laughed, "Come off it; it's not difficult to find these things out you know and these so-called psychics are very clever at reading people's responses. It only takes one or two accurate guesses."

"Ok, so you don't believe in it, but listen to this," Susan sat forward on the edge of her chair, her eyes brimming with excitement. "Just after her reading, Sally came into some inheritance from a distant relative. She finished university at the end of May, managed to get her ideal job as a primary school teacher, starting in September, and six weeks ago she met this guy called Patrick and fell madly in love. They're even talking about getting engaged at Christmas. So how about that then, you old cynic," Susan grinned.

Despite her scepticism Sarah was impressed, "Not bad," she smiled.

"The thing is," Susan went on, "I'd booked an appointment for myself and an old schoolfriend on Thursday evening, but my friend can't make it. I was wondering if you'd like to come with me instead."

"That's very kind of you, Susan, but-"

"Oh go on Sarah, it's just a bit of fun. Besides you never know, this Lola might be able to explain why you had that awful vision, not to mention the gorgeous ghost." Susan laughed, "It isn't everyone has Brad Pitt materializing in her bedroom you know."

"If only!" Sarah smiled at her friend's enthusiasm. "Ok, you've persuaded me. What time on Thursday?"

"Six; is that ok? We could go straight from work."

"Fine; count me in."

Susan jumped up and flashed a beaming smile. "Great. You won't regret this."

After Susan had gone, Sarah sat for a moment, thinking about what her friend had said. Was this medium of Susan's really genuine? She would love to hear a few things about her future and more importantly, maybe the medium *could* throw some light on the terrifying things she had seen, or at least tell her why the ghost had appeared only to her and not to Adam..

Despite her best efforts to put it out of her mind, Sarah's fear had persisted. She had become increasingly convinced that the ghost's materialisation was a sign that something awful was about to happen to her. Every day she thought about the man she had seen and worried that he was going to return. She dreaded being alone in the house, and what was worse, she still felt unable to confide in her husband. Sarah was sure Adam must have sensed how tense she had become, but he had said nothing so far, beyond comments that she looked tired and must be working too hard; comments she had tried to laugh off.

Packing up her briefcase to go home, Sarah was suddenly overwhelmed with nausea. She rushed along the corridor to the cloakroom and threw up most of her lunch. Afterwards, her face streaming with tears, she looked at herself in the mirror over the sink. She could not go on like this. What was she going to do?

Clearing up her desk at the end of another day and wishing she had not agreed to go with Susan to see the medium, Sarah emptied a plastic cup of filtered water onto the plants on her window sill, logged off from her computer and packed her case. Realisation dawned that she was the last one left on her floor. The building was a typical 1960's office block – lots of concrete and glass – and not particularly attractive. Sarah decided to take the stairs rather than the lift. Everywhere seemed so quiet – almost eerie. She ran down the stairs quickly; was glad to get outside into the car park and the evening sunshine. She did not want to be alone at all.

She had not mentioned the medium to Adam; he always saw everything in black and white. He would tease her; might even be annoyed. She remembered a documentary they had watched one time about the paranormal. She had been fascinated, but Adam had said there was a practical explanation for everything and people who visited a psychic or medium to see what the future held were weak and gullible and needed their heads examined. No; she would not mention Lola to Adam!

After they had eaten that evening, Sarah stretched lazily on their new cream-leather sofa, a glass of wine in her hand. Peering intently at the crystal cut glass she was aware that lately, alcohol was the only thing that seemed to help her to relax. She glanced around the living room. The new paintwork smelled fresh and clean; the beech units and cream-coloured walls made the room look quite trendy and the woven, brightly coloured rug in front of the plasma fire looked really great. Adam certainly had a flair for interior design.

"I love what you've done in here, Ad. This house is really beginning to feel like home. I'm glad we chose this furniture and the new blinds make it seem quite modern don't you think?"

"Yes, I'm certainly happy with it." Adam set down his glass, reached for the bottle on the glass-topped side table. "By the way, when did you take up painting again?"

Sarah shot him a quizzical smile. "Eh? I didn't know I had." She had been a keen painter before she met Adam and had attended various art classes at a local college, but had not picked up a brush for some while.

Adam topped up her glass. "Surely you can't have forgotten? The painting was on my workbench when I went in for the drill this morning."

"In the shed?"

Adam looked bemused. "Of course in the shed!"

"How strange. My paints and brushes are on top of the wardrobe. I haven't touched them for ages. The one you found must have fallen out of a packing case. Perhaps one of the removal men put it there?"

"Oh? I assumed you'd done it recently. It looked quite fresh. I brought it back to the house; it's very good – I thought we could hang it in here, maybe?"

Sarah sipped her wine, which was spreading a warm feeling through her body. "Where is it now?"

"I put it in the utility room in case it got damp in the shed."

"Just as likely to get damp in there I would have thought," Sarah said quietly, as Adam jumped off his recliner and strode from the room. A moment later he was back carrying the picture, which he carefully handed to her.

He was right, the painting seemed quite fresh; the colours bright. It depicted a young woman sitting in a garden. She looked to be about eighteen, was wearing a flared, blue skirt and white blouse. She was very pretty with long, blonde hair that was thick and curly. Her features were quite small and her lips shiny as though wet and catching the light. Sarah studied the painting carefully, struck by the subject's eyes which, even though she was smiling, seemed sad. The girl was a complete stranger and resembled nobody she knew. Sarah looked up at her husband. "I didn't paint this – I'm not that good. I wonder who she is – and where it came from."

"Must belong to the Palmers," Adam shrugged. "They left a couple of boxes behind. Could be a relative of theirs and-"

"Of course!" Sarah interrupted. "Didn't Mrs Palmer say she was a teacher? Maybe her subject is art? It looks as if this girl is sitting in our garden too; I recognise the fence and the plants behind, though it must be depicting it as it was a few years ago - the shrubs are all so small." Sarah stifled a yawn and drained her glass. The wine had made her feel sleepy.

Adam grinned, put his arm around her. "Come on sleepy head. Let's get you to bed before you doze off on me."

Moments after her head hit the pillow Sarah fell into a deep sleep and began to dream about the girl in the painting. She was sitting not in the garden, but on a chair in their living room. She was sobbing uncontrollably, shaking in fear, her eyes wide and pleading. She seemed to be reaching out to Sarah and begging for help. Her words became clearer and clearer: *I made a mistake, I made a mistake.*

Seething with frustration, Sarah stretched out her arms to the girl knowing she had to help her before it was too late, but she could not move from the spot. Something was stopping her; an invisible barrier. The girl covered her face with her hands, flung back her head and suddenly there was blood everywhere. Sarah could no longer distinguish the girl's features; her face was just a mass of red - and then the screaming started.

"Wake up, wake up. It's ok – a bad dream."

Adam was shaking her gently. Sarah woke, totally disoriented and frightened – so very frightened. Her husband switched on the bedside lamp and hugged her tightly. Realising she had just had another nightmare Sarah fought back the urge to cry. It had been so vivid. What was wrong with her? Why had she had such a terrible dream and what was causing her to be so scared? Nightmares had never been a problem before, but this was a particularly bad one. What was it about this house that was so affecting her? She started to wonder about her state of mind. Seeing ghosts and having a nightmare about a young girl being brutally murdered. Was this the first sign of madness? Nothing had ever happened to her like this before. Trembling, Sarah became aware that she was sweating profusely, unbelievably hot. She threw back the covers.

"Are you ok – do you want a drink?" Adam asked.

Sarah nodded and tried to stay calm. "I'm fine, sorry, bad dream about that picture. Feel a bit hot."

'Hang on. I'll get you some mineral water.' Adam, looking very concerned, rushed downstairs.

Feeling as though she was on fire, Sarah went into the bathroom, ran the cold tap on her flannel and slowly wiped her face and body. By the time Adam came back carrying two large glasses of ice-cold bubbling water, she felt more comfortable.

"Here you go, how are you feeling now?"

Sarah took a few sips before replying. What she actually felt was tormented and all she wanted to do was to run; get away from this house, but she could not tell Adam that, he would not understand. Might think she was going crazy. She forced a weak smile, "Much better thanks, darling, sorry for waking you up. Must have been the cheese I had for supper."

Adam grinned, put his arm around her. "You don't have to scream to get attention you know." He pointed towards their window, which was slightly open. "It'll have the neighbours talking anyway – mind you; it'll do wonders for my reputation!"

Sarah faked a laugh. She could not go on like this, she thought desperately. Tomorrow was Thursday. Hoping and praying that the medium would be able to help her or at least reassure her that it was just a passing phase, Sarah tried to get back to sleep. But deep down she knew it was not a phase at all and that something terrible was happening to her.

CHAPTER THREE

On the day they were to visit the medium, Sarah and her friend had agreed they would finish work early and grab something to eat on the way over to Lola's house. Susan had logged onto the Internet to get proper directions. It turned out to be only six miles from where Sarah lived so it did not take them long to find it and they arrived outside the medium's modern, detached house with plenty of time to spare.

"Well, the house looks pretty ordinary," Sarah smiled at her friend.

"Yes, how disappointing. I was expecting something a little different, maybe a bit dark and spooky."

They were shown into a large conservatory at the back of the house by Louisa, who introduced herself as Lola's secretary. The interior of the house was furnished as a comfortable family home; the walls hung with family photographs – or so Sarah assumed. The conservatory contained some expensive looking furniture and ornaments: clearly the woman's business was doing well. Impressed, Susan picked up some leaflets from the coffee table and sat down in a heavily padded cane chair.

"It says here that she also does ghost walks," Sarah whispered to Susan as Louisa, having offered them both a cup of tea, left them on their own to wait.

Susan raised her eye brows. "Are you getting nervous?"

"Yes I am. It feels as though we're about to take an exam. I keep wondering what the future holds and whether I'll like what the medium tells me."

Susan reached out and gave Sarah's hand a quick squeeze. 'Don't worry. Sally said that even if Lola does foresee something awful she won't tell people anything really bad."

Sarah knew her friend was trying to reassure her, but it didn't help. She felt stressed; what if the medium thought the nightmares were an evil portent; that something terrible was about to happen to her? Everything had been really good before they moved into their new house in Bluebell Close, but Adam had thought it was perfect for them and Sarah, anxious to please, had said she loved it too. It was no hardship; she loved the garden, the surrounding countryside was beautiful and the house spacious and airy. At the time, neither of them had harboured any doubts about the move, but Sarah was now beginning to wonder if it had been a dreadful mistake. Supposing Lola did give her bad news, what could she do about it? No prizes for guessing what Adam would say! Sarah looked nervously at the leaflet in her hand, skimming over the words but not taking them in. She had come prepared to enjoy this whole experience, but despite trying to remain positive, doubts kept popping into her mind. Was this the right thing to do, would the reading make matters worse or would Lola be able to help?

"I'm sure we will both have good readings," Susan echoed Sarah's thoughts. "One thing though, I meant to warn you and forgot: don't tell any little white lies just to check how accurate Lola is. She'll know if you do. Sally said it was uncanny what she knew."

Sarah sat upright, indignant. "I wasn't planning to!" Not quite true; she had thought about taking off her wedding ring to see if Lola was able to tell if she was married.

At that point Louisa came back with a tea tray loaded with porcelain cups and saucers and a plate of digestive biscuits, placed it on the coffee table and asked them to help themselves. The time seemed to pass very quickly and before they had finished their cups of tea she returned to tell them Lola was ready.

"Who is going first?"

Susan looked directly at Sarah. "You go first."

Sarah felt the ball of tension tighten in her stomach as she followed Louisa out of the conservatory and into a hall. The medium was waiting at the bottom of the stairs. She was quite tall, Sarah guessed in her early forties, with dark, straight hair cut into a bob. Her face was attractive and friendly. The wide smile seemed genuine and Sarah immediately felt more at ease.

"Hello Sarah – I'm Lola. How are you feeling?"

"Fine thanks."

"Not nervous I hope."

"Just a little," Sarah smiled, her face felt tight.

"There's no need. Would you like to follow me? I do the readings upstairs in one of the bedrooms. It's comfortable and more relaxing."

"Thank you." Sarah followed Lola up the stairs and into a small but cosy room where there was a two-seater settee and an armchair. A coffee table was positioned between them.

"Have you ever had a reading before?" Lola asked in her softly spoken voice, indicating that Sarah was to sit on the settee.

Sarah sank into it feeling increasingly relaxed, though her shoulders were still tense. "No, this is my first time."

"Normally I first ask my clients to write their address and then to comment on what they expect from their reading – perhaps that they hope to enjoy it; it helps to be in a positive frame of mind." Lola smiled and handed Sarah a notepad and pen. "While you do that I will wait for your spirit to talk to me. Do you have an item of jewellery or a piece of clothing that only you have worn? It helps me to build a better picture of you."

Sarah took off her engagement ring and the necklace Adam had bought her on their first Valentine's Day and handed them over. Lola held them gently while Sarah wrote.

After a moment Lola said, "Your spirit is a tall man with thick, wavy hair, he has a large white beard and a cheeky smile." Lola paused, smiled, "He looks like Father Christmas."

Sarah's mouth dropped open. "Good heavens! That sounds like my granddad; he used to live in America but died about two years ago." In fact she had met him only a few times, but they had got on really well and in his final years he had grown very close to her Dad.

Lola nodded. "He's telling me all about you – you are quite ambitious and have worked you're way up. Your granddad is extremely proud of you. He says you studied very hard at university and all the the nights you spent working on your dissertation paid off."

17

Sarah was amazed. Determined to achieve a good degree, she had indeed worked hard and spent many nights burning the midnight oil to complete her dissertation.

"You're a talented painter too, he tells me, but you haven't used your brushes in quite a while."

Again Sarah was at a loss for words. How could this woman possibly know these things? She was a complete stranger. There was no way she could have found out so much prior to the reading.

"You've had some bad times in the past with a previous relationship?"

Sarah nodded, but most women she knew had gone through a bad relationship at one time or another. "Yes, that's true, I always thought we'd get married at some point, but when my boyfriend actually brought up the subject, the thought of it made me feel quite ill. I had to break it off."

Lola smiled sympathetically. "Well then, you will be pleased to know that according to your spirit you chose the right man to marry. He tells me you are soul mates and could have a long and happy life together - if that is what you want. There's good news on the way too: a promotion in the next two or three months that will provide the challenges and opportunities you have been looking for."

This put a big smile on Sarah's face; could this be the Service Manager's job she was after she wondered, but the medium did not enlighten her further.

For a time Lola was silent, her head on one side as though she was listening, then she nodded and smiled. "Your spirit has gone now, so I will next do a palm reading." She returned the jewellery, picked up a magnifying glass from the coffee table and moved to sit next to Sarah on the settee, gently taking her hands and studying each palm in turn.

"Well, again it is good news. You have a long and healthy life ahead of you. I see you will have two children, a boy and a girl," Lola reached over to replace the magnifying glass on the coffee table and returned to her armchair. "How are you feeling now?"

"Fine, thank you."

"Good. Then we will look at the Tarot cards to see what else is going on in your life."

Sarah hoped and prayed the cards would not predict something bad was going to happen to her or any of her family. She was in awe of this woman; it was as if the medium was totally in control of her. Sarah had the feeling that Lola could quite easily put her on top of the world or drop her into the depths of depression. It was unsettling and she found she did not want to mention the ghost or the young girl in the painting; at least not yet.

"Can you shuffle these for me and hand them back when you feel you have shuffled them enough?" Lola held out a pack of cards.

Hesitantly taking them, Sarah found her hands were shaking. "Sorry - I'm all fingers and thumbs."

"Don't worry. Just take your time."

Sarah shuffled the pack and handed it back to Lola, who leaned forward to the coffee table. "Thanks; now I'm going to spread them out face down, and you are to pick five cards and turn them over. Take as long as you like and choose the ones you feel are right."

Self-consciously, Sarah took a few moments to pick the first card. It was strange, but after that she seemed to know exactly which ones to choose. The first one she turned over had a picture of a hand holding a branch with a few leaves on it. It meant absolutely nothing to Sarah.

"That's the Ace of Wands upright in a spread," Lola explained. "It usually means new beginnings in work and social activities; new opportunities and some excitement due to new interests. This confirms what your spirit was saying earlier, that you will be starting a new job and looking forward to the challenge." Lola was smiling as she watched Sarah turn over another card. "That's the Three of Cups in an upright spread. It means you make yourself happy by doing the things you love – as I said, you are creative, but you haven't had time to paint recently. You enjoy socialising with your friends and I feel you will travelling abroad in the near future. It will be an exciting trip that needs much preparation."

Sarah's heart felt light. The Tarot cards were boosting her confidence and making her feel really good about herself. No bad news so far.

The next card depicted a man in a robe sitting under a tree looking at three large cups and being presented with another.

As Sarah turned it over, Lola's expression changed to one of concern. A sudden pang of tension made Sarah gasp; she felt instantly nervous, afraid of what the medium would say.

"This is the Four of Cups upright in a spread. This means the focus is on past relationships, which might not be healthy. You need to be aware of a new love potential. I did say earlier that you could have a long and healthy relationship with your partner if you wanted it, but past loves might muddy the waters a little. Your partner can be a jealous man if he feels threatened emotionally; be warned and try not to lie to him."

Sarah was incredulous: Adam jealous? She loved him completely; could not imagine being without him. She would never lie to him. This was nonsense. She was about to say so, but Lola was focussing on the wall behind Sarah's head and seemed hardly aware of her.

After a moment, the medium spoke again. "This potential new love has a lot to offer and will prove a temptation, but as I said, in the end it is down to the strength of your feelings for him as opposed to how you feel about your husband. You are still very young and attractive to the opposite sex. I feel you will have many admirers and sometimes we all need to flirt a little, but be aware of the dangers this might bring."

Sarah felt a bitter taste in her mouth. Biting back a retort that she hoped she had the good sense to realise her marriage was far too important to her to ever do anything to threaten it she reached for the next and final card. It depicted a knight on horseback holding a sword above his head.

"This is the Knight of Swords upright in a spread; it usually means he is bringing news of problems and troubles."

Sarah held her breath, her heart missing a beat.

Noticing her dismay, Lola smiled kindly. "I feel sure these messages relate to someone around you. That is to say, not to you personally, but to someone close to you. Your cards are telling me that someone you will meet could be in very serious danger and will need your help - and soon. There are some very aggressive vibes; I fear something bad is about to happen and you are connected to the situation in some way. Has anything in particular been troubling you lately?"

Now was the opportunity to mention the ghost, but Sarah found she was too upset to say anything. Wordlessly, she shook her head, tears trembling on her lashes.

Lola leaned across the table and clasped her hand. "I'm sorry, please don't be upset, Sarah. I'm afraid I cannot tell you any more, but I know you will be given some signs. Your spirit will help you and when the time is right you will know what to do. You are a strong person and whatever this is I feel you will be able to get through it."

Instinctively Sarah knew she had already been given those signs. They had come in the form of unspeakable visions that had made her feel she was losing her mind. With a sense of foreboding, she grappled with what Lola had said. There were so many questions she wanted to ask. She cast her mind over the people she knew; which of her friends needed help? None of them had any problems as far as she was aware, and nobody she knew was connected to the dark-haired ghost or the young girl in the painting. What help could she possibly be to anyone? Sarah felt confused and frightened, and no nearer to understanding what had been happening to her.

Lola put the cards away swiftly. "That is the end of your reading, but remember, Sarah, you are in control. You have a husband who loves you, a good career and many friends to support you. Your life is in your hands, no one else's."

Sarah stood up warily and gave Lola a weak smile. "Thank you, it was perhaps not as enjoyable as I had hoped, but very interesting." In fact the reading had been overwhelming, her stomach was churning and the moment when she might have divulged her fears about the ghost had passed her by.

Lola led the way downstairs to where Susan waited anxiously in the conservatory. Smiling with relief, Susan stood up. "My turn now then."

Summoning an answering smile, Sarah whispered, "Good luck!" and sank down on the cane chair to wait, her mind going back to the Knight of Swords and what it had foretold.

An hour later the two women were on their way home. Susan, in a happy frame of mind having obviously enjoyed her reading, grinned at Sarah, "So, what did she tell you?"

Saying nothing of the warnings she had received, Sarah chatted about the job opportunity, and about her granddad, who, it seemed, was watching over her and would help her.

"Really? Wow! That's amazing. I suppose it's the Service Manager's job she was referring to, you jammy devil! She didn't say anything like that to me."

"So what did she say?" Sarah asked, anxious not to dwell on the disturbing things the cards had revealed. Her friend needed little encouragement and chatted eagerly as they drove home.

CHAPTER FOUR

Sarah did not tell Adam where she and Susan had been. There seemed little point in inviting her husband's sarcasm and he, assuming it was just a girlie evening out, did not ask. She supposed it was in a way, but even so it made her feel deceitful. After supper, she took herself off for a long hot soak in the bath hoping it would help her to relax, but all she could think of were the severed limbs of her nightmare. Feeling totally helpless and vulnerable, Sarah forced herself to think things through objectively. She was convinced she had been meant to find the painting of the girl in the garden. Someone or something had put it there deliberately. So, was there some way of identifying her? That might help. Maybe she could find out if there was a connection to the Palmers. Ignoring the feelings of nausea it gave her, she made herself think about the ghost, recalling how young the man had seemed and how angry. He could easily have been about the same age as the girl; maybe a little older. Was there a connection between them? Was he a relative or boyfriend? Sarah gasped with dismay. Had her nightmare been an image of a killing that had actually taken place in this house? Had she seen the ghost of a murderer? The thought made her blood run cold.

Lola had said there would be signs and that her granddad would guide her in some way. Would he? Was it possible? And why had Adam not seen anything – why only her? And were they going to be in danger? So many questions! Sarah felt such a burden on her shoulders. What did the girl in the painting want her to do and how long would it be before the bad thing happened? Or was it something that had already happened, and if so, how could she help? Her head started to ache with tension – then, suddenly, the air went cold.

Shivering, Sarah jumped out of the bath and grabbed the bath robe off the top of the linen basket. Her senses were heightened; her heart seemed to lurch. It was then she heard voices: a man and a woman having a heated argument. She strained to listen. Was it the neighbours? Suddenly a man shouted at the top of his voice and Sarah knew it was coming from inside the house.

Tightening her robe, she ran out of the bathroom, terrified, her heart beating wildly. The shouting match seemed to be coming from the end bedroom. What was going on?

"Adam, Adam?" Sarah screamed his name. "What's wrong? Who is it?"

Feeling a heavy sense of dread she moved slowly and carefully along the landing towards the noise, resisting the temptation to run downstairs. The words, "I hate you!" seemed to echo along the walls. She began to tremble. Where was Adam? Surely he could hear this too?

With her heart thumping loudly and feeling as if at any moment it would burst out of her chest, Sarah crept to the bedroom door. It stood slightly ajar. Peering through it, she had to stop herself from crying out. In her line of vision was the young girl of her nightmare; the one from the painting. How could it be? The girl was cowering in the corner of the room and looking up at someone; Sarah could not see who.

Rooted to the spot, her mouth dry with fear, Sarah heard the girl pleading. "Forgive me, I did not mean to make you angry, but Robert is my boyfriend. I thought you and I were just good friends. You said you understood that."

The man answered her, his tone softened by her words. "I'm sorry; it is just that I really care about you. I don't think he is right for you. I've seen him when you're together. He doesn't know how lucky he is, Jane. My little Jane, you are so beautiful," his voice died away to a sigh.

Sarah, horrified, unable to speak or move, watched as the girl nervously stood up straight and lifted her long tapering fingers to the gold chain about her throat. "Thank you for this, it is lovely; I adore dolphins." Sarah noticed the girl's fingernails were polished pink and that she was fiddling with the pendant as she spoke.

"I know you do. I know all your likes and dislikes. You're a gorgeous young woman, Jane. You deserve the best of everything, and if you'd only let me, I'd really look after you - much better than he ever could."

At that, the girl smiled and moved towards her companion, holding out her hands. "I know you would. I just need a bit more time."

Still unable to catch a glimpse of the man to whom the girl was speaking and desperate to see, Sarah found the courage to push the door fully open.

In an instant, the girl disappeared and Sarah was left staring into a cold, empty room. Totally bewildered, feeling as if her legs were about to give way, she stumbled across to the far wall and leaned against it. There was nobody there. There never had been. She was hallucinating again. Yet she *had* heard an argument taking place - right here where she was standing. The girl had seemed so alive, the voices so real. But they could not have been real - could they? Something evil had happened in this house, Sarah was certain of it. Was this the girl who needed her help? But how that could be? If it was the past she was seeing, what could she possibly do? Sobbing, Sarah wrapped her arms around herself and tried to stop shaking. What was happening to her? It was all too much to take in.

"Sarah – did you call? Are you ok, you look really pale?" Adam stood in the doorway, a mug of coffee in his hand.

Pushing herself away from the wall, Sarah became aware that her face was wet with tears. She dashed them away hoping he had not noticed. She wanted to throw herself in his arms, tell him what was happening to her, but how bizarre would that sound? He really would think she had mental issues; that he had married someone who needed to be institutionalised. Unless... had he heard the voices too?

"Didn't you hear them arguing?" she burst out.

Frowning, Adam shook his head, "Who? When?"

"Just a few minutes ago, a man and a girl, shouting at each other. Surely you heard them?"

"Great! We now find out the neighbours fight like cat and dog - and I thought it was a quiet area. Come to think of it, as I was backing the car off the driveway this morning the guy opposite came out with a face like thunder and slammed his door as if he wanted the whole world to know he wasn't happy. I bet it was him and his partner causing the commotion. I hope this isn't going to be the norm. No wonder you look so upset."

Sarah felt her heart sink. So Adam had heard nothing; he was not experiencing the same visions as she. Was her mind spiralling out of control? Making a huge effort to keep it all together, she tried to focus on the present. Flashing her husband a forced smile, she said, "Ah well, no harm done. Everyone has ups and downs. I'll just go and finish drying off."

Applying her moisturising cream, Sarah gazed at her stricken face in the bathroom mirror and knew she could not go on like this. She looked dreadful. What could she do? She was living in constant fear. Her earlier thoughts came back to haunt her: the young girl — Jane, her male companion had called her — must also be a ghost, which meant she was already dead and had quite possibly been brutally murdered. Surely in that case she was beyond help. It made no sense. Sarah tried to recall exactly what the medium had said: someone close to her was in trouble and needed help. But this girl was not close to her; she had never seen her before, so how on earth could she help. Sarah rubbed her forehead. It was all too much; her thoughts were going round in circles and a migraine hovered behind her eyes.

Putting her cream slowly back in the cabinet, Sarah shivered. Everywhere seemed so cold again. For a moment she wondered if there was something wrong with the central heating. Forcing her mind to focus on work she knew that with the number of projects currently underway there was no chance of taking any leave. She could not be ill — not just now. Running a brush through her hair, Sarah turned around to empty the bathwater.

She recoiled in horror. Lying under the water was the girl she had seen only moments ago in the end bedroom. Jane's face was distorted as if she had known the end of her life was close and had fought against it. The lifeless eyes were wide open, the blonde hair floating like seaweed in the water. Around her neck where the gold necklace had been was a deep, angry bruise.

Sarah dropped the hairbrush, tried to scream, but paralysed with fear she could only stand and stare, unable to breathe. Time stood still – it was as though her heart had stopped beating.

Clenching her hands at her sides, she forced herself to shut her eyes. "This is not real. When I open my eyes she will be gone." For a moment Sarah stood, motionless, muttering over and over as though intoning a mantra: "This is not real. This is not real. This is not real. This-"

The upstairs phone started ringing.

"Sarah," Adam called. His voice sounding remote and distant, as though he was a long way away, "It's Jen for you."

Sarah opened her eyes, drew a deep breath and looked into the bath.

The girl had gone and the water was clear.

Then everything went black.

CHAPTER FIVE

Sarah woke to find herself in bed, a cold flannel on her forehead. Adam was sitting next to her, his expression one of extreme anxiety.

"You passed out again, baby. How do you feel now? Shall I call the doctor?"

Sarah shook her head, wished she hadn't. Her head felt sore, she must have banged it somehow when she passed out. Shutting the murdered girl out of her mind, she drew in deep breaths; knew she was close to becoming hysterical. Aware that Adam was clasping tight to her hands, she eased them from his grasp, removed the flannel from her forehead and forced a watery smile. She had to move on, keep it together and try to figure out what the hell was happening to her. The important thing was to appear calm in front of Adam, not break down.

"I have a thumping headache, but otherwise ok."

"You must have bumped your head on the bath, how did it happen? I just heard a thud and found you sprawled out. That's the second time I've found you on the bathroom floor, baby. What is it? What's wrong with you?"

Sarah knew she had to lie. Adam would not believe what she had seen; that she had fainted because a strangled girl had been lying in their bath – and not just any girl, but a complete stranger, who happened to be from a painting he had found in their shed. She really must be going mad. "Oh dear! Sorry, darling, you'll think I'm an absolute wimp. I felt a bit weak after my bath. Before I could do anything I must have passed out. Maybe it's a bug or something," Sarah smiled, wondering how long she could keep this up.

"Maybe it is – and of course I don't think you're a wimp, daft girl, but I'm really worried about you. Best go to the doctors tomorrow." He tidied the covers and leaned over to give her a light kiss. "Better safe than sorry, eh?"

"I'm fine – honest – just need to relax for a-"

"No Sarah, no argument, you're going, if only to put my mind at rest." Adam handed her a glass of water. "I suppose it's not... that is... do you think you could be pregnant?"

She heard the nervousness in her husband's voice and almost laughed. If only that were true. It was not that Adam did not want children, just not yet. Sarah would not have minded being pregnant. It was the least of her worries at the moment, on the other hand, she might quite possibly be having a nervous breakdown. She was seeing ghosts and dead bodies in their new home and was no longer able to discern what was real. Sarah wanted to shout and scream at Adam, make him understand what she was going through, but she could not bring herself to admit the truth to this dear, caring but very sceptical man. "No, you can relax," she said. "I've just started my period."

Fleetingly an expression of relief crossed Adam's features, to be quickly replaced with worry lines. Sarah relented, "Ok, you win; I'll book an appointment with the doc tomorrow, ok?"

"Good girl." Adam hugged her tightly and after checking her forehead, switched on the portable TV. "You just lie there for a while," he said, picking up the discarded flannel. "I'm just going to the bathroom. Join you in a minute."

Later, as they lay in bed watching the news, Sarah determined that the only thing to do was to investigate what had happened – if anything – in this house. She would begin her research just as soon as she had an opportunity. First she had to identify the dead girl. At least she now had a name to go on. For the moment, Sarah decided, she would assume that she was not hallucinating. That being so, it would appear that Jane had been murdered in this house and that as amazing as it seemed, flashes of the past were crossing some kind of time boundary so that she could see them. Why only she and not Adam, she could not fathom, but Sarah was not prepared to believe she was going mad – at least not yet. She had never really thought about the supernatural, didn't know much about ghosts – that was something else she would look into – but what little she did know suggested that restless spirits materialised for a reason that was often to do with the extreme trauma of their deaths. Maybe Jane wanted people to know how she had died; needed some form of justice before she could move on.

The place to start was with the people who had sold them the house: the Palmers. Talk to them and all might be explained for surely it was only through them that Jane and the young man could have come to be in this house in the first place. Sarah knew the Palmers had bought it as soon as it was built. It pointed to their being involved in Jane's murder. But how could that be? They had seemed such a good-natured couple, very caring and clearly doting on their daughter.

With a sudden intake of breath, Sarah recalled the Tarot card that had indicated she could prevent a bad thing from happening. Had the murder not yet taken place? Could the visions she was seeing possibly be from the future? To Sarah, this seemed far worse. She began to feel paranoid, her mind teeming with questions: would she meet the girl? Hadn't Lola said she would meet someone? Oh God! Was Adam involved in some way? The thought made her feel physically sick. Surely not? It was not possible that she could be so deeply in love with someone who could commit such an atrocity. But what if he was? Did that mean she was in danger?

What nonsense, Sarah reprimanded herself, forcibly calming herself down and remembering what else Lola had said: *You are in control, Sarah*. The dreams and visions were no coincidence; she had to be seeing them for a reason. Some sixth sense was telling Sarah that a murder either had or was going to take place in their dream home and that whether she liked it or not, she was involved, so she had better pull herself together!

Despite the events of the previous evening, Sarah surprised herself by managing to get a good night's sleep and awoke feeling refreshed. She heard Adam moving about in the kitchen, his heavy footsteps coming to the bottom of the stairs.

"Sarah, don't be long darling – I've made us some breakfast."

"Just coming," she called. Feeling quite energetic Sarah put the visions, hallucinations – whatever they were - to the back of her mind. Washing and dressing quickly, she went straight down to the kitchen. Adam had made scrambled eggs with button mushrooms and brown toast.

"That looks delicious – thank you."

"How are you feeling this morning?"

"Much better." This time Sarah did not have to lie although she still felt very anxious – an anxiety that would not disappear until she was far away from this blighted house.

"Well even so, don't forget to make an appointment with the doctor," Adam said, shrugging into his coat and grabbing his briefcase from the hall before giving her a quick hug, his mind already on the day ahead.

As she was getting ready to leave for work, Sarah made up her mind to take the afternoon off. Her boss, knew she was owed almost two days' time in lieu; the workload could wait. Everything could wait. The visions were her top priority; the ghosts were really getting to her. It was more important she take steps to prevent herself from having a complete mental breakdown. Her first port of call would be the local library to suss out the history of the land on which the house had been built. She knew the surrounding fields were part of a farm belonging to a family named Digby. Had Bluebell Close also once been part of the farm? The Palmers might know. She would ring them this morning and at the same time ask them about the painting to see if they recognised the young woman. At least it was a start.

By midday Sarah had cleared her in-tray, gained her boss's approval for the afternoon off with the excuse that she needed to see a doctor – just routine, she had hastened to add - and phoned the Palmers to invite them over for tea. Having decided it might be better to discuss the painting face to face rather than try to describe it on the phone, she had told Mrs Palmer there was quite a bit of mail for them, which had not managed to get re-directed to their new address, and also that Adam had found something of theirs that was too heavy to post, which they could pick up at the same time. As she left the office it was close on lunch time. Sarah knew she should eat, but had completely lost her appetite so headed straight for the large library in the centre of town.

The library assistant was very helpful and showed her the local studies' section, which included journals, newspaper clippings and school projects on the history of the town's development since the beginning of the century. Sarah had a couple of hours to review the information and find any clues that might explain why their house was being haunted. Principally she was looking for news reports of an unexplained death – or murder. Quite quickly she found information on the Digbys and confirmation that Bluebell Close had indeed been part of their farm before the family decided to sell off some of the land. The farmhouse had been built about ninety years ago by the great granddad of the present family. There was a family tree that had been put together recently and Sarah traced all the family members to the present day. John and Diane Digby currently managed the farm and had two sons aged eight and ten years. Was it possible, she wondered, that Jane or the dark-haired man was a relative or friend of theirs? Although the family history made interesting reading Sarah found she was no nearer to discovering the identity of either ghost and became increasingly depressed.

Time seemed to be racing by. Leaving the Digbys, Sarah turned her attention to the local newspapers, going back ten years to when their house was built. She knew it was a long shot, but there was always a hope they might turn something up. She felt as if she was clutching at straws - anything to try to explain what was happening to her. All of the old newspapers were stored on microfiche and analysing each one was both time consuming and tedious. It would be much quicker to carry out research on the Internet, but that, she conceded, was impossible at the moment. She found a news item about a man who had died in the town centre after a drunken brawl. There was another story on a missing teenager, but she was only thirteen and looked nothing like the girl Sarah was hoping to find.

Then, on the front page of the local paper, dated about three months after their house was built, there it was. It took Sarah's breath away. She stared at it, unable to believe her eyes. It was a photo of the girl she had come to think of as 'Jane', beneath the headline: 'LOCAL GIRL MISSING.' It took a few minutes to digest the information. This was the girl in the painting; the girl she had seen in her end bedroom, in her dream and, horrifyingly, strangled in the bath. So the visions *were* from the past. She was not making it up; not hallucinating. This girl had actually existed. As realisation dawned, all Sarah wanted to do was to break down and cry. She sat back, completely overwhelmed, her fingers hovering over the microfiche reader. What should she do? Who would believe what she had seen? Sarah could feel herself starting to panic. Were the visions depicting what had actually happened to Jane? Surely not?

Sarah ran her hand through her hair pushing it back off her face; it was damp, she was sweating profusely and felt sick. She found she was biting her nails - something she had not done since she had left junior school. Telling herself she could handle it and taking deep, slow breaths, Sarah forced herself to continue reading convinced now that she was meant to find this information. The name of the girl was Jane Moore, nineteen years' old and a student, who lived with her parents just outside the town centre. She was supposed to travel by coach to meet up with her friends in Blackpool, but had never arrived. Her parents had not reported their daughter missing at first because they thought she had changed her mind and gone to meet her boyfriend instead; he – they did not give his name - was also on holiday in Blackpool. Jane was described as intelligent, fun loving and very independent and her parents were distraught.

Sarah felt tears pricking her eyes as she read about how the Moores, desperate to know where their daughter had gone, had appealed to the public to get in touch if they had seen her. Mrs Moore stated that they were a close family and that Jane had never done anything like this before. The parents were even offering a substantial reward. It was heartbreaking. Sarah knew what pain her own parents would have endured in similar circumstances. Ten years ago she would have been only a couple of years younger than Jane. She moved on to the following papers, anxious to find more information. A month after the report of her disappearance, Jane Moore was once again front page news. Body parts had been found in a derelict warehouse on an industrial estate three miles outside town. They had been partially burned, but were later identified by dental records as belonging to the missing student. Her disappearance had then turned into a murder investigation.

Shaken, Sarah finished the story in disbelief. She and Adam had moved to this town because they had wanted to get away from inner city life to be in a more peaceful, rural area. That such a horrific crime had been perpetrated on their doorstep – perhaps even inside their house – shocked her to the core. She had believed and hoped she would find Jane had turned up safe and well and that the visions could be explained by stress combined with a vivid imagination. But no, she had seen it with her own eyes: Jane had been murdered and cut up into pieces, possibly in the bathroom. It did not bear thinking about.

Completely unaware of the passage of time, Sarah stared unseeing at the microfiche reader. A baby's sudden scream in the children's area of the library brought her out of her trance-like state. Too upset to continue her search, she returned the microfiches to their envelopes, gathered her things together, ran to her car and in a daze, drove back to the house. Lola had said that someone needed her, that something bad was going to happen if she did not help: could Jane be that someone? Was the girl haunting their house ten years after she was murdered? And if so, what had happened to make her come back? Or had she come back before; was that the real reason that the Palmers sold the house? God! The Palmers! She had almost forgotten they were coming to tea.

Sarah felt even more frightened than before as she tentatively opened the front door. What would she be going into?

What might she see this time? Her hands shaking, she reached for the light switch and snapped on the hall light. Everything appeared normal. She took off her shoes and went into the kitchen, switching on the overhead light; although it was not yet dark, it made the place seem somehow warmer, more inviting. Filling the kettle to make a cup of tea, Sarah remembered a friend telling her once that if a person had died in unusual circumstances they could become trapped between this world and the next. She had thought it mumbo jumbo at the time, but now it came back to haunt her. Jane had certainly died an excruciating death. Was she trapped between worlds, her soul in torment? Who was her murderer? Was it someone she had trusted, here, in this very house?

'It's got to be the dark-haired man, he was so angry,' Sarah murmured. 'Was he never caught? Has he murdered again?' She was aware that she was talking to herself, but she needed to talk and there was nobody in whom she could confide – least of all Adam! Who would believe she was seeing visions of Jane Moore's murder when she hardly believed it herself? She had to find out what Lola had meant when she said that someone would need her help. Could the medium possibly have known more than she divulged? Susan said Lola never told anyone anything really bad. Had she seen something so awful in the cards that she had held it back?

'It's no good standing here frightening yourself to death with unanswerable questions, Sarah muttered crossly, checking her watch. The first thing she could do was to find out if the Palmers had known Jane; check their reactions to see if they too had seen the ghosts. Tomorrow she could go back to the library to find out if the killer had ever been caught. Find out if she was right and that he was indeed the angry, dark-haired young man.

CHAPTER SIX

Thankfully, the Palmers were late, giving Sarah time to shower and change before they arrived. As she opened the front door, Mrs Palmer was very apologetic.

"We'd forgotten how bad it was trying to go anywhere in rush hour, it's a good job we didn't have our daughter with us." She held out a box, "This is a belated housewarming present, dear, just a little something to make you feel at home."

Jean Palmer was a large woman with pale blue eyes and short, cropped hair, streaked with grey. There was something motherly and caring about her that, for an instant, made Sarah want to weep. She masked her feeling by looking inside the box; it contained a homemade chocolate cake.

"This looks gorgeous. Thank you so much Mrs Palmer."

"It's nothing, dear. And please call me Jean."

Trying to appear more relaxed than she felt Sarah led the couple into the living room. "Would you both like tea, or would you prefer coffee? I can't wait to try this delicious cake, we can all have a slice," Sarah said brightly, wanting to make them feel as comfortable as possible.

"Tea with no sugar would be lovely, thank you, but we'll pass on the cake as we are both trying to diet, though not very successfully!" Jean said.

Terry Palmer chuckled to himself. He was slightly thinner than his wife, had a ruddy complexion and thinning hair.

Jean, not at all amused, shot him a stern glance. "Goodness," she said to Sarah, "the house looks great - and so different. You have been working hard."

Sarah smiled, observing that Mrs Palmer was rapidly scanning the room and admiring the new wooden floors and beech furniture. "Thanks. It's mostly my husband's choice, but we have similar taste and I really like it. Please, do sit down," she indicated the table in the dining area and went through to the kitchen to make the tea, aware of an undertone of conversation. She had the distinct impression that for all Jean's motherliness, Terry Palmer was a little hen-pecked!

Returning with the tea tray, she pulled out from the sideboard the bundle of mail, which she had tied together with ribbon. "I think it's all here. Have you settled into the cottage?"

"Yes, thank you," Jean beamed at her. "Megan – that's our daughter - loves the big pond outside and Terry has been working very hard decorating every room."

Try as she might, Sarah could not imagine this middle-aged couple having had anything at all to do with Jane's murder, but although she did not like to deceive them, it was important to know if they recognised Jane. She took the picture off the top of the book case and passed it to Mr Palmer.

"Oh, by the way, before I forget, this is what I meant by something too heavy to post. Adam found it in the shed and we thought it must belong to you."

Sarah waited for any reaction. There was none.

Terry Palmer glanced at it and handed it to his wife. "I'm sorry; I don't think it's ours. I don't recognise it at all. Do you, Jean?"

His wife scrutinised the painting. "No I don't. What a pretty girl. Who is she I wonder? How strange you found it in the shed; I thought we had completely cleared it out. We did, didn't we Terry? And I can't remember any visitors going in there afterwards."

Terry Palmer nodded. "Yes, it was empty when we left. I even swept it out, so I would have seen the picture had it been there. It's not ours I'm afraid."

"Maybe a friend left it for you to find as a housewarming? It's really lovely," Jean said, handing back the painting.

Disappointed, Sarah took it from her and put it back on top of the bookcase, said as brightly as she could muster, "Ah well, not to worry. I'm sure we'll solve the puzzle eventually."

For the next half hour or so, they chatted about inconsequential things until Terry Palmer looked at his watch and said, "We mustn't take up any more of your time. Thank you for the tea – and for the mail. I'm sorry you've been troubled. The redirection has kicked in now, so it shouldn't happen again."

"Oh, it was no trouble, thanks for coming over, and especially for the cake."

Relieved when they had gone, Sarah concentrated on preparing a chicken casserole to take her mind off her disappointment. The uneasy feeling had returned; she'd had about as much as she could take for one day. She had so hoped the Palmers would be able to throw some light on the dead girl and explain what had happened here, but their bland reaction to the painting could not have been anything but genuine. *Someone* must have put it in the shed; the picture was a solid, physical thing, not a figment of her imagination. Indeed, it was Adam and not she who had found it.

Sarah was just thinking she would go back to the library first thing in the morning, when Adam rang to say he was on his way home. Putting the casserole in the oven, she took her mug of tea into the living room. It had been warm all day, but she felt a bit chilly. She glanced out of the window a strong wind had got up, the trees in the back garden were swaying, the saplings bending almost double; perhaps there was a thunderstorm on the way? She picked up a paperback from their new magazine rack. It was a romantic novel and she read a few pages in the hope that it would help her to relax, but found she was becoming increasingly restless, continually distracted by the noise of the wind and wishing Adam would hurry up and get home, she so badly needed someone to talk to.

After a few minutes she gave up on the novel, got up and walked over to the window, staring in disbelief at the sky, which had become ominously black. Sarah hated storms. She could feel the hairs on the back of her neck rising. Something felt wrong, but she could not put her finger on what. The living room seemed suddenly to have grown very dark. Sarah went to turn on the lamps; the switch clicked, nothing happened. Oh Lord! A power cut. She went back to the window; the rain was lashing the glass, the wind shrieking like a banshee. Staring out of the window, to her horror she realised the lights were on in the houses opposite. This was no power cut.

Sarah's heart started racing. Panic set in, should she call the police? 'Pull yourself together, Sarah Miller,' she murmured crossly to herself. Whatever was she thinking of – police indeed! It was probably just the trip switch. Both the front and back doors were locked, nobody could get in the house. She drew the heavy curtains across the window to shut out the storm. The room seemed even blacker. Why did she feel so scared? But even as she asked the question, she became aware of another presence in the room; heard above the noise of the storm the sound of someone breathing heavily. She swung round, shouted, "Who's there?"

Peering into the gloom, Sarah could see the room was empty, but then she heard sobbing; the sounds of a woman in extreme distress. "Jane," she cried, "Is it you?"

About to move towards the sound Sarah stopped in her tracks as the door leading from the hall was flung open. It crashed back against the wall and a man shouted harshly, "Charlotte?"

And then he was there, striding into the room, fists bunched. His face was in shadow, but Sarah got the impression that he was taut with fury.

She shrank back into the curtains, her heart pounding, hardly able to breathe, hardly daring to look. Had the intruder mistaken her for someone else? Rigid with fear, she heard a woman cry out: "Leave me alone!" It did not sound like Jane; the voice seemed coarser, higher pitched.

Wishing herself invisible, Sarah peered round the curtain, but could see no woman, nor work out where her voice was coming from. At that moment there was a shattering crash; the man appeared to have knocked something onto the floor. Sarah flinched; all her logic screamed at her that if he was not real, he surely could not have made contact with a solid object. She was confused, still reeling from what was happening. And who was Charlotte? Another ghost; another woman he had killed – or was about to kill?

The woman's voice sobbed: "It was your fault, you made me do it."

As Sarah's eyes adjusted properly to the dark she made out the man's outline. He was walking away from her towards the dining area, a tall, menacing figure, and in his hand something glinted: a knife?

Sarah thrust her fist against her mouth to prevent herself from crying out. Instinctively casting about for a weapon, she sidled quietly to the windowsill and felt behind the curtains for the large glass vase she knew she had left there. Whoever Charlotte was, she needed help and fast. With a surge of adrenaline, not thinking what she was doing, Sarah clasped the ornament and stepping forward raised it above her head.

Suddenly there was a crack of lightening and dining area was momentarily bathed in white light. Involuntarily, Sarah shut her eyes; saw the image against her eyelids of a woman sitting on the floor by the patio doors surrounded by strewn debris, blood pouring from a deep cut in her head. It was not Jane; this woman's hair was long and dark. Sarah swayed, put her hand out and clutched at the curtain.

"Sarah! What on earth are you doing?"

Sarah jumped, her eyes snapped open and she blinked against the light. Even before she looked towards the patio doors she knew everything would seem as normal, the woman and her assailant gone. Adam stood in the doorway to the hall, his hand on the light switch, his face creased in puzzlement as he focussed on the vase in her hand.

Afraid she was going to pass out Sarah moved weakly towards the dining area, clutched the back of a chair for support and placed the vase in the middle of the table. "I was just moving this when there was a blasted power cut," she tried to say it brightly, but her voice came out thin and reedy. She cleared her throat, turned towards her husband, "The storm must have brought the lines down."

"Well it's back on now and the storm's gone over. Are you alright? You look as if you've seen a ghost."

Aware of the irony of that remark, Sarah managed a weak smile while attempting to wipe away the images from behind her eyes. Determined not break down she held onto the tears welling in her throat. "I'm fine; just a little shocked by being plunged into darkness – and you know how I hate lightening. Tea's on, I'll check on the casserole. How was your day?"

"Not bad, the new chap on the team is really good and proving to be reliable," Adam turned back into the hall, kicked off his shoes and put them neatly on the shoe rack by the front door then followed her into the kitchen. "He didn't need much training either; a quick learner with a definite head for figures. Accountancy wasn't his first choice of career, but he flew through his CIMA exams. I think he's going to be a real asset to my team. I played squash with Mike at dinner and thrashed him so that was probably the best bit of my day. What about you? Did you see the doctor?"

Avoiding the question, Sarah went to the fridge, pulled out an opened bottle of wine and helped herself to large glassful, quickly gulping half of it down before pouring a glass for Adam as he came up behind her. "Oh, you know. Not too bad; business as usual," she said, handing it to him.

"Thanks," he took a few sips and perched on the edge of a stool by the breakfast bar, watching her busily collecting plates and cutlery and loading up a tray. She switched off the oven and pulled on her oven gloves, unable to prevent her thoughts probing what she had seen. Did it mean that Jane was not the only woman who had been killed in this house? Sarah stifled a gasp. Maybe there were more, their bodies buried under the floorboards or under the patio paving slabs. Shuddering at the thought, she bent to retrieve the casserole, placing it absently on the work surface. The situation was getting worse. It had been too dark to ascertain whether it was the same dark-haired young man she had seen before, but if it was, could he have been a serial killer?

"Hey," Adam teased, "are you planning to get drunk tonight?"

Sarah realised she had finished the first glass of wine and was pouring herself another, filling the glass to the top.

Peeling off the oven gloves, she hesitantly faced her husband, miserably holding out her hands to him. "I... I lied. Today has been pretty bad. The wine helps."

Adam set down his glass, came forward and took her in his arms. "My poor baby - things bad at work? Do you want to talk about it? What did the doctor say?"

Sarah wished more than anything else that she could share the burden. Adam was her soul mate. Together they could find out what terrible secrets this house was harbouring. Why could she not bring herself to confide in him?

"He said it was most likely stress, what with the move and everything," she lied. "I'll be ok. There's just such a lot of pressure at work at the moment. Unrealistic deadlines, but I'll cope." Sarah blushed, suddenly aware this was the first time she had ever lied to her husband. Remembering what Lola had said, it made her feel queasy.

Adam kissed her lightly on the forehead. "I know you will but don't overdo it. Take a break if you need to. I think we both need a holiday and you're due some leave." He leaned over the casserole, wrinkling his nose appreciatively, "Smells good. Let's eat, I'm famished."

Sarah nodded. A break from this house is what she really needed. She hoped the library would offer more clues tomorrow. She needed to know what she was supposed to be doing; find out who was in trouble and what she could do to help if anything. It was like living a nightmare. In her mind's eye she saw again the dead body in the bath, the limbs floating in the red water – did they belong to Jane – or to Charlotte? She prayed she would find some answers soon.

CHAPTER SEVEN

After supper had been cleared away Adam opened another bottle of white wine from the fridge and brought it through to the living room where they had settled down to watch the evening news. "What happened in the study?" he asked.

Sarah was immediately on edge. "What do you mean? I haven't been in there today."

Her husband laughed. "We must have a poltergeist then; it's a real mess. I thought perhaps you'd decided to have a clear out. There are letters and papers scattered all over the place."

Sarah forced a smile although fear had gripped her again. What had someone or something been looking for? "Oh yes – I'd forgotten," she said. "I went in there this morning to look for some old notes; thought they might be useful for a project I'm doing at work."

"Did you find them?"

Sarah nodded, "Yes, sorry, didn't realise I'd left such a mess. I'll clear up in a bit."

"Don't worry about it on my account, Adam said, focussing his attention on the news.

Twenty minutes later Sarah went upstairs to the study; it was in fact the fourth bedroom, but they used it to house their computer, a few reference books, various household files and all her old paperwork from university. Adam was right: the room looked like a bomb site, no wonder he had remarked on it. They were both organised people as a rule and liked the house to be clean and tidy, had even decided to employ a cleaner to help keep on top of it while they were both in full-time jobs. But now the room looked as though whirlwind had been through it throwing everything off the shelves. Sarah's stomach clenched into a tight ball: if ghosts were capable of moving things around like this what else were they capable of doing?

It took her the best part of an hour to restore everything to normal. She could hear Adam's laughter drifting up the stairs; he must be watching *Friday Night With Jonathan Ross*. About to switch off the light, Sarah felt her skin prickle, became aware of a presence outside the door. She shivered; suddenly the room was cold. Spinning round, she saw the indistinct figure of a man disappearing along the landing. Oh no! Not again: this was becoming ridiculous. Taking a deep breath, more angry than afraid, she followed slowly, aware of how dangerous it could be, but desperate to know what he was doing. The ghost passed through the closed door of the end bedroom. At least this time he was doing what ghosts do! Sarah thought, resorting to black humour in an effort to steady her nerves. She opened the door. The room was in complete darkness; the air so cold it was like stepping into a butcher's cold store. Snapping on the light Sarah gasped at the sight that met her eyes: the scene was straight out of a horror film. Blood was splattered all over the walls. Lying on the floor in the centre of the room, as though it had been flung there, was a hammer, the claw glistening with blood and strands of matted hair – blonde hair.

Her courage leaving her, Sarah swayed, her body convulsed with trembling. She closed her eyes tight shut, cried out, "Go away from here! Leave me alone."

A moment later she opened her eyes: the gruesome scene had vanished, everything looked perfectly normal.

Backing out of the room, Sarah switched off the light and closed the door. She knew now that she needed help. Whatever had happened in the past was taking over her life and she was losing control.

CHAPTER EIGHT

Saturday morning dawned and Sarah drove into town, telling Adam she was doing some research for a forthcoming project at work. She hated this necessity to lie, but she could hardly tell the truth. Adam would never believe her; at best he would think she was deluded, at worst that she needed sectioning. She could think of no one person she could turn to for help; nobody would believe her - that was the huge problem. Sarah knew she could not be clairvoyant: from what she had read on the subject, such people started seeing things from an early age. In all her life she had never seen anything remotely supernatural – so why now? What connection did she have to the dead girl, Jane – and this other woman, Charlotte? There must be *some* connection, but whatever it was, it eluded her.

She parked up and as soon as the library opened went straight over to the Local Studies' section and quickly found the relevant fiches to continue her search. Turning back to the story she had been unable to finish the day before, she learned that Miss Moore's boyfriend, Robert Taylor, also a student, was arrested shortly after the discovery in the warehouse, but a few weeks later he had been released without charge.

A few other suspects were taken in to 'help the police with their enquiries', but like Taylor, all had been released without charge. DNA tests had been inconclusive, but the police continued to believe the killer was a local man. They had carried out door-to-door enquiries, combing the locality for almost a year without making any progress. Sarah read through the local papers as quickly as she could, hoping to find that the case had been solved, but it was a cumbersome and painstaking task and she was running out of time. She was well aware that the library closed at noon on a Saturday. The only alternative was to use the Internet at home, but where to begin? All she could do was Google on Jane Moore and see what turned up. There were probably hundreds of people with that name. Sarah felt as though she was wading through treacle; getting nowhere fast.

A stentorian voice boomed from the desk: "Library's closing in ten minutes." A stout, sour-faced assistant glared in her direction and Sarah, feeling frustrated, felt obliged to start packing the microfiches away. This was a very slow way of trying to find out about Jane's murder. She needed help from someone with access to the right information. It was only as she was pulling out of the library car park that Sarah remembered Simon Leivers, a friend from her student days, who had applied successfully for a place on the police force's scheme for new graduates. They had lost touch since she married Adam, but surely he would be able to advise her; help her to find out if Jane Moore's murderer had ever been caught?

When Sarah got home there was a note on the kitchen table from Adam to say he had gone golfing with friends and would be back around four. She made herself a cheese sandwich and ate it while rummaging in her bag for her address book. Did she still have Simon's phone number? She and Simon had been close friends at university, helping each other out at exam time by revising together; taking notes at lectures if one of them was unable to attend. They'd had a lot in common insofar as both wanted to do well on the course and had high ambitions for their careers. Sarah had valued his friendship highly, but for her, the initial physical attraction had been only fleeting. Not so for Simon. When he told her how he felt, things had been strained between them for a while. Eventually, however, he had got over his disappointment and they had parted as friends, though it had never been quite the same as before. After university they had kept in touch with letters and the odd phone call, but eventually the gaps between got longer, dwindling to a dashed-off note enclosed once a year in a Christmas card.

For a time, Sarah sat looking at the phone, hesitant about giving Simon a call. He had declined an invitation to her wedding; it could be awkward. On the other hand he really might be able to help her. Finally, she plucked up the courage and dialled, waited, listening to the ring tone. It seemed to go on forever; supposing he had moved? She had no mobile number for him. She was on the point of slamming down the phone when it was picked up.

"Hello?" She recognised Simon's voice in her ear.

"Simon? Hi, it's Sarah, remember me? Sarah Sheldon from Uni - Sarah Miller now, of course."

After a short pause he answered, "Sarah? Hi, how *are* you, long time no hear." There was genuine warmth in his voice and she relaxed immediately.

"Wonderful, thanks. I'm sorry I've left it so long, but we've only just moved house and what with one thing and another... you know how it is. And anyway, I don't know why I'm apologising to you; I was always the one who made the effort to keep in touch, Detective Leivers – or is it Superintendent by now?"

Simon started laughing. "I wish! Ok, fair dos. I lost your phone number and I'm not much good at writing, sorry. Anyway how's married life? Sorry I couldn't make it to the wedding, but thanks for the invite."

"No worries, I know all you policemen are wedded to your jobs. Married life is really great. Look, can I update you on all the gossip when we meet for lunch next week - my treat - how's about it?"

There was a long pause. "Hello? Simon?" Sarah said tentatively.

"I'm still here. Just recovering from the shock – did you say your treat? Are we meeting at McDonalds then? I've got some of their vouchers so even less for you to spend."

It was Sarah's turn to laugh. "Cheek; I don't know how you dare – you never had two pennies to rub together. I can't remember how many times I bought you chip cobs and pints of lager on a Friday lunchtime – me, who earned a pittance working behind various bars and nightclubs while you were earning a fortune stacking shelves at Tescos!"

"Ok, Ok, I know I owe you big time. I can't help it if I was useless with money. I needed to go out every night to forget about those bloody shelves. So when do you want to meet up?"

Sarah was already checking her diary. "What about next Wednesday? I'm based in Nottingham City Centre at the moment. Where are you based now, Detective Leivers?"

"As it happens, I'm on a training course in Nottingham the latter half of next week so that would suit me. I'm working my way towards another promotion, but I'm putting in plenty of hours at the moment so I can skip off without a guilty conscience. Wednesday will be fine; about twelve-thirty ok for you?"

"Great; twelve-thirty in between the lions in Market Square - and don't be late, especially as I'm paying."

Simon sounded hurt. "Hey, you may have baled me out a few times but as far as I remember I never once let you down – gotta go – see you in the Square next Wednesday, 12.30 prompt."

"Looking forward..." Sarah started to say, but the dialling tone burred in her ear.

CHAPTER NINE

After she had put the phone down Sarah felt relieved. It had felt good to talk to Simon and she was already looking forward to their lunch date. They had always got on so well. A guilty feeling crept over her when she remembered exactly why she had contacted her friend after all this time, but the image of the murdered girl soon banished it. Sarah knew she would have to be careful about how she broached the subject; she had no wish sound foolish and would need a plausible excuse as to why she was searching for information on Jane Moore's murder. Sarah shivered. Somehow, thinking about what she would say to Simon made everything seem more real. If she could see the ghosts, surely, sooner or later, they would be able to see her? Maybe they already could. She thought of the way in which her things had been scattered about in her office; if the dark-haired man could physically move things, could he harm her? But why would he want to; what had she done to deserve his anger? That was perhaps the most frustrating thing: working out where she fitted into the horror story. She shivered again. Did she really want to know what the connection was? Another thing that troubled her was exactly when the murder had taken place. Presumably the Palmers had moved in as soon as the house was completed – or had they? Had the house been standing empty for a while? Time enough for the killer to lure the women in, safe in the knowledge that the place was deserted? If that was so, it could only have been someone local – maybe even one of the builders.

On impulse Sarah dialled the Palmers' number. Mrs Palmer answered almost straight away.

"Hi, Jean, it's Sarah. Sarah Miller. Sorry to disturb you, but I wonder if you could settle a little disagreement between Adam and me. Were you the first couple to move into this road? You bought the plot before the house was built didn't you?"

"Hello Sarah. Yes, that's, right."

Sarah could tell Jean was puzzled by the call, but there was no stopping now. "Did you move in as soon as the house was finished? I mean, literally?"

There was a pause. "Well, Terry has a better memory than I do, but I'm fairly sure we didn't move in right away because there were a few things the builders had to sort out for us. Some problem with the plumbing in the kitchen and we'd paid extra for the whole house to be decorated and carpeted throughout. I think there was about a five-week delay, but we didn't mind because we were able to move our furniture in and then go on holiday while they completed the work, which made the whole thing less stressful, and Morgan's, that's the builders, sorted it all out for us while we were away. But why do you ask?"

"Oh, no reason really, it's just that painting I showed you. Adam wondered if someone could have left it in the shed between when the house was finished and you moved in. But of course, you would have seen it wouldn't you. I'm not thinking straight."

"Well we might not have done if it got covered in all Terry's DIY stuff, but I'm sure, it wasn't there when we left. He said he'd swept it out. Still, you know what men are!"

"Yes, of course, I remember him saying that now," Sarah laughed, but we are completely mystified as to where it came from."

"Why don't you ask the builders? I'm sure I've still got their number somewhere. I wonder what I've done with it."

"Oh no, please don't worry. Look, I'm sorry for troubling you with it. By the way, the cake was delicious, thank you so much."

"It's no trouble," Jean said.

Apologising yet again, Sarah rang off. She sat down heavily on the armchair in the living room. Her mind was racing. So Jane's murder could have been prior to the Palmers moving in, but the killer took such a risk – and how did he get hold of the keys unless as she'd thought, he was one of the builders? Or unless he was connected in some other way to the Palmers, perhaps one of the removal men who had found out they were going away. It was all such a mystery.

If the killer was indeed the dark-haired man, then he must now be dead since she had seen his ghost, or was it flashbacks to the past she had been seeing, in which case he could still be alive? She knew what he had looked like back then, but he could have changed dramatically in ten years. Where did she start and would she be able to find evidence that he had killed Jane Moore and possibly Charlotte too? There could be other victims too; young women who fell for his charms. The possibility made Sarah cringe, but still unwilling to entertain the thought that she might be descending into some form of madness, she determined that at the very least, she had to identify the killer and find out if he had ever been caught.

CHAPTER TEN

The remainder of the weekend turned out to be the most enjoyable Sarah had experienced in months. It was all down to Adam, who had returned from his round of golf shortly after she got home from the library. Sarah was in the kitchen sorting out the washing basket, doing her best to keep busy in an effort to put all her tumultuous thoughts to the back of her mind.

Adam handed her a huge bouquet of white lilies; her favourite flowers. "Hi – I bought these for you. You've seemed so stressed recently, I thought you could use a little cheering up."

"Oh, Ad, they're beautiful." Sarah took them appreciatively and smiled up at him, "Thank you darling." She wished she did not feel quite so guilty. Was it fair to keep things from him? Adam was clearly concerned about her. He had no knowledge of what she was going through; knew nothing of the events that had taken place here ten years ago. Or did he? Sarah stiffened. It had been Adam who had found this house in the first place; sold her the dream about living in the country. Before the traitorous thought could take hold, she banished it firmly from her mind. "I'm sorry if I've seemed distracted, but work's been hectic with the deadlines we've been given and there've been so many problems to sort out, but hopefully it'll get better now."

"Work's not everything, Sarah. You should let other people take on some of the problems. It's not all down to you, you know; you've got a team; why don't they support you?"

"They do – they've all been doing masses of overtime lately, and besides, I-"

Adam reached out his finger and gently pressed it to her lips, "Hush a minute. Look, I thought it was about time we went out and did some socialising so I've booked table at Chico's for seven, if that's ok with you? After that we're meeting Guy and Rachael at the Blue Lounge for a few drinks. I thought I'd surprise you."

Sarah laughed in delight. "That's great. We haven't been to Chico's for *ages*, and it'll be great to catch up with Rachael. Thank you, Ad, that's just what I need."

"Good, glad you're pleased," Adam smiled at her obvious pleasure and watched as she arranged the lilies, placing them in the cut glass vase that remained on the dining room table.

Having lived in almost constant fear over the past few weeks, Sarah was really happy to be doing something normal for a change; the prospect of getting away from the house and its dark secrets, if only for an evening, was a real tonic. She had been so caught up in everything, what with the move, long hours at work and the gut-wrenching visions at home, that having fun had taken a back seat.

They spent the rest of the afternoon relaxing and watching a film before Adam took a quick shower while Sarah languished in the bath. She dressed in a figure-hugging, black lacy dress, which showed off her small waist, then took time to style her hair and apply some light makeup.

Adam gave a wolf-whistle as he walked into the bedroom, "Wow! You look gorgeous." He pulled her towards him and hugged her tightly.

Sarah so wished she could confide in him. Almost she did so. There was no denying that he loved her as much as she loved him, but in many ways they hardly knew each other and her fear of jeopardising their relationship kept her from saying anything. Instead, she gave him a mock curtsey, "Well thank you kind sir. You look very smart yourself; let's go party."

The City Centre was bustling. It was the end of the month, payday for most people and everyone seemed keen to go out and celebrate. Predictably, Chico's was busy, but the meal was excellent. They both chose Steak Diane with breaded mushrooms as a starter and ordered a bottle of Chardonnay.

"I'd really forgotten how good the food was here," Sarah said, feeling pleasantly full and relaxed. She had drunk only two glasses of wine, but already it was having the desired effect. The dark traumas of the past few weeks seemed suddenly unreal, much as if they were memories of a horror film she had once seen a long time ago. Maybe after all, it had been only her vivid imagination. Except, she had seen Jane Moore and the report of her murder in the newspaper: that had not been her imagination. Sarah gulped down another glass of wine, determined to drown her fears with alcohol.

"Yes, we've been neglecting us lately. Hey – go easy on the wine!" Adam smiled, gently clinked her glass, "Here's to us my darling. I think we should make every effort to go out for a nice meal at least once a month."

After passing on desserts they made their way to the Blue Lounge, where Guy and Rachael were waiting for them. Guy had been Adam's friend since infant school and the obvious choice to be his best man. Sarah knew him quite well: he was easy going and entertaining, always with a joke to tell; he'd made a hilarious speech at her wedding. Rachael too was friendly and fun to be around. The couple had been living together for six months and it seemed they were a good match; both wanted to travel more.

Sarah could tell from his expression that Guy was bursting to tell them some news. They had hardly sat down before he beamed and said, "Guess what. We've booked an extended holiday to Australia in October."

Adam grinned, "Lucky devils! How long for?"

Sarah knew her husband had always wanted to visit Sydney and travel around Australia. No prizes for guessing he would be green with envy. She smiled at his enthusiasm as he gave Guy all his attention.

"Six weeks, we fly to Cairns and then travel down the East Coast by train to Sydney. We've got what's called an East Coast discovery pass; you can hop on and off the train when you feel like it. It's a good way to check out the scenery."

Rachael was beaming. "Yes, the furthest I've ever been is Cyprus. I backpacked around Europe when I was a student, but Aussie's a whole different ball game."

"Yes, well we'll be backpacking there too," Guy said, "so you've got to get used to doing without ninety-nine changes of clothes and that great toilet bag of yours crammed to the gunwales with make up," he teased, exchanging an amused glance with Adam.

Rachel pouted. "That'll be a problem then. I simply can't manage without my No 7 gear, and then there's my straighteners and curling tongs and my hairdryer, which is an absolute must, and I shall need a few different outfits for going out, and jackets to match of course, not to mention shoes, and then there's-"

"Stop, stop!" A little alarmed, Guy held up his hand. "Come on Rachel; one small backpack only - remember? Besides, you'll be the one who's moaning when you can't carry it around and you needn't think I'm going to do it for you."

Sarah hid a smile, knowing only too well that Rachel, an eminently practical person, was getting her own back.

Unable to keep a straight face, Rachael gave a peal of laughter, "Oh you are daft, Guy. You must know I'm not serious."

"Oh, but surely you are," Sarah gurgled. "We girls need our accessories. I know I couldn't *live* without my straighteners and curling tongs!"

Knowing when he was being ribbed, a relieved Guy grinned sheepishly and they all joined in the laughter.

After a few drinks the four friends were deep in conversation and Sarah, feeling somewhat lightheaded, could not help but be aware she was attracting attention. Other men were openly admiring her, one even tried to chat her up. It made her feel good even though she did nothing to encourage it and for once she was glad of Adam's possessive stare; his arm tightly about her waist.

Later, Guy suggested they go on to a club and they all readily agreed. Completely relaxed for the first time in ages, Sarah was thoroughly enjoying herself, certain she could dance the night away, but when it got to past one in the morning and her heels were pinching and she was dropping with tiredness, she was almost relieved when Adam decided to call it a night.

In the cab on the way home Adam was keen to talk about Guy and Rachael's holiday. "They're visiting Thailand on the way over to Australia, a stopover for three days and then three days in Bali on the way back. It's a holiday of a lifetime. Guy said the flights were dirt cheap and the cost of living in Aussie is much lower than here."

"Sounds great," Sarah said on a yawn, resting her head on Adam's shoulder, barely able to keep her eyes open. All she wanted was to go to bed and fall into a deep sleep. The cab driver was manoeuvring his way out of town as quickly as he could, but had to pull up sharply as two girls tottered out into the road oblivious to any traffic.

The cabbie blasted his horn at them. Jolted out of sleepiness, Sarah sat up quickly as one of the girls, dressed in a short denim mini-skirt and high-heeled sandals, looked straight into the cab.

Sarah gasped, pointing in astonishment, said without thinking, "Adam it's her! Look! It's that girl!"

"What girl?"

"The one who..." Just in time Sarah came to her senses, conscious that her husband was eyeing her with a great deal of curiosity. "Oh – nobody, I must be half asleep. I thought it was a girl from work, that's all. Don't mind me." But in that one instant, Sarah had recognised her immediately: it was the girl who had been weeping in front of the patio doors, her head bleeding copiously from an open wound. The girl called Charlotte. "Adam," she whispered, "I feel sick."

The cab driver swore. "Well whoever the stupid bitch is, she's got a death wish that's for sure. Excuse my French, but if I'd knocked her down, you can bet it'd be my fault." He accelerated away as the girls disappeared down a side road. Sarah wanted him to stop, but she knew if she said anything Adam would think she was completely barking, and anyway, if she had caught up with the girl what would she have said to her? 'Excuse me, but are you the ghost of a woman who was murdered ten years ago?' They'd lock her up! Besides she conceded, maybe she had been mistaken after all. With the amount of alcohol she had consumed it was hardly surprising if her mind was playing her tricks. She became aware that Adam was talking.

"Hang onto it, darling, we'll be home in a minute. Did you hear what I said about the holiday?"

In a state of shock, Sarah tried to focus on the present, "No, sorry, I just heard what you said about Guy stopping over in Bali and Thailand."

"I said: why don't *we* go to Australia this year? I'm owed some extra holiday for all the weekends I've been working and surely the Council would let you take extended leave?"

"They might, but when are you talking about, isn't this year a bit soon? We're already into August."

"I thought maybe we could go before Christmas, it will be slap bang in the middle of their summer, which would be good, and it'll give us time to get it all organised. I would be quite happy to go over Christmas itself, but I know how much you enjoy us spending it with your family. Guy's advised me who to book with and where to go on the Internet to find out about places to stay and what have you. You know it's always been a country I've wanted to visit."

"Yes, I know, Ad," Sarah gave an exaggerated yawn and snuggled up to him, "but can't we talk about it tomorrow?"

"Of course we can, sleepy head," said Adam, kissing her lightly on the cheek.

CHAPTER ELEVEN

They did not get up until almost eleven the following morning and only then because the phone was ringing.

It was Sarah's Mum. "Hello darling, I just wanted to check how you are. We haven't heard from you for a while. Is everything ok?"

Still heavy with sleep, Sarah fumbled with the receiver, "Sorry Mum, I've been so busy lately, but yes, everything's fine and the house looks great now. Thanks again for the cheque; we used the money to buy a coffee table, it was just right for the living room." She tried to inject some enthusiasm into her voice and sound brighter than she felt. "As a matter of fact we are hoping to come down to see you next weekend if it's ok?"

"Of course it is, I've missed you and so has Dad. Steve should be here too. We could have a barbecue if it's nice."

An image of her brother popped into Sarah's head. Steve was eighteen months younger than she and they were like chalk and cheese. They had both done well at school, but unlike Sarah, who had always been determined to go to university, Steve's ambition went no further than leaving school at the first opportunity and starting an apprenticeship. Sarah smiled to herself. She could not imagine her happy-go-lucky brother ever settling down, though he always appeared to have a swarm of girls around him wherever he went. She supposed he was handsome in a sort of way with his floppy, sandy-coloured hair, large hazel eyes, straight nose and well-proportioned face. He had a great physique too; had been into weight training for as long as Sarah could remember and was proud of his musculature. As children they had fought like cat and dog, but since leaving school had grown much closer. It would be good to see him again.

"That sounds good, thanks Mum. Look, can I ring you back? We went out last night for the first time in ages and I think I overdid it a bit; feel a bit hung over."

"It's really not good for you to drink too much, dear; make sure you drink plenty of water today, and eat a proper meal."

Sarah laughed. Her mother still treated her as if she was a naughty teenager. "I will Mum, don't worry. And anyway, you know we don't drink very often. We were celebrating getting the house finished, that's all. Must go - I'll ring you tonight. Give my love to Dad."

Smiling to herself, Sarah put the phone back on its rest. She was close to both her parents, but her Mum was teetotal and disapproved of excessive consumption of alcohol, particularly in young people, which meant Sarah and Steve had always had to appear sober whenever they came home from an evening out. It had been a struggle at times and probably had not fooled their Mum for a minute!

She went slowly downstairs to the kitchen and poured herself a glass of orange juice. In fact she had not got a hangover as such. It was more to do with the fact that sleep had eluded her for most of the night. She had been thinking about the girl she had seen. Had she really recognised her – or had it been a figment of her imagination? She still could not be sure. But if she had, it made the whole situation even more confusing since the girl – Charlotte - was obviously still very much alive, which meant the dreadful scene in the dining room was not a vision of the past after all. In which case, was she seeing into the future? But how could that be? What possible reason might there be for Charlotte to be inside this house in the first place?

A terrible thought crept into Sarah's mind making her stomach lurch. Could Adam be having an affair with this girl? It would explain the connection. But surely that could not be true. She tried to think things through rationally. The girl from the painting – Jane – was definitely from the past. How could she be seeing both past and future? It made no sense. Almost, Sarah laughed at herself; as if any of it made sense! The dark-haired man she had first seen in the bedroom most certainly was not Adam. The man in the dining room had been too shadowed to identify as the original ghost, but even so, his build had been all wrong for

Adam. Besides which, she trusted her husband completely - didn't she? He would not want to jeopardise their relationship with a casual fling so soon after their marriage – would he? But try as she might, Sarah could not shrug off an uneasy feeling at the back of her mind that Adam was in some way connected with this whole ghastly business.

"Is this for me?"

Sarah started guiltily, almost dropping her glass as Adam came into the kitchen and pointed to a large glass of orange juice on the worktop. Masking her thoughts with a cheery smile, she reached for the bread bin. "Yes, I'm just doing some cheese and toast to go with it. How are you feeling?"

"Not bad, I think it helped that we stopped drinking in the club and I stayed in the shower till my head was clear. Who was that on the phone?"

"Mum. I told her we'd be coming down next weekend - that's what we arranged didn't we?"

"Yes, we haven't been for a while. I've booked next Monday and Tuesday off so we can stay a couple of days and catch up with everyone. Is Steve going to be around?"

Sarah smiled, planting a small kiss on her husband's cheek as he bent to retrieve the cheese from the fridge. He and her brother got on really well; both had the same keen interest in football and playstation games – typical boys! How could she possibly have imagined Adam had anything to do with Charlotte; it was inconceivable.

"Yes he'll be there; we'll take both sets of parents out for dinner on Sunday shall we? That is... do you think your Mum and Dad will come?" Adam's mother suffered from agoraphobia and found it difficult to socialise. The wedding had been a real dilemma for her as the guests numbered almost one hundred and fifty, most of whom were strangers to her, but she managed to cope with it all until the evening reception, at which point she and her husband had quietly slipped away.

"Yes they will, so long as it's only the seven of us."

Sarah felt mildly irritated. She found it hard to understand her mother-in-law's condition, which caused such awkwardness even around her own family, but especially when Steven was there. Yet he had always tried to be sociable with Adam's Mum. "Well at least Steve will be on his own," she said, voicing the thought. "He's without a steady girlfriend since he and Mandy split up, so that shouldn't be a problem."

"He's a bit of a lad isn't he? Adam grinned. "Mandy lasted all of seven months, which surely must be a record. Anyway, I'm going on the Internet for a bit to check out those sites Guy told me about. Have you thought any more about Australia?"

"Not really – but of course, if it's what you want and you think we can afford it, then I'm up for it." Sarah put a few slices of cheese and toast on a small plate. "Have these first, or take them up with you. By the way, I forgot to mention that I'm meeting Simon Leivers for lunch on Wednesday. We're just having a bit of a catch up."

"On his own?" Adam raised his eyebrows.

"I think so, though I didn't actually ask. It's just that he wants me to help organise a reunion with the people on our course, before we all lose touch, he said."

Adam nodded, "Did he now. I ought to do the same; I made some good mates on my course too."

"Then why don't you?"

"Maybe I will."

Sarah could tell from his expression that her husband was not entirely happy about it. He had met Simon a few times before they were married and had not liked him much, finding him a bit full of himself and difficult to talk to. Adam was perhaps a little possessive at times, but he was not really the jealous type and Sarah had never given him any reason to be. Even so, she knew he would be wondering why Simon all of a sudden wanted to renew their friendship. Once again, she was being deceitful, but she did not want Adam to know it had been she who had made the contact, for then he would demand to know why. Sarah was not yet ready to confide in him; not until she had found out more about Jane's murder - and about Charlotte - and was able to prove that she was not a nutcase.

Sarah took the opportunity to catch up on some chores while Adam downloaded information on places in Australia that were at the top of his list to visit. She had just finished the ironing and was having a cup of tea when he wandered back into the kitchen. "I can't believe how cheap these flights are. I'm going to talk to Michael tomorrow about taking extended leave. He might not be best pleased since as you know, we're encouraged to take only two weeks at a time, but-"

"You can't possibly go to Australia for two weeks that's-"

Adam frowned. "I know. Let me finish. Michael knows I'm owed a lot of time in lieu and the run up to Christmas is always slow, so there shouldn't be a problem. I've already mentioned it in passing and he seemed ok about the idea, so I don't anticipate it'll be a problem."

"Well, I have to say it's a tempting thought: all that lovely sunshine while the folks at home are coping with winter! I don't see any problem with me taking extended leave either, I'm owed plenty, but if I have to I'll take it as unpaid. Oh, Ad; can we really go? It would be wonderful!"

Adam pulled her into his arms and hugged her. "We'll go, darling. It'll be the holiday of a lifetime."

Sarah relaxed against him, raising her lips to his kiss, everything but their holiday plans pushed temporarily to the back of her mind.

CHAPTER TWELVE

The following Wednesday lunchtime Sarah was waiting for Simon in the square. It was a beautiful sunny, cloudless day, she was in a good mood but a little apprehensive about seeing her old friend. She was fully expecting the conversation to be difficult at first and wondered how the meeting would go. Years ago, when she had broken up with Andy, her first real boyfriend after Uni, who had been difficult when she ended their relationship, Simon had been really supportive. When later she had told him about Adam, he had seemed disappointed. She remembered him asking her out and saying he had hoped after Andy that he might be in with a chance. Sarah had thought he was joking, but looking back with wiser, more experienced eyes, she was not so sure. She hoped he realised now that it was never going to happen. Dread the thought that he imagined she was after some kind of an affair! Sarah knew she would have to approach with care her reason for wanting to see him; she did not want him thinking she had got in touch simply to make use of him - even if it was true.

"Hi." A tall, well-built man with short-cropped, spiky hair walked right up to her. He was wearing chinos, a linen jacket and an open-necked, white shirt that showed off a delicious looking tan.

It took a few moments for Sarah to recognise him. "Simon? Hi – wow, you look so different..."

He smiled, revealing perfect white teeth. "Is that good different?"

Sarah returned his smile, "I'm disappointed; had imagined you'd be in uniform."

"Well thanks a lot - and you look great too," he grinned. "I'm on a course, didn't I say? They let us out of uniform lest we frighten the horses!"

Sarah giggled, unable to believe how much he had changed in little more than a year. The Simon she remembered had been thin and weedy, rather studious looking, his hair almost reaching to his shoulders, but usually tied back in a pigtail and he had worn John Lennon specs. The man who stood in front of her now was a hunk: very much in shape, slim-waisted and broad shouldered. The cropped look suited him as did his new physique. He must be wearing contacts because the specs had gone too.

"You've been doing weight training," she said accusingly.

"You noticed."

She had also noticed, but did not say, that he looked tired. "Right," she said, "let's go and eat, are you hungry?"

"Yes, I didn't get a chance to have any breakfast at the station."

They walked across the square into a trendy pub that also served food. Sarah, distracted and not sure what to say, picked up a couple of menus and chose a table by the window.

As they sat down, Simon seemed perfectly at ease. "It's great to see you, Sarah – it seems longer than a year. Are you and Adam still living in the same house?"

"No, we moved almost three months ago."

"That's a shame. I really liked your old place."

"I did too," Sarah said, wishing she and Adam had been more content to stay in their old house. Oh God - if only.... She noticed Simon looking at her, his eyes brimming with curiosity. She had never noticed before how blue they were. Were the contacts tinted? Surely not. "But we wanted to buy somewhere together," she added hastily.

"Ahh! How sweet."

Simon's tone was mocking and it made her laugh. "Be careful or I might make you pay for your lunch after all!"

"Ok, ok," Simon held his hands up in pretended horror. "So how's work? Are you still in IT?"

"Yes, I really like working on software problems and I got promoted a few months ago to Team Manager. Anyway, how's life in the fast lane?"

"Very hard, long hours and an unbelievable amount of paperwork, but I love it. I couldn't imagine doing anything else."

"I bet it's very rewarding, what sort of cases do you investigate?"

"Well, no major cases so far, but I've been involved with a lot of street crime, which has included one or two rape cases unfortunately, but yes it is rewarding when we catch the bad guys. I've been lucky to work with some very good DIs and hopefully, if I keep my head down and work at it, that's what I will become eventually."

"You've never been involved in any murder cases then?"

"I've been present at some interviews with murder suspects, but no, I haven't been directly involved in any murders. Can I get you a drink?"

"A diet coke would be good, thanks."

Sarah watched Simon move over to the bar still unable to relate him to the man she had known. That he was tired was obvious from the heaviness around his eyes, but she had to admit he looked far happier than when she had seen him last – and devastatingly attractive. What a transformation – it was like Cinderella in reverse. All she needed was a glass boot. She was still giggling at the thought when he came back with the drinks.

"What's so amusing then?"

"Oh, nothing really, I was just thinking how much you've changed."

"Have I? Well, yes, I suppose I have." He grinned, set her coke down in front of her and taking a sip from a tall glass of what looked like mineral water, sat down beside her. Noticing her raised eyebrows, he grinned, "Daren't drink alcohol in the middle of the day, I'll fall asleep at my desk. You were asking about murders. I've come across some real lowlife I have to say. I've had to learn to keep hold of my temper and not let some of the bastards get to me. The training in this area is excellent on our force, but I have felt at times that I could really lose it, you know? My work mates tell me they've felt the same way at some point or another; it helps to talk about it."

"So your colleagues are really supportive then?" Sarah was impressed. Undoubtedly the job had changed her old friend. He seemed to have matured a good deal since university, was no longer quite the joker she remembered; the one who had always said that life was there to be enjoyed. Even so, he had always knuckled down when it came to exams and coursework, which was presumably why he was doing so well now.

Simon smiled. "The people I work with on a daily basis are not so much colleagues as close mates. We support each other; we work together and socialise quite a bit too. Most policemen do – you know, hang out together after work. We have a lot of respect for each other and one thing I've realised is how much I've come to rely on them. When you're working a case or dealing with some vicious characters, you need that support. Not one of my mates has ever let me down yet." He tapped the table, "Touch wood they never do and that I never let them down either." He broke off and grinned as Sarah's stomach audibly rumbled.

She blushed, "Sorry, but I've got to order now; I'm starving. You have just two minutes to choose what you want or I'll eat without you."

Simon quickly surveyed the menu. "I'll have the 'Steakwich' with salad and fries. He leaned across the table and lightly touched her hand as she got out her purse, "but put that away, I'll get these."

"No you won't. It's my treat; you can pay next time."

He shrugged, "Fair enough."

Whilst they were waiting for their food they talked about old times and gradually Sarah found herself slipping back into the easy, teasing, laughter-filled relationship they had once had soon after they had first met: two greenhorn students in their first year away from home. The conversation barely paused as the food was delivered to their table and they got stuck into their meal.

"They give very generous portions here don't they; I'm stuffed," Sarah pushed the last few mouthfuls away from her. "So you're still single then? Not met Miss Right yet? Surely there are a few decent-looking police women?"

Simon stared at Sarah intently for a few seconds and cupped his hand over hers. "I met Miss Right, remember, but she didn't want to know."

Yet again, Sarah could feel herself blushing.

Simon cracked out laughing. "Just look at your face! If you must know, I've had a few relationships since we parted - one of them actually lasted eight months, but it ended because of the hours I put in on my job, which is sad in a way, but I love my work, so no, no decent love life yet."

Relieved, not only that Simon had been teasing her, but also that he was still single, though not sure why she should feel that way, Sarah inwardly reprimanded herself. What was she thinking of? She was behaving like a teenager just because an attractive man was flirting with her. Giving herself a mental shake, she focussed on the real reason she had invited Simon to lunch. Jane Moore. The lunch break was moving along all too quickly, it was now or never.

"Before I forget, there's something I wanted to ask you, Simon – that is, about your work."

"I'm all ears."

"I was in the library doing some research the other day – I'm working up a project about town planning. Anyway, I was looking through old newspapers on microfiche and I happened across a story about Jane Moore."

"The name seems familiar. Do I know her?"

"I doubt it, but you may have heard of her. She was murdered ten years ago. It sparked my interest because it happened to be near to where we now live - and I believe after that another girl was murdered - Charlotte somebody - but I didn't have enough time to read up on it." Sarah gave a small smile, trying to sound nonchalant. "And there was I thinking it was quite a nice place to live. I just wondered if the killer was caught - thought you might know."

Simon shrugged, finished his drink and shook his head. "Every town has its fair share of trouble, that's not bad going – two murders in ten years. You want to see how many murders happen each month in the country and sometimes the killers are never found, but I don't want to scare you. We do a good job overall, but you always get the psychos around. Actually, if you look at the stats like I had to a few months back, a high percentage of victims know their attackers." He pointed to Sarah's empty glass.

"Can I get you another?"

Fully intending to pursue the conversation, Sarah nodded. "Yes please, another diet coke?"

While Simon stood at the bar, Sarah had time to acknowledge that she was enjoying his company far more than she should; not only that, but she wanted to prolong it. She knew she had slipped into dangerous territory. Since she and Adam had been on their first date she had always been totally faithful – never even looked at another man. She was annoyed at herself for finding Simon so attractive; it felt disloyal to Adam. Yet she could not deny that she and Simon had chemistry and she was aware from his attentive behaviour and the warmth behind his eyes that Simon still fancied her. As he returned with the drinks she found herself wondering if getting him involved with her quest was such a good idea.

"You were saying that some murderers are never caught," she said as he slid into the chair beside her. "Is that still the case? I thought the police managed to catch suspects from cold cases these days because of DNA testing?"

"That's true, but it depends upon what information and evidence we have on the victim. We're a lot more thorough now when collecting evidence, but I am always amazed how Forensics manage to find enough DNA to test."

"Supposing I wanted to find out about an old murder case, where would I start?"

"What's this got to do with town planning?" Simon sat up straight and looked directly into her eyes. "I feel that there's something you're not telling me, Sarah." He frowned, said suspiciously, "Are you in some kind of trouble? Or is Adam?"

Sarah laughed and shook her head. "Don't be silly, Detective Leivers. It's the local history aspect that intrigues me. And if I'm honest, the fact that a killer might still be on the loose so near to our new home makes me feel a little uncomfortable."

"The Jane Moore case you mean."

"Yes. It was awful. She was only a teenager, strangled apparently and cut up into pieces. They found her remains in a warehouse near to where we live. A neighbour of ours is convinced she was murdered actually inside our house before the new owners moved in not long after it was built. It's probably only gossip and her evidence is sketchy, but you know me. I'm so nosy and also I just freaked out that something so horrendous could have happened in my home." Sarah shrugged, "But it was only a thought. Not to worry if you don't want to talk about it."

She had tried to sound neutral and hoped the lie about the neighbour sounded plausible; she wished she could tell Simon the truth and make him understand how horrified and scared she really was, how terrifying visions and ghosts were taking over her life.

"No, it's alright; go on, I'm intrigued."

"The houses in our close had only just been completed at the time of Jane Moore's murder and this neighbour, who obviously had only just moved in, said she was convinced she saw Jane sitting in our garden, and then saw her again, only that time going into the house with a man." Sarah paused, thinking on her feet. Goodness, but she was getting too adept at lying!

"Go on," Simon said intently.

"Well, she said she heard them having a fierce argument. The weird thing is that the Palmers, the people we bought the house from – they were the first to own it - didn't move in for about five weeks whilst the place was being decorated, and so there was indeed an opportunity for someone to gain access while the house was standing empty. So I wondered, who was this man and why was Jane with him in an empty house? It's all quite strange."

Simon looked puzzled, "I agree, it's more than a bit strange, but how come this neighbour told you all about it? Was the murderer never caught?"

"That's exactly what I was wondering, which is why I mentioned it." Sarah shifted uneasily in her seat, she really hated lying, but if Simon knew the truth he certainly would not be so keen to help her and would dismiss her as some sort of crackpot; there was no hard evidence, no real witnesses to the murder; just her own sixth sense portraying strange visions of what might have happened. "I read in the paper that Jane's boyfriend was arrested initially, but later released. It must have been in all the papers at the time, but I can't remember it. We didn't live in the area ten years ago, and anyway, in those days I was probably too busy partying to watch the news!"

"Do you think your neighbour could be making it all up, after all you don't know her that well yet...?"

"True, but she seems pretty sensible and quite intelligent, though she is certainly lonely. Her husband works away quite a bit. But why would someone make it up, especially when we'd only just moved in?"

Simon gave a wry grimace. "You'd be surprised how many sensible people make up stories to get attention. Some of them must have really vivid imaginations, but it makes our job difficult; you get so many time-wasters it can be very annoying. What does Adam think about it?"

"He doesn't know. I didn't want to worry him, and anyway, he'd probably laugh at me for entertaining mindless gossip from a crackpot neighbour. He can be a bit critical of me at times." Sarah inwardly cringed at her disloyalty. As soon as the words left her mouth she wished she had not spoken them.

"Ah." Simon arched his eyebrows and looked at her thoughtfully, but said nothing more.

"I think she's not just craving attention though," Sarah continued. "She seems very agitated by it and also the fact that the police didn't take her seriously, even though she described the man with Jane in great detail. I think she just wants closure and to know what really happened. It's got me intrigued too, and as I said, I'd like to find out more about the case if I can, but I'm not sure where to start."

"Don't think I'm raining on your parade, but I disagree about the attention seeking. I suspect your neighbour has nothing better to do than fantasise about a murder that happened ten years ago. We get them all the time. She might have seen someone who looked like Jane going into the house. It could just as easily have been someone looking over the house with a view to buying a similar one in the same road, especially if it was empty – a good opportunity for a snoop. I'm surprised you gave your neighbour's story credence, but I can see that it concerns you."

Simon emptied his glass, put it gently on the table and leaned forward. "Tell you what, just to put your mind at rest about your new home I can look through the station archives and dig up the case notes. It might take me a few days though as I've got some heavy shifts coming up. But I guess you're not in a hurry – it happened ten years ago after all!"

To her annoyance, Sarah found she was welling up. Dashing a hand over her eyes, she said, "I'd be really grateful, Simon, thank you. I know the killer was probably arrested and convicted years ago and everything sorted out, but it would be such a relief to know for sure," she gave a weak smile, "it'd stop me having nightmares for one thing."

"I thought there was something you weren't telling me. You've been *really* worried about this haven't you?" Simon took hold of her hand and gave it a gentle squeeze. "Hey, don't let it get to you. Like I said, I'm sure your neighbour was mistaken. She's probably been watching too much television, or was trying to frighten you for her own amusement."

Acutely conscious of his fingers caressing hers, Sarah pulled her hand free and glanced at her watch. "Goodness, look at the time; it has gone so quickly. I'd better get back to work much as I would like to sit here all afternoon. It's been really great to see you again and catch up."

"Likewise, I'll give you a ring as soon as I find out anything, but try not to worry, eh? Can I have your mobile number? Here, let me give you mine."

When they had exchanged numbers, Sarah got up, planted a light kiss on Simon's cheek and went to the bar to pay the bill, only to find it had already been settled. Shaking her fist at Simon in mock anger, she grinned, mouthed 'Thank you' and hurried out of the pub.

Simon had come up trumps as she supposed she had known he would – but the feelings he had stirred in her, which she was trying desperately to deny, were unsettling. Why was she so attracted to him when she never had been before – well, not since their first few weeks at Uni anyway? Surely she was not so shallow as to have fallen for his physique and transformed looks? Worried, Sarah hurried to work, arriving red-faced and out of breath just before the core flexitime ended.

CHAPTER THIRTEEN

Feeling much more positive, Sarah waited for her computer to boot up, conscious that she should get on with her work, but unable to resist reflecting on her lunch date. She had so much enjoyed it – she smiled to herself - rather too much in the circumstances. A sudden thought struck her and as though Lola was speaking into her ear, she heard again the medium's soft voice: *This is the Four of Cups upright in a spread. This means the focus is on past relationships, which might not be healthy. You need to be aware of a new love potential.* Oh no, surely not! Surely the medium had not meant Simon. Admittedly he had achieved quite some makeover, indeed, he was now extremely handsome, but underneath it all he was still the same old friend from Uni, still teasing her and cracking inane jokes. For a moment she toyed with the image of how he might look in uniform; he must surely have many female admirers. What was wrong with her? She was happily married to Adam – he was everything she wanted. She was certainly not a bored housewife, and she did not want or need to flirt with an old flame just because he found her attractive and had somehow changed into a hunk! Forcing herself to concentrate on resolving the system integrities that had landed on her desk, Sarah knuckled down to work and the afternoon passed quickly by. It was almost six when her mobile beeped: it was Adam.

"Hi, how are you?"

"Not bad, I'm just about finished. I can't really complain as I had a two-hour lunch break."

"Oh yes; Simon. How was he?" Adam's voice was strained, as if he was forcing himself to sound cheerful. "Hopefully he's changed for the better since we last saw him?"

"Well he really loves his job, if that's what you mean. I didn't notice that he was any different, but it was good to catch up." She quickly changed the subject, "Are you going to order something for tea? I forget to take any meat out of the freezer."

"Yes, no problem, I've just got home. I'll nip down the shops and get us a ham and pineapple pizza and some garlic bread." There was a slight pause. "Is Simon married now?"

"No, only to his job - I gather he's always at work; no time for any social life beyond the force, he said. That was why he wants me to help organise this reunion thing – but it probably won't be for a while, he's tied up on some training programme for several weeks evidently." Sarah listened to herself and was aghast that she could so easily lie; but they were only white lies weren't they? No point in worrying Adam for no good reason. No harm done.

The relief in Adam's voice was palpable. "Ok I'll see you later, take care. I love you."

"I love you too – very much."

Feeling guilty, Sarah tidied her paperwork away. She had never been in love with Simon. He had simply been a good friend, nothing more. He was just doing her a favour that was all; there was nothing to feel guilty about. I mean, she thought to herself, you don't feel guilty for finding Brad Pitt attractive do you? It doesn't mean you want to leap into bed with him. But she knew she was spinning herself a line; sensed that Simon still wanted her and there was nothing more seductive. He had been very pleased to see her and had looked at her with open admiration. Could she handle that if they met again? Maybe it was best if she restricted any further communication between them to the telephone. Sarah knew she had to be careful, her marriage was everything and she loved Adam deeply.

As soon as she entered the house she could smell the pizza and garlic bread. "Hi Ad, I'm home. That smells wonderful." Sarah went through to the living room. The fire was on, the room warm and cosy. On the coffee table were two glasses of wine. She felt a rush of contentment; who would believe this house was haunted, let alone that terrible events had taken place here. It all looked so ordinary.

Adam came in balancing a tray in each hand. "I thought we'd have it in front of the telly if that's ok with you?"

"Great idea darling, thank you. I could eat a horse." Aware that it saved her from having to think of innocuous things to say about Simon, Sarah squashed a treacherous feeling of relief as Adam switched on the TV.

After they had eaten, Sarah cleared away and loaded up the dishwasher. It was an unwritten rule in their marriage that whoever got the meal was spared the clearing up. When she had finished, she sat down next to her husband on the sofa and kissed him lightly on the lips. "Thank you, that pizza was exactly what I needed; I'm stuffed."

Adam smirked. "Well I would have cooked something more substantial if I'd known you wanted a horse, but I didn't know how hungry you'd be after going out for lunch."

"It was nothing special – just a pub lunch, you know the sort of thing, baguettes and a side salad. I didn't fancy the chips."

"So, has Simon been in touch with anyone else from university?"

"He's seen one or two from our old tutor group, but I need to organise a proper reunion some time. I think between us we've got everyone's mobile number or email address, but like I said, it won't be for a while – and besides, I've got much too much to think about planning for our holiday," she gave him a bright smile.

"So are you going to meet up again?" Adam asked, sliding his arm about her waist.

Sarah heard the note of jealousy in her husband's voice and knew he was attempting to appear cool and calm. "Probably not for a while, like I said. Perhaps next time we can fix it so you can come too, you might be able to help – especially if you are planning to do the same sort of thing with your old mates." Anxious to change the subject, she added, "Have you found out any more about Australia?"

Adam beamed at her, "Yes, we need to sort out where we want to go, get some sort of itinerary together. Michael has agreed to my taking extended leave provided I train up someone else to cover the basics while I'm away. The new guy – Toby - has already picked up on most of what he needs to know, he's bright and is keen to learn. It's his second career; evidently he started off as a-"

"Toby?" Sarah interrupted, "that's an unusual name; makes me think of jugs and highwaymen!"

"Does it?" Adam smiled. "Well he's not in the least like either. Anyway, I was saying, I think the team will cope without me for a few weeks, particularly since it'll be a quiet time anyway in the run up to Christmas. It's afterwards the insurance claims start coming in thick and fast. You know - all that spilled red wine on cream carpets!"

Sarah giggled, "Well all I need to know are the dates. My boss is fine about it. She says it's just a case of making sure everything keeps ticking over. None of my team is planning any leave before Christmas anyway; most of them have tacked it onto New Year, so that's ok."

His face alight, Adam hugged her. "That's great; I can't wait. I'll write the dates down for you to take in tomorrow."

It seemed he had forgotten all about Simon. For that at least, Sarah was thankful.

For the remainder of the evening they snuggled down to watch a film, but Sarah found her mind kept wandering. She could not really blame Adam for being jealous. She would feel the same if he were to have a lunch date with an old flame, especially if it was one who still carried a torch for him. No matter how self-confident her husband appeared, Sarah knew he suffered from insecurity at times. It was the odd things he said occasionally, which led her to believe he wanted constant reassurance that she still loved and wanted him. Maybe it was a hang-up from being adopted at six weeks' old and growing up only child. Adam had often told her how grateful he was to his adoptive parents. They had brought him up in a loving family home; often going without so he could have a good education and always supporting him in whatever he chose to do. But however much his mother had reassured him that he was loved and wanted, there was always that lingering question as to why his birth mother had given him away. As an adult, Adam had uncovered the answer to that, but by then his insecurities were too much a part of his psyche to change. He had spoken to Sarah about his birth parents only once. According to the adoption agency, his mother had been a young teenager when she became pregnant and her boyfriend – Adam's father - had dumped her. Without supportive parents to help her and unable to cope alone, she had reluctantly given up her baby for adoption. Sarah could sympathise with her dilemma. A baby was a huge responsibility at any age, but for young teenagers it must seem an insurmountable problem and so drastic a change in their lives: plans for a future career brought to an abrupt halt; dreams of a happy marriage potentially destroyed. Few young man are prepared to take on a ready-made family; the situation must have seemed bleak for Adam's birth mother, no matter how devoted she was to her baby. Sarah knew if it had happened to her she would have been utterly reliant on her parents. The pressure would have been unbearable and she may well have ended up resenting her own child as much as she did the absent father. Every child deserved loving parents. Sarah could not begin to imagine what a heartrending decision it must have been for Adam's birth mother and what a wrench to part with him, but to Sarah it seemed such an unselfish act; she had made the sacrifice to give her son a better life.

Giving up on the film, Sarah was just considering having a bath when Guy phoned Adam's mobile. She waited a few minutes, but it was clear Adam would be on the phone discussing Australia for ages, so she pointed upstairs to him and mouthed, 'Going for a bath'. He nodded and blew her a kiss. She turned down the sound on the television and left him to it.

It seemed suddenly cold going from the living room to the hallway. Sarah checked the central heating thermostat and turned it up a little. Intending to collect some fresh towels from the airing cupboard, she switched on the landing light on her way upstairs to the bathroom. Ever since those first nightmarish visions she had hated going in there, dreaded opening the door, but it was something she would just have to get over – or so she told herself. She noticed that the door to the small spare room was open and out of the corner of her eye saw something black standing on the carpet – it looked like a full bin bag. Dumping the towels in the bathroom and turning the bath taps on, she went to check. Adam had been talking about getting rid of some of his old clothes in response to a plea from the charity shop that had been distributing plastic bags around the close – but surely they were white? Obviously not: there were three large black sacks lying on the floor tied tightly at the tops. Maybe he had decided to throw in a few extra things and used bin bags instead. She found it hard to believe that Adam had got rid of quite so many clothes; he'd have hardly any left at this rate.

Sarah went through to their bedroom and looked inside the wardrobe, puzzled to find it was still as full as before. That was odd; where had he got all those clothes from and why had he left them in the spare room instead of taking them downstairs for collection? Sarah shivered and feeling a little uneasy walked back along the landing to the bathroom. As she did so, she caught a whiff of something in the air: an unpleasant, pungent smell. Unable to place it, and remembering the taps were still running, she hurried to turn them off.

Curious to know what exactly Adam had thrown away, she returned to the black sacks wondering if he had put in some of her clothes too. Fair enough, but he might have asked her first. She supposed she had better take a look. As she bent over the first sack, the peculiar smell seemed stronger; whatever was it? Had he chucked in some old trainers? 'Men!' she muttered to herself.

The knot was very tight, but with her long nails she managed to undo it. Suddenly, the smell was overpowering; a rotten, musty stench. Sarah retched, covering her mouth and nose with her hand. It was then that she noticed a line of red coming from the bottom of the sack, seeping into their cream carpet. Dropping to her knees as realisation dawned, Sarah, her eyes streaming, felt glued to the spot. How could she not have recognised the stink of putrefaction? Her senses screamed at her to leave the sacks alone and run away, but the urge to look inside was too strong. Dreading what she would find, she ripped through the plastic. What looked like a bundle of thick towels spilled out onto the carpet; they were sticky, completely soaked in blood.

Feeling the bile rushing up her throat, Sarah scrambled to her feet, ran to the loo and vomited instantly and violently. With tears still streaming down her face, she tried to shake the images away. It isn't real, she told herself. And yet it seemed so very real. Was it Jane's blood, had she been slaughtered in that very room? What kind of a monster would be capable of doing such a thing? No normal person could have done this.

CHAPTER FOURTEEN

"Have you finished in the bathroom?"

The question made Sarah jump. She could not speak. Were the sacks real?

Adam's voice came again as he climbed the stairs. "I heard you retching. Was it the pizza? My stomach's feeling a tiny bit dodgy too." He came into the bathroom. "Are you ok? Lord, I hope I haven't poisoned us both. It thought it was well within its use-by date, but I may have misread the label. Can I get you anything?"

She nodded and sat on the side of the bath breathing deeply, trying to regain her composure. "Will you just check in the little bedroom for me," she said hoarsely, "I think I left my bath towels in there? I had to be sick and it came on suddenly."

"Sure. You should get in the bath, your teeth are chattering. Hang on a minute, I'll just get your towels and then I'll come and scrub your back." He went out of the bathroom and Sarah got straight into the bath. She felt so cold, like a block of ice, which the hot water did little to expel. Her throat was sore from being sick and every time she closed her eyes all she could see was the blood; so much blood.

She heard Adam's footsteps coming back along the landing. "Did you find the towels?" she called. "If not, I may have left them in the bedroom."

He did not reply.

The door pushed open. It was not Adam who stood there, but the dark-haired ghost. In his hand he held a saw, the blade smeared with blood. He wore a white T-shirt that was splattered with red dots. The rage and cruelty in his face were frightening, but he was not looking at Sarah: he seemed utterly self-absorbed.

Sarah covered her breasts with her hands, lay motionless, not daring to breathe, but the man looked right through her, appeared not to see her at all. After what seemed like forever he turned and walked out of the room. Sitting up, Sarah gulped in some air, her chest heaving.

"No – you didn't leave the towels in there, the room is completely empty – and they're not in the bedroom either." Adam walked into the bathroom and saw the towels where she had left them on the floor. "Hang on, aren't these they? You're getting forgetful in your old age, babe," he smiled, looked at her and exclaimed: "Goodness! Your face is as white as a sheet. Have you been sick again?"

Sarah splashed herself with bath water, the horror of what she had just witnessed making her want to cry out: to shout and scream at Adam for not seeing it too. One minute she was cold and shivering, the next so very hot. She held back her tears, drew her mouth down, "No, but I don't feel too good. Will you wash my back now?"

"Yes of course. Hope you're not coming down with something."

"Me too; I haven't been sleeping too well lately, it's probably just that I'm tired.

Adam put some soap on a sponge and began to lather Sarah's back. "The sooner we get you into bed the better in that case."

"Oh that does feel good," she said, leaning into his hand as he gently sponged her back. She was perplexed that Adam had noticed nothing untoward. He had come into the bathroom almost at the same moment the ghost had left it. How could he not have seen it - or at least feel something as they passed so close to each other? She turned to look up at his face, "Did you think the house felt a bit cold just now? The small bedroom felt like an ice box when I looked in there."

"Cold? No, I'm only wearing a T-shirt and I feel really warm. And anyway, that room gets the sun all afternoon. I think you might be coming down with a virus."

Sarah shrugged, said absently, "Maybe." She could not explain what was happening to her, but whatever it was she was becoming increasingly anxious that they might both be in danger. The dark-haired killer was clearly insane.

Adam squeezed out the sponge and bent to drop a kiss on Sarah's shoulder. "Is that ok?"

"Lovely, thanks. I'll just have a soak for a while."

"Ok, but don't get cold." He turned to go, but not wanting to be alone, Sarah caught hold of his hand. "Will you stay and talk to me?" she wheedled, knowing she sounded pathetic.

"Of course I will." Adam hesitated, his eyebrows knitted together. "Are you sure you're ok?"

Sarah nodded, "Just want some company that's all." She could see he was concerned about her. Who could blame him when she was acting so strangely? What must he think of her? Once again, she almost blurted out what she had seen, but as before, something stopped her. She could not bear the thought of him not taking her seriously and treating her like some crazed child, or worse, insisting she see a psychiatrist. Would he stop loving her if he thought she was deranged? She knew she had to confide in someone soon; it was too heavy a burden to carry alone and would lead to a breakdown if it went on. Perhaps she should go and see a doctor after all, maybe get some tranquillisers or something. Their dream home had turned into an evil nightmare; a place she no longer wanted to live in. She wanted to sell up and move away; as far away as possible. But how could she say that to Adam when he was so pleased with the house?

He sat on the edge of the bath and chatted about Australia. Sarah listened with only half an ear, not saying much as he excitedly listed the places they would visit and the things they must see and do. She could see he was disappointed by her lack of enthusiasm, but she could not help it. Her mind was too taken up with the terrible events that were unfolding before her eyes and had left her anxiously wondering where it was all leading and how it would end. Would she be forced to see the killer actually committing the murder – severing Jane Moore's limbs? The thought made her shrink inside herself with horror. She had never felt so helpless and out of control. How long could she go on pretending to everyone else that everything was normal?

CHAPTER FIFTEEN

For the remainder of the week, Sarah made a point of ensuring she was never alone in the house. Adam must have noticed she was being a bit clingy, which was not like her, but aside from giving her a few odd looks, he had not remarked on it.

At last it was Friday afternoon and they were getting ready to go and see her parents. Sarah could not wait to get away.

"It's only for a few days," Adam said, slightly exasperated as Sarah carried her overnight bag into the hall. "Whatever have you got in there - it's bursting at the seams."

"I know, but I need to take a few different outfits just in case. I'm going out with Jenny on Saturday and then we've got the family dinner on Sunday night - and you never know if it'll turn cold, so I've put in a few warm jumpers as well."

Adam grinned, "Just a few, eh? Sure you haven't got the kitchen sink in there as well?" He hefted the bag onto his shoulder, "Come on, we'd better get going. If you don't mind, I'd like to pop in to see my Mum on the way. I know we'll see them on Sunday, but I'd just like to say hello. If the motorway's not too bad we might make it for about seven-thirty."

Sarah smiled sympathetically. "Yes, of course."

He in-laws were quite a few years older than her Mum and Dad and perhaps because Adam was their only offspring, they missed him a lot. He had always felt guilty for moving so far north and he and Sarah tried to see both sets of parents as often as possible. It was not a problem while they had no children, but Sarah could imagine it would be much more difficult with a baby in tow. Her own parents had often talked about moving further up north to be closer to them; she wished they were in a position to do that right now, she had never felt so isolated.

They made their destination in good time, had a cup of tea and a few sandwiches with Adam's Mum and Dad, and soon after nine, Sarah was at last enveloped in her own parents' warm, welcoming hugs. They had always been close and Sarah still missed the girly chats she used to have with her Mum; talking over the phone just wasn't the same.

Mrs Sheldon held Sarah away from her and looked her up and down with a critical eye, "You've lost weight - and so has Adam by the look of him. I hope you're looking after yourselves you two." Sarah's Dad rolled his eyes at his son-in-law and murmured, "I'll beat a hasty retreat and make us a cup of tea," which made Adam laugh.

"Well we've been eating plenty," Sarah reassured her mother. "It's not easy to cook a proper meal every night of the week when we're both so busy at work and don't get home much before seven, but we manage; it's not all takeaways, Mum, honest."

Mrs Sheldon looked unconvinced. "Well I've made a nice shepherd's pie. Dad and I have already eaten, but there's plenty keeping warm in the oven. I wasn't sure how hungry you'd be," she said, ushering them into the lounge.

"Thanks, that sounds great," Adam grinned, "but would you be awfully offended if I passed? Mum made us some sandwiches, so I'm not very hungry at the moment."

Sarah nodded. "Me too - we'll have it tomorrow, if that's ok?"

"Of course - if Steve leaves you any." Mrs Sheldon smiled wryly, "He's out with one of his mates. He said not to wait up. He'll be back late and ravenous as usual I daresay. You won't say no to a slice if cake though, will you Adam?"

He laughed, "How could I resist?"

Pleased, Mrs Sheldon smiled. "I've been doing a lot of baking recently; stocking up the freezer so you'll have plenty of ready meals to take back with you, if it helps."

"That'd be great, thanks Mum." Sarah said, as her father emerged from the kitchen carrying two mugs of tea and his wife's fabled chocolate cake. With a contended sigh, Sarah stretched out in the leather armchair and watched her mother slice up the cake whilst Dad and Adam chatted about football. It was so good to be home. Watching her parents, Sarah was as always surprised by how little they seemed to age; they had hardly changed at all in thirty years of marriage. Her mother's blonde hair was cut into a bob that framed her heart-shaped face. She was slim and active; had always made a point of walking everywhere she went in order to maintain her slender waistline. Much to Mrs Sheldon's chagrin, her husband was naturally lean and never saw the need to try to keep fit. He looked much younger than fifty-one, his hair still thick and dark with no traces of grey. They made an attractive couple and Sarah was proud of them. "I must say you both look wonderful," she beamed from one to the other.

Her Mum smiled. "Thanks love; must be down to the mini-break we had the other week. It was so relaxing, though I think your Dad got a bit bored. He had to leave his golf clubs behind."

Sarah laughed, "Surely not! I thought he took them to bed with him. He'd like it where we are, there's a really nice golf club – or so Adam tells me. He plays there occasionally. Are you still considering moving to our neck of the woods?"

"Funny you should ask. We had the house valued only the other day. You'd never believe how much it has gone up in value since we bought it. I was amazed."

"Well it was twenty years ago, Rose," Mr Sheldon chipped in disparagingly.

His wife shot him a dark look. "I know that, but as I was going on to say, Sarah, if your Dad accepts the redundancy package his firm is offering and we get close to the valuation figure, he'll be able to take early retirement and moving won't be a problem. Then he can spend all his days on your golf course!"

Mr Sheldon winked at his daughter, "Are you sure you want your old Mum and Dad living closer to you and cramping your style?"

Sarah wanted to shout out, 'Yes, yes, yes, I can think of nothing I want more, especially right now,' but not wishing to worry them by sounding over-enthusiastic, which was sure to give them the idea that something was wrong with her marriage, she said only, "You both know we would love to have you living closer to us. Is Steve still planning to move to Spain by the way?"

A pained look crossed Mrs Sheldon's face. "Yes, he's convinced that he and his friends can make much more money over there. Once they've saved up enough, they plan to set up in business back here, hopefully in no more than a couple of years' time."

Sarah was impressed by her brother's aspirations. "He'll be fine Mum, he's going with his two most sensible friends; they'll all look out for each other."

"I know; I just worry about him that's all. I'm so afraid he's being overly optimistic.

"They'll certainly need plenty of money behind them to get the business started," Adam said, "but Sarah's right. I've met Steve's friends and they all seem pretty keen to make a go of things."

Mrs Sheldon visibly relaxed. "Have you two made any plans for tomorrow morning? If not, I thought you and I might go to town, Sarah. I want to buy some clothes. Which reminds me, I saw Jenny the other day; are you planning on catching up with her while you're here?"

Jenny had been Sarah's best friend since Junior School. They had always made the effort to keep in touch despite the distance between them. It always surprised Sarah how every time she saw her friend it was as though they had never been apart; they just seemed to pick up where they had left off. There was always plenty to talk about and they had a mutual respect for one another. She trusted Jenny completely and had already made up her mind to tell her about Jane Moore and the ghosts. She knew Jenny would take her seriously: it would be such a relief to get her opinion about what was going on.

Sarah smiled up at her Mum, "Yes, I'm going out with her tomorrow evening; we'll probably catch a film or something. No plans for the daytime though. I'd love to go shopping with you. Can't remember the last time I went to London."

"That'll be nice, dear. More cake anyone?"

There was no sign of Steve the next morning. "He's probably having a lie-in," Mrs Sheldon said as she and Sarah cleared away the breakfast things. "Goodness knows what time he got in last night."

Sarah, who had heard him come in at around two o'clock, laughed. Her brother would be unlikely to emerge before lunch time. She wondered if it had really been 'a mate' that he had been with last evening – more likely a girl, but she did not want to drop him in it. Soon after breakfast, Adam had gone off for a round of golf with Dad and now that she and her Mum had the place to themselves, Sarah sensed a slight tension in the atmosphere. She guessed what was coming. She had never been able to hide anything from her Mum.

"It's none of my business, Sarah, and I don't want to pry, but is everything alright between you and Adam? I get the feeling that there's something you're not telling me. It's not unusual to go through a bad patch once the honeymoon wears off, you know. Do you want to talk about it darling? You know you can talk to me about anything."

"Adam and I are fine, Mum, stop worrying about us. It's work that's the problem. I'm just a bit tired, that's all. We've had a lot of tight deadlines to meet and it has all been rather stressful lately, but it will slow down next month. I'm coping and Adam is really supportive. It's nothing to worry about, honestly."

"I know you're ambitious, love, but don't overdo it, make plenty of time to enjoy yourself. You and Adam are both so young; you need to relax together more. You know what they say about all work and no play...."

"I know, we have resolved to improve our social life and we are planning to have a long holiday before Christmas. In fact, guess what: Adam's taking me to Australia. It's something he's always want-"

"Australia?" Mrs Sheldon shrieked, putting put down her tea towel and turning to face her daughter. "Oh Sarah, that's wonderful news! I want to hear all about it. Where are you going?"

"I'll tell you on the bus, Mum. We really need to get a move on if we want to get in some serious retail therapy."

Later, after they had walked many miles across London visiting as many clothes shops and department stores as they could fit in, they made their way home. Sarah had thoroughly enjoyed herself, especially when they had stopped to rest their aching feet and have a coffee, at which point she had consumed a very wicked hot chocolate fudge cake as a mid-morning snack. She had seriously considered telling her Mum about the murder case she was investigating, if not about the haunting, but in the end decided not to. It would only worry her and spoil their weekend.

CHAPTER SIXTEEN

On the way back from London, loaded with so many shopping bags that she and her Mum had to sit in separate seats on the bus, Sarah pulled out her mobile and phoned Jenny. "Are you still ok for this evening? Shall we go for a pizza at Zizi's or go and see a film? There's a good one showing at-"

Jenny cut across her, "Let's go for a pizza and a few drinks. I need to catch up with my best friend," she laughed, "it's been a long time; too long!"

"Great; I'll pick you up at seven." Switching off her mobile, Sarah pondered on how Jenny had sounded: she had not been as bubbly as usual and her laugh had seemed forced. Maybe it was just that she was tired. That would not be surprising in the circumstances. Jenny and her partner, Vinny, both had full-time jobs, and at home they had been up to their elbows in DIY for a very long time and were still, as far as Sarah knew. They had been together for nearly eight years and were soul-mates, or so it seemed: always teasing each other and larking about, both shared the same sense of humour and laid-back attitude to life. They had bought a dilapidated old house three years ago and had been renovating it to a very high standard of finish ever since. Sarah admired Jenny for persevering with the project. Living surrounded by constant mess and coming home from a day's work to start plastering walls and laying floors was not Sarah's idea of fun, but apparently they loved it. Vinny was a qualified joiner and skilled in most areas of DIY, while Jenny was the creative one with a flair for interior design. Last time Sarah had seen them they were talking about selling up and investing in another house to restore. Not only had it become their main hobby, but it could well turn out to be a lucrative source of income, Jenny had told her. Thinking about her friend, Sarah found herself hoping it was only tiredness that had made her sound so unlike herself.

By the time Sarah and her Mum arrived home, Steve was up and waiting for them. Grinning, he opened the front door. "Lord, it's the last of the big spenders." Giving his sister a bear hug, he eyed all the shopping bags. "Do I detect a spot of serious retail therapy by chance?"

"Whatever gives you that idea," Sarah laughed dumping the bags on the floor to return his hug. "You look good, Steve. Been working out?" It was a joke: the gym was his second home.

Steve flexed his biceps, "Maybe just a little. Not bad, eh?"

Her brother had filled out since she had last seen him; Sarah guessed he was over six foot now, his body well-toned and sporting a healthy tan. She giggled; all he needed was a surf board under his arm! Gazing critically at the handsome, chiselled face grinning at her beneath the untidy mop of hair, she could see why young women found him so attractive, but she was not about to tell him so.

They strolled out into the garden and chatted about Steve's plans for Spain, until it was time for Sarah to get ready to go out. 'The boys' – as Mrs Sheldon liked to call Dad, Adam and Steve - were going off somewhere for a few 'glasses of lemonade' with some mates. Her brother winked at her and Sarah giggled. She need have no worries that Adam would be happily entertained in her absence. Having declined the remains of her Mum's shepherd's pie and settled for a cup of tea when they got back from London, Sarah was anticipating stuffing herself with pizza and garlic bread and looking forward to some girlie chat. She kissed Adam lightly on the cheek as he handed over the car keys. "Enjoy yourself, darling, but make sure you pace the booze. You know Steve's mates will drink you under the table."

"That's for sure," Adam nodded, "but your Dad will keep an eye on us and Steve will look after me."

Sarah laughed, "That's what I'm afraid of!"

It was only a fifteen-minute drive to Jenny's home. Parking in front of the house, Sarah paused to look up at the mullioned windows. The place looked as though it had come from the pages of a glossy magazine, much like those she drooled over in her dentist's waiting room. As lovely as it was – and she had to admit her friends had done a great job - Sarah had no ambitions to live in an antique. Give her a nice modern home like hers and Adam's any day. The thought brought with it a pang of sadness. Had things been different she would have looked forward to describing her new house to Jenny. As it was the oppressive shadow of evil that hung over her dream home had destroyed it for her.

Jenny looked good as she opened the front door, her hair straight and feathered complementing her petite, delicate features. Sarah lost no time in telling her so. "Wow! You look fantastic! I love your hair – and what a great jacket; suede is so trendy."

Smiling a greeting, Jenny gave Sarah a hug. "Thanks, but you've lost some weight girl. I don't want my best mate turning anorexic on me."

"It's more to do with the stress of work and marriage," Sarah smiled, as they walked back to her car. "It's good stress though, and I eat like a horse, honest."

"Well I can sure as hell sympathise with the marriage bit."

Sarah started to laugh, but her friend looked so serious she turned it into a cough. "Hey Jen, that was a bit barbed. Is everything ok with you two?"

"Not exactly - fact is, we're not getting on too well at the moment," Jenny admitted, as they got into the car.

"Oh Jen, I am sorry." Sarah gave her friend's hand a quick squeeze, "I just knew there was something wrong. Is it serious? Do you want to talk about it?"

With a sigh, Jenny sat back in her seat. "It would be a relief, I haven't been able to talk to anyone else, but I know you don't judge and won't just side with me simply because we're best mates."

"Of course I won't," Sarah lied, putting the key in the ignition, but not starting the car.

Jenny stared out of the windscreen and they sat in silence for a few moments. "This is going to sound really awful, but I'm not sure I want to be with Vin any more. Everything he does at the moment just seems to irritate me. Even the way he puts his socks on in the morning is starting to get to me. How daft is that? I know I must sound like a real bitch, but I can't help it. He leaves every room in such a mess most of the time. It didn't bother me when we were working on the house and not actually living there – let's face it, you wouldn't have noticed the mess then, but now I seem to spend all my time clearing up after Vin and it's driving me nuts. We both have full-time jobs, yet I have to do *everything*. It's always me who has to deal with the household accounts, get out the vacuum, do the washing and ironing, go for the shopping, wash the dishes, make the bed, do the sandwiches for the following day, while he just sits around watching TV or playing on his X-box. It's 'woman's work', he says if I have a moan. He never even gets around to cutting the grass until I can't stand it and have to do it myself before the neighbours start complaining! Honestly, Sarah, I feel like an unpaid skivvy, or worse, a slave."

Sarah made sympathetic noises, but did not interrupt. It was as though Jenny in releasing her feelings for the first time had uncorked a bottle of fizz.

"We haven't had any sex for about six months now," Jenny went on, "and the worst thing is that we can't be bothered. We're neither of us thirty yet, Sarah, but you'd think we were well past retirement – like an old married couple! And we never go out – at least, not together: I still go out on girlie nights occasionally. I exercise at the gym after work, and play badminton and tennis with my colleagues, but when I go out for lunch it's always with friends or with my Mum. In fact, I socialise more with my family than I do with my partner. Vinny and I share the bills and the mortgage, but that's about all we have in common at the moment. Since we finished the house it's like we lead separate lives and I've got to the stage of wondering why we are still together at all. I don't love him any more, Sarah," Jenny ended on a sob.

Sarah was taken aback by her friend's outburst. Whenever she'd seen the pair of them together, they had always been laughing and joking. She had thought they were truly happy. Despite her surprise, Sarah was only too well aware how couples could put on a show to mask their problems. She had experienced something similar with Andy. She remembered how she had become increasingly bad tempered, always finding fault and picking a fight, but not wanting to hurt his feelings and lacking the courage to end it, she had continued in the relationship until she had come almost to hate him. Yet none of their friends had ever had any inkling that anything was wrong between them. Surely it had not got that bad for Jenny – at least, not without good reason? Her best friend was not the sort to be bothered about household chores; would at one time have chivvied Vinny into giving her a hand and laughed about it. Maybe this was just a bad patch they were going through; no matter how compatible the couple, no relationship was a bed of roses all the time. Even she and Adam had their moments!

The more she thought about it, the more Sarah was convinced there was something Jenny was not telling her. Tentatively she asked, "But why don't you tell Vinny how you feel, work out some kind of housework rota or something? He never struck me as being a lazy guy – he did masses of work on the house. You both did. How come things have changed so much between you? Has something else happened? He isn't playing away from home, is he?"

Jenny shook her head, her face etched with misery. "I don't think so. Actually, it's more likely to be me! I suppose it all started when I got a new manager three months ago. Gary – that's his name - is such a great guy. He's really fit and such a gentleman. Not very tall, but good looking in a Tom Cruise sort of way, you know? Most of the women at the bank fancy him rotten, but this man's so easy to like; he takes real care of his body and always looks so smart. Plus he's quite dynamic and has already made huge changes to our working practices, which have made things much easier for everyone. Gary is so into the open door policy; if you have any problems you are encouraged to talk to him and it's not just for show; he really means it. I work quite closely with him and we've developed a great working relationship. He asks my opinions on procedures, and if they need updating he listens to my ideas from a non-biased point of view. He makes me feel special, Sarah. It's not just that he's easy to get on with at work either; he's keen to promote social activities outside work as well. Says he wants to get to know all of us properly. Honestly, Sarah, he's like a breath of fresh air after some of the old-fashioned, narrowed-minded managers we've had in the past. I've got to the stage where I'd rather be at work than at home. I know I shouldn't say it, but Vin seems such a drag by comparison."

Sarah gave a wry smile, "Is this Gary keen to promote social activities with the rest of your colleagues too, or is it just with you?" She said it teasingly, wanted to lighten the atmosphere, but glancing across at Jenny was perturbed to see her friend was blushing.

"Of course not; he's the same with everyone," Jenny snapped defensively, adding sheepishly, "well, I suppose he did give me a gorgeous bouquet for my birthday. But when we met our investment targets a few weeks ago, he bought a huge box of Thornton's chocolates for me to share with my team. He does things like that and it means a lot, like you're a real person and not just some lowly employee, you know? Gary's ambitious, easy to talk to - and single, which really doesn't help matters! Then, when I go home, it's like Vinny is getting so *boring*. He doesn't want to go out anywhere even though the house is all finished. All he wants to do is play on his X-box. As I said, we don't make love much anymore. He's put on a paunch since he packed in going to the gym and doesn't seem bothered by it either – like he doesn't care what I think any more. We are getting more and more distant with one another, but whenever I try to talk about it, Vin finds some excuse not to."

"Men always do," Sarah smiled. "They run a mile if they think you're getting all emotional. But surely you can patch things up, Jenny? You both had such a good thing going. Isn't it worth finding a compromise?"

"I'm not sure any more. Vin seems to think there's nothing wrong, like everything's normal, but I'm beginning to wonder if buying a house together was a big mistake. I didn't really have any proper relationships before he came along and I now feel like I've missed out. My new boss certainly isn't helping, although he's never shown any indication of being interested in me beyond a professional capacity – which, given the way I feel, is just as well!" Jenny laughed, but Sarah could hear the tears behind her voice. "I know I shouldn't, but I find myself fantasising about him a lot and that must surely be a bad sign."

Sarah chose her words carefully, "Ok, so I'll admit Gary does sound quite appealing at the moment, Jen, but remember they all do until you get to know them properly. Familiarity breeds contempt and all that! It sounds to me as if you're going through a bad patch and it's only natural to fantasise about a dishy guy, but you have been with Vinny a long time and had a lot of good times together. It can't be smooth sailing all of the time and the romance goes out the window unless you make the effort. That butterfly feeling you have at the beginning of a relationship soon disappears, you know, but if you let it, it can be replaced by something much deeper and more satisfying, believe me." Sarah paused, suddenly aware that this was true for her and Adam too. The butterflies had long gone, but her feelings for him were deeper now than they had ever been. Yet even she had experienced a frisson of excitement when she had been with Simon and to her consternation had found herself fantasising about him. If she and Adam were having a bad patch, it would be all too easy to give in to it – and for what? Risk everything for a few hours of illicit pleasure, which in all probability would turn out to be nowhere near as good as she had imagined? Dread the thought!

"But as I said, only if you make the effort," Sarah added hastily, putting thoughts of Simon firmly aside. "Vinny's clearly taking you for granted. He's got to be made to realise that you are still young and attractive and not be so complacent. And you've got to try to make him understand how he's letting you down. Why don't you suggest that you go to the gym together or play squash or badminton like you used to? From what I remember you both used to enjoy that, but if Vinny doesn't fancy the gym, there are other ways of keeping fit. What about going for walks in a nice country park or out on a bike ride? It would get you both out of the house and Vinny away from his wretched X-box! You've got to let him know how you feel, Jen. I know what Adam's like when he's on his computer. He forgets how long he's spent on it until I have a go at him. Is it really worth throwing in the towel at this stage in your relationship for the sake of a flirtation with your boss, which, apart from anything else, would probably lose you your job – and anyway, how do you know Gary would welcome an affair with you? Don't misunderstand me; I'm not saying you should stay with Vinny just for the sake of it, but are you quite sure you no longer love him enough to turn things around? Why not give it a trial period and see if he makes the effort?"

Sarah pulled into Zizi's car park and stilled the engine. "On the practical side, just because you have a house together doesn't mean you have to stay together, you know. You can always sell it and start over. All I'm saying is, make sure it's what you *really* want and is not just a passing phase."

Jenny nodded. "I hear what you're saying and you're right, of course. I think I'm feeling vulnerable just now. It's a long time since I've had a crush on anybody and it shook me up I suppose. It's only ever been Vin. He seems to have changed, but I guess he's been really stressed with getting the house as we want it on such a tight budget - and it doesn't help that my hormones are all over the place – PMS and all that."

"Join the club!" Sarah said wryly. "The week before I start I feel I could kill somebody and it's usually Adam; certainly that's the time when we argue the most. That's very normal, Jen."

"I know. I've painted you a black picture, but it's not all bad, Sarah. Fact is; Vinny has suggested we book a holiday, spend some quality time together."

"There you are then," Sarah smiled, unbuckling her seat belt. "Perhaps he notices more than you think."

Jenny nodded, returning Sarah's smile. "Thanks for listening, I feel so much better talking things through with you. You always have a way of sorting out my problems."

"I feel the same way about you too. Are you hungry now? I don't know about you, but my tummy is rumbling."

Jenny chuckled. "Let's go and pig out. I could eat a ton of chips! But please don't tell Vin; I've banned his favourite biscuits and have been restricting him to rabbit food lately!"

"Poor chap, no wonder he prefers his X-box."

Laughing as they made their way into the restaurant, Sarah could not help reflecting that listening to her friend's problems had taken her mind off her own. She felt as if she was living a normal life again. If only it could last.

CHAPTER SEVENTEEN

They ordered ham and pineapple pizzas with garlic bread and a side order of chips; chose a starter from the salad bar and found a nice quiet table.

"So," Jenny said, picking at a plateful of mushrooms in garlic butter. "How are things with you - any gossip?"

Sarah gazed thoughtfully at her friend. She had been looking forward to telling Jenny all about the horrifying things she had experienced in her new home, but now it came to it, she wondered if she should. Jenny had troubles enough of her own. And besides, what if her friend laughed at her and told her she was imagining it all? Suddenly tongue-tied, Sarah cast around for something else to talk about. "Fine, work's busy and I've applied for a Service Managers job, which I really want and think I stand a good chance of getting. Adam's doing really well too. We are hoping to go to backpacking in Australia before Christmas."

Jenny's eyes lit up. "Wow! I'm impressed. That's great. How long are you going for?"

"A month, hopefully, but I haven't negotiated the time off yet, though my boss is fairly laid back and I'm owed stacks of leave. Adam is putting an itinerary together. The idea is to travel around by train once we've arrived there and stop off wherever we feel like it."

"Sounds wonderful," Jenny said enviously. "We were hoping to get to Egypt one day. I've always fancied a cruise on the Nile and Vin wants to see the pyramids, but I'm not sure the budget will stretch to it now."

Sarah took a sip of her diet coke. "It'd be great if you could - just what you need. You and Vinny have a lot more in common than you think, you know."

"I suppose."

There was a brief pause in the conversation as the pizzas were delivered to the table. Sarah broke off a piece of garlic bread.

"I forgot to tell you, I went to see a medium a few weeks ago with a friend from work. I didn't really want to go, but she needed the company. And actually, it turned out to be quite interesting," she laughed, "though I'm not sure I really believe in all that stuff. And yet she said some things about my life that she could not possibly have known. It was weird."

"Goodness. What did she say - anything interesting? I would love to know what was going to happen to me in the next few years," Jenny said wryly.

"She said I would be promoted in the next couple of months and the job would be challenging; that Adam is the right man for me and we would have two children – a boy and a girl."

Jenny smirked, "That's all good news then. I wish someone would tell me that Vinny is the right man for me and that things will get better between us!"

Sarah trusted Jenny completely, always had. Her friend was the most level-headed person she knew. Why was she finding it so difficult to talk about what else Lola had said? She had to talk to someone and Jenny was her best mate. She drew in a deep breath, said, "It wasn't all good news, Jen. Lola – that was her name – warned me that a past love would come back into my life and that it could be dangerous to my happiness if I wasn't careful. I concluded that what she was really saying was that I would be faced with a choice as to whether to stay faithful to my husband - or not."

"Come on, Sarah, you don't need a medium to tell you that! Every married woman has that choice - and let's face it, we all get tempted. A woman who says infidelity has never crossed her mind is probably lying, but not you. Adam is really good for you and I know how much you love him. It sounds like a load of mumbo jumbo to me."

"Yes; actually I was a bit miffed about it - as if I would ever betray Adam!" Sarah pushed the remains of her pizza round the plate; the ball of tension was back, her appetite suddenly gone. "There's more though. It was as if Lola was talking to someone else in the room, but there wasn't anyone else there."

"That's what mediums do, dear."

"Yes, well she said it was my spirit and from the way she described him it sounded just like my granddad. Then she said he was using her to tell me someone is in mortal danger and needs my help, that there will be signs and I will know what to do when the time is right." Sarah gave her friend a weak smile, "It was quite scary actually."

Jenny frowned. "Did your spirit say who this person is?"

"No."

"Did he say what form the signs would take?"

Again, Sarah shook her head.

"Well how are you supposed to help if you don't know?"

Sarah swallowed hard. This was going to be difficult. She pushed her plate to one side, nibbled on a bit of lettuce. "Some very strange things have been happening to me since we moved into the house and I think it must be connected to whoever is in danger."

Jenny stopped eating, her loaded fork half way to her mouth. "What sort of strange things?"

"How long have we known each other, Jen?"

"Must be at least twenty years, why?"

"Would you say I was a pretty sensible person?"

"The most sensible person I know." Jenny put down her fork, "Look, what is it Sarah? What's troubling you?"

"Promise you won't laugh or tell me I'm going mad?"

An expression of sheer bewilderment crossed Jenny's face. "Come off it, as if I would." She grabbed Sarah's hand and gave it a quick squeeze. "You can tell me anything, you know you can."

Sarah nodded, "I know." She bit her lip, "I've been seeing ghosts, Jen. I think our house is haunted, which is really weird because it's only ten years old and I thought only old properties like yours were haunted – lost souls from long ago and all that. But just after we moved in I was upstairs putting up some pictures when I felt a real chill in the air like there was a cold draught from somewhere, yet it was a really still, hot day. Anyway I went into the bathroom and ran a bath, then turned to look in the mirror, but it was all steamed up. I wiped it clean and saw someone standing behind me – just a glimpse. I spun round, but there was nobody there. And then I saw the bathwater had turned into blood and there were what looked like severed limbs floating on the surface."

Jenny gasped, put her hand to her mouth. "God, that's awful!"

"Tell me about it! It was like a scene from a very scary horror film. I actually passed out. When I regained consciousness, Adam was next to me and the bath was completely clear and clean. He said I must have had a nightmare, sleep-walked into the bathroom. It seemed the logical answer and at first I put in down to the stress of the move and my hectic workload."

"Did it happen again?"

"Yes; the very next day. I walked into our bedroom and there was a man there. A young man with dark hair, he looked angry and I thought he was real and was going to attack me. I've never been so scared in my life, but when I cried out, he just walked right through me. It was why I agreed to go and see the medium. I thought she might be able to help."

"And instead she frightened you rigid and by the sound of it was no help at all."

Sarah nodded miserably.

"What does Adam say about it?"

"Well to be honest, I haven't told him. I'm so afraid he won't believe me and will think he's married some kind of nutcase and I don't think I could bear that."

For the next few minutes, Sarah related to her friend all the other things she had seen, about the painting of Jane Moore, the research that had led her to believe that at least one girl had been brutally murdered in her new home. She could see Jenny was taking her very seriously and trying to digest what she had been told; her face had paled significantly and it was a couple of minutes before she spoke.

"First of all, I certainly believe you and I don't think you're at all mad, so you can stop worrying about that. I'm desperately sorry it's happening to you, Sarah. It's awful. No wonder you've lost weight! It seems clear to me that someone – this 'Jane' by the sound of it - needs you to know what happened in your house and that these visions are the signs the medium told you about."

"Do you believe in ghosts, Jen?"

"As it happens, yes I do. I've never told anyone this before, but I'm positive I've seen one. When I was about seven years' old Mum and Dad took me and my sister round an old castle that had been renovated by the National Trust. Of course, we were both really excited and went running around all over the place. I wanted to hide from my sister and when the tour guide wasn't looking I crawled under the ropes and went into an area that was closed to the public. I found myself in what looked like a child's nursery; there was a tiny desk and chair, a cot and a few scruffy looking wooden toys on a shelf. There were bars at the window too, except one that was boarded up, I suppose because there was a fearsome drop to the ground. Anyway, this little boy was sitting on the floor playing with a toy steam engine. I wondered why he was there all on his own; he looked only about four or five, but he smiled at me and seemed quite content; started chatting about his train. He had like blue velvet pedal pushers on – real old fashioned; even to my young eyes it looked a bit odd."

"What happened?" Sarah was curious noticing that the colour had drained from Jenny's face as she described the scene.

"The door opened and the tour guide came in with my parents. The boy simply vanished into thin air right in front of my eyes. I got a right telling off for trespassing, of course, and I started to cry, which made my Mum even crosser. She didn't realise I was crying because I was scared stiff. Then I heard the tour guide explaining to my parents that when the castle was lived in years ago one of the bars had fallen out of the window and the owners' little boy had squeezed through the gap and fallen to his death. It was why they were keeping that area of the castle roped off until they got more funds to renovate it. I have always been convinced it was the dead boy I talked to. It really freaked me out for a while I can tell you. But your experiences are very much worse than mine, and I agree with you, the best thing to do is to find out exactly what happened in your house; whether your dark-haired ghost was the murderer. Perhaps Jane will leave you alone once she has made you aware of her story."

"That's just what I think. I'm so glad you're taking it seriously and not just humouring me." Sarah felt as if a burden had been lifted from her shoulders. "It's like trying to fit together pieces of a jigsaw puzzle. The hammer, the towels soaked in blood, the limbs floating in our bath. It's the scariest thing that's ever happened to me and I don't understand why Adam appears not to be seeing anything out of the ordinary."

Jenny moved her hand to her stomach. "Yuck! I feel a bit queasy. Do you think you might have any connections to this Jane Moore or her family? If it's just with you that might explain why Adam doesn't see her maybe."

Sarah shook her head. "I'm pretty sure I don't – she was a nineteen-year-old student ten years ago, long before I was at Uni. I don't think we have any relatives in the area and we've never lived anywhere near there till now. It's a good point, though. Perhaps Jane's a distant cousin or something. I hadn't thought of asking Mum, but I wouldn't want to worry her."

"Was anyone ever charged – did they find the murderer?"

"That's what is so frustrating – I don't know. It was such a painful process going through the old papers on microfiche and I didn't have time to search back more than a few months after it happened. So I called Simon. You remember Simon?"

"Your student friend: the weedy looking guy with the long hair tied up in a pigtail?"

Sarah giggled, "That's the one. He's a policeman now and anyone less weedy you couldn't imagine! We had lunch the other day and I have to say he's really fit now. I was amazed how much he'd changed. Anyway, I have enlisted his help to see if he can help me."

Jenny stared at her friend in disbelief. "You told him what has been happening? Did he believe you?"

Sarah laughed out loud, covering her mouth with her hand when she saw some of the customers were looking across at her.

She blushed, quickly put her head down. "No. I don't want him to think I'm completely barking. I made up an excuse, which he seemed to accept. I'm waiting for him to get back to me. I don't know what else to do. But I'm scared, Jen. I can't bear to be in the house on my own. I've been following Adam around like a wet lemon all week! I know he's beginning to think there's something wrong with me."

Jenny nodded her head slowly. "I don't blame you. I still can't believe this is happening to you; I know how much you and Adam wanted that house and I know how awful you must feel spinning him a line."

Her friend's sympathy and understanding brought tears to Sarah's eyes. "That's one of the worst things about it; I feel so deceitful. Sorry, I don't mean to cry," she said, mopping her face with her paper napkin. "It's been so awful not having anyone to talk to."

"Look, you aren't on your own, Sarah. We will sort this out together and find out why it's happening. If the medium is to be believed your granddad is trying to warn you. If we accept that Jane's murder took place in your house, it seems to me the suspects must be quite limited. Either the Palmers are lying or you're right and it was someone who worked on the house and took his chance while it was empty. We'll get to the bottom of it, you'll see. It'll be alright."

Sarah felt as if the bond between her and Jenny had become even stronger and for the first time she felt a rush of excitement. It made a huge difference having someone to share things with. "The builders were called Morgan's; somewhere in all the paperwork we should have some information on them. There must be a warranty on the house – it's only just ten years' old. I could try to find out who actually owns the firm and if they are still in business, and something about the staff if possible. I know we are talking about a long time ago, but there might be something."

"That's going to be a tall order. Why don't we both try? I could ask Vinny; he's done jobs for building companies all over the country. He might know someone who has worked for Morgan's if they are a big company."

"Oh no, Jen, please don't. I'd really prefer it if you didn't tell V-"

Jenny cut across her. "Calm down, Sarah, obviously I won't tell Vinny why I'm asking - I'll just say it's about the warranty or something. The other thing we could do is Google on Morgan's. They're sure to have a website; most reputable companies do these days."

Feeling much better, Sarah smiled ruefully at Jenny's obvious enthusiasm. "This could all be a wild goose chase you know. There is always the possibility I'm hallucinating; the start of a mental breakdown perhaps - that has been worrying me as much as anything."

"You don't really believe that though, do you? Much more likely is that you are experiencing paranormal events and I'm convinced from what you say that it's for a specific reason. The man you keep seeing could be still out there, alive and dangerous."

"Not if he's a ghost!"

"Good point. But even so, he's obviously very violent and dangerous - and what about the other poor girl you saw in the living room; Charlotte was it? Was she murdered too – are we talking about a serial killer here?"

Sarah felt a rush of fear. "I thought that too, but I really don't know. I sincerely hope not."

"At least you've seen his face, although if he's alive he'll be ten years' older. Some people don't change that much though. I don't think we've changed much since we were teenagers."

"You certainly haven't," Sarah smiled. "You're right though. There's got be a reason why the ghosts are appearing to me after all this time. I mean, why didn't they appear to the Palmers?"

Jenny looked thoughtful. "Are you sure they didn't? You don't suppose it could be an anniversary of some sort, do you, and that some other young woman is in danger?"

Sarah knitted her eyebrows together and bit her lip; she could feel the tears welling up again. "It might be me," she said in a small voice.

"It's not you, Sarah. Remember what Lola said. You are there to try to help when and where you can. Like I said, we are going to face this thing together and find out what we can. Hopefully your policeman friend can help out too, especially if he tells you the case was never solved. At least then the theory about someone else being in danger makes more sense." Jenny broke off, glancing over her shoulder. "Shall we pay the bill and move on? Our waiter seems to be hovering – probably hoping for a tip. Fat chance! There's a trendy bar across the road that shouldn't be too busy tonight."

Sarah giggled tearfully, "Good idea, let's cheer ourselves up with a drink and talk about something else."

CHAPTER EIGHTEEN

The bar was dimly lit and quiet with only a handful of customers. Jenny ordered two glasses of white wine and led the way to a table by the window.

"Hey, I'm driving," Sarah protested.

"You can have one, surely. The glasses are quite small and after what you've been going through you deserve some alcohol. I'm surprised you've not been hitting the bottle and turning into a complete nervous wreck! I'm sure I would be."

Sarah gave a watery smile, "You're right, I have been feeling as if I'm losing my nerve recently. Well maybe just one then, thanks."

As they sipped their wine, Sarah could see that Jenny was preoccupied and it came as no surprise when her friend raised the subject of the ghosts again. "I know you said let's talk about something else, but I was just thinking about this man you keep seeing – the murderer or so we think. He must have been very charming to get two young girls to go with him into an empty house. They say more often than not a victim of abuse knows her attacker. I wonder how well they knew him and how he enticed them."

Sarah grimaced, "From the little I've seen of him he was very good looking; a bit like Brad Pitt, except with jet black hair, but he had those same classic 'Adonis-like' features, you know? And he was at least six foot tall; slim, but strong looking."

"Bit of a dish then."

Sarah grimaced, "Put it this way: if we were single and had seen him in a club, we'd have been really hoping he'd ask us out. But there was something scary about his eyes, they were sort of wild looking; menacing almost. After what I've seen and heard I'm pretty sure he was capable of murder. He looked as if he was out of control, you know?" Sarah shuddered at the memory. "I forgot to say, I actually saw him come into the bathroom carrying a saw and covered in splashes of fresh blood."

"Ugh! That's so horrible. I wonder what the young women did to make him so angry."

Sarah shrugged, "Turned him down, perhaps."

"Could be," Jenny mused. "When you heard him and Jane arguing, did you hear what it was about?"

Sarah hesitated. She had tried so hard to blank it from her memory that it was difficult now to recall in any detail. "Well, it was certainly heated, but I didn't actually see who Jane was talking to, I just assumed it was the same guy. Jane was cowering in the corner looking really frightened. She kept touching a gold pendant she was wearing and thanking him for it."

"Ok, but what were they arguing about?"

"Jane said she needed more time, that she thought he understood she just wanted to be friends and that she already had a boyfriend. He responded by saying that her boyfriend didn't appreciate her beauty and didn't deserve her. Then he said that if she would only let him, he could look after her much better – or something like that. I don't remember the exact words, but I got the feeling she had rejected him in favour of her boyfriend and he was mad about it."

"It sounds like he knew her quite well then. Obviously he wanted her boyfriend out of the picture - hey – would that be the one who was accused of her murder and then released?"

"I guess so. Robert Taylor was his name according to the newspaper. Like I told you, the next time I saw the ghosts was during that thunderstorm, only it wasn't Jane I saw that time, and he called her Charlotte. I didn't get a good look at the guy, it was so dark and the lights weren't working."

"How can you be sure it wasn't Jane?"

"Jane has ash blonde hair; I'm sure the girl I saw was dark, and she sounded different. She was shouting at him to leave her alone, but I was scared and confused. I could have been mistaken."

"Well whoever the killer is – or was - he obviously can't take rejection. I think he must have seduced young women by giving them expensive gifts to buy his way into their affections and then turned nasty when they twigged what he was really like."

"Could be; certainly it seems he was unstable. Jane obviously didn't care enough about him to finish with her boyfriend. Perhaps at first it was a novelty to have this dishy guy flirting with her, but then when she tried to back out, things got out of hand. It is quite likely no one else knew about their friendship. It is equally likely that the same thing happened with Charlotte."

"You could be right; maybe he became obsessed with young women and couldn't accept it when they didn't want him as much as he wanted them. It could be a motive for murder if you were insane, I guess. You know the sort of thing: 'If you won't have me, then I'm not letting anyone else have you.'" Jenny frowned, "It could have been a power thing, especially if he was insecure and needed to feel he was in control of these women. When he found he could no longer control them, he murdered them. Fact is, Sarah, he was probably little more than an unhinged bully!"

"That's a bit of an understatement! He certainly killed Jane, though we don't know for sure that he killed Charlotte, but yes, you could be right about the power thing. I wonder if he raped them first." As she spoke, Sarah recalled how Simon had reacted in their second year at Uni when she had told him there was no future for them as a couple and all she wanted was his friendship. She remembered being quite scared when he had slammed his fist against the wall in frustration, so hard he had made his knuckles bleed. Afterwards he had gone out of his way to avoid her, not speaking to her for several weeks. They had sorted it all out eventually and become friends again – though never as before. But Simon was a normal guy. What if he had been unstable like the dark-haired man? Would he have smashed his fist into her instead of into the wall? It was an appalling thought; she took a gulp of wine, said, "Clearly, Jane's murderer is or was mad. Like you say; emotionally insecure and quite probably immature – certainly he seems to have had an explosive temper. Incidentally, I don't think

I told you this, but when Adam and I went out the other night, on the way home I thought I saw Charlotte in Nottingham City Centre. I don't mean as a ghost, but as a real living person. It was a shock I can tell you. We'd had a few to drink and of course it was after dark, but it got me wondering if I was seeing flashes of both the past and the future." Sarah shrugged, "I don't know, Jen, it doesn't make any sense. I think I'm starting to mix up real life with the visions."

"It's completely understandable considering what you've been through. Let's hope you are right and Charlotte at least is still alive. It is such a bizarre situation. I feel very sorry for both women, but especially Jane Moore." Jenny gave Sarah a lopsided grin, "And I don't want my best friend having a nervous breakdown because of something that happened ten years ago. We have to get to the bottom of it – and soon." She took another sip of her wine and stared unseeing at the long-stemmed glass in her hand. "You know, it occurs to me that the killer must have been in a position of some authority to have been entrusted with the keys to your house for as long as he was – five weeks, you said?"

Sarah nodded, "That's how long the house stood empty before the Palmers moved in – according to Jean Palmer anyway."

"Then he may have visited your property more than once, perhaps taken Jane there a few times, which suggests he was more than just one of the builders. If the house was already finished, which we presume it was, and the murder occurred in the five weeks prior to the Palmers moving in, he would have had no excuse to go in there again unless he was the boss."

"That's true. The Palmers were the first to move into Bluebell Close, and there's only the farm at the back so everywhere would have been quite private; nobody to overhear. He would only have known that if he was connected to the building company." Sarah emptied her glass and Jenny quickly followed suit.

"Want another?" Jenny asked, her eyes sparkling with excitement.

"Better not. I'll have a diet coke. I'll get them." Sarah got up to go to the bar, turned back. "Hey Jen, this isn't one of your beloved crime novels you know. There's no need to look as if you're actually enjoying it!"

Jenny laughed, "Sorry, but I can't help wondering about it. I mean, do you think the murder was premeditated or that it just happened on the spur of the moment?"

"From what I've seen I'd say he must have been thinking about it beforehand. If we assume the visions are portraying what really happened, this man was clever. He made sure he never got caught and that no evidence could be linked back to him; he seemed pretty well prepared, what with the towels, the hammer and everything – and pretty quick to dispose of the body. God, Jen: he cut her up! Now can we change the subject?" Jenny's face paled and she shivered, clasping her arms about herself as Sarah turned towards the bar. When she came back to the table she could tell Jenny was still not going to let it go.

"Go on then, spit it out," Sarah said with a wry smile. "I can see you are itching to say something else."

"Not really, I was just thinking that your friend Simon is sure to know if the case remains unsolved. He should also be able to find out if anyone other than the boyfriend was arrested as a prime suspect, which could give us a lead. Also, could he look to see if anyone at Morgan's had a criminal record do you think? Why don't you call and ask him?"

Sarah put the drinks on the table and sat down, "I'm sure he'll do what he can, but he's a busy man, Jen, it may be ages before he gets back to me. Besides, I-" Sarah looked down, her face suddenly hot. She looked up again to meet her friend's curious gaze.

"Besides what?" Jenny grinned, "He hasn't still got a thing for you has he? Oh Sarah, look at your face!" Her grin turned to laughter at her friend's embarrassment, "He has hasn't he? And hey – isn't he your past love? You're not tempted to get your hands on those delectable pecs of his are you?"

Blushing, Sarah held her hands up, "Certainly not! I know what you're thinking, but it's got nothing to do with what Lola said. Simon and I were never in a relationship as such, and therefore he can't be counted as a past love, can he? And anyway, I am totally besotted by my husband, remember?"

"That may be so, but if Simon still holds a candle for you, you need to be a bit careful girl, because there's nothing so seductive! From the way you described him he's a right charmer and if he thinks you are interested in rekindling a relationship on a deeper level – after all it was you who contacted him – well, I'm only saying it could be a bit tricky, that's all."

Sarah nodded. Jenny was right: Simon could be a real threat to her marriage if she let him, but she was not about to confess that to her best friend, however close they were. She quickly changed the subject and for a while they chatted about work and then about shared memories, until it was approaching last orders and they decided to call it a night.

They were quiet on the way home, both lost in nostalgic thoughts of the past. As Sarah pulled up outside the house, Jenny yawned, said, "Coming in for a coffee? Vin would be glad to see you. I expect he's still up – glued to his X-thingy."

"No, I won't thanks, Jen. I'd better get back, but I've really enjoyed catching up."

"Me too; it's been great – really interesting and I mean that. Nothing could have prepared me for what you've told me, but remember, you're not on your own any more, ok? We'll sort this out together. I'll try to find out as much as I can about Morgan's and I'll get back to you as soon as I have anything to report."

Sarah hugged her friend tightly. "Thanks. I can't tell you how much that means to me. It's felt like I've been living in a different world; slipping away from reality, you know? I feel so much better now and so relieved that you believe in what's been happening to me and don't think I'm a head case! Look after yourself, Jen. I hope you work everything out with Vinny; you make a great couple, but whatever happens, you know you can rely on me for support."

Jenny, her hand on the car door, turned back, "Thanks, we'll try to sort things out. I'm a great believer in fate, if it's meant to be and all that jazz. Feel free to ring me any time..." Jenny paused, looked as though she was going to say something else, but whatever it was she decided against it.

Sarah smiled, "Thanks, I will and I'll let you know straight away if anything else happens."

CHAPTER NINETEEN

When Sarah arrived home her Mum was still up, watching a late-night chat show. Sarah smiled to herself; here she was approaching thirty and her Mum still wanted to make sure she was home safe as if she were still a teenager. It gave her a warm, secure feeling and she could not help reflecting that the only place where she felt unsafe at the moment was in her own home, it was ironic. But she could not say that to her Mum, not without worrying her. She put on a bright smile and went through to the lounge. They chatted over a cup of coffee until Mr Sheldon came home with Adam and Steve in tow, clearly merry and unable to conceal they'd had more than a few drinks. But after one sharp glance at her husband, Mrs Sheldon smiled, "Well you've all had a good time! I'm off to bed. Goodnight darlings."

Sarah settled into the weekend finding it all very relaxing. The dinner party they had arranged with Adam's parents went off well, and for a time Sarah almost forgot about her visions, but when Tuesday morning dawned and she was re-packing her bag, she was gripped by a feeling of dread. What was she going back to? Slightly panicked, she almost found herself begging Adam to extend their stay for a few more days. Her Mum always got very upset when it was time to say goodbye and Sarah too found herself becoming very emotional - and not just because she was leaving her family behind.
    With heavy traffic and jams on the motorway the journey back was slow, and Sarah, who did most of the driving, was exhausted when they finally pulled into their driveway. The house felt warm and welcoming, but Sarah peered warily into each room before plucking up the courage to go upstairs. It all seemed normal. She ran a bath and started to unpack, leaving Adam to prepare a meal. Sarah could imagine nothing worse than having to

set about cooking dinner right now. She and Adam had always shared everything. Poor Jenny!

Having emptied the cases she was just about to slip into a hot bubble bath when she heard voices. She had been half expecting it, but it still made her cringe, her fear creeping up her spine and raising goose-bumps on her skin. The voices sounded light-hearted and were coming from the main bedroom. There was a sudden shout of male laughter and a woman was giggling. Sarah slipped on her bath robe and went quietly across the landing. The bedroom door was slightly ajar. With adrenaline pumping through her, afraid of what she would see, she peeped through the gap. Jane Moore was sitting on a wooden chest of drawers in front of the bay window and held a glass of white wine in her hand. She looked relaxed and happy and very much alive. Sarah's mouth was dry, her breath coming in short gasps, but since telling Jenny about these visions she felt somehow braver than she had; ready to face whatever was happening to her. Heart thumping, she pushed the door wide open, determined this time to see who Jane was talking to. He had his back to the door, but Sarah could see he was the same height and build as the man she had seen before – and he had jet black hair. He was standing opposite Jane, just a few feet away from her and from the tone of his voice he was in a jovial mood. The room looked very different, decorated in pastel shades – pink and lilac. Sarah could smell fresh paint and the scent of newly laid carpet. There were no ornaments around that she noticed, just a few bits of furniture, which looked as though they had been dumped there and not yet arranged. Sarah stood stock still gazing at the scene before her and knew she was seeing it as it had been ten years ago while the Palmers were still on holiday.

"So, you're a man of many talents – an artist as well as a quantity surveyor, my, my!" Jane giggled again and glanced up at her companion from under her lashes in classic Princess Di style, as if aware she looked stunning. She was quite clearly flirting. She wore a blue, halter-neck top and her jeans were skin tight showing off her slim figure. Her skin was tanned as if she had recently been abroad her beauty was captivating. She must have had plenty of admirers Sarah thought sadly, it was easy to see why this man had wanted her. He in turn seemed so charming and debonair; how could he have been so callous, so brutal? Sarah felt tears stinging her eyes.

"Well I'm only a trainee surveyor and a lot of people are good at painting. The question is, am I talented enough for you? You know what I want, Jane. Can you honestly say you don't want it too?"

Jane smiled provocatively, revealing perfect white teeth. "Even if I did, I'm going out with Robert, remember?"

He laughed, "I know, but couldn't we just go out as friends? Go on, say yes. Let me take you somewhere really special. I've got a steady girlfriend too, so we will have to keep it a secret, but what they don't know won't hurt them and we could have such fun. We're two of a kind you and I."

Sarah wanted to shout out a warning: *Don't listen to him, Jane, he's lying!* but even as she drew breath the ghosts were fading, the room shifting before her eyes and returning to normal. As it did so, her fear receded to be replaced by stark pity; mostly for Jane, but also for herself that she was being forced to witness these terrible events as they unfolded. Once again she had failed to catch a clear view of the man's face, but she was certain it was the angry young man she had seen that day standing in front of her bedroom window, and then again spattered with blood in the bathroom. That poor girl; she'd had no idea that she had been playing with fire. Too immature to see her handsome seducer for what he was, she had clearly been impressed by him, not suspecting his motive in encouraging her to keep their relationship a secret – so artfully done by mentioning his own girlfriend. Had there been one? Was it Charlotte? Whether he was lying or not, Jane would obviously not have wanted Robert to find out about her assignations with this man. If she had told no one, not even her best friend, it might explain how the killer had got away with it. Had he got away with it? Sarah still did not know, but she was convinced this dark-haired man had been Jane's murderer. In none of the visions had there been anyone else in the house who might have perpetrated that horrific slaughter; there was no one else it could have been.

Had Jane really fallen for this guy or had it simply been a meaningless flirtation? It may have been extremely unwise, but it was not a crime. Sarah had a great deal of sympathy for Jane, recalling how she had herself enjoyed flirting, especially as a teenager when it had meant so much to have boys fancying her, making her feel attractive and sexy. Prior to meeting Adam, she had rarely been totally faithful to her boyfriends. It had been just a game in those days - playing the field. They had all done it, boys as well as girls. The pity for Jane was that she had picked the wrong man to flirt with – and by the time she realised what he was really like it was already too late. Sarah was certain that she and Jenny were right: the murderer had wanted to control Jane and had scented easy prey in that inexperienced and very beautiful girl. Perhaps he had never intended to hurt her, only to use her, but when she rejected him and he felt he had lost control, he had been driven to kill her.

Sarah knew she was seeing these visions for a reason. This one was another piece of the puzzle: now she had a clue to go on. The man had been a quantity surveyor, which meant he could well have worked for Morgan's. It was also reasonable to assume he would have had access to the house. Sarah knew what a surveyor's job entailed: they were there from the beginning to calculate the quantity and cost of the materials and then to ensure the estimates were not exceeded as work progressed. It fitted perfectly. A quantity surveyor would have needed to be on site frequently, solving problems and ensuring the work was carried out to the architect's specification. None would have questioned why he needed access to the house; he would just have been seen to be doing his job.

Her mind busy, Sarah carefully checked all the other bedrooms before going back to her bath. One thing puzzled her: why were the visions so random and out of sequence? She had seen Jane's body and the severed limbs first, yet now she was seeing what looked to be the start of her illicit relationship with this killer. Why was it going backwards? And what about Charlotte - was she another victim? Or was she the one who needed help to prevent an excruciating death such as Jane had endured? It was a disturbing thought.

Early next morning while she ate her cereal, Sarah pored through all the paperwork they had on the house. It had taken her a while to find because when she had tidied up the study after it had been ransacked, she had misfiled the information she sought. It occurred to Sarah that it might have been exactly what the ghost had been searching for, though it proved to be not particularly useful. There was an address and phone number on one of the letters Mr and Mrs Palmer had received from Morgan's, but when Sarah tried the number she found it had been disconnected. She was a little disappointed, though not surprised. The builders were not going to be easy to find.

After she had arrived at work she rang directory enquiries to get an updated number for the address. Again she drew a blank: the address was now owned by the Halifax Building Society. Sarah cursed under her breath in frustration. She would just have to trawl the Internet to see what she could find - if anything – on Morgan's Building Company. The pressure was getting to her; she could not shake the feeling of dread that someone was depending on her and she was running out of time. 'Granddad; are you there?' she whispered. 'Please help me.'

After a short lunch break Sarah came back from a team meeting to find a note on her desk. Simon had called and left his work number for her to contact him. As soon as she got a chance she gave him a ring.

"Sergeant Leivers," his voice sounded very business-like.

"Hi Simon, it's me. I got your message. How are you?"

"Thanks for ringing me back, Sarah. I thought I'd better ring you now. I'm going away this weekend on another course. I've found some information in the archives that should interest you. I haven't got time to explain just now and I'd rather not discuss it on the phone. I know I don't need to tell you how confidential this all is, but is there any chance you could meet me on Friday?"

Sarah felt the hairs rise on the back of her neck; another meeting with Simon was just what she had hoped to avoid. On the other hand, she so needed his help. She checked her diary. Friday morning was full of meetings and a software demonstration would probably take up most of the afternoon: something she could not get out of with her boss away on holiday. "Sorry, Simon, my diary's full all day. Is there any chance we could meet up after work?"

There was a slight pause. "Yes, that should be ok. What time?"

"Whatever is easiest for you; you're doing me the favour here."

"Ok, let's say five-thirty in the same pub as before. Sorry, got to go now. See you Friday."

Almost as soon as Sarah put the phone down, Adam called her mobile. With a twist of guilt, she took the call.

"Hey, how's my best girl?"

"I'm fine. I'll be doing some overtime though, what with all the testing we've got to do and the deadlines so tight."

Adam laughed. "Welcome to the real world. We have to work to ridiculous bloody timescales all the time in the Private Sector. Anyway, I only called to say that Guy just phoned. It's late notice I know, but he and Rachel wondered if we would like to go out on Friday night. A new Italian restaurant has just opened near their place and it's supposed to be really good. He said we could share a few bottles of wine and stay over at theirs."

Sarah silently cursed; it was sod's law. Why Friday and not Saturday? There was no way she could mess Simon around when he was putting his neck on the line to help her. She would have to make an excuse. "I'm really sorry, Ad, but I've just arranged to take my team out after work on Friday. I can't let them down – and anyway, it's all booked up." She knew she was gabbling lie upon lie, but she could not tell the truth. It would lead to an argument with Adam and she could not handle that. Not right now.

"No worries, I'll tell Guy; it was late notice anyway."

Relieved to hear that Adam sounded neither hurt nor disappointed, Sarah said on impulse, "Why don't you ask them round on Sunday for dinner or something? You know I enjoy creative cooking and I haven't had time for that lately – in fact we haven't done any entertaining at all since we moved in."

"That's a great idea; I'll do that - and don't worry about Friday, babe. I hope you get everything done and I'll see you later."

"Thanks, Ad. I'll aim to be home about seven." With a heavy burden of guilt settling on her already over-burdened shoulders, Sarah rang off.

The rest of the week seemed to fly by. Attending various Senior Management meetings to give updates on software projects, and then a round of performance reviews, meant she had little time at her desk and was working later and later to catch up. By the time she got home she was mentally exhausted. The last thing she had wanted to do was to go on the Internet to look for any information on Morgan's.

"Will you be having a few drinks tonight?" Adam asked over breakfast on Friday morning. "You look very smart."

"Do I?" Sarah knew full well that she had selected her best suit to impress Simon and felt immediately guilty. "No, I don't think so. We'll probably just have something to eat, why?"

"I was going to offer to drop you off at work and pick you up later. I'm not going out tonight and it would mean you could leave your car. Your hair looks nice by the way."

Sarah instantly felt worse. More lies: "Oh, Ad, how thoughtful, but I'd rather take the car; that way I know I can leave when I want to. They're all younger than me and will probably want to go on somewhere afterwards."

"Ok, if you're sure? Only I was thinking of joining you for a quick drink when I picked you up. But not to worry, we'll go out another time."

He hugged her, but Sarah could hear the disappointment in his voice and wanted the ground to open and swallow her up. She did not want to shut Adam out, but her need to find out the truth about Jane Moore's murder had become an obsession. She had lied quite deliberately to the man she loved more than anything in the world and that she was capable of doing so had shaken her to the core, but it was too late to change things now. She could tell him neither about the supernatural happenings taking place under his nose, nor about Simon's involvement – especially about Simon's involvement. When Adam had come home on Wednesday night he had seemed really down. Eventually he had told her why: he had found out that a married female colleague, one whom he had always respected, was having a torrid affair with a senior manager. He was appalled by her behaviour and went on at length about scheming women and the evils of marital infidelity. Sarah, afraid of sounding defensive and making him suspicious, had shrugged it off, when what she really wanted to do was to point out that it takes two, while reassuring Adam that such a thing could never happen to them. She had done neither of those things.

Now, driving to work, Sarah evaded the questions that were swimming around in her head and tearing her in two. Why had she found it necessary to lie to Adam? And why had she felt the need to dress to impress when Simon was merely a friend doing her a favour for old times' sake? But try as she might to curb it, Sarah anticipated their meeting with increasing excitement and as before, had to keep reminding herself that it was not a date.

CHAPTER TWENTY

She was a little late getting to the pub where she was to meet Simon. Late that afternoon, one of her senior colleagues had wanted to go through a few queries with her. She could hardly put him off; not if she wanted promotion to the Service Manager's job, but it had been difficult to concentrate as she saw the clock hand creeping round to six.

Simon was waiting at the bar.

"Sorry I'm late," Sarah gasped, getting her breath back, "I had to run all the way here; couldn't seem to get away from work. I should be used to it by now!"

"No worries; it happens to me all the time, which is probably why none of my relationships ever work out." He smiled, "looks like we're both married to the job." He gestured to the bar, "What can I get you? A large Scotch by the look of you!"

Sarah returned Simon's smile, already relaxing in his company, "Tempting, but no thanks, I'll have a diet coke please. Hope I didn't get you into trouble?" she said as they ordered some food and found a table.

"Trouble?" Simon quirked his eyebrow; it made him look rather comical and Sarah giggled.

"Yes, spending your precious time looking up an old murder case."

He chuckled, "No – no trouble and we call them cold cases these days; at least we do if they are unsolved."

Sarah's stomach lurched. "Jane's murder was unsolved?"

"No - quite the contrary."

"Are you saying her murderer was convicted?"

"Don't look so surprised; we're not completely incompetent you know."

"Sorry, I didn't mean it like that, it's just that my neighbour said... or at least, implied that-" she broke off aware that Simon was frowning.

"You should forget about her, Sarah, she was nothing but a lonely old gossipmonger. In fact the murder had nothing to do with your house. As it said in the paper, the body parts were found on an industrial estate just outside your town, but the murderer was arrested. It was Jane's boyfriend, a Robert Taylor."

Sarah's mouth dropped open. "But that can't be right; it also said he was released without charge."

Taking a pull at his beer, Simon carefully replaced the glass on a beer mat. He looked up at Sarah, shrugged. "He was at first, but then the SOCOs-"

"SOCOs?" Sarah frowned.

"Sorry – jargon - Scene Of Crime Officers - found the murder weapon: a hammer, hidden inside Taylor's car. It seems he battered her to death before he cut her up. There was blood on the back seat, later confirmed by the lab as Jane's. Some of her friends had said the couple had been seen arguing a few days before she went missing. I read all the case notes and Taylor's alibi didn't check out either. Basically he didn't have a leg to stand on, although he kept protesting his innocence – but they usually do, of course. We found out from Jane's parents that Taylor had asked her to marry him, but she thought they were too young and turned him down. Obviously he couldn't take the rejection."

"Surely there's more to it than that? Rejected teenagers don't usually resort to violence, never mind actually killing the person who rejected them." Without thinking, she added, "Hell, I rejected lots of boys. It happens to teenagers all the time. None of them was ever violent towards me." Suddenly aware of what she had said, Sarah blushed, smiled weakly, tried to cover it, "He must have completely lost it - that's awful."

If he had noticed her insensitive slip, Simon, gave no sign. He shrugged, "It's all too common I'm afraid; the lad grew up on a sink estate and had to be tough to survive. He had a history of violence. It seems he had a temper and quite often got into a fight, usually in a pub; on one occasion he had to be pulled off some guy before he caused serious damage and would have been arrested for GBH had the witness been reliable. His parents said he'd got in with a local gang and that it wasn't his fault. They also said he was besotted with Jane and would never have harmed her, but the prosecution surmised that he was unstable and lost his temper when she tried to cool things off. The defence tried to change their plea to manslaughter, said it was an act of unpremeditated passion, but it was overturned. The jury returned a verdict of guilty and Taylor was given a life sentence for murder. It's a shame because he had a promising future - he was in his second year at university and doing well, but like I said, it was in the report that he and Jane and been seen arguing. What is more, a close friend stated that Jane had confided she wanted to finish the relationship because Taylor was getting too serious, but he frightened her and she wasn't sure how he would take it. There was no doubt he was guilty, Sarah, there was no one else in the frame. It was damning evidence – cut and dried really. So that's it, case solved and nothing for you to worry about."

Sarah bit back an angry retort, 'No one in the frame that the *police* knew about!' she wanted to say. She could not believe what she was hearing and was convinced Robert Taylor had been set up. It was disappointing – and so frustrating: the dark-haired man had been clever, she already knew that. He could easily have planted the murder weapon and smeared Jane's blood on the back seat; he was both smart and callous enough. It was clear now to Sarah that the murder had been premeditated. The killer had probably made it his business to find out about Jane's boyfriend; knew he had a history of violence, may even have provoked him to lose his temper in some pub. He must have followed Jane and Robert, knew they had been seen arguing, must have reasoned that since nobody knew of his own association with Jane, the boyfriend would be the prime suspect. That Robert had got into a few fights meant nothing; just because he was handy with his fists it did not make him a murderer – if that was the case, Sarah thought, her own brother would have been locked up years ago! Robert had obviously cared deeply for Jane and would have been upset when she rejected him. She might easily have exaggerated her fear to her best friend. Sarah too had been in relationships where she was scared to finish with the guy in case he reacted badly; had said as much to Jenny at the time using such words as: 'He'll kill me!' But it was just something one said; it meant nothing. To her way of thinking the evidence against Robert Taylor was circumstantial; there was more to this case than Simon and his colleagues knew. But what could she say? That the truth was being brought to her attention by a ghost? Hardly! This vicious killer was more than likely still out there and some other girl or woman was in danger: he had succeeded once – at least once - what was to stop him trying it again? Perhaps she herself was a target. Was that why Jane was showing her what had really happened? Sarah swallowed, her mouth suddenly dry, took a swig of her coke.

Simon's voice broke into her thoughts. "Hey, are you ok? You don't look as relieved as I thought you'd be." He gave her a gentle smile, "Relax. I know it's gruesome to think about what happened to Jane Moore, but good news for you, surely? No need to worry that her killer is still lurking in your shrubbery!"

"Yes, sorry, of course I'm relieved. I just don't understand why my neighbour said what she did. Obviously she was trying to scare me. Maybe she thought it was a good joke or didn't like the look of us, or something."

"All I can say is that she must have a warped sense of humour, stupid cow."

"Yes, well I don't have much to do with her. Anyway, thanks ever so much for finding out about the case for me. I owe you one."

"No problem. If you need to know anything else just give me a shout. I mean it."

Sarah smiled gratefully, "Thanks again. Ah, here comes the food. Not sure I've got much appetite after that conversation!"

Over their meal, they talked about all sorts of things, falling into the easy relationship they had enjoyed years ago, before it had ended in tears. Sarah was surprised to learn that Simon was clearly fond of his two-year-old nephew, talking at length about the child's antics and making her laugh. "I thought you hated kids," she smiled.

Simon chuckled. "That was when I was a lot younger and couldn't begin to contemplate being responsible for another human being. Things have changed on that front: I'd love to have a couple of kids one day, God willing. How about you? You'd make a great Mum you know. Any plans in that direction?"

"Maybe," Sarah knew she was blushing. "But right now I'm so busy at work I wouldn't have the time – besides we can't afford children just yet. We're planning a long holiday in Australia this year."

"Wow; that sounds great. Tell me more."

The time seemed to fly by and Sarah was amazed to see that it was already after nine. She bit her lip, "I'd better go. Adam will be wondering where I am."

"I'm sure he knows I'll look after you."

Again Sarah found herself blushing, but she was not about to confess her deception. Unable to meet Simon's eyes, she stood up, laughed, 'Trust me I'm a policeman, eh?"

"Something like that," Simon pushed back his chair and stepped forward as if to give her a hug, but at the last moment he held back, his hands dropping to his sides. "I've really enjoyed tonight, Sarah. I'd forgotten what it was like to be so relaxed in feminine company."

Sarah gathered her belongings. "Me too and thanks; we must keep in touch. Have a good weekend." She kissed him lightly on the cheek and turned quickly away, aware that Simon was gazing at her, a look of regret – had she imagined yearning? - standing in his eyes. He raised his hand, made to say something else, but whatever it was, Sarah did not hear it. She was already hurrying away. She had to sort out her feelings; she seemed to be rapidly becoming infatuated with this handsome, caring guy. What the hell was the matter with her? She was playing with fire. Just like Lola had said. Relieved to be in the dark isolation of her car, she took a shuddering breath and set about squashing her hopes that she and Simon would meet up again.

CHAPTER TWENTY-ONE

Sarah felt a wave of tiredness sweep over her as she opened the front door. Partly, she knew, it was because she would have to tell yet more lies, and partly because she was so anxious and unsettled, not only by her emotional response to Simon, but by what she had learned about Robert Taylor.

Adam's voice drifted through from the living room. "Hi love, enjoy your evening?"

Sarah took off her coat and went through to him, kicking off her high-heeled boots along the way. Adam was perched on the sofa eating some toast and jam.

"Yes thanks, the food was good and everyone always relaxes when they are away from the office. Is that all you've had to eat?"

"Yes, it's not worth cooking a meal for one. I wasn't very hungry earlier anyway. Who did you go with then?"

Suddenly Sarah wished she could just stop it, right here and now; tell him everything - not have to lie any more. She hesitated. He would be hurt, angry, worried about her state of mind. No, she could not tell him. She felt a surge of irritation: why did he have to question her, forcing her to lie? Failing to keep the edge out of her voice, she said, "Oh, you know, just some team mates and colleagues from Accounts. Anyway, why are you asking? Don't you trust me?" She'd meant to say it teasingly, but it came out sounding defensive.

"Just making conversation, that's all. Anyone get drunk and fall over?" Adam quipped looking looked slightly hurt by her rebuff.

Sarah felt wretched. It wasn't his fault; it was she who was in the wrong. Despairingly, she ran her fingers through her hair. "No, no one was really drinking much. Sorry, didn't mean to snap. I'm just tired that's all; it's been a long day. I was tied up with my Senior Manager until nearly seven – and on a Friday too."

"Not literally I hope," Adam smiled, obviously trying to lighten the atmosphere.

"You're joking! He probably knew we'd arranged to go out and was miffed he wasn't invited. I think I'll make a cup of tea. Do you want one?"

"Yes please."

Sarah went into the kitchen, hoping her husband would let it rest. She abhorred lying to anyone at all and rarely did so – apart from those little white lies to save hurting people's feelings – but to lie to Adam of all people – it made her feel sick. She was all too well aware that it was becoming a habit recently. It had to stop. Her feelings for Simon were beginning to bug her, making her feel that she was being unfaithful, which was nonsense. Nothing had happened between them and nothing was going to: *Then why are you lying?* Ignoring the little voice in her head, she made the tea.

Later, while Adam was watching the last few minutes of a documentary, Sarah went upstairs to get ready for bed. Hearing the TV was still on in the living room, she took the opportunity to give Jenny a quick call. She had been meaning to do it all week, but this was the first opportunity. "Jenny? Sorry it's so late. How are you? I hope I haven't woken you."

Her friend sounded sleepy, "No, I'm fine - you sound a little excited though, what news? Have you heard anything from Simon?" There was a muffled yawn on the other end of the phone.

"Look, I'm sorry; I shouldn't have called at this hour. I'll ring you tomorrow."

"No, it's fine - I'm wide awake now. Go on."

Keeping her voice low, Sarah related everything she had learned from Simon, ending with the conclusions she had drawn.

"Oh God, that's awful," Jenny said. "I believe you're right, they convicted the wrong person. The poor guy was framed for his girlfriend's murder and has been in prison all this time for no good reason. We owe it to both him and Jane to uncover the truth. The real killer might be still out there somewhere and possibly about to strike again."

"That's just what's worrying me," Sarah said. "I'm scared stiff, Jen."

"I'm not surprised, but try not to be. Just keep your eyes open and don't talk to any tall, dark-haired, handsome strangers."

Sarah had to laugh. "You're a tonic, girl!" She could feel her spirits lifting; it was so good to hear Jenny's voice in her ear.

"I've made some progress on the Internet," Jenny said. "I've found a website for Morgan's. The company appears to have sub-contracted out to smaller, local firms. I'm just trying to eliminate any that were not in business at the time."

"That's great, thank you so much, Jen, I'm really grateful for your help. I haven't had time to do much research this week. I've gone through the paperwork on the house though. Nothing useful I'm afraid, just contact details of premises they apparently sold years ago. But I've learned something else about the ghost: he was definitely in the building trade."

"How do you know that? Don't tell me - another vision?"

"Afraid so; he and Jane were talking in our bedroom and I overheard her say he was an artist as well as a quantity surveyor. He must have painted that picture we found."

Jenny sucked in a breath. "Goodness. Well at least it means we're on the right track and the killer had something to do with Morgan's. I know the Internet sites won't give me a list of employees, but if I can narrow it down to the sub-contractors that fit the bill, we can take it from there. At least we have an old address to go on – better than nothing. A quantity surveyor is a specialist job. If I took an educated guess I'd say he had to have a degree at least and possibly some other qualifications relevant to the job; he was probably a fellow of some chartered institute or something. There can't have been that many of those who were working locally at exactly the right time – not as many as there would have been bricklayers anyway!" Jenny chuckled, her excitement bubbling over the phone.

Sarah wished she felt the same. She endeavoured to dampen her friend's enthusiasm. "But even if we are able to identify him, what can we prove? My visions are not going to stand up in court. They'll write me off as some weirdo!"

"Yes, well we'll cross that bridge when we come to it. Besides, think positively. Remember that Jane is trying to communicate with you and may be able to lead you to some evidence. If you have any more visions try to remember the exact details: which rooms they were in, what Jane and the man were wearing, the date and time of day, whether it was fine or wet – anything at all that might help. There has to be *some* evidence somewhere. It might be ten years ago, but the police have arrested people for murder as many as twenty years after the event. I watched a documentary the other day about the strides they are taking in forensic science. As recently as this year they have been able to match up DNA from the tiniest of samples. It would have been inconceivable ten years ago. Someone or something is obviously trying to guide you in the right direction, Sarah. Don't give up."

Sarah was forced to agree; she was about to say something else, but heard Adam's footsteps on the stairs. "Jen, I'll have to go, but I'll keep you posted, speak to you soon." She rang off abruptly as Adam strode into the bedroom. Was it her imagination or was he eyeing her suspiciously? How stupid to have cut the conversation short when she could simply have changed the subject; Jenny would have understood right away.

"Who was that?"

"Jenny. Her cocoa was boiling over and she had to cut me off," Sarah attempted a laugh and was relieved when Adam appeared to relax, loosening his tie and unbuttoning his shirt.

"Still the same old scatterbrain then - how is she?"

Sarah peeled off her clothes down to her bra and pants and hung her suit in the wardrobe. "She's having a bit of a crisis at work, but fine otherwise. Did you get our train tickets through – the East Coast discovery passes?" she said, changing the subject.

Adam's face broke into a smile. "Yes, the flights are booked for 30th November and the passes arrived in the post today. I've done a bit of an itinerary for us if you want to have a look. Shall I go and get it?" He turned back to the door, hesitated, "Or are you too tired?"

"I'd love to see it, Ad. Golly, November - it's not that far away now is it?"

Adam's eyebrows shot up, "You sound excited. I thought you were a bit ambivalent about going away."

"Whatever gave you that idea? Of course I'm excited, and no, I'm not too tired, but I will be soon if you don't stop dithering in the doorway."

Laughing, he ran downstairs and was back in a trice with a fistful of paperwork. He grinned at her, his eyes alight with enthusiasm. "As you know, we're flying to Cairns after a three-day stopover in Thailand. It will take us about fifteen hours to get to Bangkok from Gatwick, so we'll be really shattered when we get there, but the hotel I've booked looks fantastic and would be considered a five-star rating over here." He held out a brochure.

"It certainly looks expensive. Goodness, it's got a pool and a Jacuzzi – and what huge rooms. Are you sure we can afford it?"

Adam's face flushed with pleasure, "No worries; I've worked out all the costs, darling. I know you hate flying, but there's no other way I'm afraid. We'll have loads of time to get over our jet lag once we get to Cairns."

"Never mind that; this is the trip of a lifetime. It will all be worth it."

Dropping a kiss on her head, Adam sat on the bed and spread out a map of Australia. "It's such a huge country – difficult to imagine. We're only going to be able to see a tiny bit of it."

Sarah kneeled to peer over his shoulder, her arms round his neck. "So we'll be travelling down the Gold Coast?"

"Yes," he said, stabbing his finger at the map. "We'll actually have three weeks there, and with these train passes we'll be able to hop on and off with our backpacks. We'll just have to make sure they are light enough to carry because we'll be doing a fair amount of walking around places of interest."

"Not forgetting the beaches and those wonderfully exotic parks Guy was telling us about?"

"Absolutely - Australia has some of the best beaches in the world."

Adam's enthusiasm was infectious and despite herself, Sarah began to feel excited. The thought of sunbathing on beautiful white sandy beaches suddenly seemed real and not just a dream. She made a mental note to pack stacks of sun lotion. "How *ever* are we going to decide what to see?"

"We will, you'll see. I've done a fair amount of reading up on the Gold Coast. Pointing at the map, he talked her through the itinerary, using words to paint images of all the delights in store."

Despite her worry and stress, Sarah's eyes lit up. She grabbed Adam's hand and kissed it. "Oh darling, it sounds wonderful, I can't wait."

"Hey, steady on, you're creasing the map!" Adam laughed, gently withdrawing his hand to smooth out the creases.

With her head full of sunshine, of turtles and exotic fish swimming around in clear, sparkling water and of koala bears and kangaroos, Sarah lay back on the pillows, flung her hands above her head and stretched languorously, completely unaware of the sensuous picture she made. "Can we go to the opera when we get to Sydney?"

"If we conserve our cash, we might be able to manage it. I've heard the Aussie youth hostels are very clean and cheap. It's also cheap to eat out over there – cheaper than here at any rate."

Sarah giggled, "You mean if we are very careful with our money we might be able to afford to eat once a week?"

"Well as I'm holding the purse strings, maybe once every two weeks." Adam leaned over to kiss his wife lightly on the lips. "Seriously though, I can't believe we are actually this close to going to that wonderful country. It's a totally different culture over there; they have such a relaxed approach to life, which I think is great."

"You would!" Yawning, Sarah pulled her husband against her and hugged him, her lips against his hair.

"So remember," Adam leaned up on his elbow to look down at her face, "our backpacks *must* be light. All we will need is

T-shirts and shorts with a couple of jumpers. Only the basics since we won't be clubbing and-"

Sarah laughed and stopped his mouth with her fingers, "I've got it, darling, no dresses, curling tongs, etcetera. I'll manage, you know I will."

As Adam gazed down at her, the look in his eyes made her catch her breath. Reaching behind him to toss the map on the floor, he leaned over her, teased her bra straps down from her shoulders and nuzzled her neck, his lips making her skin tingle with delicious anticipation. "Oh, Ad - I love you so much," she whispered as he began slowly to remove her clothes and then his own. Gently he eased himself onto her. For a fleeting instant she thought of Simon. How could she ever have imagined she had feelings for him beyond friendship? *This* was what it was all about; not a trivial, passing fancy most likely born out of her stressed state of mind, but this feeling of total, almost overwhelming love. How stupid she was. She raised her face for Adam's kiss.

Suddenly he stopped, leaned back onto his elbows, his face creased in a frown.

"What's the matter?" Sarah gasped.

"Sorry, darling. I'm just a bit concerned about this house."

"What do you mean?" Sarah's passion subsided like a pricked balloon her fear making her voice squeak. "What's wrong with the house?"

"Nothing's wrong with it, silly – it's just that it suddenly occurred to me that it'll be empty for a full month. I know it's not a bad area, but there's a sink estate not that far away. We've got a lot of expensive items between us. It might prove too much of a temptation for some people."

Breathing a sigh of relief, Sarah smiled. "I hadn't thought of that. I suppose we couldn't ask Mum and Dad to housesit for us?"

"I doubt they'd want to in the run up to Christmas. It is pretty remote and the town's not much cop for serious shopping."

"Don't worry, Ad. We can tell the local police and ask the neighbours to keep an eye. The alarm system is pretty good and if you're worried about anything in particular, the computer and laptop maybe, I guess we could store them somewhere else. Dad would have them in his garage."

"How sensible you are. You're right, of course. I'm worrying about nothing. Now then, where was I?" he laughed, bent to kiss her again.

Just before she was swept away by her husband's lovemaking, Sarah could not help wondering what might happen here while they were away. Supposing Jane's killer learned the house was again standing empty? Was *that* what someone or something was trying to warn her about? The thought made her blood run cold.

CHAPTER TWENTY TWO

Sarah groaned, surely it was not morning already, but she could see from the digital alarm that it was almost seven. She felt completely befuddled and her mouth was as dry as a bone. Careful not to wake Adam, she slid out of bed, pulled on a tracksuit and went downstairs to fetch a glass of mineral water. The sun was streaming through the kitchen window; it was going to be another glorious day. For a moment she had a mad impulse to go out for a walk, but tiredness won and she went back to bed.

Try as she might to get a bit more sleep it eluded her and after tossing and turning for half an hour, Sarah once more slid out of bed. 'A walk would've made more sense,' she muttered to herself. Adam was lying on his back, his mouth slightly open, each breath whistling softly between his puckered lips. Sarah was tempted to lean over and kiss them, but it seemed a shame to disturb him. A shower would sort her out and since it was still quite early, it was a good opportunity to go on the Internet and see what she could find out about Morgan's.

When she came out of the shower, Adam was awake. He pushed back the duvet, stretched and yawned. "You're up early – couldn't you sleep?"

"Well I might have done if someone hadn't kept me awake half the night!"

Adam grinned, "I wonder who that might have been."

Sarah bent to kiss him, "My lover," she laughed.

"That's nice," he said. "How do you fancy going into Derby today? We could do some shopping for the holiday. We might find a bargain or two, they should be selling off summer stuff quite cheaply now."

Sarah pulled out a T-shirt from the chest of drawers and slipped it on. "That's my cheapskate husband – always taking care of the pennies."

Adam picked up his pillow and aimed it at Sarah. "Hey that's not fair."

She caught it and threw it back. It hit Adam square in the face and laughing he leapt out of bed and made a grab for her. Sarah squealed, "I didn't mean it, no, stop, stop!" She giggled as he tickled her ribs and breathless, twisted out of his arms, caught her foot in the duvet and they both landed in a heap on the floor.

It seemed such a long time since they had been carefree like this, Sarah thought, as her husband helped her to her feet and kissed her. It was important to spend some quality time together away from the house. Morgan's would have to wait. "Yes, let's go to Derby, good idea. We haven't shopped there for ages and I hear there's a really good food hall opened up there now. We can grab a bite to eat when we've finished bargain hunting. It'll be fun."

Adam gave her a cheery smile. "Ok, give me fifteen minutes to make myself presentable and we can be on our way."

They headed towards the Eagle Shopping Centre. The town was very busy and finding a parking space took ages, but Sarah's carefree mood persisted; one of her favourite occupations was shopping for clothes and it took her mind off Jane Moore. Adam managed to find a free space on a side street and hand in hand they strolled to the shops.

After two hours of wandering around the main clothes stores, Adam had had enough. "Phew, it's much too hot for shopping, I'm bushed. Let's go and get an ice cream on the square."

"That's the trouble with men – no stamina," Sarah grinned, handing him another carrier bag. "But an ice cream would be nice and I have to admit even my feet are aching."

"Thank goodness for that!" Adam steered his wife through the crowd of bustling shoppers until they got to the square and found an empty bench.

"I'll go," Sarah said, "You mind the shopping." She strolled over to the ice cream van, which to her surprise, given the sultry weather, did not have much of a queue. She was studying the pictures on the van window and trying to decide what to have, when a deep voice said in her ear: "I'll have a large 99 please and don't forget the flake."

Sarah spun round, momentarily taken aback. Standing there in his uniform, his eyes twinkling and a broad smile on his face was Simon.

"Simon, hi – what a surprise, I didn't expect to see you here." Sarah lifted her hand to shield her eyes from the sun and looked up at him. The dark blue suited him. He looked taller in uniform, Sarah thought - and much too damned attractive! She felt her face growing hot and prayed it did not show.

"I work in Derby sometimes, but I'm on a course here today – didn't I mention? Just needed to pick up a few things and thought I'd skive off for a bit as it's such a beautiful day. Have you been doing some shopping?"

Sarah swallowed hard in an effort to regain her composure. "Yes, we've been bargain hunting, but it's so hot in all the shops. We're hoping some ice cream will help to cool us down." She slightly emphasised the 'we' and the 'us' and felt suddenly quite sick. If Simon came over to say hello to Adam, which was only natural, he was sure to say something about last night. *'Be sure your sins will find you out'*, said the little voice in her head.

Simon raised his eyebrows and looked around the square. "You're with Adam? Where is he?"

"Over there waiting patiently for his cornet," Sarah looked over to where her husband was sitting, put on a bright smile and waved.

"Oh yes, I see him," Simon nodded in Adam's direction.

Sarah panicked. "Simon, I know this will sound odd and please don't make anything of it, but could you not mention last night, only..." she faltered, not sure what to say without giving away how deceitful she had been on the one hand, and being terribly disloyal to Adam on the other.

Simon looked down at her, "Only you didn't tell him you were with me?"

Miserably she nodded. "I was going to, but-"

"Look, it's none of my business," he cut across her. "And anyway, I haven't got a lot of time. Please give my apologies to Adam," Simon pulled out his wallet, "but let me at least buy you both an ice cream before I go."

"No, please, I'll buy you one," Sarah smiled, unable to hide her relief.

"Absolutely not, I insist." He nodded at the vendor, who was leaning out of the van window watching the exchange with interest. Simon held up three fingers and a ten-pound note.

Before Sarah could argue, three large 99s were passed to Simon and he handed her two of them.

Embarrassed, she looked up at him about to apologise for her subterfuge, but suddenly tongue-tied, she hesitated.

"You'd better go before they melt." Simon grinned, and eyeing her lasciviously he ran his tongue slowly up the side of his cone to catch a runnel of ice cream.

Sarah flushed, a twist of desire curling in the pit of her stomach. She looked quickly down at her feet. "I seem always to be thanking you," she mumbled, confused.

"No worries. Take care - see you again soon." He winked, gave her a teasing smile and turning, sauntered away.

Simon's parting words had sounded more like a question than a statement, Sarah thought hurrying back to Adam. Her husband was standing up watching her. As she got closer she saw that he looked cross: his lip was curled, his face all red and mottled and his eyebrows drawn together in a frown.

"Who the hell was that?" he snarled.

Sarah, brought up short, said defensively, "Nobody - just an old friend." She shrugged, held out his cone.

"Well it didn't look like nobody to me." Adam knocked the ice cream out of her hand and roughly grabbed her by the wrist, "Which old friend? Anyone I know?" He sneered, "*You* certainly seemed to know him pretty well." Holding on to her, he raised his other hand. His fingers spread as if to slap her, stopped just short of her cheek. He drew back his lips, hissed, "Hussy!"

Sarah gasped, flinched backwards, "Stop it, Adam! Why are you behaving like this?" She gazed at him, perplexed. He was like a different man, not one she liked very much. How was this possible when they had been so close last night? Feeling her temper rise, Sarah snatched her wrist away, threw her cone into the bin and fished out a tissue to wipe the sticky mess off her fingers. She did not want to tell her husband it was Simon she had been talking to. It would only make matters worse and the whole incident would be blown out of all proportion. She was being made to feel guilty, yet had done nothing wrong. Adam was behaving like a spoilt child and ruining their day.

"I'll ask you again," Adam shouted. "Who was he?"

"Someone from my old course, alright? Just drop it. I was only being polite." Sarah rubbed her reddening wrist, which stung where Adam had gripped it so hard his fingers had left imprints on her skin. "What's your problem, Adam?" She was conscious that her voice had risen several octaves and that passers by were staring at them. Humiliated, she hoped and prayed that Simon had gone; could not bear the thought that he was watching this, but did not dare look to see.

Adam's face contorted with rage, spittle glistening on his lips. "I'll tell you what my problem is. My problem is that you're married to *me*, and yet there you are chatting up some bastard in uniform and looking at him the same way you look at me. You're *mine*, I tell you. How dare you come on like that to someone else! What were you doing? Trying to make me jealous - because if so, you bloody well succeeded! Tell me who he was."

"That's simply not true, I wasn't chatting him up. I told you; I was just being polite. Adam, please stop this, you're frightening me." Close to tears now, Sarah stared up at her husband unable to believe this was happening. It was as though there was no trust between them; no love. He was treating her as if she was his possession and she hated it. He had never been like this before in all the time she had known him. But then, she told herself, she had known him for not much longer than a year; they had been married only a few short months. Had she made a dreadful mistake? *I've made a mistake; I've made a mistake.* The words went round and round in her head and sounded so real she almost turned to see who had spoken them. And then she remembered, and into her thoughts swam an image of Jane's look of terror and the dark-haired killer's eyes, blue and cold as ice: the jealous lover who had killed so violently and so brutally because he had lost control.

Sarah shuddered, conscious that Adam was glaring at her, waiting for an explanation, but instinctively she knew there was nothing she could say that would satisfy him. There was no point in even trying. "Don't get so mad, Ad, I was just talking and I don't like what you're implying. Whatever's going on in your head, forget it! It's all in your imagination. I think you must've got heatstroke or something. Go cool your head!"

With that, Sarah swung round and stalked off. Ever since she had started seeing the ghosts and trying to understand what had happened to Jane, she had wondered how it was possible for someone to get so out of control they crossed over the line of sanity into madness. Now, by some quirk of fate, Adam was showing her. Even a regular, caring guy such as he had always seemed, could suddenly be driven by the powerful emotion of jealousy to act out of character. It was devastating. Not sure where she was walking, blind to what was going on around her, tears streaming down her face, Sarah strode on.

Minutes later she heard someone running, heavy footsteps pounding up behind her. "Sarah, baby, wait - please." Adam, out of breath, overtook her and blocked her path, one hand clutching all their bags, the other held behind his back. "I don't know what came over me."

She looked up at him, speechless.

"Oh God, darling, please don't cry, I'm so sorry, I was just being stupid. Please don't let it spoil our day. Maybe you're right and the heat got to me. I'm stressed out with work and I'm taking it out on you. Forgive me? I love you so much, sometimes I'm so afraid of losing you it just curls me up inside." From behind his back, Adam brought out an ice cream and held it out to her,

"Peace offering?" He gave her a lopsided smile and Sarah felt her anger melt away, much like the ice cream was doing, dribbling onto Adam's hand and splashing onto the pavement.

She took out a tissue from her pocket and wrapped it round the cone. She could no more have eaten it than fly to the moon, but she had to go through the motions. Her husband looked like a small boy on the naughty step. "I'll let you off this time, but don't ever let it happen again. You're not going to lose me, Ad. You've got nothing to be jealous of. You're the only man in my life; you must know that. If we don't trust each other our marriage is a sham."

As she spoke, Sarah's stomach gave a nasty lurch. Who was she to talk about trust when lately she had betrayed that trust with lie upon lie? She was forced to acknowledge that however much she loved her husband – and she did - she was undeniably attracted to Simon. There was chemistry between them that was not something she could easily control. It was lust, pure and simple. She had no idea why; it had never been there before, but however inexplicable it was, somehow Adam's antennae had picked it up and if it went on it threatened to kill her marriage. She was not prepared to court disaster.

"So I'm forgiven?" Adam asked hesitantly.

"Yes, darling, you're forgiven."

"You don't have to eat that you know," Smiling, he took the cone and dropped it into the gutter, then he held her sticky hand and they made their way back to the car.

As they walked, Sarah heard Lola's voice in her head: *We all need to flirt a little, but be aware of the dangers this might bring.* The medium had been right after all. Clinging to her husband's hand, Sarah made a resolution: there would be no more lies and she would never see Simon again.

CHAPTER TWENTY THREE

Bored, Jenny sighed heavily as she re-read the last paragraph of her training notes. Glancing at her watch she realised it was way past going home time. She was alone in the office. Gary, their new line manager, was in Birmingham for a management meeting. The place seemed dull without him. Idly flicking through the remaining workload occupying her in-tray, Jenny gave another sigh. Nothing really appealed; it was all routine stuff. Would she bother to deal with it now or leave it for tomorrow? Tomorrow was likely to be busy: Gary would be back and had scheduled a meeting to talk through some new initiatives for their branch. In her capacity as Senior Financial Adviser, he had asked her to head up some new projects. It had really motivated her and she could not wait to get started. After five years at the bank she was ready for some new challenges and Gary, obviously keen to develop his staff, had sensed it straight away. And that, she told herself, was all it amounted to. Gary had never once indicated that he might want more than a working relationship with his Senior Adviser!

Staring unseeing out of the window, Jenny found that once again she was fantasising about her new boss and gave herself a mental rap across the knuckles. The trouble was the fantasy gave her so much pleasure in her otherwise humdrum existence that she did not want it to stop. She knew she was acting like a schoolgirl who has developed a crush on her teacher, but had convinced herself there was no harm in it; it was just a passing infatuation. Sure, she found Gary devastatingly attractive, but Vinny was her partner; they were just having a bad patch that was all. And yet...

Jenny sighed, 'Comparisons are odious' someone once said – she could not remember who - but she could not help comparing the two men. Gary was at least six foot tall and muscular with it. No problem wearing heels in his company, Jenny smiled to herself. Vinny, at five foot seven, was barely a couple of inches taller than she was and heels had always been difficult. Until recently he had been quite thin, wiry and strong, but was now running to fat. His bright blue eyes and baby-blond hair had looked so boyish when she first fell in love with him. Now he had begun to recede at the temples and compensated by wearing his hair untidily long. Gary's eyes were hazel, his hair short and jet black, so crisp and curly looking it made her want to run her fingers through it. But she should stop this right now. It would not do. Things between her and Vinny had really improved since her chat with Sarah. She had to give him a chance. Swinging round in her chair, Jenny pulled her focus back onto the training notes. She would go home when she had read them through again.

Try as she might, Jenny could not concentrate; her mind kept drifting back to her partner. At last she had managed to get him to listen to her and after a productive talk he had acknowledged their need to spend some quality time together, especially now the house was finished and they had more opportunity. Taking her completely by surprise, he had then given away his beloved X-box, complete with games, to his young cousin. Perhaps even more surprising was that he had joined the gym she went to so they could work out together. It was clear he had taken her seriously and wanted their relationship to work. After all, until recently they had lived happily together for more years than some couples stay married; it seemed foolish to throw all that away without at least trying to mend things.

As good as his word, last evening Vinny had come home with the most beautiful bouquet of red roses. After supper he had helped her wash up and taken the wind out of her sails completely by revealing his plans for a romantic weekend away. It was so unlike him that Jenny, still unable to believe the change in him, found herself wondering cynically how soon it would be before he slipped back into the same old ways that had been bugging her for months. But she tried to think positively: they had agreed to take one day at a time and see how things worked out. In some ways she felt it might be best if they got married. Maybe they should consider starting a family, but something felt wrong and Jenny knew it was a really bad idea to imagine that a baby would make things right. She concluded that just now it was more important for her and her partner to find ways to be happy with each other and then, maybe, marriage and babies would follow. Yet she could not dispel a niggling doubt that no matter how much effort Vinny made, she would not be with him for much longer. And no matter how much she tried to convince herself that he was the right man for her, in her heart of hearts she was afraid he was not. The plain fact was that she had fallen out of love with him and nothing he did could bring it all back.

Realising she had yet again read through the notes without taking them in, Jenny forced herself to concentrate and this time succeeded. About to pack up to go home, it occurred to her that with the office empty, now was a good opportunity to log onto the Internet and do a bit more research for Sarah. Jenny had always known her best friend to be level headed - the most sensible person she knew – and had no doubts at all that the ghosts and visions were genuine. Distressed for her friend, Jenny was determined to help in any way she could. She had already found twenty building companies trading under the name of Morgan's and based all over the country. Now what she wanted to do was to narrow down her search and if possible identify Jane Moore's killer and importantly, find out if he was still alive. Except, of course, if Sarah's dark-haired man had done the dreadful deed he must be dead, given that he was now a ghost! But the whole business was so surreal anyway that Jenny did not allow that to put her off. Besides, if it was true, an innocent man was still languishing in prison.

Feeling slightly guilty for using the office computer – but her own one at home was so old and slow – she logged on. The first company she viewed gave a list of housing sites and price ranges. There were colourful photographs of show homes and a raft of information about their various specifications, but little on the actual company beyond contact details. She jotted these down before moving on to the next website. It proved to be similarly lacking in useful information, as did all the others she tried. A few gave the name of their Managing Director, which she surmised could prove useful. What she planned to do was to phone likely companies, pretend to be interested in one of their housing developments and try to find out the names of - or even get to speak to - their quantity surveyors. Obviously, any of those who had qualified more recently than ten years ago could be discounted. Once she had a list of potential candidates, she could ask casually about other building projects they had worked on, get a list of locations, perhaps pretend that she would like to see their work for herself before she contracted their company. It was a long shot but it was worth a try. And it would take some nerve, but Jenny prided herself on her ability to extract information from anyone, regardless of their status. Her communication skills had greatly improved since she had been promoted to Senior Financial Adviser. It was part of her job now to sell the bank's investment products to both new and existing customers and she knew she had exceeded expectations in that direction.

Just as she had finished shutting down her PC, Gary breezed into her office. He left his briefcase by the door and smiled down at her. "You're working late. How's it going?"

Her heart giving a little skip, Jenny returned his smile. No matter how much stress he was under, Gary always seemed so pleasant and friendly. He never had a bad word to say about anybody and if there was a staffing problem, his approach was firm but always fair. "Not bad, I've just finished the training notes. I'm ready for tomorrow and the briefing on the next project, unless you wanted to go through things now?"

Gary pursed his lips and shook his head, a slight frown creasing his forehead.

"Is there a problem?" Jenny said, added tentatively, "Have I done something wrong?"

He pulled a chair up to Jenny's desk and faced her directly. "No, you've done nothing wrong. It's quite the reverse actually. As you are aware, Head Office monitors every bank's performance statistics and our branch has been doing extremely well. Out of all the branches we've been in the top ten consistently for the past twelve months, if not longer."

Jenny nodded, unsure where this was heading but with the distinct impression that she was not going to like the outcome. "They surely can't be unhappy about that can they?"

Gary laughed, shook his head, but to Jenny his laughter seemed forced. Conscious that her stomach had knotted with tension, she waited anxiously for what he was about to say.

"No," he said after a moment. "I gather they are extremely pleased about it, but because we are doing so well and they are aware it is people like you have produced such impressive results, they have decided in their wisdom to move you and one or two of your colleagues to branches where the targets over the past year have not been so good."

Jenny, her face suddenly hot, blurted out in dismay, "But that's so unfair!"

"I know it must seem that way and not much of a reward for all your hard work, but I've been instructed today to offer you a £5,000 pay rise to compensate. You will not have to move home if you don't want to, but I'm afraid the branch to which you are allocated is a good hour's commute from here. I have to admit I was shocked at first and I will be sorry to lose you, but think about it Jenny: when you've been noticed by senior management the opportunities for promotion are endless."

Jenny, not at all happy with this turn of events, decided to be frank, "Come off it, Gary, we both know it will result in more pressure on those of us involved. What if we can't improve performance? Besides which, I really like working here. The people are great; there are plenty of new challenges and opportunities ahead to keep me interested, especially with the new projects I'm supposed to be heading up. Plus it's a convenient location for me here. Do I actually get a choice?" She was conscious that her voice was raised and tried to soften it with a smile.

"No, sorry; the decision has already been made and if you refuse it might affect your future prospects with the bank."

Jenny shrugged, "Then I'll just have to go somewhere else. In the last five years I've built up some valuable experience in all areas of banking. My qualifications must count for something – I averaged eighty per cent on the exams last year - makes me pretty marketable I would have thought," she retorted.

"Of course other financial companies would want you. I've no doubt about that. But you would still have to move from here, so why not to one of our branches? What's the difference?"

"The difference is I don't like being pushed around," Jenny snapped heatedly.

Gary looked visibly upset. "I'm sorry, Jenny. I can't believe those idiots at Head Office want to do this. It pisses me off that we should have to suffer because another branch is constantly under-achieving, especially when you have consistently helped us to meet our performance targets. You are an excellent team player; a real asset to this branch in my view."

Jenny blushed, looked down at her hands. "Thanks for saying that, Gary. Your opinion means a great deal to me. So where do we go from here? Should I give in my notice?"

"No, don't do anything hastily. Maybe I can think of a way to change their minds." Running his hands through his hair, Gary sat back in the chair. "It may depend on how your colleagues take the news; if enough of them jump at the chance to improve their pay prospects it might let you off the hook. You know I'll support you all I can. Let me talk to one or two of my contacts." He pulled out his mobile phone, stood up and walked quickly over to his own office, shutting the door firmly behind him.

Jenny slowly packed up her briefcase, went through to the adjoining office to lock up the safe, pocketed the keys and came back for her jacket. For a moment she loitered by Gary's door, but could hear nothing beyond the low murmur of his voice. Deciding to hang around until he had finished his calls, she moved over to the window and gazed out at the rush-hour traffic. There was quite a breeze; the trees in the car park were swaying. The litter bin was overflowing and empty plastic cups were blowing about and scuttling under the cars. A man sat huddled on a bench. He was smoking, a can of drink in his hand, a plastic bag at his feet.

Some fifteen minutes later, Gary emerged, a broad smile on his face. "I've spoken to a friend who, as it happens, works at

Head Office. He's suggested a way we might persuade the powers that be to let you stay – as well as those of your colleagues who feel as you do, of course," he added hastily.

"That's great news," Jenny beamed at him, "but how? You're not going to get yourself into any trouble on my account I hope?"

"Lord no; I just need to get you heavily involved straight away in those new projects so that when I say you are indispensable I'm not lying! I've been told very precisely what to say to swing things in my favour. It hinges on my being able to demonstrate that to move you now would radically alter our projected profit margins. The bank wants to improve the performance of those other branches, but not, I imagine, at the expense of this one! As ever, it's all about the bottom line."

Jenny heaved a sigh of relief. "Thank you. You didn't need to do this. I'm very grateful." Without thinking, she leaned over and kissed him lightly on the cheek. No sooner had she done so than she could have kicked herself; whatever would he think of her? How could she have been so crass?

Flushing to the roots of his hair, Gary moved sharply away from her as if she had scalded him. "It's as much for me as it is for you, I don't want to lose good staff. Anyway," he checked his watch, "look at the time. I think we'd better lock up and go home now, don't you?" Getting the relevant keys together he promptly dropped them, bent to pick them up and moved to the door, dropping them again in the corridor and cursing under his breath. Clearly he was flustered, Jenny thought, a little surprised. It may have been a bit unprofessional, but she had only pecked him on the cheek, it was not as if she had flung herself at him. Yet his usual cool demeanour seemed to have utterly deserted him and she wondered why. A sudden thought occurred to her: was he gay?

With the doors locked and the alarm set, they walked in awkward silence to where their cars were parked side by side. Jenny noticed that the man on the bench had gone. Fumbling in her bag for her car keys, she pressed the lock release and tried desperately to think of something to say that would dispel the cloud of embarrassment.

Forestalling her, Gary said rather formally, "I'll talk to Management tomorrow, but I'm confident you won't need to move." He turned to his car, "Goodnight."

Taken aback by his abrupt manner, Jenny could not let him go like this. "Gary?"

He looked back over his shoulder, "Yes?"

"Look, I'm sorry. I didn't mean to offend you. It was most unprofessional. Please forgive me, it was just..." she floundered, her voice tailing away.

Gary threw his briefcase into his car and turned back. "There's nothing to forgive. I'll admit I was a bit shocked, but I'm really glad you kissed me."

He moved towards her. There was no time to think; suddenly she was in his arms, his mouth covering hers. Powerless to resist, Jenny lost all track of where she was and what she was doing. It was her fantasy come to life and Gary's lips against hers felt even better than she had imagined. All her senses clamoured for this to go on and on and never stop.

When eventually it did, Gary moved away from her and looked down at his feet. "I didn't mean for that to happen. I couldn't help myself. And just when I thought I was doing such a good job of masking my feelings!" He shrugged, "Sorry."

Clinging to his hand, Jenny smiled up at him, "You were doing a great job. I didn't suspect for a moment that you felt the same as I did."

A look of relief spread across his face. He pulled her towards him, looked down at her searchingly, "Really?"

Reading the desire in his eyes, her head swimming, Jenny nodded, "Really," she whispered.

Gary smiled, "If I'm honest I fancied you from the moment I first saw you. I made it my business to find out if you were unattached." He shook his head, turned his mouth down, "I was really upset to discover you were in a long term relationship;

knew I would have to back off. When you kissed me back then, I assumed it was just gratitude. I never dared hope..."

She stopped his mouth with her kiss. His lips were soft and warm; his tongue probed hers insistently, making her tremble. She had never felt anything like this – not even with Vinny. Vinny! Awash with guilt, she faltered, but only for a second. Gary was irresistible; it was utterly different from anything she had ever experienced. This man was intelligent, caring, responsible, attractive and perceptive – she ran out of adjectives. In short he was everything she could have wished for in a man. Without question, this was the real thing. He held her hard against him, his need too obvious to ignore. "And to think I thought you might be gay," she murmured with a smile.

Gary threw back his head and laughed and feeling a sudden urge to justify herself, Jenny pulled away from him. "I don't want you to imagine that I make a habit of this," she said shakily. "I know this is going to sound as if I'm spinning you a line, but I've had doubts about my long-term relationship for quite a while. Lately it has seemed as if it is only our shared interest in the house that is keeping us together and I had already decided to end it." She looked up at Gary's face. He was gazing into her eyes and his expression made her feel weak at the knees.

"You don't have to tell me this, you know," he said, gently teasing a strand of hair back from her face.

"I know, but I wanted you to understand. It's not just me. My partner would agree with me if he was being honest. We practically grew up together and we're good friends, but we're not right for each other, not any more. When you came along it helped me to acknowledge what I already knew - and anyway, I'm not the sort of person who would be comfortable about two-timing."

Gary pressed his lips into the palm of her hand, closing her fingers over his kiss. "I'm so glad about that, but I don't want to put pressure on you. This is all rather sudden. Go home and sleep on it, and if you decide this was all a big mistake, I'll understand. No harm done."

She shook her head emphatically, "It's no mistake, Gary. I need to go home now and sort things out, but I'll call you later if that's alright?"

Gary nodded, relaxing almost imperceptibly, "Of course, any time. You've got my mobile number?" Wordlessly, she nodded. He kissed her once more and they parted company.

Jenny drove home slowly. She was deliriously happy but hated the thought of facing Vinny. She knew he would be extremely upset, particularly given their recent reconciliation and the effort he had made, but what she had said to Gary was true. She did not want to demean herself or Vinny by two-timing; it would not be fair on any of them, least of all her soon to be ex-partner. She thought fleetingly of calling her best friend, remembering how it had been for Sarah when she had contemplated ending her relationship with Andy, how distressed she had been and how scared of what her boyfriend would do to her. But Jenny was not scared of Vinny, only of hurting him. And anyway, it had been different for Sarah; she had not met Adam then. Once she did, she was happier than Jenny had ever seen her, had admitted she had never really been in love with Andy and was right to end it when she did instead of prolonging it out of habit. Recalling her friend's words, Jenny found herself wishing she had gone with her instincts and ended things with Vinny weeks ago. What had happened tonight had muddied the water, made her feel she should be guilty, when in fact even if things did not work out with Gary, she would still not be able to stay with Vinny. How right she had been not to marry him; their relationship had run its course.

She pulled into their driveway and looked up at the house, feeling a tug of remorse, but whether it was for the home they had made together, which she would now have to leave, or for Vinny, she could not have said.

CHAPTER TWENTY FOUR

The first thing Jenny noticed as she entered the house was how tidy it looked. Vinny had obviously made an effort to clean the kitchen and put away his clothes instead of leaving them on the floor wherever they fell. Her heart felt heavy: he was really trying his best to please her. She saw a note on the dining room table; picked it up and read it quickly. He had gone to the gym and left her some cottage pie in the oven. The note was signed, *Loads of love, Vin.*

Her eyes brimming with tears, Jenny ran upstairs, undressed quickly and got into the shower. She gave up trying to stifle her sobs and let the tears come, utterly confused by her emotions. It was all so sad, but staying with someone out of sympathy was not the right thing to do under any circumstances, even had there not been the chance for her to be truly happy with someone else. She thought back a few months to how it had been before Gary came on the scene. Had all her and Vinny's problems stemmed from that moment? Was she guilty of deceiving herself as well as her partner? But no; she would never have fallen for Gary if she had still been in love with Vinny, there would have been no room in her heart.

Throwing on a clean pair of jeans, a T-shirt and a warm sweater, she packed some of her clothes and toiletries into an overnight bag. There was no way she could stay in the house tonight. Her parents would put her up until she found a place to rent. As soon as Vinny came back she would tell him and would not give him the chance to persuade her to stay. They could sell the house. It was in excellent condition. If Vinny wanted to buy her out and stay on, then that was fine. Renovating it had been fun and she liked what they had done to it, but she would not be sad to go, not really. They had talked about selling up anyway; it had been a means to an end, more of an investment than a home – or so she told herself. Vinny would get over it. They were both young and could start again with other partners. Jenny surprised herself that she was being so practical about everything. It was further proof, if any were needed, that Vinny was not the right man for her or how would she be able to think things through so logically?

She went into the living room, her gaze suddenly caught by the roses Vinny had given her. Their heady scent seemed to fill the air. They were beginning to drop already; a scatter of red petals lay on the table. Jenny felt herself welling up again. She dialled her parents' number, pleased when her Mum answered the phone. She sounded sympathetic and not at all surprised. "I've had my doubts about you and Vinny for some time, love, and so has your Dad. Just come over as soon as you have your bags packed and don't worry about anything. Take care and come as quickly as you can."

"Thanks Mum, I won't be long, but I must wait for Vinny, it wouldn't be fair to leave without saying goodbye." Jenny had decided not to mention Gary to her Mum; there was no need for anyone else to know. And anyway, he was not the reason why she was ending her relationship with Vinny - he was simply the catalyst.

Vinny did not arrive home until after nine. He looked relaxed and cheerful as he came into the living room where Jenny was waiting with her coat on. She knew it was going to be one of the worse moments of her life. They'd had their fair share of rows over the years, but never had they come close to actually splitting up.

He looked at her in surprise, "Are you cold? I was going to put the kettle on. Shall I do you a hot water bottle to cuddle? Do you want a cup of tea?"

Jenny felt sick and empty; she had barely eaten since breakfast. "No, I'm fine, I'm going out shortly. I was just waiting for you to come home." She could barely get her words out her throat was so dry. "Vin, we need to talk."

"What's up? You look very serious," he sat on the leather settee opposite her. "Go on then, I'm all ears."

Fleetingly she wondered why he did not give her a hug, but Vinny had never been demonstrative; never shown his emotions - he barely even held her hand these days. She had learned to live with it over the years, but it still hurt sometimes. The fact was that they were more like brother and sister than partners, but even so, Jenny knew this was going to be difficult. Vinny clearly had no idea of the bombshell she was about to drop and she felt awful.

She drew in a deep breath, "I know we've talked about things and about you making more of an effort and believe me, I know you've been trying and I really appreciate it, but I just think we're not right for each other. We're not making each other happy. I'm really, really sorry, Vin, but I want out." Jenny knew she was speaking too quickly. She looked at the floor, swallowed, her tears not far away.

Vinny sat in shocked silence, his face had paled and his hands clenched into fists on his knees. After a moment he spoke. "Just like that?"

Jenny nodded miserably, unable to speak.

He shook his head in disbelief. "Why do you say we aren't right for each other? Things are good between us. We have a lovely home and no ties; we can do whatever we want. Ok, so money's a bit tight just now, but it won't be like that forever," he paused, bewildered, pushed his fingers through his hair. "What do you mean we're not making each other happy? I'm happy. I love you. I thought you felt the same."

Vinny's eyes were pleading, glistening with unshed tears. His face was all crumpled and he sounded so broken. Jenny knew she had just wrecked his life and she felt as though her heart was breaking. For a moment she almost rushed over to fling her arms about his neck, tell him she had made a mistake and that everything would be alright. Anything to dispel that look on his face. But she knew it would be wrong to lie: kinder by far to cut it now, cleanly and quickly, than give him false hope. It would be a mistake to pretend she was happy. She had shared a good few years of her life with this man and she was fond of him, but she was no longer in love with him – if indeed she ever had been. It was hard to remember how she had felt in the early days, but there was no going back now. So instead she said, "I can't remember the last time you said that to me. We don't love each other, Vin. Not as a couple. It is habit and friendship that have kept us going." Jenny's voice broke, all she wanted to do was weep, but she could not afford to give way to her emotion. "We've been together a long time; you've just grown used to me like I have you. I care about you deeply; you know I do, but..."

"But it's not enough. You want the marriage and family thing don't you, is that what this is all about? So let's get married. I want that too. It's just we've never got around to talking about it. We can do it straight away – I'll see about getting a licence tomorrow." He gave her a tight little smile, "Hey – we can go to Egypt for our honeymoon. You'd like that wouldn't you?"

It was all going wrong; Jenny knew she had to leave and quickly. She pushed herself up from the chair, "We never got around to talking about it because we both knew that it wasn't right for us. I'm not forcing you into anything, Vin. I don't want to marry you. I'm so sorry, but it's over and I'm going to my Mum and Dad's."

As she said that, Vinny's attitude seemed to change. His mouth compressed into a thin line and despite the tears that were coursing down his cheeks, his face looked suddenly hard. "Oh no you're not! You're not going anywhere until we've sorted this out." He leapt off the settee and running to the back door, stood in front of it barring her way.

They rarely used the front door and Jenny knew it would be locked and bolted. Vinny would stop her before she had a chance to slide the bolts. Feeling very vulnerable, she followed him into the kitchen. "Stop it, Vin, there's no point. You can't stand there all night."

"I will if I have to. Come on, Jen, you've had a bad day and are not thinking straight. It'll be ok. I know our relationship isn't perfect but we can work it out. Tell me what you want and I'll do it; I'll do anything. Let's talk about it. Talk to me, Jen, please."

Jenny attempted to stay calm, but she was tired and her frustration was making her angry; his keeping her imprisoned was not going to improve the situation. She tried once more to get through to him, "There's nothing more to say. I don't want to hurt you any more. I'm trying to be honest and tell you how I feel. Please don't hate me and make things more difficult than they need to be. Let me pass, Vin. This is hard for me too."

"Hard for you is it?" Vinny sneered. "How do you think *I* feel? I love you; I always have. You know it's true. We've never been the kind of couple to say 'I love you' every five minutes, but so what? I thought we were happy with each other, knew each other well enough not to need constant reassurance. In all the years we've been together it's never once crossed my mind to cheat on you. Not like my mates: never mind that they already had a wife at home, most of them couldn't wait for the opportunity to get off with other women. But not me; you were always the only girl for me and I thought my love life was sorted. Ok, I'll admit I got a bit lazy, maybe took you for granted, but since we talked about it I've really tried. You know I have – and it's not been easy, but I've lost weight and I'm getting fit. I've made a real effort to be what you wanted." Vinny began to sob, his breath coming in shuddering gasps, his voice getting louder. "And now you tell me you've decided it's all over. *You've* decided. Eight years and that didn't mean anything to you? Goodbye Vinny; just like that?" He was shouting now, his face red, a vein throbbing on his forehead. His left hand balled into a fist and he moved towards her.

Just for a moment Jenny thought he was going to hit her. She had never seen him so angry and it scared her. She could see he was losing control, he was visibly shaking. Her heart was beating so loudly it almost hurt, the blood pounding in her ears. She saw him looking at the worktop, followed his gaze, saw a knife lying there. Jenny gasped, took a step backwards. Suddenly she heard Sarah's voice in her head: *Someone close to me is in danger.* Was she the one in danger? She wished she had called Sarah before Vinny had come home; asked her advice. Maybe finishing with him like this had been too sudden; tipped him over the edge. She should have taken more time, given him more signs that things were not right and let him down gently. She could have suggested a trial separation to see how things went. It was too late to think about that now – or was it? Would he let her go if he thought she intended coming back?

"Calm down, Vin. Of course it meant something to me, you know it did. We've had a lot of good times together, but now I want different things and I've let it get to me. You're right, I'm not thinking straight. Let me go, Vin, please. Just for a day or two, give me time to think. I need some space away from here to sort out my head for a bit." Jenny's breathing was ragged. She had done exactly what she had told herself she would not do and given him false hope, but that was before she had been so scared.

Vinny wasn't hearing her. He seized a kitchen chair and smashed it on the quarry-tiled floor. He kicked the pieces out of the way and slammed his fist down on the worktop making the plates jump and rattle. The knife was only inches from his fingers. "Why are you looking at me as though I'm a bit of dirt you've just scraped off your shoe?" he yelled, shaking with rage. "I've done nothing wrong. All I've done is try to make you happy. I've bent over backwards to do things your way and yet you can't wait to get away from me, can you." Panting, he bent over as though in pain. Swaying on his feet, he grabbed onto the worktop for support. Suddenly the tension left him, his shoulders slumped and he drew in a sobbing breath. "Do you hate me so much?"

Close to tears, her fear forgotten, Jenny ached for him. "How can you think that? You know I don't hate you. It's not you, it's me. I've changed, and I'm so very sorry. Maybe we can work things out in time, but right now I just need a break. Please try to understand, I never meant to hurt you."

He looked at her then, his mouth twisted in the mockery of a smile. "I want to believe you, but we've both known loads of couples who've had a break and none of them ever got back together. It's just an excuse." Vinny pushed himself away from the worktop and moved back to the door. His gaze softened; his expression wistful. "Do you remember the first time we met? I can remember it like it was yesterday. I fancied you like hell. You were wearing black jeans and a white crop top. You looked absolutely bloody gorgeous and I couldn't believe you weren't with anyone or that I stood the remotest chance of getting you to go out with me."

"Yes, I remember," she whispered. He seemed to have relaxed slightly and Jenny surreptitiously eyed the door. Dared she try to rush him?

Vinny read her thoughts and his lip curled. "So you want a break, eh? If you need time to think about whether you really want to be with me, then it's obviously over." He gave a resigned shrug and stood aside. "Go then. Get out of my sight. Take with you whatever you need because I'm telling you, there'll be no second chance. Walk out that door and we're done; finished. We'll sort out the house through solicitors. I won't want to see you again – not ever, understand? It's your choice." It was his last throw of the dice.

Jenny nodded. She had hurt him badly and knew he was attempting to sound strong; keep his pride intact. Relieved, she brushed past him, but as her hand reached for the latch she hesitated. She was walking out on eight years of her life and Vinny would never speak to her again. Suddenly it felt as though she was falling over the edge of a cliff and the ground was a very long way down. She stood for a moment, heard the wall clock ticking, the tap dripping, Vinny's harsh breathing. Squaring her shoulders, she grasped the latch and pulled open the door. "I'm so sorry, Vin." There was nothing more to say. It was over.

Only as she was getting into the car did Jenny remember she had left her overnight bag in the hall. Wild horses would not drag her back inside the house. It did not matter; her Mum would sort her out for now. As she drove away she caught sight of Vinny in the rear view mirror. He was standing on the back step gazing after the car. He looked so terribly alone.

Jenny began to weep, barely able to see she absent-mindedly switched on the windscreen wipers before realising it was not raining. In her mind's eye she saw Vinny's fingers inching towards the knife. Fortunately it had not occurred to him to ask if there was someone else. Had he done so and had she told him, she thought he would probably have killed her.

CHAPTER TWENTY FIVE

Disorientated, Sarah sat up in bed. There was a faint musical tone coming from her bag; someone was calling her mobile. The radio alarm on the bedside table registered almost 10:30 p.m. She had been asleep barely twenty minutes having decided to get an early night. She sighed, fumbled for the lamp switch, reached for her bag and took the call. "Hello?"

"Sarah, it's me, Jenny. I'm sorry to call so late."

"Don't worry, is everything ok?"

"It's Vinny. We're finished. I've just left him. It was so awful and I feel terrible. I'm sorry to land this on you, but I have to talk to someone." Jenny started to sob uncontrollably.

"Hey, it's alright, what are friends for?" Sarah rubbed her eyes and tried to think what to say that would not sound trite. "Everything's going to be ok. You're bound to be distressed after all the years you've been together. But you've obviously thought about it and believe it's for the best. Let's face it; you've had doubts about you and Vinny for quite a while. There's no point staying in a relationship if it's not right – and it could be worse, Jen, at least there are no children to worry about." Sarah was relieved to hear Jenny's sobs starting to subside.

"I know, but having to tell him I don't really love him was hateful. He was so dreadfully hurt. He said we could get married and have a family. I couldn't make him understand that I don't want that any more – at least, not with him. Then he lost his temper and wouldn't let me go. He was so angry, Sarah, I thought he was going to hit me and it made me think of what your medium said and I wondered if it was me who was in danger. I saw Vinny looking at a knife on the worktop and I thought for a minute he was going to grab it and turn it on me. I've never been so scared. It was like I was standing outside myself watching it happen to someone else, not to me and Vinny. It doesn't seem possible; it was as if he hates me."

Sarah felt a wave of compassion for her friend, who was clearly distraught. "Hang on in there, love. I know it's hard, but you're out of it now. If Vinny meant to hurt you he would have done it there and then on the spur of the moment. He's not going to come after you once his temper has cooled and he's thinking rationally again."

"I guess so. It was like he accepted it in the end – he just stood aside and told me to go; said he never wanted to see me again."

"I think you've made the right decision. You have a chance to make a clean break and start again. Maybe in time you'll meet someone else who is more right for you. That's what happened to me and I've never looked back." There was silence on the other end of the phone. "Jenny? You ok?"

"Actually, Sarah, I think I have; that's what made me finally decide to call it a day with Vinny." Jenny cleared her throat, obviously embarrassed.

"Is it Gary by chance?"

"Spot on! I don't suppose it took a lot of guesswork - you knew how I felt about him, but earlier tonight I discovered that it's mutual. Oh, Sarah, I've never felt like this about anyone before. It's amazing."

Sarah laughed. "I'm very happy for you, so long as you're not jumping out of the frying pan into the fire. But you were right to be honest with Vinny; it wouldn't have been fair on either of you to two-time him, not after all the years you've had together."

"I wasn't totally honest," Jenny said in a small voice. "That is, I didn't tell him about Gary."

"There's no point in rubbing his nose in it, Jen. Besides, it's not as if you've slept with Gary or anything. You haven't, have you?"

"No! But I've thought about it. Vinny really would hate me if he knew."

Sarah could hear the tears coming back into her friend's voice. "It's bound to be a painful time for you, Jen, but you'll get through it. So will Vinny; he'll be ok. I know it's a bit of a cliché, but time is a great healer. By the way, where are you? I take it you're not going back to the house?"

"No, I'm at Mum and Dad's – back in my old room. They said they had been half expecting it and are being really sympathetic. As it happens, they're going off in the caravan for a few days tomorrow, but they've given me a spare key. Being on my own seems like heaven at the moment although Mum's not sure about it."

"She might be right. Are you sure you want to be on your own just now? I mean, just in case Vinny takes it into his head to try to persuade you to go back to him. Then you'd have to tell him about Gary and it could get nasty. Why not come up here for a few days to get away from it all. I can take some time off and we can go shopping in Nottingham. We could pretend we're tourists: there's Sherwood Forest and Nottingham Castle to see, not to mention the exclusive viewing of a haunted house that I could lay on for you – you might even get to see a ghost or two!"

Jenny giggled. "No thanks! Seriously though, it's a tempting offer. I'll come up as soon as I can get away, but I'll need to give some notice at work. I've been offered another job at a different branch, by the way. I wasn't too keen at first, but given the circumstances, I'm wondering if it's too good an offer to refuse. I'd get a bonus too, which would be useful now I'm on my own again." Jenny paused, "It's going to take a bit of getting used to."

"That's great news. Yes, a fresh start is a good idea. It'd be a bit tricky staying where you are if you're in a relationship with the boss. Let me know as soon as you can get up here and I'll arrange a few outings for us. We'll have some fun. Sorry you've had to go through all this, but it will pass, Jen, believe me."

"It's no worse than what you've been going through and you are managing to keep it together. You're the only person I wanted to speak to and as usual you've made me feel so much better. Incidentally, I've got a list of builders trading under the name of Morgan. I'll bring all the information with me when I come up. We could try to track down the company that built your house."

"That's great, Jen, but I want you to relax and enjoy yourself, not help me try to solve a murder case that happened all that time ago. And anyway, it could all just be my mind playing tricks on me..."

"Nonsense - you're the most level-headed person I know. If you're a crackpot there's no hope for the rest of us! Besides, trying to establish what happened to Jane Moore's killer will help take my mind off my current problems."

"Well if you're sure; thanks, Jen." Sarah glanced at the clock. "Look, I'd better get some sleep; I've got meetings all day tomorrow. Try not to worry. I'll pop back to the office around lunch time - call me then if you want to talk any more. Call me anyway so I know you're ok."

"I will. Thanks for listening."

As soon as they had said their goodbyes Jenny saw she had missed calls on her mobile. Vinny had been trying to contact her. She switched her mobile off. Any conversations with Vinny just now would be sure to turn into massive arguments. If only she had not stopped loving him, how much easier everything would have been, but there was no going back. Like he had said, they could communicate through solicitors. Oh damn! She was welling up again. She grabbed a tissue from the box her Mum had thoughtfully placed on the bedside table, and wiped the tears away. Closing her eyes, she tried to re-capture the wonderful floating feeling of being in Gary's arms, his lips on hers, his breath warm on her face, but the trauma of the last few hours had rubbed it out. It was just after eleven; the house still and quiet, but Jenny was too upset to sleep. She thought about the new job. It would mean more money, which she would need now; living on her own would be expensive and it would be some time before she got her share of the proceeds from the house sale. She certainly could not live there any more, whatever Vinny might say. A fresh start was exactly what she needed. He would guess she was going to live at her parents' place, at least for a while. It was not unusual; most of their friends still lived at home. She and Vinny had been lucky to be able to afford a house of their own – even if it had been a wreck when they bought it! She would just have to keep a low profile until the dust had settled and everything was sorted out.

Rolling over to turn off the bedside lamp, a thought suddenly occurred to her: what if Vinny found out about Gary? Would he try to cause trouble? It was highly likely. She would have to ask Gary to be patient. He would understand. Maybe it was a mistake to dive headlong into another relationship so soon anyway. Her feelings for Gary were very strong at the moment, but supposing her emotions were playing her false. Could she be wrong? Life with Vinny had become so boring and then along had come this Prince Charming. It was only natural that she had fallen for him, but was it just an antidote? Had she mistaken infatuation for love? After all, she hardly knew Gary outside work. It was one thing to fantasise about having a relationship with your boss, but quite another to actually go and do it. And relationships could be so complicated. Maybe it was best to cool it with Gary and enjoy being single again; live a little; use her freedom to explore new things – she had been so young when she hooked up with Vinny. Now she could experience all the things she had missed out on; do what she wanted when she wanted without having to worry about anyone else. Besides, she would need to put most of her energy into her new role at the bank. It was not going to be easy: the staff at the new branch would be sure to resent an outsider swanning in and telling them how to do their jobs. Would Gary be offended she had decided to move after all his efforts to keep her? No, surely he would understand.

Settling down to try to sleep, Jenny's mind wandered to Sarah's ghosts. She knew her friend had been trying to cheer her up when she had joked about the haunted house, but there had been an edge to her voice. There was no question that Sarah was still very frightened. So would I be in her shoes, Jenny thought. What had Jane Moore done to deserve so brutal a fate? Her killer must surely have been insane. Did he feel betrayed by her? Did Vinny feel that way too? Jenny shivered, recalling the look on his face as he had smashed the kitchen chair, as if it wasn't a chair at all, but her. She had really thought he was going to hit her; that she was only seconds away from having a knife thrust into her. In the blink of an eye her old, lovable Vinny had become a violent stranger. Was that what had happened to Jane?

CHAPTER TWENTY SIX

Jenny was woken by the alarm and for a moment could not work out where she was – the window was on the wrong side of the room and everything looked different. And then she remembered and bile filled her throat. Swallowing hard, she waited for the nausea to subside. She had barely slept; watched the hours crawl by until the early hours, re-playing over and over in her head the dreadful scene in the kitchen.

She could ring in sick, but would that be sensible? Work would take her mind off things. After a long, hot shower Jenny felt refreshed enough to make a real effort with her appearance, taking time to disguise the dark circles round her eyes with foundation and carefully applying her makeup. She chose a bright pink lipstick, telling herself that today was the first day of her life: a new beginning.

"Jenny, love, your breakfast is ready," her mother's voice floated up the stairs.

Still feeling slightly queasy, Jenny groaned. Eating was the last thing she wanted to do, but her parents would worry if she did not at least try – and she had eaten nothing at all for almost twenty-four hours, which may account for how she was feeling now.

She put on a bright smile and ran downstairs into the kitchen. "Thanks Mum."

Her mother seemed relieved, "You look a little better than you did last night, Jen, that's good. I'm afraid it's only cereal and toast. I didn't get much in as we were going away."

"It's fine, Mum. I haven't got much of an appetite this morning anyway," Jenny said, glad she had ladled on the makeup. "Morning Dad."

Mr Peters looked over the top of his newspaper and smiled at his daughter. "We're thinking of cancelling our trip, it's not important and we can go another-"

"No, Dad," Jenny cut across him. "You and Mum both deserve a break, especially now the weather's so nice. There's no need to stay on my account, really, I'll be fine. Besides, I'll be at work until late most days. There's so much to do. And anyway, Sarah has invited me to stay at hers for a while, which will be great. I shall take some time off as soon as I've cleared my in-tray." She forced a smile, "So you see, you must go or I shall feel terribly guilty."

Her Dad frowned. "What about Vinny – he's not going to keep coming round here is he? After what you said last night, we're worried about what he might do."

"He won't do anything, Dad – you know Vinny, he's not the violent type. And anyway, he'll be concentrating on going out on the pull with his mates to prove he's not bothered. He'll most likely say he was the one who finished it – male pride and all that. No, you two carry on with your plans. It will make me feel worse if you don't go away. I just want to get on with my life."

To Jenny's relief her Mum smiled and gave her a hug. "Alright love, but we will do some shopping before we go, won't we Brian. We can't leave Jenny with all the cupboards bare!" She looked across at her husband, who grunted assent from behind his newspaper. "Could you do Jenny a list of the club sites and contact numbers, dear, then she can get in touch with us if she needs to - and if you change your mind, Jenny, and want us to come home again, you only have to say. We're not going far, probably only to the coast."

"Thanks, Mum."

Half an hour later, Jenny arrived at work and was soon engrossed in a pile of customer queries that needed her attention. She had noticed that Gary was in his office with some junior members of staff, but he did not look in her direction. She was on the point of making another customer call, when Sue, a young counter clerk, came rushing over to her desk with a huge grin on her face. "Oh, Jenny, someone has sent you the most beautiful, huge bunch of flowers. I've put them in the kitchen for you in some water."

Jenny, still holding the telephone receiver, smiled up at her. "That's kind, thanks. I'll pick them up later."

Looking a little wistful, Sue said, "Is it your birthday or something?"

Before Jenny could answer, the inquisitive clerk was called away to the counter. Jenny breathed a sigh of relief. It was nice of Gary to send her flowers and very romantic, but a little unwise. People would talk: so much for keeping a low profile!

At coffee time Jenny wandered through to the kitchen. The bouquet was overflowing the sink and her heart sank; it was full of lilies; very expensive. They were also her favourite flowers, but Gary could not possibly know that. Vinny did, of course. It was ironic. In all their years together she could count on one hand the number of times he had bought her flowers. The bouquet was tied with shiny, purple ribbon, a tiny white envelope attached to the bow and bearing her name: 'Jenny Peters'. Recognising the writing straight away, she ripped open the card. *I'm sorry. I didn't mean what I said. I need to see you. Please can we talk. All my love, Vin.*

Jenny swallowed and shoved the card angrily in her pocket. Why couldn't he accept the relationship was over? Did he think she was regretting what she had done; that it had been an easy decision to make? They had never split up before. Surely he must know she was serious to have taken this drastic step? What more was there to say? Jenny knew all he wanted to talk about was getting back together. The best thing she could do was to ignore his plea and make no contact for a while. Let him see this was permanent. She poured a cup of coffee from the machine – it was too hot and scalded her tongue. She would take the flowers home to her Mum – no, they would not have room in the caravan for that great bouquet. Besides, they would be long gone before she got home. The rich honey scent made her feel ill; she would just have to chuck the lilies away, though it seemed a shame to waste them. Oh bother Vinny! Why could he not let her go? Jenny recalled that Sarah had gone through exactly this sort of thing when she had split up with Andy. He had refused to accept they were through and bombarded Sarah with letters and heated phone calls for months on end – almost up until she had met Adam, in fact. How long would it be before Vinny accepted the inevitable? Jenny had been so sure he would put on a brave front and pretend not to be bothered. He was young, he would meet someone else. She hoped it would be soon; it would be so much easier and she would not have to feel guilty any more. Jenny realised with some surprise that she felt not a trace of jealousy. She nodded to herself; yes, she would be genuinely happy for Vinny to move on. Lost in thought, she did not hear the door open.

"How are you today?"

Jenny spun round. Gary stood looking at her, his expression faintly anxious. "You made me jump," she smiled. "I'm fine, just a difficult time at the moment."

He nodded towards the sink, "Are they from your boyfriend?"

"Ex-boyfriend. Yes they are. He's trying to make me feel guilty." Mortified, Jenny felt tears pricking her eyes and sliding down her cheeks.

Gary fiddled with his tie, clearly unsure what to do. He looked round at the door to make sure they were alone before giving her a quick hug. "Look, if there's anything I can do just let me know. I'll ring you later if that's ok? Obviously, we need to keep this out of the office."

Jenny gave him a watery smile, "Yes, of course. I'll be ok. I just need some time."

"Of course you do, take care," he hesitated then hurried away.

For Jenny, the rest of the day passed in a blur. Fortunately it was Friday; a busy day at the bank, which was just as well since it kept her mind fully occupied. Before the end of the day, she took the bouquet to Sue, "Here, you have these. It was a nice gesture from an old friend, but they give me hay fever, you'd be doing me a favour. Watch out! Mind the pollen, it can stain."

Too overwhelmed to ask questions, the clerk took them gratefully.

At 5.30 Jenny was getting into her car when she spotted Vinny's white van on the other side of the road. She swore. The last thing she wanted was speak to him. Pulling quickly out of the car park, she headed into the traffic hoping he would not follow her. How long had he been waiting outside the bank? She glanced in the rear view mirror, could not see the van. Jenny felt very both wary and annoyed: if it had been the other way round and Vinny had wanted to finish with her, she would have accepted it no matter how painful it was, not gone chasing after him. There would have been no phone calls, no letters, nothing. Her parents had always taught her to have a sense of pride. Vinny was being pathetic. Ignoring her sense of uneasy guilt – they had, after all, being together for eight years and if she was honest, she had not given him much of a chance – she told herself that any sympathy she might have had for him had now completely disappeared.

Checking the mirror again, Jenny could see no sign of the white van. Had she been mistaken? Maybe it was not Vinny after all. Even so, she was reluctant to go back to her parents' place straight away, especially as the house was empty. Most of her close friends lived a good few miles away and besides, it would be rude to drop in without warning. After driving around for several minutes, she found herself at a superstore on the edge of town. "I need some shopping anyway," she muttered, talking to herself helped her to feel calmer; less nervous. Checking there was still no sign of Vinny, she went into the store and bought some groceries, quite forgetting until she got to the checkout that her Mum had said she would stock up before they left.

It was after seven when Jenny pulled into her parents' drive – a big empty space with the caravan gone. Putting her car away in the garage and checking everything was locked up properly, she carried her shopping into the house. Her mobile phone was bleeping, which meant there was another message. It might be Sarah; Jenny suddenly realised she had forgotten to call her friend at lunch time. Deciding to ignore it until she had put the groceries away, she went up to run a bath. Eating had been low of her list of priorities, but now she actually felt quite hungry. She would cook something in a minute. "Stress – it's better than any diet!" she said, battling to maintain her sense of humour. Late sunlight was filtering through the blinds in the bathroom as she slipped into the hot bath of bubbles. She felt herself begin to unwind, heard her mobile bleep from the bedroom, shouted, "Go away!" and ducked her head under the water.

Almost an hour later she got out of the bath and wrapped in her mother's bath robe, padded across the landing to fetch the mobile. There were six text messages: the first three were from friends, including Sarah, just asking how she was. The next one made her catch her breath: R U OK? PLS RING. NEED 2 TALK.

It was Vinny. She felt compelled to read the next message. BITCH, TALK 2 ME!

Jenny gasped; fear lurched into her stomach and coiled into a knot of tension. Vinny had never called her 'bitch' before. Nor had he been particularly violent. He had been involved in a few fights just after they had met and could defend himself well enough, but he had never threatened her, not ever – even when he lost his temper as he had on occasion. His text frightened her. She had turned his world upside down and clearly he could not handle it.

She turned to the final message and a shiver ran down her spine. WATCH YOUR BACK, BITCH. I KNOW U R ALONE. I'M COMING 2 GET U. Jenny's heart skipped a beat; the tension made her want to be sick. "Get a grip girl," she shouted at her reflection in the mirror. Vinny was just being immature, acting like the tough guy. Did he think that this threatening behaviour would send her running back to him? Maybe, she thought, he has been talking to some of his more yobbish mates. One or two of them, she had been horrified to discover, did actually hit their partners. Jenny had always thought Vinny abhorred violence as much as she did, especially violence against women.

For a moment she stood rooted to the spot, her imagination running wild, Lola's warning to Sarah coming into the forefront of her mind.

A sudden loud bang made Jenny scream. Her heart tripped and skidded. What was that? What should she do? All the windows had locks on them. Both the front and back doors were padlocked and a six-foot fence enclosed the rear garden. Plus there were security lights that lit up both back and front. No one could get in; she should be safe. Despite this, Jenny felt more vulnerable than she had ever done. She went onto the landing, leaned over the banister straining her ears; heard nothing. The bang must have been a car backfiring. What else could it be?

Crossing the landing, she went to look out of her parents' bedroom window, which was at the front of the house and gave a good view of the whole street and surrounding area. Everywhere seemed quiet and peaceful. There appeared to be no-one hanging around. She jumped as the phone in the hall started ringing. Vinny? She could not face a barrage of abuse. Her nerves were in tatters. She ignored the phone and after a while it stopped. Immediately afterwards, her mobile ringtone jangled out a melody, she picked it up and a wave of relief swept over her as she saw it was Sarah.

"Hi, Jen, how are you?"

Jenny's hands were sticky with sweat. "Not good – Vinny's trying to scare me. He's sent some horrible texts. The last one said he was coming to get me – and I'm pretty sure he's been following me around today."

Sarah gave a low whistle, "I know this sounds a bit dramatic, but have you contacted the police? He's obviously very angry and being stupid. People do some strange things when they're upset. If he knows the police are around it might put him off trying to contact you."

"You're right. I'll give them a ring just to be on the safe side. I'm beginning to wish my parents were here; could do with the company. My imagination's running wild. I know how silly it sounds being afraid of someone you've lived with for eight years, but..."

"It's not silly at all. Vinny's acting out of character. His behaviour is unpredictable to say the least. I wish I could get my hands on him frightening you like that. Look, why don't I come down? It's the weekend and the traffic will be practically non-existent by now."

Jenny was horrified. "You can't drive all that way on your own in the dark."

"It won't be dark for quite a while, and Adam will come with me anyway. It's not a problem."

"No, I can't let you do that, but bless you for suggesting it. I think I'm overreacting, Sarah. I'll do as you suggest and ring the police; make them aware I've had some threatening texts. There's a sergeant lives just down the road from here, perhaps he'll come over. There must be a contact number somewhere." Talking to Sarah had made Jenny feel much calmer. This would all blow over soon; Vinny would come to his senses. After all, what could he do to her - she was being silly. "It'll be fine, Sarah. Don't worry about me. I'll be ok."

"Well if you're sure. But remember, we're only a phone call away. I'd really feel happier if you were not on your own. Ring your local copper and set my mind at rest. I'll ring you in the morning. Take good care."

Jenny rang off and put the mobile in her pocket. It was too quiet in the house for her liking. She felt a bit chilly wearing only a bath robe. She turned up the heating, closed all the blinds and curtains and switched on the TV for company. Remembering there was a bottle of white wine in the fridge she walked through to the kitchen and poured herself a generous glassful. On her way back to the living room, she stopped in the hall to look up the number of the local police station and keyed it into her mobile's memory. She would maybe phone later, like Sarah said, just to be on the safe side.

Jenny curled up on the settee with her drink and watched a sit-com, which helped to lighten her mood. After twenty minutes the alcohol began to do its job. More relaxed, she felt her eyelids becoming heavy: she had not had a lot sleep last night; no wonder she was so tired. She let herself drift off to sleep.

Jenny woke with a start. In a daze, she checked her watch - almost 1:00 a.m. - she had been asleep for a good couple of hours.

Grabbing the remote, she killed the sound on the TV and strained to listen, trying to identify the noise that had woken her. It came again; a tapping sound. Jenny felt an uncontrollable sizzle of horror. Someone was tapping on the window. It sounded as if it was coming from the patio. How could anyone have got into the back garden? The back gate was always kept locked. As quietly as she could, she got up from the settee, switched off the lights and clutching her mobile to her chest crept up the stairs, her heart pounding like a drum. She went into her old room and peered out of the window into the garden. Nobody was there: had she been mistaken? Maybe the tapping was in her imagination or the wind had knocked a branch against the glass. She stood for a moment, undecided, was about to turn away when the security light came on.

Jenny gasped. Someone was moving about in the shadows by the shed at the top of the garden. It could only be Vinny and he was horribly near. Fumbling with the keys on her mobile, she dialled the police, explained she was on her own and there was an intruder outside. They took the details and her mobile number and promised to send someone out as quickly as possible. Jenny sat on the side of her bed and hugged her ribs, swaying backwards and forwards and moaning to herself: 'Please come quickly, please come quickly.'

She almost jumped out of her skin as her mobile rang. Thinking it might be the police, Jenny answered straight away. "Hello?"

"So at last I get to talk to you," Vinny said. "Why are you doing this to me? It's driving me insane. I can't live without you."

Trembling, Jenny could barely get her words out. "Are you outside the house?"

"What's it to you? I don't know what to do. I can't eat, sleep or work. You've destroyed me. What have I done to deserve this? What did I do wrong?"

Vinny's words sounded slurred and Jenny could tell he had been drinking, which made things even worse. Her heart plummeted. She tried to sound calm, "Why don't we meet up tomorrow? It's late and I'm really tired. We'll both sleep on it. Things will look better in the morning."

"I don't want to sleep! Don't you realise, you slag, that I can't be without you? I'm coming to get you, bitch."

He was shouting down the phone and Jenny, gripped by helpless fear, could only hope and pray the police would get here soon. Surely one of the neighbours must have heard or seen Vinny - he was not even trying to be quiet. Why was he being like this? Jenny felt trapped. If she ran outside he would surely go after her. She would never be able to get to the car in time. But what if he tried to smash his way in? She tried again to calm him down, keep him talking. Each precious minute brought the police nearer. "Don't call me names, Vin. It doesn't help. I know you're upset. Why don't we sort this out tomorrow? I will come over to the house and we can talk properly."

Vinny gave a humourless laugh, his voice sounded strange, not like him at all. "Don't feed me crap, Jenny. I know you won't come. It's too late for that anyway. There's someone else isn't there?"

Jenny got up from the bed and looked out of the window. The security light had clicked off and she could no longer see anyone by the shed. Backing away, she left the bedroom and went to the top of the stairs, talking into the mobile as she slowly went down into the hall. "No, there's no one else. I thought I had explained. I just think we need a break – or at least, I do. Look, Vin, hang on a moment, I need to go to the loo, could I ring you back?" She was trying to stall for time; anything to delay him, give the police a chance to arrive.

"Don't bother. Do you have any idea much I hate you? Rich isn't it. I hate you and yet I can't live without you. And I'll call you all the names I want: bitch, bitch bitch! Like I said, I've been watching you. I'm still watching you. And don't expect anything from the house either because you and lover boy are not getting-"

Appalled, Jenny cut him off, unable to listen to any more. She was petrified. Vinny was drunk and so full of anger and aggression. She could not believe he was being so nasty nor understand the change in him. In all the years she had known him, he had never behaved like this; he clearly hated her for what she had done. Subsiding onto the bottom step, Jenny clung to the banister and started to weep, the tears running hotly down her face.

Suddenly there was a crash of breaking of glass.

"Oh, God!" Jenny cried out. She covered her mouth to stifle the scream and willed herself to go back upstairs. What could she use as a weapon to defend herself? What if Vinny had a gun or a knife?

Then she heard voices. The police! Weak with relief, Jenny's legs gave way and she collapsed on the stairs dropping her mobile, which bounced down into the hall, flashed and went black. She heard someone calling her name. The security light came on at the front shining into the hall.

Pulling herself up, Jenny rushed to the front door, without thinking drew back the bolts and pulled it open. Saw her parents running up the driveway. The police were right behind them. Of Vinny there was no sign. She was safe.

Jenny rushed sobbing into her father's arms, "Oh thank you. Thank you for coming home."

CHAPTER TWENTY SEVEN

Sarah woke from a nightmare, mouth dry, chest tight and images of the dark-haired man still vivid in her mind. Incongruously, they had all been sitting round the dining table, herself and Adam, Jenny and the dark-haired man. He had been invited to dine with them and everyone was talking and laughing as if it was the most natural thing in the world. And then the man brought out a knife and lashed out at Jenny who started to scream, her hands clawing at the blood streaming from a cut on her face. Sarah ran to her, repeatedly calling for Adam to help, but he just sat the table laughing until the tears ran out of his eyes.

It was a ridiculous dream! Sarah threw back the quilt; it was so hot and stuffy in their bedroom. Adam was still asleep; snoring lightly. Sarah glared at him, filled fleetingly with desperate anger, but it was just the dregs of the nightmare. She shook off the feeling and chastised herself for being silly. She glanced at the clock: six-thirty, another Saturday morning. Where had the week gone? She settled back on the pillow, her thoughts turning to Jenny. From what she knew of Vinny, he had never been aggressive; quite the contrary, had always seemed so passive. Now he was apparently acting like a madman. Deciding it was too early to ring her friend just yet; Sarah thought about Jane Moore. If only that poor girl had been content with Robert Taylor and not felt the need to flirt with someone else, she might still be alive. Sarah had the horrid feeling that there was almost a parallel with Jenny and Vinny. Undoubtedly that thought had been in her subconscious and brought on her nightmare. Sarah snuggled up to Adam. She loved him deeply and found it hard to imagine not feeling content with their relationship. The streak of jealousy he had allowed her to see last Saturday had completely disappeared as though it had never been, and in her mind it had somehow lessened. She now felt she must have exaggerated it. And in a way, however much she had protested her innocence, she knew she had given him cause, if only in thought.

The phone was ringing. Adam picked it up. Sarah realised she had drifted off to sleep again. It was now nine-thirty.

"Hi, Jenny, I'll hand you over." Adam passed the phone to Sarah and mouthed 'I'll make a cup of tea.' She nodded gratefully, feeling slightly guilty that she had gone back to sleep and wasted so much of the morning already.

"Jenny, are you ok?"

Her friend sounded tired, her voice strained. "Yes, I'm fine now, but it's been a bit traumatic," said Jenny, relating what had happened last night.

Sarah gasped, horrified to hear that Vinny had tried to break in. "How awful - I can't believe it, he always seemed such a gentle person. I knew I should have driven down to you."

"You would never have got here in time, and anyway, Mum and Dad arrived at the same time as the police."

"Thank God for that! Are the police keeping tabs on Vinny?"

Jenny gave an angry laugh, "As much as they can, but nobody saw him last night, he must have scarpered when the police arrived. It's his word against mine that he actually threw the brick at the window and so as far as the police are concerned he hasn't committed any crime. I've filed a complaint about his threatening behaviour, but I don't suppose they'll do much about it; it's just another domestic to them. So I'm going to have to try to carry on as normal, but at least I'll be moving out of the immediate area soon, so we won't be bumping into each other all the time. Mum and Dad are going to help me look for a place, but I'm hoping to get some time off before I start my new job so that I can come up and see you. A break is just what I need right now; it's all so stressful. I still can't take in what has happened. I had no idea Vinny would react like this."

"I'm so sorry. Have you had a chance to speak to Gary yet?"

There was a pause. "Not yet. I'll ring him in a bit. Vinny already suspects I'm seeing someone. If finds out for sure it will only make things worse." There was another pause. "To be honest,

Sarah, at the moment I don't feel like getting involved with anyone else. It seems a bit soon, I'm so exhausted and emotional just now – and anyway, I don't want Gary getting any trouble from Vinny."

"Oh, you poor thing," Sarah said on a wave of sympathy for her friend. "I know what you mean, though. However much you like Gary, you need some time to recover from your ordeal. Tell him how you feel; if he's the right one, he'll wait."

"Yes, I will speak to him. As you say, if it's meant to be then things will work out. Anyway, thanks for listening. I'll catch up with you later. Mum's calling me so I'd better go."

As Jenny entered the living room, the glazier was just leaving having already fixed the patio door. On the dining room table was another huge bouquet of lilies. Mrs Peters bit her lip, and got up from the settee, anxiety written all over her face. Jenny noticed how tired she looked; it was a trying time for them all.

"These have just been delivered for you. I'll make another pot of tea." Tea was her mother's answer to everything!

Looking at the flowers, Jenny felt so nauseous that for a moment she thought she was going to be physically sick. She held her hand to her mouth until the feeling subsided. Why could Vinny not leave her alone? There was a large envelope leaning against the flowers. Feeling the tension in her neck, Jenny tore it open. There was a card inside: a picture of a huge, floppy-eared rabbit looking very sheepish and the word '*SORRY*' written across it. 'Bastard', Jenny whispered under her breath, her nausea turning to anger. She forced herself to open the card and gasped in amazement as a wad of crisp £50 notes dropped onto the carpet. She scooped them up: there were ten of them. Where had he got that kind of money? The note inside the card was brief and did not look much like Vinny's handwriting, which was normally very poor. He must have made a deliberate effort to keep it legible:

Jenny,
I'm so sorry about last night. As you probably gathered I went into town with a few mates to drown my sorrows, but I got drunk too quickly. You know I can't hold my booze! It's no excuse I know,

but my anger got the better of me. I still can't take it all in. The police have been round to caution me and warn me to stay away from you and I will. I'm truly sorry for the pain I caused you and hope you will forgive me. I wasn't in my right mind. The house is going up for sale next week. I'm taking some time off work to sort out my head and don't worry, I'll look after this place so we can get the best price. Hopefully it will sell quickly and then we can both get on with our lives. I hope the enclosed covers the cost of repair to your parents' patio door. Tell them I'm sorry. I'm really ashamed - it isn't like me at all. I suppose I just lost my cool. If you let me know the name of your solicitor I'll keep them posted about the sale of the house.
Sorry.
Take good care.
Vinny.

Jenny's emotions were in turmoil; could she believe what he had written after all that had happened? Or was it simply that he had he been forced into doing this because of police intervention? Vinny must surely know now that there was no way they could ever get back together. Jenny stared at the lilies; for her own sanity she had to believe that what he had written was genuine; that he was really sorry and the nightmare ordeal over. Feeling more positive, she went through to the kitchen where her parents were preparing breakfast.

"Here's some money from Vinny to cover the cost of the repair to the door, Dad. He says he is truly sorry for the inconvenience." Jenny knew Vinny's behaviour had really upset her father; she was their only child and had always been 'Daddy's girl'.

Jenny handed the crisp notes over to Mr Peters who was drinking a cup of coffee and eying his daughter carefully. "It didn't cost anywhere near that luckily. The glazier was a friend of mine."

"Well look on it as compensation. It's my fault you've missed out on your holiday."

Mr Peters ran his large hand through his thinning grey hair then put his arms around his daughter. "We don't need the money, love. You're the one who needs compensation. Never mind about the holiday; I just couldn't rest, yesterday. Had to come back - wouldn't have been able to enjoy it anyway knowing you were here on your own. We should never have gone. What did the card say?"

Jenny smiled brightly; determined to convince her parents that everything was going to be alright. "Vinny's very sorry for all the trouble he's caused. He admitted he got drunk and it's totally out of character for him. The house is going up for sale as soon as possible. I believe he does really regret what he did. Clearly my ending the relationship came as a big shock to him and he couldn't handle it, but he's calmed down now." Jenny passed the card to her Mum who read it carefully.

"You're not going to go back to him are you?"

Jenny snorted, incredulous that her mother could even ask the question. "No, even if he hadn't scared me half to death, I don't love him anymore, Mum. It just took me a while to realise it. There's no way I'm going back. It's been very painful, but it had to be done."

Mr Peters grinned. "That's my girl. You are very brave you know. Many girls would have just accepted the situation and tried to make the best of it, especially with sharing a house and all the effort you put into it."

Her Mum nodded and patted Jenny on the shoulder."Like I always say, our girl takes after you, Brian: brains *and* determination!"

Laughing, Jenny heard her mobile ringing and went through to the living room to answer it leaving her parents to finish their breakfast. It was Gary.

"Are you ok? I tried calling you a few times last night. Your mobile was either busy or switched off. Why didn't you call? I've been worried about you."

Jenny was suddenly pleased to hear his voice. She had really missed him and it seemed ages since they had last seen each other. In reality it was less than 24 hours, but such a lot had happened.

"I'm fine now. Last night was a bit hectic and stressful but everything seems to have been sorted out." Gary would be wondering what had actually been sorted out and if she was regretting what had happened between them. He did not know all the details. Jenny wanted to make things clear. "My partner..." she corrected herself, "ex-partner that is - his name's Vinny - and I are definitely over. He's going to sell our house as soon as possible and I'm staying with my parents meantime."

There was a pause. "There wasn't any trouble then? It's good that he's accepted the situation. You should be able to get a fair price for your house, especially with the market being so good at the moment."

"Fingers crossed. I hope we both do well out of it after all the hard work we put in doing it up." As she spoke, Jenny wandered upstairs to get some privacy. She did not want her parents to know about Gary just yet. They would say she was getting involved with someone far too soon after only just finishing with Vinny, especially after all the trouble they had just been through. She went into her room and closed the door.

"Actually, Gary, he took the split very badly, so badly that the police have had to caution him. I won't go into details, but you and I are going to have to tread carefully for a while. I don't want to aggravate the situation. Also, my Mum and Dad are worried about me. They mean well, but I really don't need a lecture about not getting involved with anyone else so soon. So as much as I want to see you – and I really do - we may have to wait a little while. I hope you understand."

"Of course I do. There's no pressure from my side. Take time to get your head together and I will ring you tomorrow evening when hopefully things have calmed down a bit. We don't need to rush into anything. That's not to say I'm not missing you because I really am, but by the sound of it you've been through a traumatic experience and I can be patient."

He was being so very understanding. Jenny felt a warm glow spreading through her body. There was a strong bond between them; she just knew it. "Thank you for that. Is it possible to take some time off before I start my new job?" Jenny sensed Gary was momentarily taken back and realised she had not mentioned her decision before. Everything had happened so quickly.

"Er... the new job – yes – of course. You've changed your mind about it, obviously. It's probably a good idea in the circumstances. Fortunately, I haven't said anything about the projects to the Assistant Directors yet. They will want you in the new role as soon as possible, but they are expecting a handover period of a few weeks. Why don't you take a few days at the end of next week? We'll talk about it on Monday - that's if you feel up to coming in?"

"Yes, I feel fine now." It was true, Jenny thought, surprised, she did. The nausea had disappeared and she felt much more like her usual self. "To be honest, Gary, the sooner I move the better. The new challenges will keep my mind occupied... and besides, I think perhaps it would be best if we were not working in the same branch, don't you?"

"Maybe, but you're a hard worker Jenny - very driven, which has clearly been noticed by the powers that be. Speaking as your line manager I'll be sad to lose you – and that's an understatement - though it's a pity we couldn't have worked together for longer. Some of your good ideas have made my job a lot easier."

Jenny giggled, "Well, if you hadn't kissed me..."

"I'm sure I recall that you kissed me first!"

Still laughing, Jenny said, "Ah well, you'll just have to work harder for your money now then. Seriously though, we couldn't have a proper relationship if we worked together; every time you did anything for me it would only lead to accusations of favouritism. It's better all round if I leave."

"I suppose you're right, much as I hate to admit it. Anyway, I will ring you tomorrow evening. Take care of yourself. And try not to worry. I understand perfectly that you need some space and like I said, I am happy to wait as long as it takes."

"Talking to you has made me feel tons better. See you soon." Wishing with all her heart that Gary was with her right now and wondering how she could have contemplated cooling the relationship before it had properly begun, Jenny rang off.

CHAPTER TWENTY EIGHT

Still worried about Jenny and alarmed by Vinny's aggressive behaviour, Sarah was all for driving down to London to see for herself that her best friend was ok. Jenny had sounded so fraught on the phone. But Adam dissuaded her, pointing out that it might only make matters worse if Vinny thought everyone was ganging up on him. Jenny had her parents with her and the police had been alerted. It was best to leave them to sort themselves out and not interfere. Sarah supposed Adam was right, but the whole episode had brought back painful memories of her breakup with Andy – that together with the awful nightmare and niggling anxiety that her best friend might be the person Lola had implied needed her help, had made Sarah feel tense and upset. Sensing it, Adam had suggested they go out for the evening – perhaps see a film - and she had jumped at the idea.

While Adam was getting ready, Sarah took the opportunity to water the garden. There had been hardly any rain lately and although the evenings were turning slightly chilly, the days were still warm and the borders bone dry. Sarah loved their garden. It was so colourful now in the back end of summer. She was standing with the watering can admiring the roses behind the bench and enjoying the scents of early evening, when Jane Moore materialised a few feet away from her.

Sarah's heart missed a beat. Jane appeared to be shielding her eyes from the sun with her hand and looking up at the house. In her other hand she held a drink in a tall glass. She was smiling, looked happy and carefree and Sarah stared at her perplexed. It was the closest she had been to the ghost and unlike before, when Jane had seemed so solid and real, this time she was slightly transparent so that Sarah could still see the bench outlined behind her. She could also see how really pretty Jane had been: her skin was flawless, her long hair a silvery ash blonde, and her natural smile lighting up her heart-shaped face. She could have been a model. As in the past, Sarah's fear was drowned by overwhelming sadness that this young woman's life had been summarily cut short by a vicious killer, the dark-haired lover who had robbed her of her right to live that life, denied her the chance of a career, marriage and children.

Gently putting down the watering can, Sarah moved forward slowly holding out her hands, desperate to make some form of contact. Could Jane see her? As Sarah watched, the apparition turned towards her and to her horror she saw a dribble of dark blood oozing out of Jane's mouth and running down her chin. Sarah started forward, called out to her, tripping over the watering can in her haste to reach the young woman whose mouth was now pouring with blood. As Sarah struggled to her feet, a look of sheer terror crossed Jane's face. She began to fade; the bench came once more into sharp focus and she was gone. Sobbing, her knees trembling, Sarah caught hold of the bench and sat down. Had Jane seen her? Why was her mouth bleeding? She had looked one minute so happy and the next so petrified. Was it that she did not want to be forgotten? "I am trying to help you, Jane," she whispered. "If you can hear me, don't worry. I *will* find out who did this to you and then I will tell your story." Sarah sat for a moment, listening, but all she could hear were the birds twittering in the trees as they prepared to roost.

"Sarah, are you ready?" Adam called from the patio. Picking up the watering can, she went back to the house.

"What were you doing in the garden? I could see you standing like a statue by the bench."

Her mind racing, Sarah locked the back door, "I was looking at the roses, and watering my plants. It's been so dry, but they are flowering beautifully just now."

"Thought perhaps you'd taken up yoga or something," Adam grinned.

As they left the house Sarah was nonplussed that once again Adam had seen nothing. She wondered if it was because he was a man; women were often much more intuitive; maybe being a woman, she was more able to sympathise with the ugly things Jane had endured at the end of her life - or was it because Jane was linked to her in some way, but not to Adam. Sarah still had not asked her mother if she knew of any people called Moore in their family. She made a mental note to call her.

Monday morning dawned bright and clear. Jenny, although feeling decidedly sluggish, got out of bed as soon as the alarm went off. There were so many things she needed to sort out at work and booking leave was at the top of her to do list. After showering, dressing and hurriedly swallowing a bowl of muesli, she was out of the house before seven. The roads were clear and there was no sign of Vinny or his van on her short drive to work. She was relieved: it was better if they did not see each other.

Gary's car was already in the car park and it was not even twenty past seven. Jenny smiled to herself. He was very conscientious. She found him making a coffee in the tiny kitchen. With a quick look over her shoulder to ensure the corridor was empty, she dropped her bag on the floor and went over him.

Gary kissed her passionately. "God, I've missed you."

"Me you too, but they say absence makes the heart grow fonder," Jenny said breathlessly when he released her. "Is it ok with you if I book my leave now? I thought I'd spend the day writing notes on where I am with my present workload. It'll make the handover that much easier."

Gary nodded. "Yes, we can have a progress meeting later if you like and I can tell you what I know about your new role. Like I said, the Assistant Directors are keen for you to start as soon as possible. They're offering a generous relocation package too."

"What sort of trouble is the branch in then?" Jenny asked, wondering about the new challenges she would have to face and keen to stay work-focused, which was not easy given the way Gary was looking at her.

He smiled. "It's a bigger branch than here and I've heard there have been one or two personnel issues, but the powers than be are more interested in expanding the customer base and trying to get increased take up of the bank's financial schemes. With your knowledge and experience you have nothing to worry about. You have a very great deal to offer them."

"Thanks," Jenny blushed at the compliment. "I'm glad about the relocation package because I fully intend to move. At least it's forty miles away. I can easily travel home at weekends. I'm going to rent a place for a while until I'm settled. It gives me the opportunity to look elsewhere if I don't like it and-" she broke off as a call came through on her mobile, mouthed 'sorry' to Gary and took the call without checking who it was, thinking it must be her Mum.

It was Vinny and Jenny's smile disappeared. Why was he ringing her so early? "Hi Vinny, how are you?"

"I'm not too good really but that doesn't matter. We need to meet as soon as possible before I talk to my solicitors about the house." He sounded emotional and straight away Jenny was on edge.

Gary pointed to the door and moving towards it, blew her a kiss, but she held out her hand and shook her head. He edged back into the room.

"Can't we just talk over the phone, Vin?" The situation was awkward. She really did not want to see him; not now, not ever.

"Can't you even bear to see me?" Vinny's voice broke. "After all the time we spent together is it really that bad? You may be able to cut all feelings, but I can't. I've tried."

Jenny kept her voice calm and steady. "Look, Vin, I know it's hard for you. I am really upset too, but it's for the best. If we see each other now it will just lead to massive rows and prolong the agony. The most important thing is that we both have space. There needs to be time for the wounds to heal." Jenny bit her lip; knew she had said the wrong thing. She glanced up at Gary, saw he was watching her closely and looking faintly embarrassed.

Vinny's voice sounded in her ear. "What wounds? There are no wounds. I think you're scared in case when we see each other you'll regret your decision to finish the relationship. You're probably regretting it already, but I'm not angry just upset. If we can just talk things through we can sort any problems out. I know we can. We've been through worse things before. What about all the problems we had with the house when we first bought it; we got through that ok didn't we? Eight years together must mean something. Give us a chance, Jen, please."

Her anger surfacing, Jenny's face flushed. Vinny had lied; he clearly had not accepted their relationship was over and had no intention of leaving her alone. She tried to be patient with him, "I'm not scared about seeing you, but there really is no point. We are definitely over and nothing you can say or do will make me change my mind. I really am sorry, but things haven't been right for a while. You deserve someone who really loves you. Please don't make this any more difficult than it already is."

"You really are a witch, aren't you? I can't understand how I never saw it before. Don't worry I'll soon get over you. You've done me a favour, you b-"

Jenny immediately switched off her mobile, feeling the hairs rise on the back of her neck, the ball of tension settling into her stomach. The flowers and card had just been a ruse to lull her into a false sense of security. It was apparent he was determined to hurt her one way or the other. She looked across at Gary with a sense of helplessness, her eyes filling with tears.

He came forward, took her hands in his and caressed her fingers. "I can see that was hard. Are you ok?"

She shrugged, turned her mouth down. "Just when I thought he had come to terms with the situation and moved on, it seems we are back where we started. He's not being very nice I'm afraid..." Jenny's voice tailed off.

"Why don't you tell me what happened between you?"

For a moment Jenny hesitated, and then it all came out: Vinny's behaviour when she had broken the news, how he had followed her home and sent threatening texts, and then the broken window. Finally, she told Gary about the flowers and the note." All the time she was speaking, Gary caressed her hands, his gaze never leaving her face, his look of concern deepening.

When she had finished speaking, he gave her a gentle hug. "I don't want to alarm you, but how far do you think he might go before he actually does come to terms with it? Is a broken window just for starters? I wonder how far he would have gone had the police not arrived when they did."

"I'm rather glad I didn't have to find that out!" Jenny gave a tight smile.

"Me too. Obviously he has a temper. Look, Jenny, tell me to mind my own business, but has he ever lost it and threatened you before?"

"Oh, we've had rows – what couple hasn't, but he's never laid a finger on me. In fact, until the other evening in the kitchen I'd not really seen how aggressive he can be. Usually when we argued he'd just go off and sulk for a while, but he always came round in the end. He used to get into the odd fight with his mates when they'd been drinking – and it doesn't take much to get Vinny drunk – but that was years ago. I hardly knew him then. He has tended to drink very sparingly since we got together – apart from the other night, that is. But we've not even come close to splitting up before. I suppose he's never had a situation like this to deal with."

"Has he got any family to support him or close friends?"

"Both: he has three best mates he's known for fifteen years or more – since school – and his family are very close; he used to see a lot of his brothers. I'm wondering if he's actually told any of them. I should have smelled a rat when I started getting those bouquets; he's hardly ever bought me flowers before. He probably thought it would bring me round, as if we'd just had a little argument or something." Jenny paused, gave a shy smile, "Not wanting to wish away the time that we have left to work together, but I have to say I can't wait to get away from this place now."

Gary nodded. "I think you should go as soon as it can be arranged, and I will instruct the staff to keep your whereabouts confidential no matter who asks. In fact, why don't you go home now and take the rest of the week off. Go and see your friend – Sarah is it? The one who lives in... Nottingham did I hear you say?"

"Yes, but no," Jenny frowned. It was tempting, but she did not like to leave unfinished business. Nor did she like the feeling that she was being hounded out of town - and for what? All she had done was to finish a dead relationship. Just how dead it had become she was only now coming to realise. "Thanks, Gary, that's a great offer, but I want to sort out my workload for my replacement. I'll take Friday off and some days next week and thank you for being so very understanding. I will need to give Sarah some notice anyway, and I'd prefer to be at work, it keeps me sane."

"Sweet girl; committed as always no matter what. Well it's your decision, of course, and I know you're a really strong person, but I think you need to be careful. Vinny sounds a little unstable to me. He could be dangerous if he gets drunk again. At the very least contact the police once more, let them know what's happening. They can go round and give him another warning. If necessary you can take out an injunction against him. Do you have a solicitor? I can put you in touch with one if it helps. It would give you some protection: he is less likely to harass you if he knows it could land him in prison."

Jenny swallowed. How had it come to this? "That sounds pretty drastic," she said. "But if it gets him off my back perhaps I should. It's like living in a constant nightmare at the moment."

"Talk to the police; ask them about it. Will you do that for me?" Gary put his head on one side, listening. "I think I can hear people arriving. We'd best make a move." He took her hand and kissed the palm, closing her fingers over his kiss as he had done the first time. It made Jenny tingle all over, and for a moment she wanted to fling herself into his arms and beg him to stay.

As if sensing her hesitation, Gary whispered, "Hang on in there, my darling, it will all be over soon. You will go away and he will get fed up."

She gazed at his departing back, her fingers still holding onto his kiss, his words 'my darling' still sounding in her ears.

Jenny spent most of the morning on the phone, updating her clients about her proposed move and informing them of what was happening and who would be taking over from her. She kept herself busy writing handover notes and updating documentation. At lunch time she broke off to check her mobile. There were five text messages from Vinny and one from Sarah. She read Sarah's first and gave her a call.

"Hi, Jenny, how are you?" Sarah's voice sounded bright and cheerful, making Jenny feel a little happier.

"Not too bad. Would you believe, Vinny is still not accepting we are over; he's already called me and now he's bombarding me with texts. I daren't read them; he seems to be getting more and more abusive. Anyway, I have to be quick. Would it be ok to come up on Friday and stay for a long weekend? I need to get away from here."

"Oh, Jen, how awful for you - come as soon as you can and stay as long as you like. I'm really looking forward to seeing you. I've already warned my boss I'll be off for a few days next week and it's not a problem. Why not come after work on Thursday? The roads will be quieter - and I'll cook us a meal for when you get here. Don't worry; there will be plenty of white wine in the fridge; you sound as if you need it! I'll get Adam to go out with his mates and we can have a natter. It will be like old times."

Jenny was relieved. "That sounds great – I'll do that. See you on Thursday then; can't wait."

"I'll fax you directions. It's a bit remote, but I can meet you wherever you want and lead you in."

"No need, I'll be fine; I'll call you if I get lost. See you soon."

Ringing off, Jenny looked down at her mobile and steeled herself to read Vinny's texts. They were as bad as she had feared. The first four were accusing her of two-timing him, along with a barrage of abuse about herself and her family. The final one made her blood run cold: I'LL MAKE U PAY 4 RUINING MY LIFE.

Jenny now knew that Gary was right and as much as she disliked the idea, she had to contact the police again. This was not Vinny any more; this was some stranger. A vindictive madman who intended her harm - and she honestly could not say how far he might take things. Any lingering sympathy she had harboured for her ex-partner had completely gone. The man was mentally abusing her and she was seriously worried, not just for her own safety, but also for that of her friends and family.

CHAPTER TWENTY NINE

At lunch time Jenny went to the local police station. Gary, having looked at the texts on her mobile, insisted on going with her. It was quiet inside reception. Most people were also on their lunch break, Jenny supposed. A woman with two young children and a baby in a buggy occupied the only seats. She looked weary and anxious, her gaze fixed on the large notice board on the opposite wall that was covered in 'What to do in case of...' posters. The officer on duty at the desk looked up as Jenny, Gary's hand protectively at her waist, came through the door. He was a friendly looking guy, quite young, with dark, thick lashes, a full mouth, and dimples in both cheeks when he smiled. His nose and cheeks were peppered with freckles. His sympathetic manner as he listened to her story made Jenny feel at ease right away. He took time to look through Vinny's texts before saying with a reassuring smile, "Please excuse me for a moment while I show these to my Sergeant." He carried the mobile through to an adjoining office. Moments later he reappeared with a policewoman, who looked to be in her forties and had an air of quiet authority, but gave a friendly smile as she came forward holding out her hand. "Hello, I'm Sergeant James. Would you come this way please, Miss Peters," and leaving Gary in reception, she led the way into her office, closed the door and invited Jenny to sit opposite the desk. Feeling awkward, Jenny perched on the edge of the chair, her gaze drawn to a picture of the Queen resplendent in all her regalia.

Sergeant James settled herself behind the desk, "I'm sorry to make you go over it all again, Miss Peters, but would you mind telling me exactly what's been going on between you and your partner?"

"My ex-partner," Jenny corrected.

"Yes, of course, sorry," the policewoman smiled, listening carefully as Jenny once again described Vinny's threatening behaviour since she had tried to end their relationship. When she got to the incident at her parents' house and could not stop her tears, Sergeant James pulled out a box of tissues from her desk drawer and with a sympathetic smile placed it at Jenny's elbow.

When Jenny had finished, ending with the call and texts she had received this morning, the policewoman nodded. "Thank you, I know this is hard for you, Miss Peters, but you have done the right thing in coming to talk to us. My advice would be for you to take out an injunction against your ex-partner."

"What does that mean exactly?" Jenny asked nervously.

"It means that if you are granted a court order against molestation – and I have no doubt that you would be, and quite quickly, given the evidence of threatening and potentially violent behaviour – then if your ex-partner breaks the order and continues to harass you, we can arrest him even if he does not actually physically harm you. You can either apply through a solicitor, or direct to the civil court yourself."

"I'm not sure," Jenny said, "it seems so drastic."

"Well it is your decision, of course. In the meantime you can make a formal complaint against him." She handed Jenny back her mobile, reached into a filing cabinet behind her chair and drew out a sheaf of paperwork, "Sorry, but it seems everything these days has to be done in triplicate!" Asking for details of Jenny's full name and date of birth, her former and current address, and similar details about Vinny, Sergeant James proceeded to fill out the relevant forms. When she'd finished, she showed Jenny where to sign. Feeling uncomfortable and shocked that it had come to this, Jenny was led back into reception and was relieved to see Gary still standing there. Grateful for his reassuring presence, she gave him a watery smile as they took their leave of Sergeant James. As they left, the tired looking woman was trying with limited success to control her bored infants under the benevolent gaze of the duty officer.

Within forty-five minutes, Jenny was back at her desk and immersed in a pile of account queries. It was gone six before the tasks were finished and she was able to leave the bank to go home.

Gary was not yet back from a meeting and most of her colleagues had already left.

Getting into her car, Jenny had the feeling that something was different about it, but could not put her finger on what. She glanced at the back seat, but could see nothing unusual, it looked clean and tidy, no rubbish left lying around, which was her pet hate. She was about to put the key the ignition when she realised what was disturbing her: the passenger seat had been moved forward. Jenny's heart started pounding. No one besides herself had been in the car for the past week. On impulse she checked the glove box and saw a piece of writing paper folded on top of the DVD's. It had not been there this morning, she was sure of it. Jenny felt the blood drain in a rapid whoosh from her head down to her ankles. Gingerly pulling out the paper, she carefully unfolded it.

WE WILL ALWAYS BE TOGETHER

The words were typed in bold, large letters in the centre of the page. There was nothing more. Jenny gasped: it had to be Vinny. How dared he! What did he mean by *we will always be together*? There was no guarantee she would have found the note for ages. What had been the point of leaving it there? As she puzzled over it, the significance of Vinny's words came home to her with sickening dread: the only way they would be together always was if they were both dead.

Retrieving her mobile, she bolted out of the car and punched in the number the policewoman had given her. A man answered and promised to send someone over as quickly as he could. Jenny stood back from the car and looked it all over, her mind running wild wondering what else Vinny might have done, his words: *I'll make you pay*, sounding a warning in her head. Her hand shaking, she keyed in her parents' number and was relieved to hear her Dad's voice. Quickly, she explained what had happened.

"Don't worry, love. I'm on my way. Whatever you do, don't try to start the car." Jenny could hear the panic in his voice;

knew he would break the speed limit to get to her. Sure enough, less than fifteen minutes later Mr Peters was hugging his daughter tightly. Jenny could see he was frightened; his face was quite white and there were tears in his eyes. "I can't believe what that stupid man is doing to you. He's lost his grip on reality and needs to be locked up."

Jenny's anger had passed now and she felt completely numb. Again she wondered how this could be happening to her. Vinny was making life a living hell for all of them. "I'm sorry, Dad," she sobbed, "it's all my fault."

Mr Peters pulled gently away from his daughter and resting his hands on her shoulders looked into her eyes, "No, Jenny, it is *not* your fault. It takes a lot of courage to do what you did, but you made the right decision. You didn't love Vinny and it would have been wrong to stay with him in the circumstances. Your Mum and I always knew this day would come, knew you and Vinny weren't right for each other, but we never said anything; you needed to find it out for yourself in your own good time. He isn't on your wavelength, never has been and never will be, but he's even more stupid than I thought if he thinks that scaring you like this is the way forward. He's a fool and like I said, he should be locked up – and if I have my way, he will be. We'll sort this out, love, don't worry. No man is going to hurt you while I'm around, and that's a promise."

Jenny, feeling like a comforted child, sniffed and reached in her bag for a tissue. Her father forestalled her, handing her a neatly folded, white handkerchief from his top pocket. She had never seen him so angry; he was normally such a passive, easy-going person. "Thanks, Dad. I've called the police. They said they would send someone shortly to look over the car. I don't understand how Vinny got in; my only spare set of keys is in my handbag. The alarm was on too."

Mr Peters shook his head, "I'm afraid breaking into a car is not difficult when you know how and he could easily have cut the wires to the alarm. You know Vinny – always did know his way around a car. Besides, no one seems to bat an eyelid when an alarm goes off these days."

"I thought I knew Vinny," Jenny murmured sadly. "I realise I don't know him any more, Dad."

"I know, love, I know."

They sat down on an adjacent bench to wait and with a wave of gratitude Jenny snuggled up to her father as he put his arm around her. He smelled of aftershave and pipe tobacco; a comforting smell from her childhood. Her parents had always been so supportive. What would she have done without them?

They did not have to wait long. A police car drew into the car park and a young constable, who looked to be in his early twenties, broad shouldered and at least six foot tall, got out of it. He was accompanied by an equally large man in overalls.

"I must be getting old," Mr Peters muttered in Jenny's ear as both men approached the bench. "They say it's a sign of old age when policemen look like overgrown schoolboys."

Jenny stifled a giggle and wondered if she was becoming hysterical.

"Miss Peters?"

"Yes, hello; thanks for getting here so quickly," Jenny stood up. "This is my Dad. I didn't want to drive the car in case my ex-boyfriend has tampered with it in some way. He's a little unstable at the moment..." her voice tailed away.

"I understand, Miss Peters. Sergeant James briefed me. You were right to call us." I'm Sergeant Hardy," He gestured to his companion, "and this is PC Baxter, a specialist police mechanic. He's going to give the car the once over, check it's safe to drive."

"Thank you," Jenny said gratefully, handing over her keys. Surely Vinny would not have stooped so low. Now she had calmed down, she could not really believe he actually meant to harm her physically; he was just trying to scare her. He knew how fussy she was about her car and that she would notice the seat had been moved. It would be only natural to then check the glove box. Her nerves were getting the better of her - Vinny had succeeded; she had been scared out of her wits.

PC Baxter took his time, first getting down on his hands and knees and then rolling onto his back underneath the car. After a couple of minutes he emerged, dusted himself off, winked at Jenny and opened up the bonnet to inspect the engine. He then got into the driver's seat, looked in the fuse box and checked the wiring. Finally, he got into the back seat and meticulously examined the interior of the car. After some ten minutes he had finished his inspection. He nodded at his colleague, said, "Clean as a whistle."

"Ok, Miss Peters," Sergeant Hardy smiled, "it is safe to drive, but would you mind coming back to the station and filling out a report?"

"Yes of course and thank you for helping me out. I'm sorry to have wasted your time." Relieved, Jenny smiled at her father, who was standing beside her, his hand on her shoulder. "Do you want to go on, Dad? I'll be ok now."

"No, love, I'll follow you and we can go home together." Jenny did not try to dissuade him; knew he was concerned that Vinny might be watching from some hidden vantage point. She had wondered that too; it was a creepy feeling.

After completing the necessary paperwork at the police station, Jenny drove home, closely followed by her Dad. Her Mum's car was parked in the driveway by the caravan. Jenny pulled up behind it and switched off the engine. She was indescribably weary and supposed it was reaction setting in. No sooner had she got out of the car than her Mum appeared at the front door. She looked distressed, her cheeks stained with tears.

"Thank God! You're safe. Your Dad phoned to tell me what had happened. I've been worried sick. I can't believe what that awful man is doing." She looked up as her husband squeezed his car in beside Jenny's, her relief at seeing him plain to see. "Let's go in. I'll make a pot of tea."

Tired and distressed as she was, that predictable comment made Jenny smile as she followed her Mum into the house.

A few minutes later they were all sat in the kitchen sipping cups of refreshing Earl Grey when Mr Peters suddenly slammed his hand onto his knee. "This has gone on long enough, I won't put up with it. It's got to stop and if that bastard thinks-"

"Not now, Brian, dear," Mrs Peters gently reprimanded, "we'll talk about it later. Let Jenny drink her tea, you can see she's falling asleep on her feet. Give her time to get over what's she's just been through. At least she's safe and in one piece. We can be thankful for that. You go up and have a nap, Jenny, love. I'll wake you when supper's ready."

Gratefully, Jenny did as she was told. A couple of hours later, feeling somewhat refreshed, she rang Sarah to tell her what had happened, had just finished speaking to her when Gary called her mobile. Once again, Jenny related the events of the afternoon.

"This is getting beyond a joke," Gary said, angrily. "I hate to tell you this, but it appears that several of your colleagues have seen your ex-partner hanging around the bank. He must have broken into your car only minutes before you went down to the car park when he knew most people would have left."

"Oh, Gary, I don't know what to do." Jenny knew her voice was rising by several notches. "I believe he is only trying to frighten me and doesn't intend to actually harm me, but it's really getting to me now. I'm so tired and yet I can't properly relax. I don't think I can go on like this."

"Hang on in there, my love, things will get better. You're going away soon and after that you'll be moving. Your ex will soon stop all this once he knows you've left and are out of his reach, especially with the threat of prison hanging over him. Incidentally, I've told everyone in the office to keep quiet about where you will be based. I tried to protect your privacy and do it without broadcasting what's been going on, but Kirsty seemed to know. It was she who first noticed Vinny loitering outside evidently."

"Yes, I had to tell Kirsty. She knew Vinny from the old days; used to go out with one of his mates. She was always asking after him and I hate to tell lies, so I mentioned we had split and that he was taking it badly. It's awful, Gary. I feel like a prisoner; unable to go anywhere without constantly looking over my shoulder. I've even asked Mum if she'll drop me off and pick me up from work until Thursday."

"Good idea and what a boon to have such supportive parents," Gary said.

"I thank my lucky stars daily," Jenny managed a laugh, "especially for my very supportive boss!"

After they had said their goodbyes, Jenny sat for a while gazing unseeing at her mobile. Gary was indeed supportive – and not just because of how they felt about each other. She knew he would have been equally concerned about any member of his staff in a similar situation. He was such a dear man. She prayed Vinny had not somehow found out about their burgeoning relationship. In his present state of mind there was no doubt he would vent all his anger and frustration on her boss. She would have to make doubly sure they were not seen together outside work. Jenny sighed; she knew she was going to miss Gary dreadfully, but even so, she longed for Thursday to come.

CHAPTER THIRTY

Sarah put the phone down, appalled by what Jenny had told her. Even though Vinny had apparently done no damage to the car, there was something decidedly sinister about the way he had deliberately set out to frighten her best friend – and what if it was a precursor to physical violence, which, given his evident instability it could so easily be? Jenny had told her about the possibility of applying for a court order, but had also voiced her doubts that it would be effective. She seemed to feel that Vinny had gone past caring and in that state of mind he could quite easily be dangerous. Sarah had done her best to reassure her friend, but was frightened for her and very glad she was coming to stay in a few days' time. Even if Vinny discovered she had gone away and guessed where to, he had no clue where they now lived. If he was determined to come after Jenny and make her life a misery he would eventually find out, of course, but they would have to cross that bridge when they came to it. At least Jenny would not be alone and they could have some fun days out together, which would give them both a much needed lift.

Since the incident in the garden last weekend, Sarah had not had another vision. Ever since her reading with the medium, she had automatically connected Lola's warning to Jane Moore – or possibly to Charlotte. Similarly, she had thought the visions were the 'signs' Lola had mentioned. Now, the more she thought about it, the less likely it seemed. Neither of those young women was close to her. Her mother had confirmed that they had nobody named 'Moore' in their family so far as she knew – Sarah had fielded her curiosity by saying she was getting quite interested in genealogy in her spare time, which was not exactly a lie, but she had then been forced to dampen her mother's enthusiastic offer of help! As the time slipped by and her visit to the medium seemed increasingly remote, Sarah had begun to feel that it had been just so much mumbo jumbo after all and the only reason she had found

Lola so convincing at the time was because her nerves had been shredded by the horrendous supernatural experiences at home. But there was still a lingering anxiety in her mind that if the medium's prediction *had* been genuine, then someone somewhere needed her help. It had been only natural to think then of Jenny. But Vinny had never appeared in Sarah's nightmares and nothing seemed to fit. It was all so confusing. Did that necessarily mean Jenny was not the one who needed her help? Maybe the nightmares were not connected at all. She and Jenny were certainly close and it would seem that her friend was in danger. It was a very worrying thought. Sarah determined that she would do everything in her power to protect Jenny and would even go so far as to ask Simon's advice, though after that dreadful incident in Derby with Adam, she had decided not to make contact with him again. But what harm could a phone call do? They were just old friends, after all.

Jenny's Mum drove her to work next morning. They were nearing the bank when they saw Vinny walking along the main road. Jenny's heart sank - please no, not again. She wriggled down in the seat hoping he would not spot her.

"Just ignore him, Jen," her mother said. "He can't do anything in broad daylight."

"He looks terrible though, doesn't he Mum?" His clothes were dirty and dishevelled; his hair greasy and unwashed and Jenny noticed as they passed him that he was unshaven. He was shambling along like some down-and-out wino and fleetingly she recalled the man she had seen sitting on the bench in the car park. Had that been Vinny too? She was filled with pity.

Mrs Peters frowned and increased her speed. "Well, he's got nobody but himself to blame. I can't understand what's wrong with him. He's got no pride. Why doesn't he accept the situation and why aren't his family helping him? If he carries on like this he'll end up losing his job - that is if he's not lost it already. It's not your fault love. You've done right thing. Feeling sorry for him is no reason to go back to him. Forget him; he's no longer your concern."

"I know, but I can't help it. We were together a long time. I can't just stop feeling concerned about him, even though I no longer love him. But there's nothing I can do. If I agree to see him, which is what he wants, it will only make matters worse, make him think I've changed my mind. I'm not going back to him, Mum, no matter how sorry I feel for him; not in a million years. It makes me wonder, though, what state our house is in with Vinny looking like he does. I can't help thinking he might have trashed it. This whole business is really getting to me, Mum."

"I know it is, love, and I'm not surprised. Are you sure you want to go in to work today? From what you say, your boss will understand if you want to stay home. He seems extremely supportive, taking you to the police station and everything. It's very good of him; I hope you thanked him properly."

"He'd have done the same for anyone," Jenny said quickly, feeling a tiny bit guilty at deceiving her mother, but not yet prepared to come clean about her involvement with Gary. "And of course I thanked him. I'll be fine, Mum, there's good security at the bank and the police are keeping an eye on Vinny anyway."

They pulled up outside the bank's car park and Mrs Peters patted her daughter's hand reassuringly. "Don't worry about the house, dear. You're Dad and I will go round and make sure it's alright. I've still got a spare key you know."

"Mum, no!" Jenny cried out. "Please don't do that. It's very good of you to suggest it, but we don't know what Vinny is capable of doing – the change in him is shocking. He's not in his right mind, I'm sure of it. What if he turns violent and hurts you to get at me? I'd never forgive myself. Please, Mum, promise me you won't. The house doesn't matter to me; I don't care about it any more. The solicitors will sort all that out anyway. Just keep out of his way."

Mrs Peters nodded, "Ok, love, if that's what you want, I promise." She smiled, "I hope you have a good day with your nice boss. Give us a call when it's time to come and pick you up."

Jenny kissed her mother on the cheek, "I will, Mum – and thank you."

Hurrying into the bank before Vinny came round the corner and saw her, Jenny was soon in her office and trying to organise her files. There still seemed so much to do. The new Senior Financial Adviser would not be in place for some weeks, and Jenny needed to leave copious notes for her colleagues to tide them over. She was working on the last file when the phone calls started. Every time she answered her extension there was a silence; then heavy breathing.

After the fourth call her temper flared. "Look, Vinny, I know it's you. Stop being so pathetic and stop calling this number. We are finished. You're not going to achieve anything by harassing me like this. Leave me alone or I'll call the police."

A few moments later, the phone rang again. Jenny switched it off; she was fairly certain it was Vinny. If it was a customer call, it could not be helped. Weary and tense, she could not wait for the day to end and wished she had stayed at home after all. Gary was not in evidence today and his car was not in the car park; she assumed he was at Head Office. She wished he would call her mobile, but did not like to call his in case he was tied up in a meeting.

Five-thirty came at last and Jenny phoned her Mum. She was just tidying away her desk when Karen, a senior bank clerk who had worked for Jenny for a couple of years, came into her office. She looked anxious. Jenny sighed; what now?

"I just thought I'd better let you know that Vinny has been spotted loitering in the car park – about ten minutes ago."

"Oh lord, not again! Thanks Karen. Luckily Mum's picking me up tonight - thank God." Jenny covered her eyes with her hands, "It's getting so stupid. He's been ringing me all afternoon. It seems even the police being involved has not put him off. I don't want him to go to prison, Karen, but I don't think I can take much more of this. I'm sorry for blubbing all over you."

"Don't be silly," Karen said, coming up behind her and massaging Jenny's shoulders. "I'd be blubbing too if it was me. Goodness, you're all knotted up. Mind you, I'm not surprised. I would never have expected it of Vinny, but men can be such bastards when they don't get their own way. Life is so unfair. But look on the bright side, Jen, only one more day and you are away from here. He can loiter in the car park as much as he wants; you won't have to face him any more and if I see him I'll give him a piece of my mind I can tell you!"

Jenny was forced to smile through her tears; everyone was being so kind and supportive. "I know, thanks Karen. If you ever get tired of banking, you'd make a wonderful masseuse!"

Feeling apprehensive, Jenny walked out into the car park accompanied by two of her colleagues. There were quite a few people around; the sun was shining, both her parents were waiting in the first parking bay. Smiling with relief, she walked towards the car.

Just as she reached it, she heard someone harshly shouting her name. Mr Peters opened the car door for her just as Vinny emerged from behind a parked van. He seemed to be swaying as he tried to walk towards them.

Jenny heard her Dad swear. "Just get in, love, don't look at him. We didn't notice him in the car park. He's drunk; bloody fool!"

They drove off at speed. Jenny compelled to look back, saw Vinny staggering after the car. He tripped and fell, sprawling like a heap of rags in the road. She felt beads of sweat forming on her forehead, anger and compassion warring in her head. They travelled the remainder of the journey in shocked silence.

Getting wearily out of the car, Jenny watched anxiously as her Dad made sure he had locked the gates to the driveway securely, and then shot the bolts on the front door. They all trooped into the kitchen. Mrs Peters immediately seized the tea caddy and switched on the kettle before pulling a meat pie out of the oven. She dished it out, and passed a plateful to her daughter. The smell of the hot, steaming gravy turned Jenny's stomach; normally she enjoyed her mother's pies, but she simply could not face it. She pushed the plate away, "Sorry, Mum. It looks lovely, but I just can't I'm afraid, not right now."

"You've got to eat, love, just try a little bit," Mrs Peters coaxed. "It's your favourite steak and kidney; I made it specially."

"I know, Mum, I will in a while, thanks. I'll just get changed first; have a shower."

"Ok, dear, you go and do that. I'll keep it warm for you. Take a cup of tea up with you; it'll make you feel better."

As soon as she was in the shower, Jenny let her emotions spill over. The past week had been the worst time of her life. She had wanted to remain on friendly terms with Vinny; they had been friends for so long she could never have imagined things could possibly turn so sour between them. Now he had succeeded in making her feel guilty; he was obviously having a breakdown and she felt responsible. He had become a completely different person: a pathetic and vindictive drunk, possibly even dangerous. Not her friend Vinny at all. What if they'd had children? Would it have made a difference? But it did not bear thinking about; she would have been tied to him forever or risk what he might have done if she had tried to take them away. She would never have been able to trust him not to harm them to get at her. On reflection, she'd had a lucky escape.

The next day was Thursday – her last day at the bank. Vinny had obviously cottoned on that her parents were giving her lifts to and from work and since he recognised both their cars, Mr Peters had hired another for Jenny's use while she was in Nottingham, in the hope that Vinny would not follow her. Driving it into work that morning, her Dad following along behind at a discreet distance, but Jenny saw no sign of Vinny.

During the morning, Jenny received another string of abusive text messages and voice mails from Vinny, which she duly reported to Sergeant James. They would caution him again, the policewoman told her. Had she thought any more about taking out a court order? She might also like to think about going to Women's Aid, who may be able to accommodate her in a safe house, at least until the threat from Vinny had been removed. She gave Jenny a contact number, but could not give her an address, which, for obvious reasons was highly confidential. Jenny thanked her, but explained it would not be necessary as she was going away for a few days and when she came home she would be moving out of the immediate area.

She worked through her lunch break and by mid-afternoon, was reasonably satisfied that she had done all she could to make life easier for her colleagues after she had left. She was just thinking about calling it a day and sloping off quietly, when several of her colleagues filed into her office carrying a large mixed bouquet and a bottle of champagne. They had also all clubbed together to get her some vouchers to spend on clothes. It was a surprisingly large amount and Jenny knew Gary must have put a lot of money into the collection. He was standing at the back of the room, but came forward with a huge card that all the staff in the bank had signed, and then gave a speech, thanking her for all her efforts in the past and wishing her well in her new job. Fortunately, he kept it short and Jenny, tearful, knew her face was as red as a beetroot and hoped everyone would think it was from pleasure – which it was in a way.

Gary escorted her to her car, keeping his distance, and managing to look terribly formal by shaking her hand – just like a boss who was merely saying goodbye to a valued member of staff. He opened the car door for her, stood back, assumed a bored expression and said in an undertone, "I am giving you a mental hug and several kisses, and I'll call you around nine. Take care."

There was no sign of Vinny and Jenny, still smiling, got back to her parents in time to devour a ham salad sandwich before setting off for Nottingham. Her parents came out to the car, her Dad carrying her borrowed suitcase and her Mum clutching the bouquet – not the lilies - they had been thrown on the compost heap days ago – but the one her colleagues had presented to her.

"These are so lovely, Jen. Why don't you take them for Sarah? Dad and I will probably go off for a few days while you're away and they'll only be wasted if you give them to me. We were thinking perhaps we might go up to the Peaks, you know we love it there and we won't be that far away if you need us in Nottingham.

We thought we'd drive over to your new branch first and see if we can find you a nice place to rent. Much as we like having you here with us, love, we both think it would be best if you move away as soon as possible."

Wordlessly, Jenny hugged her Mum, and then her Dad. "Just make sure you call us as soon as you get there," he said gruffly, "and give Sarah our love."

Jenny was surprised how hard her Dad hugged her. It was as though she was never coming back. At least, she thought, they could relax knowing she was safe with Sarah and Adam.

Mrs Peters planted a kiss on her daughter's cheek. "Forget about everything that's happened and just concentrate on having a good time. You deserve it."

"I will, thanks for everything. Bye Mum; Dad; I love you both so very much."

The traffic was busy and Jenny was glad she had already warned Sarah that she might arrive a bit later than expected. She hoped to be in Nottingham before eight if at all possible. She felt very positive and happy to be going away, and so glad that Gary had found a way to speak to her before she had left. She looked forward to his call. Maybe they would be able to meet up in Nottingham over the weekend. Sarah was keen to meet him. At least they would be able to spend some time together without fear of gossip – and even worse, that Vinny was lurking around the next corner. Jenny relaxed. Her mobile started to ring, but she ignored it. Gary had said he would call at nine, she had already spoken to Sarah and her parents would not call her when she was on the road. Anyone else could go hang; especially Vinny!

Turning onto the M1, Jenny saw a white van about half a mile in front of her and she swallowed hard. It looked so much like Vinny's - it even appeared to have the same coloured sign on the side. Jenny slowed down and let another car come in between her and the van. She was not sure what to do. Her brain was telling her it could not possibly be Vinny. How would he know where she was? Before the panic had properly set in, the van turned into a service station. Jenny breathed out slowly, her hands shaking. To take her mind off Vinny, she switched on the radio and the rest of the journey went quite quickly. Ninety minutes later, when she came off the motorway, her positive feeling had returned.

CHAPTER THIRTY ONE

Sarah's directions were quite straightforward and the road to Bluebell Close only a few miles from the motorway. As Jenny came off at the appropriate junction the scenery became far more picturesque; trees and farms, very green. The mobile rang; she pulled off into a lay-by. It was Sarah.

"Hi, how are you and more importantly where are you?" Her friend sounded very excited.

"I've just come off at Junction 27 and turned left at what must be the big island you mentioned. I'm on a dual carriageway now, probably only about a mile from your road?"

"Yes, well done. You will come to another smaller island shortly, turn left and then a sharp right past Dobb Park, it's clearly signposted. Our road – well, it's more of a lane really - is a right-hand turn at the bottom of the hill. There's a big oak tree on the corner."

"Great, see you shortly. By the way it's very beautiful round here. It really feels as if I'm out in the country."

Sarah chuckled, "Well there's a farm right behind us and you will experience the country air at first hand; they are doing plenty of muck-spreading at the moment!"

Thanks to Sarah's clear directions, Jenny found Bluebell Close quite easily, pleased to see that it was only 7:15; she had made excellent time after all. The houses still looked new and each one was well presented. She quickly spotted Sarah's little red sports car parked in the driveway and pulled up behind it as instructed. Jenny had been somewhat envious when Sarah had bought it after her last promotion, but as she had pointed out, it was a bargain and she had wanted a sporty model while she was still young enough to get away with it! Looking up at her friend's house, Jenny found it hard to believe what had been happening here; it looked so ordinary. The garden was full of colour and the hanging baskets still in bloom making the overall effect very pretty; the atmosphere one of tranquil prosperity.

"Hi!" Sarah opened the front door. Her hair was scraped up in a pony tail and she was wearing a pink crop top and a pair of light blue hipster jeans, which revealed an enviably flat stomach.

Jenny's first thought was that if she was not such a close friend she would have been quite jealous. Sarah was one of those women who could wear a potato sack and look good. As it was, Jenny was delighted see her friend looking so well, if a little tired about the eyes. "Hi! You're a sight for sore eyes - you look great!"

"Thanks, so do you and your hair is lighter – have you had highlights?" Sarah said, coming forward to hug her.

"No, I expect it's bleached in the sun." Jenny knew she must look skinny; she had lost quite a bit of weight in the last few weeks and her clothes were loose; almost baggy. She was thankful Sarah did not remark on it, but in fact they were both much trimmer than they used to be and it was hardly surprising given all the stress they had lately endured. This was yet another thing they had in common and Jenny felt a wave of warmth as Sarah kissed her.

"Give me your case, are you hungry? I've made some tea; follow me."

Jenny laughed, "You sound like Mum!" Her appetite had returned and there was a delicious smell of garlic wafting through the air. "I'm starving and if that's supper it smells gorgeous. Don't let me forget, there's a bouquet of flowers for you in the car. I should confess I didn't actually buy them – but I'd like you to have them anyway. And also, this," she brought the bottle of champagne out from behind her back.

"Wow! Now that's more like it," Sarah, laughing, dropped Jenny's case at the foot of the stairs. "I've tried out a new Valentina Harris recipe – Adam gave me her latest book for Christmas, he loves Italian! I've done us roasted chicken breasts in a special sauce, plenty of herbs, spices and garlic - it's a good job we're not going out tonight. We'd be knocking people out in one breath."

Jenny followed her friend through to the living room, which was open plan, very spacious and modern. "What a lovely room, it's huge. The suite looks so comfy and the colours in the rug really stand out. That's one of those new plasma fires isn't it – very trendy. So who's the interior designer here? Everything is so perfect."

"I must tell Adam," Sarah looked pleased, a grin spreading across her face. "He seems to have a flair for it; we both like the simple, modern look, minimalist, but not too much so. He's gone out for the evening – I've got him well trained!"

"I don't like to think of Adam having to slope off to sit in some lonely bar on my account," Jenny said, only half joking.

Sarah hooted with laughter, "Don't waste your sympathy, he's gone out with Toby, a mate from work. Adam's been looking for a chance to get to know him socially. I haven't met him yet, he only joined the company recently, but he sounds really nice. Anyway, take a seat and kick off your shoes. I'll put the champagne on ice and get you a glass of wine – or would you prefer a cup of tea?"

"You're joking!"

Sarah grinned. "Is white ok or would you prefer red?"

"White will be great." Already feeling at home Jenny sank into the cream sofa and did as she was bid with a contented sigh. For the first time in ages she felt able to relax and forget about Vinny. She looked all round the room while Sarah went through to the kitchen. "I look forward to having the grand tour," Jenny called after her. "I know exactly what you mean about the house, though." She found it hard to believe it was haunted here; it was all too new and modern. Jenny loved it; knew she could easily live in this house, which surprised her. In the past she had always preferred an old house with lots of character, beams and what have you.

Sarah came back carrying a misted bottle of chilled white wine and two crystal glasses, setting them down on the stylish coffee table, its glass top so clean it looked as though the wine was suspended in mid-air. "What do you mean, you know what I mean?" she handed Jenny a full glass. "It's a dry one, hope that's ok."

"Lovely, thanks. I mean haunting is usually associated with dark old places with a history. Your house is so light and airy, so modern, it's impossible to believe there are ghosts here. Don't misunderstand me, Sarah,' she said quickly, noticing her friend's sudden anxious frown. "Of course I believe you; it just seems so unlikely that's all. Anyway; I hope they'll be kind and leave us alone for a day or two, I'm afraid my nerves are not up to much right now."

"Poor you," Sarah turned her mouth down sympathetically, after a moment she said, "No disrespect, Jen, but do you think Vinny was always a bit unstable? I mean, he never appeared to be, but this unpredictable behaviour seems so sudden. To me he always came across as a very confident sort of chap with a good sense of humour. He seemed to get on with everyone, but I know people can put on a front socially. I guess I never knew the real Vinny."

"You and me both," Jenny said wryly. "I've been thinking about that a lot lately," she took a gulp of wine. "Looking back, I'm remembering things that I didn't take much notice of at the time, you know, the odd flash of temper; childish frustration. Yes, he did seem to be the life and soul of the parties we went to, but I believe it must all have been an act. I think he tried to seem confident to hide his insecurities – he was like a small boy who never really grew up. For example, I bent over backwards to get him to apply for promotion to a managerial position – he's well capable - but he always made some excuse. Vinny never really had to deal with stress of any kind, you see, and he shied away from responsibility. Said he just didn't need the pressure and if we had to have more money he'd simply do more overtime. He liked to work at his own pace, you know? I knew his parents had helped him out financially on a number of occasions before we met. When I came along it was me who had to stretch the budget, juggle the household bills, pay the mortgage and scrimp to make ends meet. There were times when it all got too much and I was worried sick about how we were going to manage. I tried to tell him; ask for his support, but he was really lazy about all that stuff and just shrugged it off with a smile. 'I know you'll sort it, Jen,' he used to say. And stupidly, one way or another I always did! He'd got used to being babied by his Mum, being her youngest, I suppose – the sun always shines out of his backside as far as she is concerned! I think I just allowed myself to become a mother-substitute. So in a way, I feel I'm to blame. I simply carried on where she left off, more fool me. I think that's why us breaking up has hit him so hard, pushed him over the edge. He's heading for a breakdown if he's not already having one." Jenny took another gulp of wine. "I hate to see him like this, Sarah, I feel so responsible."

Sarah topped up the wine, reached out to lay her hand on Jenny's. "You mustn't torture yourself, Jen. As harsh as it sounds, Vinny has brought this on himself. There has to be mutual support in any relationship for it to work, but it seems to me that in your case you were doing all the supporting and Vinny was using you as a crutch, and that's not right. It's no wonder you fell out of love with him. You had to walk away from it. From my own experience with Andy, I know a little of what you are going through – though it wasn't so bad for me; I mean, Andy never got abusive, he just kept pleading and weeping down the phone. The guilt wore me down in the end and I'm not sure what I would have done if I hadn't met Adam; I might even have gone back to him."

"Dread the thought," Jenny smiled.

"Tell me about it! Anyway, I'm so glad you are moving. It will be much safer and the new job will give you more opportunities to progress in your career without all the worry and hassle."

"I know, I just wish Vinny and I could've remained friends – we've been mates for such a long time and if I'm honest, I miss that."

It's early days, you're bound to," Sarah said sympathetically.

"I guess so. We couldn't be much further away from that at the moment. He has really scared me; become a completely different person. He has made me afraid of him and I know my parents are worried about what he might do next." Jenny ran her finger around the rim of her glass, said hesitantly, "I couldn't help wondering if the medium you went to see was talking about me; you know, the friend in danger?"

Sarah got up from her chair and went over to the sofa, putting her arm round Jenny's shoulders. "I've thought about that too, but it couldn't be you. I know your ex is doing silly things, almost stalking you, but I think you're right; he's having some sort of breakdown. Vinny's not a killer, Jen. He's just not thinking straight, but I'm convinced you're not in serious danger. All the things he's done lately, aside perhaps from breaking your parents' window, have been verbal abuse rather than physical violence. It's hateful enough, lord knows, but he's never actually hurt you, has he – and there must have been opportunities if he was that way inclined. Anyway, I'm not sure any more that the ghosts have anything to do with Lola's prediction. And I'm beginning to think that if there is someone who needs my help, then I really don't know them that well. When Lola said it was someone close to me, I assumed she meant close in an emotional sense, but she might just have meant near, you know? I mean, nearby. Like someone in the street about to get run over or something."

"You think? I hadn't thought of that, but you could be right. I guess it was only natural to link the haunting with what Lola said – but it might not be connected at all. Have you seen them recently – the ghosts?"

"Yes, I didn't tell you because I thought you had enough on your plate." Sarah grimaced, her voice a little strained, "I saw Jane in the garden last week; she was bleeding around her mouth. It was awful. I know it might be fanciful, but it's almost as if she needs to keep reminding me about her murder, as if her spirit doesn't want me to forget; like it depends on me to tell her story so that she can rest. Or even that she knows her killer is alive and will murder some other young girl – Charlotte, maybe, and is trying to warn me. I still don't quite understand how I can see *him* – the dark-haired man – if he's still alive, but if this guy's out there somewhere, he could be a serial killer, like we said before."

"That's *awful*," Jenny shivered, her skin springing into goose bumps. Poor Jane – and poor Charlotte; we have to do what we can. I've brought with me all the information I've dug up on likely building companies; I've filtered out the ones that weren't around ten years ago. It's a start, especially as we think the killer worked for Morgan's. We have to stay positive. I think we should give Jane's dark-haired man a name, call him 'Fred' or 'Bob the Builder' or something. It would feel less creepy."

Sarah laughed, "I'm not sure he looks much like a Fred or a Bob!" She gave Jenny a quick hug and got up from the sofa. "I can always rely on you to make me laugh, Jen, you're such a treasure. We can go through what you've found tomorrow. I've done a bit too, so we can pool what we've got and think what to do next. Adam's going to be late - to give us a chance to catch up on all the 'girly gossip' he said. Let's have supper first though. It should be ready by now."

The Italian recipe was gorgeous and every bit as good as it looked. After they had eaten, while Sarah made the coffee Jenny insisted on clearing away and loading the dishwasher. "This kitchen is amazing; very state of the art. When did you get it fitted?"

"About five weeks ago. The old one was quite dated. Adam did all the plans and a friend came to fit it." Sarah smiled, "We both laid the floor and amazingly we hardly argued at all while we were doing it!"

Jenny sat down on one of the bar stools wiping her hands on a tea towel. "I wish our house was as big as yours. It's really only got two bedrooms: the third is more like a box room."

"Yes, but it's got loads of character and you can still sell it as a three-bedroom house I would think. Will you put it on the market soon or will Vinny try to buy you out? It would be a lot less trouble if he did."

"Unlikely. Vinny is on a good wage, but only because he does so much overtime. I doubt he will be able to afford the mortgage on his own. The way he's behaving at the moment I very much doubt he will want to sell it, but then there is the problem that I will still be paying my half of the mortgage as well as rent on another property. I've already contacted Mum and Dad's solicitor, but there's so much red tape to go through. It could be quite a few months before anything is sorted out. Things could get very nasty too."

"Why don't you cancel the mortgage direct debits? If you speak to your bank about the situation I'm sure they would understand. Vinny would be forced to sell then and the ties would be cut a lot earlier, as well as making things easier for you financially." Sarah reached across to top up her friend's wine.

Jenny, beginning to feel quite light-headed, put her hand over her glass. "I think I'd best go easy, this wine is lovely, but very strong, at this rate you'll have to carry me upstairs!"

"It'll do you good; it isn't as if you have to drive."

"Oh, go on then," Jenny smiled, holding out her glass. "Cancelling the direct debit might be a good idea as a last resort, but I'll wait to see what happens first. Maybe Vinny's Dad and brothers will talk some sense into him. I think it's only Vinny's Mum who hates me; she wants to protect him and I was never good enough for her precious boy so she's sure to run me down to him."

Sarah nodded, "Andy's Mum wouldn't hear a bad word against him either. If they only knew it, over-protective mothers simply make the situation worse for their sons. Anyway, enough of Vinny, tell me about the new man in your life. Is Gary coming up while you're here? I can't wait to meet him."

"I hope so," Jenny smiled, her eyes lighting up at mention of Gary. "Honestly, Sarah, I feel like a giggly schoolgirl where he's concerned. He's going to call me later, so perhaps we can arrange something. He's been so good to me over Vinny, very supportive and sensitive, you know, keeping his distance outside of work so as not to make things more difficult for me than they already are."

Sarah pursed her lips, "How serious is it exactly with you two? You're very vulnerable right now. You don't think it's a bit soon? I'd hate to see you getting hurt, especially now."

Jenny's face flushed; she looked down at her wine. "I know you're thinking 'out of the frying pan into the fire', but it isn't like that, Sarah. I'm really attracted to Gary and it seems he feels the same way about me. I'm sure he's not just taking advantage of me. He's behaved entirely properly. If you must know, it was me who made the first move. It's been so hard not to be able to be like a proper couple and get to know each other outside work. He's only two or three years older than me and I know he shares the same ideals. We just seem to fit, you know? It all feels so different to my relationship with Vinny even when we first got together. I liked Vin because he seemed a nice guy and wasn't bad looking, we kind of drifted together, but with Gary there's such passion. I really want to be around him, can't keep my hands off him!" Jenny looked up, meeting her friend's gaze, "It was what you said about how it was for you and Adam that got me thinking in the first place that Vinny wasn't right for me. I know you said the butterfly feeling wears off, but in fact there never were any butterflies with us, he was just a good mate really. I look at you and Adam and it is obvious to me that you are still very much in love even after three years together. That's what I want." Jenny shrugged, "Ok, I know it's a cliché, but it feels like Gary's the one."

"Oh, Jen, I do hope so. Let's drink to that! And you're right about me and Ad; I'm even more in love with him now than when I married him. Somehow, learning about his weaknesses-"

"You mean he's got some?" Jenny laughed.

Sarah grinned, "Ok, so I know I'm always telling you how perfect he is, but Adam does have a slightly jealous streak. In that at least, Lola was right. It surprised me no end I have to say. But anyway, the imperfections seem somehow to make me love him more. I can't ever imagine being without him. I really hope you find the same thing with Gary. You deserve all the happiness in the world."

Sarah knew she had not been totally honest with her friend; Adam's childish tantrum – which was how she now thought of the episode in Derby – had been rather more than slight. In fact, on the strength of it she had decided against contacting Simon to ask his advice about Jenny. It seemed best not to court disaster. Adam was still unaware that it had been Simon she had spoken to by the ice cream van that day and Sarah wanted to keep it that way. She could not bear the thought of ever again seeing her husband completely beside himself with jealousy.

The two women were quiet for a while, both lost in their thoughts. Outside it had grown dark and moths were twirling around the patio light. Sarah got up to pull the blinds, peering outside afraid of what she might see, but there was nothing. "Shall we go and sit in comfort? More coffee?"

"No thanks, I'll be up all night." Jenny slid off the bar stool, "By the way how are plans progressing for the Aussie trip? It's less than six weeks away now isn't it?"

"Yes, I can't believe how fast the time's going." Sarah led the way through to the living room, "Don't ask Adam about it, he will bore you to death. He has everything planned out down to the finest detail – where we are going to visit, how long we'll be staying at each place; all the details on places to stay for backpackers. It will be a fantastic holiday, but I can't stop thinking about Jane. I want to help her out. I don't want to go away with the murder still unsolved. There's a reason why I'm seeing the ghosts – I am sure Jane is telling me that I must prevent another murder taking place, but I feel so useless, Jen."

Jenny sank into the sofa while Sarah closed the curtains and switched on the lamps. The soft lighting made the room feel warm and cosy despite its size. "Don't worry, Sarah. Tomorrow we can get stuck in; start early and ring round those companies. It will be quicker if we do it together. We will get to the bottom of it. I'm sure there will be a way of identifying Bob the Builder and finding out what has happened to him over the last ten years."

"I hope so; it still makes my skin crawl every time I go into the bathroom." Sarah sat in her chair and smiled across at her friend, "But I don't want us to spend all day on the phone – the weather is so nice now; all set for an Indian Summer they reckon. We must take advantage of it. I thought we could go shopping in Nottingham in the afternoon. It has so many clothes shops to look around – and shoes, of course. They really do seem to cater for everyone's tastes. And there's a really nice coffee shop near the castle for when we've had enough retail therapy. If it's alright with you, though, I thought we could do the sightseeing bit on Saturday when Adam can come too. The castle is a must, and I want to take you to the oldest pub in Europe – a quaint little place that's built into the castle rock. There's a museum to look round too and then-"

Sarah's flow was interrupted by Jenny's mobile. "Sorry, that'll be Gary, shall I take it-"

"It's ok," Sarah smiled, "take it in here. I need to go upstairs anyway. I'll carry your case up while I'm about it." She turned back at the door, "If he can come up, ask him to stay with us. I'd love to meet him and I'll square it with Ad; that'll be fine."

Smiling her thanks, Jenny took the call.

Ten minutes later, feeling slightly dazed, she was putting her mobile back into her bag when Sarah returned brandishing a bottle. "Now then, how's about another drink? More wine? Shall we open the bubbly, or would you prefer something a little stronger? Adam keeps a nice brandy for special occasions – and judging by the expression on your face, this certainly qualifies!"

"Oh Sarah, he's so lovely. He is coming up tomorrow after work and would love to stay. I don't know how to thank you."

"No problem. It's the least I could do after everything you've been through recently." Sarah walked over to the music centre and selected an easy listening CD, turning down the volume. "So he'll be able to do some sightseeing with us on Saturday and perhaps I'll push the boat out and cook us something for later. In which case, if it's ok with you, we'll save the champagne." Sarah poured two balloons of brandy and brought one over to her friend. "Aside from which, I owe you one for believing my ghost stories and not packing me off to the nearest mental institution."

Sniffing the brandy, Jenny relaxed, aware that she had a stupid grin on her face, but with Gary's voice still sounding in her head unable to wipe it off. "That'll be great. And of course I believe you; no doubts whatsoever. I've seen a ghost before remember. You have always been the sensible one. It's not something you'd make up. Who knows, maybe I'll see them tonight - although with this delicious brandy on top of all the wine I'll be out like a light - talking of which, I think perhaps I'd better go and find the bathroom..."

Sarah jumped up from her chair, "Oh goodness, what a sorry hostess I am. Yes, of course. Let's take the grand tour now and I'll show you where it is and where you'll sleep."

Following her friend up the stairs, Jenny suppressed a shiver and found herself hoping she did not come face to face with anything even remotely supernatural tonight, but somehow she could not shake the feeling that she was being watched.

CHAPTER THIRTY TWO

Sarah tossed and turned; looked over at the alarm clock, it was just past one in the morning. Adam had disturbed her when he came in at around midnight. He had tried to be quiet, but without his customary warmth beside her, she had slept only lightly until she knew he was home. Now wide awake, she was finding it difficult to get back to sleep and to add insult to injury she could hear Adam's gentle snores. It always amazed her how quickly he could relax and fall into a deep slumber from which nothing ever seemed to wake him, not even a thunderstorm. There was a creak on the landing and Sarah suspected Jenny had got up to get a drink of water; doubtless trying to minimise a hangover in the morning. Sarah grinned to herself; her friend had consumed rather a lot of brandy. She heard a door close. The thought of chilled spring water made Sarah feel thirsty. She was loath to leave the warmth of the bed, but the more she thought about it, the thirstier she became. In the end she gave up, slipped out of bed and into her silk nightgown and crept downstairs. After such a humid day, it now felt quite chilly and autumnal. Sarah tightened her nightgown and wrapped her arms around herself as she went towards the kitchen. The light was on and she could hear a scraping sound coming from the utility room. "Jen – are you ok? The spring water's in the fridge."

The kitchen was empty. The scraping noise came again. "Jen?" The utility room door was open. Sarah went towards it – and froze, rigid with terror. The dark-haired man was standing in front of the sink; horribly near. In his hand was a large kitchen knife, which he appeared to be sharpening. For a few moments she watched almost mesmerised. He was being so careful, cool as ice, scraping the blade on a stone, back and forth, back and forth. Sarah realised she was holding her breath and slowly, quietly exhaled, never taking her gaze off him, but powerless to move. After a moment he held the knife up to the light, running his finger along the blade. Did he know she was there? Could he see her?

Suddenly, as though he had read her thoughts, he turned and faced her. For a split second she saw his face clearly: his eyes were bloodshot and surrounded by dark shadows, he was unshaven and his hair looked unkempt; lank and greasy. Not at all the handsome, debonair young man she had seen before. Sarah, rooted to the spot opened her mouth to scream, but no sound came out. He advanced towards her, the knife clutched tightly in his fist and pointing at her chest.

And then he passed right through her as if she was not there and all she felt was an icy blast as though she had collided with an iceberg. Edging against the wall for support, Sarah continued to watch him, knowing now that he could not possibly see her and all her logic telling her that she could not, therefore, be in danger. Remembering Jenny saying that even the tiniest detail might be helpful, Sarah forced herself to look around and observed that the room had changed back to its original state before she and Adam had stripped it out. She knew instinctively, beyond a shadow of a doubt, that this was exactly how it must have looked when the builders had finished, just before the Palmers moved in and that what she was witnessing had happened ten years ago.

Sarah transferred her gaze back to the man. He was bending down to a cupboard and pulling out some black bin bags. Next, he went to the cupboard under the sink and retrieved a box of what looked like an assortment of cloths and cleaning products. He sifted through them carefully. Apparently satisfied he pushed the box back into the cupboard. He stood and appeared to be cheerily whistling. Sarah could see his lips were pursed, his cheeks puffing, but there was no sound – and then he calmly walked to the back door, opened it and went out into the night. It was as though she was watching a film, and yet it was all so frighteningly real.

She drew in gulps of air and waited for the utility room to shift and change back to the way it should be. When it did not, she pushed herself away from the wall and crept forward. Was the ghost still here; could he simply appear and disappear at will? Her eye was caught by a red smear on one of the taps. Walking slowly forward, she saw the bowl in the sink was full of dark, viscous blood. Gasping, her hand to her mouth, Sarah spun round, rushed to the downstairs cloakroom and vomited up her supper. The horror was continuing; it was a nightmare from which she seemed unable to wake.

Splashing water over her face, Sarah went dazedly back to the kitchen, alarmed to find that it had still not reverted to the present time. Fearfully she went through to the utility room. The bowl was empty; the blood had gone, the sink and taps were gleaming and the smell of bleach hung heavily in the air. She might almost have imagined the blood. No wonder the killer had managed to get away with murder; he had meticulously cleaned up behind him, leaving not a trace of evidence. If his relationship with Jane had, as Sarah suspected, been a closely guarded secret, he would not even have been a suspect in her murder investigation. The police may not have thought to question the builders – there was nothing to connect Jane's murder to this house.

Confused by the fact that she still appeared to be in the past and so afraid of what might happen next, Sarah's legs gave way and she sank to her knees on the floor of the utility room. As she did so, she noticed something white sticking out from beneath the cupboard under the sink: a piece of paper? Had the murderer missed something? Crawling over to it on all fours, Sarah pulled it free. Turning it over she saw it was a coloured photograph. It was creased and scorched along one side, as though someone had screwed it up and then tried to burn it, but she could see it was of him; the dark-haired man, his arm around a pretty girl who, despite the poor quality of the photograph she could see was Jane. They were both smiling happily into the camera. In complete contrast to the way he had seemed only minutes ago, he looked well-groomed, handsome – sexy - but the smile did not reach his eyes - such blue eyes. They stared out at Sarah, cold and hard. She studied the background, but it was impossible to tell where the photo had been taken. Who, Sarah wondered, had taken it? Charlotte? Was that why her life was in danger, because she knew this man had seduced Jane? Or was Charlotte already dead? And how, Sarah thought, feeling the photograph between her fingers, could she actually be physically holding onto something that was clearly very real, yet was in the past. Here at last was hard evidence that Jane had been with this man; the killer had made a mistake. Sarah slipped the photograph into the pocket of her nightgown, pulled herself up from the floor and desperate for a drink of water, went back into the kitchen. As she reached up to the cupboard for a tumbler, she felt something touch her on the shoulder. She screamed.

"Sarah, sorry it's only me. I came down for a drink; didn't mean to scare you."

Shaky and weak from shock, Sarah leaned against the breakfast bar, realised that the time shift had happened at last and she was back in her own kitchen. Weak with relief she managed a smile, "I'm ok. I didn't hear you and I guess I'm just a bit nervous at the moment."

"Of course you are. I'm not surprised." Jenny pointed to the kitchen stool. "You sit down and I'll get us some water. My throat is parched. Are you ok? You look very pale, not that I'm looking or feeling so good it has to be said," she grinned.

Sarah sat down. "I've been a bit sick, but I'm ok now. There's some spring water in the fridge." She waited until Jenny had got the drinks and was sitting down on the stool opposite her before saying abruptly, "I've just seen Bob the Builder. He was in the utility room sharpening a knife."

"What?" Jenny's face registered shock and she looked around nervously. "Is he still here?"

"No, he's gone."

"No wonder you were sick. What happened?"

Sarah described what she had seen, carefully feeling for the photo in her pocket half expecting it not to be there. But it was. She handed it to Jenny.

Jenny studied it, fascinated. "The girl is Jane?" She looked puzzled as Sarah nodded. "But how can you have this photo – it's real? Has it been in the house all this time?"

After all that had happened to her, Sarah found she could believe in just about anything; could even begin to fathom why she was being allowed to see into the past so vividly. She shrugged, "I suppose it might have been hidden somewhere. But given we stripped out the kitchen and utility, it's very unlikely. Don't you see, Jen, this is proof that none of what's been happening is in my imagination. I believe I was meant to find this and it's probably something the murderer thought he had destroyed. He's a very dangerous, clever man; he obviously got rid of all the evidence very carefully, but somehow, Jane managed to retrieve this and put it where I would find it. It's like she is reaching out to me across time. It is all I can think."

Jenny shivered. "It's all so awful. This man was a cold-blooded killer; how did he deceive that lovely girl? Look at those eyes, they're so hard. He must have been completely insane. How could anyone sane cut someone up? And from what you say he had a relationship with her. She must have trusted him, which kind of makes what he did to her even worse in my book. What made him hate her so much? And what of Charlotte? Did he cut her up too? It doesn't bear thinking about."

"I know." Sarah shifted uncomfortably on the stool, aware that it was nowhere near as chilly as it had been when she left her bed. How had she not remembered that her visions were always accompanied by a sharp drop in temperature? She should have been more prepared. "Who knows what was going through this man's mind when he did what he did? I agree; he must have been insane. He looked to be in a bad way, as though he had been neglecting himself, and yet he seemed so calm when he was sharpening the knife. I would swear that he was whistling, as though he did not have a care in the world." Sarah paused, reflecting on what she had seen. "But at least we have a picture of him now," she mused, "and we know what his job was and possibly who he worked for. All these vital clues haven't come to me by accident, Jen. Someone wants him caught and so do I. I'm now convinced he's not a ghost, as such. Jane is, I'm sure of that; she actually looks like a ghost at times – you know – in the way she fades in and out of focus. But I believe he's still alive; he is solid and real; as real as you and me. So I'm sure the visions I've been having are a sort of time shift and I'm seeing what happened ten years ago – and not necessarily in the order they happened, but in random glimpses of the past. In a way, it makes me feel less frightened. I used to think that we – Ad and I – were in danger, but I don't think that any more."

Sarah yawned, rubbed her eyes. "Sorry, Jen, I feel suddenly exhausted. Remind me to show you the painting tomorrow. I meant to show you last night, but I forgot and I'm too tired now. It occurs to me that like the photograph that too somehow crossed over into our time. The whole thing is completely weird and I can't even begin to puzzle it out just now. We'll talk some more in the morning."

"Good idea," Jen smiled. "We'll work it out, you'll see. Bob the Builder's days are numbered; we're going to make sure of it." She gave Sarah a quick hug, "Try to get some sleep. It's another day tomorrow."

CHAPTER THIRTY THREE

The next morning came all too soon for Sarah. Why was the bed always at its most comfortable when it was time to get out of it? She sighed sleepily, watching Adam as he headed off for a shower, a large bath towel slung over his shoulder, and thinking not for the first time what a fine specimen of a man he was.

Aware of her appreciative scrutiny, he grinned back at her, "You look delectable lying there. Wish I didn't have to go to work early! Ah well, you can have a lie in today, can't you? You look as if you need one - did you girls drink *all* of my brandy last night?"

"Not quite – and I don't feel that tired," Sarah lied. "Besides, I don't want to waste the day; we're going into town to do some shopping."

"Now why doesn't that surprise me," Adam chuckled.

Sarah stretched lazily, "I'm looking forward to showing Jenny what Nottingham has to offer. And by the way, her new boyfriend's coming up and I've invited him to stay over. I hope that's ok. I told you about Gary didn't I? I want to meet him, see what he's really like. Jenny's too besotted to see beyond her nose at the minute and I don't want her getting hurt, especially now when she's still reeling from finishing with Vinny."

"Of course it's ok. You don't have to ask my permission, daft girl. Why don't you book the four of us a table at that Italian place that's just opened up in town? Give us a chance to suss it out – and him too, poor chap!"

"That's a nice idea – and it will save me having to cook. We could take them to our favourite pub too - I don't mind driving." Sarah pulled a face, "It's no sacrifice; I couldn't face another drink for at least a week!"

"Serves you right," Adam grinned. "Sounds good, I'll make sure I'm home by six at the latest."

By the time her husband was putting on his tie, Sarah had already made breakfast and watered her flowers. It was going to be another hot day; the sun was shining and the temperature already rising. Coming back into the kitchen, she smiled across at Adam sitting at the breakfast bar.

"This is a treat," he said, his mouth full, "we don't normally have croissants."

Sarah rested her hand on his shoulder. "I got them in for Jenny. I want to spoil her a bit – she's had such a bad time lately. There's some strawberry jam; real butter in the fridge too, help yourself."

Adam raised his eyebrows. "She'll have to come and stay more often."

"Did you enjoy your evening out with Toby?"

"Yes, we get on really well. Do you know, I can honestly say I look forward to going to work these days - the team seems to be getting on so much better since he arrived. He's been a godsend, taking on extra work, always staying late to get his tasks done. He makes my job a hell of a lot easier I can tell you."

"I'm so pleased, Ad, that's great." Sarah had noticed the positive change in her husband lately. He seemed far less stressed and his worry lines had started to recede. Toby was proving to be a real asset. "You'll have to invite him over, darling. I've spoken to him on the phone a few times when you've been in meetings and he sounds really nice, quite efficient too. In fact I think I might have seen him when I met you from work the other day - tall guy, sexy looking?"

Adam rolled his eyes, "You too eh?" He spread a generous helping of jam onto his croissant. "Yeah, that'll be him - he's certainly a big hit with the ladies – the girls at work swoon all over him; it's sickening to watch!"

"I hope you're not envious!" Sarah laughed.

"What have I got to be envious about? He's welcome to any of them as far as I'm concerned, just so long as he keeps his hands off *my* girl!" Adam swivelled on his stool to give her a sticky kiss.

Sarah was still laughing when Jenny came into the kitchen in her dressing gown, her hair wrapped up in a thick cotton towel.

"Hi Adam, great to see you again – you look a lot better than I feel! Morning Sarah, hope you managed to get some sleep."

Sarah nodded, pouring her friend a cup of de-caffeinated coffee. "Is decaf alright? You should have had a lie in, Jen. You're on holiday remember; I was going to bring you breakfast in bed."

"Decaf's fine, thanks. Actually, I slept like a log – very comfy – and I feel much better than I deserve to after all that brandy."

"It's alright for some," Adam's eyes twinkled, his face a picture of mock outrage, "croissants and fresh butter – *and* breakfast in bed. This is just sheer favouritism. I never get treated like this. What does a guy have to do around here?"

Sitting down beside him at the breakfast bar, Jenny kept a straight face, "It's sisterhood, Adam," she explained. "Afraid you're not eligible. By the way, I couldn't help overhearing: who makes all the women swoon? He sounds interesting!"

Adam wagged his finger at her. "Hands off – you've got Gary coming later, and there's only so much one woman can take on."

"Try me!" Jenny laughed, sparkling.

"We were talking about Adam's new team member," Sarah said, smiling at their banter. "He's very appealing to the opposite sex apparently. I've yet to meet him so I can't really confirm that."

"Certainly is if the women in my office are anything to go by," Adam winked at Sarah.

"Ah, I see; he's stolen your limelight," Jenny grinned. "Never mind, Ad, from what I can see you've got my best friend here pretty much under the thumb; she's like a besotted teenager where you're concerned even if she is married to the job. No threat there that I can see."

Sarah turned round to jab her finger in Jenny's ribs. Adam snorted. "That's where I went wrong, you see. I should have steered clear of career women and married someone content to stay at home, be the dutiful housewife. A woman's place and all that..."

Both Jenny and Sarah rounded on him and pummelled his chest. Laughing, Adam held his hand up. "Pax! I'm only joking. Anyway must go before you do me an injury. Enjoy your shopping and I'll see you both later." He stood up, brushed the crumbs off his jacket, hugged and kissed his wife, grabbed his briefcase from the hall and hurried out to his car. Still laughing, Sarah blew him a kiss from the window.

"That's what I was on about last night," Jenny said wistfully, watching her friend and helping herself to more coffee.

"I'm sorry?" Sarah turned back from the window as Adam's car scrunched out of the driveway and disappeared up the lane in a cloud of dust.

"What you two have. Real love and respect for each other. Did you know that you light up the room when you're together? Are these all for me?" Jenny was eyeing the three remaining croissants.

"Yes, go ahead. Thought I'd treat us and we need some energy to keep us going."

Jenny devoured a buttery croissant. "That was gorgeous. No hangover to speak of thanks to all the water I drank last night. How about you, do you feel ok this morning?"

Sarah ran her fingers through her hair. "A bit tired, but aside from that I feel good despite what happened."

"Mm," Jenny said, "well don't forget we are in this together. We can start contacting those companies this morning – no time like the present."

"Don't rush, Jen. We have plenty of time - and thanks. I don't know what I would do if I hadn't got you to talk to."

"You still haven't told Adam?"

"No. I couldn't bear it if he didn't take me seriously – or worse, thought I was a mental case. I'll tell him eventually of course."

"Well at least you've got some hard evidence now with that photo and with any luck it won't take too long to track down Bob the Builder once we get on the phone. Then you'll be able to tell Adam everything won't you and no harm done."

In Sarah's view Jenny was being overly optimistic. It was unlikely that the building companies would be willing to divulge information about their employees to strangers. Were she and Jenny even heading in the right direction or was it just a waste of time and effort? But she wanted to appear more positive than she actually felt so she smiled at Jenny and said, "I'm sure you're right. We'd best get started."

By nine, the two friends had cleared away breakfast and were sitting in the lounge on the large woven rug in front of the plasma fire. Spread out around them was all the information on the various building companies they had accumulated between them. Morgan's seemed to be quite a common name; there was a surprising number.

"I think all these companies have been going at least ten years or longer but we could take a pile each; see if we can make sure," Jenny said, sifting through the printouts. "It's a pity the Palmers didn't have any paperwork on Morgan's. I suppose they didn't have anything on the estate agents who sold them the house by chance?"

Sarah rolled her eyes and clapped a hand to her head. "Oh Jen, what a fool I am! The builders must have used local estate agents. Why didn't I think of that? I'm certain there's something about the agents in the file — it might help."

"Ok then, you go and dig out the file while I sort out the stuff we've trawled from the Internet. Depending on how detailed it is we can probably discard quite a few. Tell you what though; I still haven't seen that painting of Jane. You told me to remind you. Can I see it now?"

"Yes, of course, it's just here." Getting up from the floor, Sarah went over to the bookcase. The painting was not where she had left it. She searched all the shelves, looked around the room, puzzled. "I'm sorry, Jen, it's not here. I could have sworn I left it on the shelves."

"Perhaps Adam's put it somewhere? Don't worry for now. We'll ask him later."

Sarah nodded. "Ok. Just going up to the study, shan't be a tick." She ran upstairs to the filing cabinet, pulled out the relevant file and promptly dropped it, cursing under her breath as papers spread out all over the carpet. 'More haste less speed,' she muttered to herself, bending to retrieve them and noticing a letter that had landed at her feet. It was headed, *'Harpers, Flitch and Parker Estate Agents and Fine Art Auctioneers, Established 1897'*, the logo 'HFP' stood out, embossed in bright red. Sarah picked it up. She must have seen it before, but had been so focused on Morgan's it hadn't occurred to her to think about estate agents. How odd that of all the stuff in the file, that particular letter should fall at her feet. It was addressed to Mr Palmer, confirming the vendor's acceptance of his offer and asking for details of his solicitors. Convinced she was on the right track, Sarah shuffled through the pile of papers, but could find nothing more. She crammed everything back into the file, shoved it in the cabinet and ran downstairs.

"Here it is," she waved the letter at Jenny. "Good news, I've got a number and address. It's from the estate agents who sold the house to the Palmers. I'll give them a call."

Jenny stood up, stretched and kicked the paperwork to one side. "Great, I'll go and make us some more coffee. This could be a long morning."

"Thanks – not decaf this time, eh?" Sarah grinned, reaching for the phone. "There's a pack of cappuccino coffee in the cupboard over the fridge." The number rang for quite a while before someone answered.

"Good morning, Harpers, Flitch and Parker, Sadie speaking, how may I help you?"

Good, Sarah thought; the estate agents were clearly still in business. She cleared her throat. "My husband and I want to extend our house, which is in Nottinghamshire, and I'm trying to track down the builders to confirm a few things about materials. I believe you were the agents who sold our house to the previous occupants, a Mr and Mrs Palmer, just after it was built," Sarah said, attempting to sound efficient and professional. "We've tried the last address and phone number the Palmers had for Morgan's

Building Company, but to no avail. I know it is ten years ago now, but we really would like to match up the bricks if we can. I was hoping you might be able to provide me with a contact number."

Luckily Sadie appeared to be both helpful and efficient. "Afraid I've only been here for four years, but I'm pretty sure we still sell for Morgan's. If it's the company I'm thinking of, it's a family firm, based in Yorkshire – Leeds I think. Could you hold a moment?"

There was a pause. Sarah gazed unseeing at the bookcase, still puzzling about the painting. Why would Adam have moved it? Sadie's voice sounded in her ear. "Sorry to keep you waiting. It's a bit hectic today; we've got a sale of antiques tomorrow and lots of valuations taking place. Could I take your name and number and get back to you? As soon as I get a chance I'll look up a contact number for Morgan's."

"Yes, please do, and thank you for your help. My husband will be so pleased." Sarah gave the woman her details and put the phone down with a satisfied smile.

"I take it from your expression that it was a successful call?" Jenny reappeared carrying two steaming cappuccino's.

"Yes and no; well it's a start at least," Sarah said, telling Jenny what had transpired. "I suppose it must be the same Morgan's, though it seems odd that they've moved to Yorkshire."

Jenny sipped her coffee thoughtfully. "Not necessarily if it's a small family firm. Let's look through these companies and see which ones are based in Leeds. Surely there can't be that many."

They began sifting though the paperwork. "Eureka!" Jenny shouted after a moment. "There's just one Morgan's in Leeds; it's got to be this one, Sarah, it says it was established in 1975 - and apparently they're still in business. Here, look, see?" She handed the printout of a brochure to Sarah.

"Brilliant!" Sarah scrutinised the black and white photos of the houses. "Some of these are similar to ours, but it looks like Morgan's are going in for a more executive style these days; these are all four-bedrooms and more," she tapped the bottom of one of the photos, "and just look at the prices! Morgan's have moved up in the world it seems – if it's the right company. I suppose it might not be."

"Well my gut feeling is that it is; it would be too much of a coincidence that there were two Morgan's selling through HFP, but there's only one way to find out. Are you going to ring them now or wait for the estate agent to ring back and confirm the address?"

Sarah's eyes widened. "Let's go with your gut instinct and ring them now. I can use the same excuse as I used for the agents. I'll ask if I can speak to one of the surveyors – say I want to talk to whoever was responsible for Bluebell Close - or do you think I should say we are interested in one of the new developments and want more information?" Sarah took a sip of coffee and tried to calm down. Her hand was shaking slightly. "Oh, Jen, I'm so very glad you're here," she grimaced. "Supposing they put me through to their surveyor and it really *is* the dark-haired man-"

"Bob the Builder," Jenny interrupted with a quick smile.

"Yes; him," Sarah knew Jenny was trying to defuse her anxiety, but she was too wound up to respond. "How will I know it's the right person? What shall I say – and suppose he senses I know something?"

"Let's cross that bridge when we come to it. It may be best not to mention Bluebell Close directly, though. Try to keep the query vague. Do you want me to make the call?"

"No, I'll do it – see how far I get, but thanks for offering."

Taking a deep breath, Sarah reached for the phone. A friendly voice answered almost straight away; a bright, young-sounding woman. As before, Sarah explained that she needed to match up some bricks and tiles on a Morgan's house built some ten years ago in Nottinghamshire. She then asked as casually as she could whether it might be possible to speak to one of the surveyors – she assumed she was speaking to the right company?

"Yes, I believe the company did build a housing development in Nottinghamshire, though it was before my time, but I'm sorry; both our surveyors are out on site at the moment. Perhaps I can take your name and number and get one of them to ring you when they return. They might be able to help, although I can't promise anything. Ten years is rather a long time."

Thanking the young woman profusely for her trouble, Sarah noticed Jenny was wildly gesticulating. She frowned, put her hand over the phone and breathed, "What is it?"

"Don't give them your name and address; give them mine – and my mobile," Jenny whispered urgently.

Sarah nodded. The young woman was still speaking: "Not at all, it's no trouble. Actually, I've just had a thought; if he's available, Paul Morgan may be able to help you himself. He knows everything there is to know about the company. He's sure to know what bricks and tiles they've used."

Sarah's heart missed a beat; she could not get her words out quickly enough. "That would be very helpful if he's not too busy. Does he own the firm?"

"Oh yes. As far as I know he started it up some time in the seventies - before I was born!" The young woman gave a small chuckle.

Sarah immediately ruled out Paul Morgan as the dark-haired man – he must be at least in his late fifties, quite possibly in his sixties - but it would be very interesting to talk to him. "He's not retired yet then?" she said conversationally.

The woman snorted, "Well we all tell him he ought to be, but in fairness he's very fit for his age and good to everyone here. In fact, Mr Morgan is funding my degree; I'm actually hoping to become a surveyor myself you see. We have two on the books currently and one trainee, but I'm hoping a vacancy will come up when I qualify so that I can stay on."

"He sounds like a good boss," Sarah said, keen to continue the conversation and take advantage of the girl's chatty friendliness, "degrees are so expensive these days. Is either of the surveyors likely to leave? It will be nice for you if Mr Morgan has a position for you."

"I wish! Unfortunately they are both quite young - only in their late twenties – and seem to like it here, but I live in hopes."

Late twenties would be the right age, Sarah thought, resisting the temptation to ask any further questions about them in case the young woman thought it was a bit odd and said something to her colleagues. One of them could so easily be the dark-haired man: Jane's killer. Sarah swallowed, made a face at Jenny and said more calmly than she felt, "Well, good luck with your degree. I mustn't take up any more of your time, but it's been nice talking to you. If Mr Morgan could ring me I would be very grateful," she gave Jenny's name and mobile number and ended the call.

"Well done, a round of applause for Sarah Miller!" Jenny clapped her hands together. "You played that really well. What was she chatting about: do any of the surveyors fit the bill?"

"Yes, both of them are qualified and in their late twenties, which would be about right. We may be barking up the wrong tree, but something feels right. I don't know why, but my sixth sense is telling me we need to carry on."

Jenny finished her coffee and sprawled out on the rug. "While you were on the phone I was looking through the info on the company. It actually makes a selling point of being a family firm. I was wondering, could Bob the Builder be linked to the family do you think? I gather Mr Morgan is too old, but could it be his son or a nephew?"

"Quite possibly," Sarah shrugged pensively. "If the killer was the son it would explain how he came to feel so comfortable in this house; you know, one of the houses that Daddy built. Don't you think it's a bit suspicious how they left this area to move up to Yorkshire? That's quite far away?"

"I agree, it is a bit suspicious. On the other hand, maybe there was too much competition in Nottinghamshire or maybe the land is cheaper in Yorkshire." Jenny shrugged, "Who knows? It might not mean anything, but we can try to find out. I've been thinking," she waved the printout in the air, "what if I ring up one of the sites ostensibly to ask about the houses and as tactfully as I can find out more about the business; it's employees and what have you? You can try your luck with the surveyors when Mr Morgan rings. Don't forget when he does that you're Jenny Peters and not

Sarah Miller! I thought it was a way of avoiding a direct link back to here - just in case... you know."

"Thanks, Jen. That was quick thinking." Sarah got up from the floor and walked over to the patio window. The sun was flooding into the garden lighting up the late flowering shrubs. "We shouldn't waste the day; it's gorgeous out there." She turned back, "You know, I'm really not sure what we will be able to prove even if we do identify Jane's killer. Am I supposed to say, 'I know you murdered your girlfriend ten years ago,' and expect him to breakdown and confess? This isn't an episode of *Midsomer Murders*, Jen. John Nettles is not going to come striding over the horizon to solve all our problems. This is real. Jane's murderer is a vicious killer, he could be highly dangerous. I'm wondering if perhaps we have enough now to go to the police rather than try to do it on our own."

Sitting up, Jenny curled her arms around her knees and rested her chin on them. She gazed up at her friend, shook her head. "I don't know, Sarah. If you go to the police with what we have, it is highly likely they'll laugh at you and send you on your way – or send you for urgent psychiatric treatment more like! All we have, in seriousness, is a series of visitations by a dead girl, your visions and a strong hunch. The only *real* thing is a burnt photograph. None of it adds up to much – certainly not in the eyes of the world. But all this is happening for a reason; I'm convinced you are right about Jane Moore: she is urging us to solve her murder and eventually we will find hard evidence. Then we can go to the police. Until then, you can only do your best. I feel we are doing the right thing, someone may be in trouble and if we can prevent another murder taking place, then it must be worth the risk – so long as we are careful. But having said that, you are far more involved in this than I am and if you want to try going to the police now then of course I will support you in any way I can."

Feeling suitably chastised, Sarah nodded. They had to help poor Jane and do whatever they could to save other potential victims, but she could not help feeling that the closer they came to identifying the murderer, the greater the danger. He would not want anyone stirring up trouble, especially after this length of time. And he had killed before... horribly.

"You're right, Jen, don't mind me; I just get a bit scared sometimes." She glanced at her watch, "Look, it's ten-thirty already. The Estate Agent's got my mobile number and Paul Morgan's got yours, so it won't matter if we go out. I think we both deserve a break don't you?"

Jenny shot her a relieved smile. "I agree; we can do some serious shopping in Nottingham. My credit card has no balance on it at the moment so we can go a bit mad. I need something to wear tonight too." Jenny hugged her knees tightly to her chest, "I can't wait to see Gary. I've missed him so much; it sounds really girly, but talking on the phone is just not the same. At the same time I feel really nervous about seeing him – not nervous exactly, but excited and a bit anxious, you know?"

"I do indeed. I remember what I was like with Adam. That butterfly feeling. In truth I still feel like that sometimes even after all this time. I'm really looking forward to meeting your Gary." Sarah clapped her hand to her head. "Goodness, I meant to call the restaurant. I'll do that now. Hope you both like it. It's new, set in a really nice park and it's had great reports - as well as being Ad's favourite food; Italian again I'm afraid. Gary is staying over isn't he? We can give you some quality time tomorrow - keep out of the way."

Jenny pushed herself up from the floor and playfully poked her friend in the ribs. "You don't have to do that, silly. We'll do something as a foursome; it'll be much more fun. I think I can persuade him to stay over, if you're sure it's ok. It'll be the first time I've been able to enjoy his company without having to keep looking over my shoulder. You can't imagine how good it will be to act like a proper couple."

"Oh I think I can," Sarah laughed.

There was a faint musical tone coming from the kitchen. Jenny shrieked, "My mobile, I forgot, I left it on the work surface. Good job it's so quiet in here." She ran into the kitchen, came hurrying back – it's Morgan's, for you. I've switched it to loudspeaker."

"Jenny Peters?" a man's voice enquired.

"Yes, speaking," Sarah said nervously.

"Paul Morgan here: my assistant told me you were enquiring about one of our houses. I gather you are in Nottinghamshire, so it must be at least nine or ten years old, is that right?"

He sounded quite gruff, but relaxed and friendly and Sarah felt quickly at ease. "Yes, that's right. Thank you for ringing me back so soon."

There was a slight pause. "Not at all; you want to build an extension I believe and need advice on matching up the materials. That's no problem. Have you pen and paper to hand? I can give you the names of the bricks now if you like. The tiles may be a little more difficult; we used three varieties back then, but quite honestly they are all very similar and once they are weathered they'll blend in."

Sarah was impressed: the builder was going out of his way to help her. Most men in his position would have passed a query like hers onto a colleague. He wasn't making any money out of this after all.

Jenny was standing behind her listening carefully. Sarah pulled out an address book and pen from her bag, "I'm grateful Mr Morgan, and very impressed with your memory."

There was a slight chuckle. "Unfortunately my memory overall isn't very good, but I do remember what materials I use on my houses – we only use top quality. This is going to sound really sad to you, but I know the colour of your brick is Charmwood Red Natural. We used it all the time when we were building in your area. It's still a favourite on some of the sites." He proceeded to reel off the rest of the materials used, together with the type and colours.

Sarah jotted it down, wondering as she did so why she was bothering. "Thank you, my husband will be impressed. We both love the house especially the layout. It's really spacious but we want to add a few extra rooms. Look, I know this is a bit nosy of me but why did you decide to leave Nottinghamshire?"

"It was for a variety of reasons really. My son suggested we move further north. His research indicated people in the Midlands were not buying the larger houses we wanted to build, nor were they prepared to pay the higher prices – there was quite a bit of unemployment in Nottinghamshire at the time, although the smaller developments sold really well; I imagine yours must be one of those? But there were other considerations too: land was cheaper in Yorkshire, and my wife's family were from Leeds so she was keen to move back there. As it happens, my son's suggestion proved to be the right thing to do and we've never looked back. The business has gone from strength to strength. But forgive me for bending your ear: as you will have guessed, houses are more than just a business to me."

Sarah gulped: so Paul Morgan's son had suggested moving. She tried to play it cool. "I'm very pleased it worked out for you, Mr Morgan. How nice to have a son to carry on the business. Did you make him a partner?" What a daft question, Sarah thought. It was a family firm for goodness sake; of course the son would be a partner. "Only," she added weakly, "I wondered why you're not called Morgan and Son."

Mr Morgan gave a throaty laugh and Sarah surmised he was a heavy smoker. "Sadly, no; after a few years my boy decided a career in the building industry wasn't for him. I think he wanted to make it on his own without his Dad's help, which was a great disappointment to me at the time. However, my daughter has now joined the firm and is doing really well – she's an architect, designs quite a number of our range and-"

He broke off. Sarah heard someone talking in the background. "Sorry about that," Paul Morgan said, "but my secretary has just told me I'm supposed to be in a meeting, I shall have to go. Nice talking to you Mrs Peters. If you have any more queries do give me a call."

Sarah thanked him again for his help and rang off. She handed the mobile back to Jenny whose brow was furrowed in thought. "I wonder what the son is doing now," she said. "I suppose you can hardly ring back to ask, Mr Morgan might get suspicious. Still, we've come a long way today; much further than I thought we would."

"We certainly have. I'd imagined it would take us all our time just to find the right company and now I've actually spoken to Paul Morgan. It's amazing."

"Two heads are better than one," Jenny grinned and started putting the paperwork into neat piles. "I was trying to piece it all together while you were talking. I think your hunch might be right. It could be that Paul Morgan's son is Jane's murderer. Things went sour with the new love of his life and being tipped over the edge he decides to murder her. He's obviously very clever: plans everything in great detail. Plants evidence in the boyfriend's car; puts some research together to prove to his Dad the company needs to move so he can get away from the murder scene as quickly as possible. Probably persuades his Mum that she would be better off moving to where her relatives are. My guess is that he then went overseas for a while. Perhaps he decided when he came home that a change of career would suit him better; help him to remove himself from any connection to the murder scene; make a fresh start."

"I hope you're right; if that's the case then he's less likely to be a serial killer. Maybe it was a one-off. But then where does Charlotte fit in? Poor Jane; it was all so calculating and awful. Meticulously planned - the worse thing is that if he thinks he got away with it once, what's to stop him doing it again when another unsuspecting young woman riles him. Will he turn on her too?" Sarah bit her lip, gave Jenny an anxious frown, "I could try ringing the trainee surveyor on reception again, see if she can remember the son; at least she should know his name."

"No!" Jenny gripped Sarah's arm. "Don't do that for goodness sake. Whatever reason could you give to be interested in Paul Morgan's son? It would be sure to arouse suspicion. Supposing he really is the killer and his father knows and is covering for him? It would be better if I try to get through to the surveyors' section. I can use an assumed name and we can devise some questions that sound plausible."

Sarah felt the tension building in her head, the onslaught of a bad headache. "Thanks, Jen, maybe later. Let's go into town now, take a break. We've done pretty well and I feel in need of some retail therapy to take my mind off everything. Is that ok with you?"

"I thought you'd never ask!" Jenny grinned. "I'm ready when you are. I'm dying to spend some money and see the sights of Nottingham."

Smiling at her friend's enthusiasm, Sarah grabbed her bag. "Right, I'll drive us down to the station and we can get the tram into town. It's really quick and it beats getting stressed trying to find a parking space.

Neither of them noticed as they left that the house had grown suddenly cold.

CHAPTER THIRTY FOUR

Jenny undid the straps on her shoes, kicked them off in the hall, sat on the stairs surrounded by shopping bags and rubbed her ankles her feet. "My feet are killing me," she groaned. "We must have walked miles. I'd no idea Nottingham had so many shops!"

"Sit down in the living room and I'll make us a drink," Sarah went into the kitchen and switched on the kettle. She was in a happy mood: the day had been a great success. The woman from Harpers, Flitch and Parker had rung back as promised with Morgan's telephone number and confirmed that HFP had acted for the builders in the sale of the Bluebell Close development. It was the same number as she had called this morning, not that Sarah had doubted she had spoken to the right company or that Paul Morgan had built her house. She tried to quell her feelings of excitement and certainty that she had taken a step closer to discovering the identity of Jane's killer. She had to remind herself that she was, after all, acting only on a hunch: the dark-haired man might be someone entirely unconnected with the builders. The next thing to do was try to find out if Paul Morgan's son had been a quantity surveyor. There was no reason to suppose, even then, that he had murdered Jane Moore, and yet it all seemed to fit. If only she could get hold of a photograph of him, but how? Sarah made herself stop thinking about it; concentrated instead on what she was going to wear this evening. She and Jenny had both managed to find a few new outfits in the Autumn Sales.

"I really liked the Trip to Jerusalem - is it really the oldest pub in Europe?" Jenny asked as Sarah carried two mugs of steaming coffee into the lounge.

"It's supposed to be. That dank cave smell really puts me off though. I certainly couldn't eat in there. We'll visit Nottingham Castle and the caves over the weekend. Maybe Gary would like to join us. Has he got to go back on Sunday?"

Jenny, having received a text message from Gary to say he was on his way, was in a fever of excitement and crossing her fingers that he would stay over until Monday, but she did not want him to feel obliged to if he did not want to. She smiled up at Sarah, "I'm not sure. He wouldn't want to impose on you. I'm hoping he'll want to stay the full weekend, but I'd like to play it by ear if that's ok; the last thing I want is for him to think I'm a bossy cow! I'll ask him later. Nottingham is a fantastic city; great tourist attractions and so many nice pubs – not to mention the shops. It's not hard to work out why you and Adam like it so much. I could easily live here."

"Hey – you're only staying for a few days, not permanently!" Sarah laughed. "Seriously though, I'm so glad you like it and of course Gary is welcome to stay over until Monday. Adam won't mind, in fact I think he'll enjoy the excuse to go out for a beer or two in the interests of male solidarity! You may not see much of Gary on your own."

"I don't mind. It will be good for him to get out and great for us both to be in a more relaxed environment; ghosts or no ghosts! Things have been pretty stressful for him too, Sarah. I feel so at home here; much safer. Thanks to you, I've almost forgotten about Vinny. What time's the table booked for?"

"Not until seven-thirty so you have time to have a long soak in the bath if you want. Glad you feel at home. I'll even allow you to use my special Covent Garden bubble bath. What time will Gary arrive?"

"I guess around six-thirty, depending on the Friday traffic. He finished work early to give himself plenty of time." Jenny started looking through her shopping bags. "What do you think I should wear? Is the restaurant quite posh?"

"Yes, really smart," Sarah nodded, "the décor is expensive and the reception area has a lovely marble floor. There's a notice banning jeans so I guess most people dress up. You'll love it: there is such a great outlook; a beautiful lake and fountain in front of the building and the menu looks fantastic. Why don't you wear the black silky dress you've just bought? It really compliments your hair. I've got a diamanté necklace you can borrow that would look good with it." Sarah smiled, pleased that Jenny seemed so much less stressed than when she had arrived: there was more colour in her cheeks and her eyes were brighter.

"Right," Jenny grabbed her bags, gulped down her coffee and headed for the door. "I'm going to phone Mum and Dad - they said they were going to try to find me somewhere to rent today – and then I'll take you up on the bath idea and then try on that dress again. What are you wearing? Why don't you go for the designer top – the red strappy one - it really shows off your fantastic figure?"

"Yes, I might just do that. I've got a pair of black satin trousers that would go really well with it. I'll take a shower while you're in the bath, then we can relax while we wait for the boys. Ad said he'd be home by six." Sarah checked her watch: "It's only half past four, we've got masses of time."

Recalling the visions her friend had described, Jenny was slightly apprehensive as she went upstairs to fill the bath. She did not want to see any severed limbs floating in bloody water or ghosts coming in and out of the room. She need not have worried; the bathroom was fresh and clean, the pastel colours making it seem warm and inviting. It was a large room and the house plants that Sarah had dotted about gave it splashes of colour. Even the bath mat was soft and inviting and there were some cream towels folded on the shelves. Jenny relaxed; everything, appeared very normal. "I love your bathroom," she shouted, "I could in here for hours."

Sarah's voice drifted back: "I'm glad you like it."

Some time later, the two women met in the kitchen. "Wow!" Sarah exclaimed. "You look fantastic! Gary won't be able to take his eyes off you."

"Thanks; so do you," Jenny blushed. She sounded nervous, but her eyes were sparkling.

"Adam will be home in a minute, let's have a glass of wine to get us in the party mood." Sarah grabbed a corkscrew from the kitchen drawer, pulled a bottle of Chardonnay out of the fridge, grabbed two glasses and led the way through to the living room just as her husband's car pulled up outside. Sarah's face lit up. Pouring Jenny a full glass of wine, she went through to the hall as the front door opened.

"Hello gorgeous girl," Adam smiled, threw his briefcase to the floor and drew her into his arms.

Taking his hand, Sarah pulled him into the living room. "Wow! Another gorgeous girl in my house - I must have done something right today," he grinned appreciatively at Jenny. "You both look fantastic. I take it Sarah took you shopping in Nottingham, Jen? I'm surprised you're all ready to go out. You must have set out early this morning. He took the glass of wine Sarah handed to him and mouthed 'thank you.' "Hope you haven't broken the bank!"

"Not really – we were quite circumspect all things considered," Jenny laughed. "The sales are on and we are the original bargain hunters as you know. Besides, we work hard for our money and deserve a few treats."

Jenny liked Adam. He had always been easy to get on with; made an effort to get to know people, although she knew he could be very protective of Sarah. Jenny had long suspected he was a touch possessive and wondered if it might cause problems, but her best friend looked giddy with happiness and once again, Jenny found herself regretting her wasted years with Vinny.

"Yuck – the sales," Adam rolled his eyes, "rather you than me. What time is Gary getting here? I need some male company, no offence girls, but you won't want to talk about football or have a beer."

"Don't worry – Gary should be here any minute. Sarah kissed her husband on the cheek, the scent of his cologne making her senses swim. "Did you get changed at the gym?"

He shot her an old-fashioned look, "Yes, with two women in the house I didn't think I'd get a look in either bathroom."

Sarah laughed. "What a cheek. You spend as much time preening yourself as we do." As she spoke, the doorbell chimed.

"That'll be Gary," Adam put down his wine. "I'll get it."

Hearing the sound of male voices in the hall, Jenny perched on the edge of the sofa and fiddled with the straps on her dress. Sarah said in an undertone, "Don't worry, you look incredible, he's the lucky one remember."

Gary came into the room, glanced quickly around until his gaze rested on Jenny. He crossed the room and leaned down to kiss her lightly on the cheek. "How are you? You look great. It makes me realise how much I've missed you."

Momentarily speechless, Jenny looked up shyly and smiled, found her voice and murmured, "I've missed you too."

Sarah came forward and shook Gary's hand. "Jenny's told me all about you; I'm pleased to meet you at last."

"Me too – and thank you so much for inviting me."

"Can I offer you a glass of wine, or would you prefer one of these?" Adam came striding through from the kitchen brandishing some cans of lager.

"A can would be great, thanks," Gary beamed, sat next to Jenny and clasped her hand. "You look so well," he said, looking into her eyes, "much more relaxed than when I saw you last. I was afraid you–"

"I'm ok, Sarah's been looking after me," Jenny interrupted, squeezing his hand.

"I confess I've been worried about her," Gary explained, smiling up at Sarah.

She returned his smile warmly. "We've been looking after each other. It's such a pleasure having her here. Jenny's my oldest and best friend. Did she tell you we were at school together?" Sarah could see immediately why Jenny was attracted to this man. He appeared very confident, a strong, dependable type. He was slim-waisted, his dark, short-cropped hair suited him; his lips were full and eminently kissable, his teeth white and even and his face unblemished and pleasantly tanned. In fact he reminded her not so much of Tom Cruise as Jenny had said, but Johnny Depp – except that Gary was taller. Sarah was surprised Jenny had not seen the resemblance; the gorgeous Johnny Depp was her favourite actor.

Before Gary could respond to her query, Adam grinned, "Well that's the introductions all over with thank goodness. Does anyone want any nibbles? Do you want to show Gary where he'll be staying, Jen? He can put his bags up in your room. We kind of assumed you'd want to be together, but the bed's made up in the spare room if you'd prefer." He checked his watch. "We should be getting off fairly soon. You still ok to drive, darling?"

Sarah nodded; "Fine." She had restricted herself to only a mouthful or two of Chardonnay. How tactful her husband was. It was obvious that Gary and Jenny needed a few moments alone. She could tell Adam liked Gary; they seemed to have hit it off straight away, but for herself, she had some reservations; a slight prickle of unease. She could not put her finger on why; Gary was extremely personable, pleasant, polite and well turned out: his suit looked expensive and unless she was very much mistaken, he was wearing a silk shirt and handmade shoes. There was nothing to dislike about him, unless it was that he was almost too perfect. Sarah found herself wondering if it was all a big act. She decided she would reserve judgement until she got to know him better. She was probably being over-protective of her best friend; for now it was enough that Jenny looked so much happier.

"Yes, of course, thanks Adam," Jenny, her face bright red, pulled Gary up from the sofa. He smiled at his hosts. "Thank you - and thanks again for letting me stay, I really appreciate this. You're both very kind."

"No problem – you can come and stay any time. We're very grateful you came up," Adam said, looking faintly embarrassed. "Jenny's been through a tough time. It's good to know you are there for her. She's my wife's best friend - but of course, you know that – and any friend of Sarah's is a friend of mine."

Sarah eyed her husband, a little surprised by this uncharacteristic speech. His face was flushed and his words slightly slurred. Surely he had not been drinking at the gym? It would be most unlike him. Was that why he had so liberally applied his cologne? Ah well, what did it matter if he let his hair down occasionally? She moved over to him and put her arms about his waist. "I love you so very much, Ad," she whispered.

Once they were alone, Jenny rushed into Gary's arms and kissed him passionately. "I've missed you so much," she breathed. "I'm so glad you came. I can't tell you how good it is not to have to think about Vinny, what he's up to, where he is. We can just enjoy ourselves. Isn't it fantastic? If you want, tomorrow we can spend the day on our own. Sarah and Adam won't mind. I daresay they would welcome some time alone too. Weekends are precious; they both work so hard."

Gary caressed her shoulders, "They seem a really friendly couple. It's good of them to put me up. This is a huge house and I love the design of it. A day on our own sounds blissful, but if Sarah has made plans it's not a problem. As long as I'm with you it doesn't matter to me who else is there. I was able to get Monday morning off, so I don't have to rush back, though I don't want to outstay my welcome. Will it be alright to stay over tomorrow do you think?"

"Absolutely - Sarah and I had a good girly shopping day today and we caught up on all the gossip last night. Anyway, we'd better go downstairs; the restaurant's booked for half-past-seven. I don't know how far it is. Do you need a shower or anything? I don't want to rush you."

Gary shook his head, "No I'm fine, I had plenty of chance to get ready before I left and it took less than two hours to get here." He pulled her towards him and kissed her again, murmuring in her ear, "You're blowing my mind – not to mention other portions of my anatomy. I don't think I can get enough of you, Jenny Peters."

Jenny giggled, "Well I'm afraid you'll have to make do for now." She put on a stern expression, "Under two hours? I hope you weren't speeding."

"Of course not," Gary held his hands up in protest, "the traffic wasn't too bad for a Friday and I know a few short cuts.

Come on then, I will be patient a while longer – and I confess I'm starving."

The restaurant was packed out, the decor expensive: there was a large chandelier in the reception area reflecting in the polished marble floor. On a nearby table a huge bowl of pink lilies scented the air. Glancing around the room as they were shown to their table, Jenny was impressed. It was an old building, but had been beautifully restored and the atmosphere was great. The surrounding land was beautiful too. All that could be seen from the windows was the lake and beyond it fields and hedgerows, no houses at all, even though it wasn't too many miles away from Nottingham City Centre. Jenny whispered to Sarah, "Eating at this place doesn't mean we have to take out a mortgage does it?"

Sarah laughed. "No, it's very reasonable at the moment. It hasn't been open long. I think they're trying to encourage as much custom as possible. Compared to the prices down your way, it's quite cheap."

Knowing Gary would want to pay for the meal, Jenny was relieved. She would feel guilty if the bill was astronomical. He looked very comfortable with Adam; the two men hadn't stopped talking, mostly about the European Cup, but it made her feel more at ease. She wanted Gary to get on with her friends and was happy to join in the conversation even if football did bore her rigid.

Sarah was enjoying the evening too, but try as she might, she could not shake her feeling of dislike for Gary. The attraction between him and Jenny was very apparent; they touched at every opportunity, but there was something not quite right about him. He was clearly making a real effort to get to know them, so what was it? Sarah knew Gary was older than Jenny, but only by a couple of years or so. Although he had black hair, he looked nothing like Jane Moore's killer so she felt she could rule out any connections in that direction, but the more he talked the more irritated she became. Sarah was angry with herself. Gary seemed genuinely likeable; very sociable. She and Jenny were so close. Whatever was the matter with her? She became aware the he was addressing her.

"This is gorgeous!" Gary blew a kiss into the air. "The steak and the sauce are cooked to perfection."

Adam agreed. "Yes, and have you seen the desserts? I can't wait to see my wife getting her mouth round the chocolate fudge cake!"

"I might pass this time," Sarah said with a smile, "this chicken dish is very filling."

Jenny grinned, a glint in her eye. "Come on, Sarah, chocolate fudge cake is your favourite, you have to have dessert or I'll feel too guilty to try one."

"In that case, I'll try to make room. I'll just have to go to the gym for a few hours tomorrow."

"Dread the thought," Jenny made a face and patted her stomach.

After desserts and leaving a generous tip, they went on to a few pubs, working their way by stages towards home. By the time they got back, it was after midnight. Adam went off to make some coffees, but Sarah was exhausted. "I'm sorry, tonight was great, but I am so tired. I think I'll turn in now if you don't mind. It was great to meet you, Gary. Do whatever you want tomorrow. Treat this place like home. We probably won't be up early so please help yourself to breakfast. Jenny knows where everything is."

Gary flashed Sarah a smile. "Thank you. It's so kind of you both. I don't think it will be long before I'm in bed, but I could do with a coffee first."

He looked as if he was several sheets to the wind. Sarah wasn't surprised; Adam had insisted on buying a few shorts on top of all the wine and beer they had consumed. She thanked her lucky stars that she had elected to drive or unable to resist, she would have been under the table by now! Gary had his arm around Jenny and to Sarah, they looked the perfect couple. She still could not fathom why she found it impossible to like him. It was so unlike her to make snap judgments.

She went upstairs, took off her makeup, had a quick wash and applied her moisturising cream. In less than five minutes she was climbing into bed. Her last thought as she dropped off to sleep was of Gary. Perhaps she would feel differently about him tomorrow. Her negative reaction could only be because she was so anxious for Jenny; her best friend was extremely vulnerable right now.

CHAPTER THIRTY FIVE

Sarah sat up with a start. Her head felt thick and muzzy and she knew she had been dreaming, but could not quite remember what it was about. What had woken her? She felt as if she had been asleep for ages and was amazed to see it was barely half an hour and that Adam had not yet come up to bed. Straining to listen, she heard muted laughter downstairs; he must still be entertaining their guests. Slightly annoyed, though not sure why, Sarah took it out on her pillow. Roughly fluffing it up, she plonked herself down with an irritated sigh, pulled up the covers and determinedly closed her eyes. She was just beginning to drift off again when she heard a peculiar noise outside the bedroom door. It sounded as though something was being dragged along the carpet. Swearing under her breath, Sarah switched on the bedside lamp, called out, "Jenny is that you?" But even as she spoke, she felt the sudden chill in the air and the familiar prickling sensation of the hairs rising on the back of her neck, and knew it was not Jenny.

    Warily, Sarah got out of bed, grabbed her robe and creeping to the door opened it softly. The hall light had been switched off and the landing was quite dark, but she could see the shadowy figure in the corridor. He had his back towards her, but she would have known with her eyes shut that it was Jane's killer and that she was having another vision. Was he still alive or was he dead? Was she seeing what had happened in the past or what might happen in the future? Was he – or had he been - Paul Morgan's son? So many questions, none of which she could answer. The apparition appeared to be half-carrying, half-dragging something along the corridor. Sarah could not make out what, only that it was something large and shapeless. Her eyes widened and she gasped in horror: was it a body - Jane's body? Was she seeing the moments directly after the murder?

    Thrusting her arms into her robe and holding it tight about her, Sarah followed, but as she crept nearer to the dark-haired man and his gruesome burden, he disappeared. Leaning weakly against the wall for a moment, Sarah drew a breath, summoned up her courage and forced herself to check all the rooms; nothing. Racked with frustration she snapped on the light in the smallest bedroom. There was no sign of the man or whatever it was he had been dragging behind him; the room was empty. She was about to switch off the light when something caught her eye: a small, carved wooden box in the corner nearest the window. Sarah was certain it had not been there before. It looked homemade, like a relic from a schoolboy's woodwork classes. She stared at it; knew it did not belong to Adam. It was smeared with what looked like blood - Jane's blood? What was in the box? Why had it suddenly appeared? She was about to go forward for a closer look when she heard heavy footsteps on the landing. The door was pushed wide open and the dark-haired man sauntered in.

"Ah; there you are," he said with a satisfied smile on his face.

Sarah shrank back against the wall, but he was not speaking to her. As always he seemed oblivious to her presence.

He went over to the box, "I wondered what she'd done with you," he murmured, bending to pick it up. He opened it, looked inside and gave a small chuckle. Snapping the lid closed, he turned back to the door and carrying the box, walked out of the room.

Her heart thumping, Sarah waited for a moment, thinking hard and wishing she had been able to look inside the box. His words came into her mind: *I wondered what she'd done with you.* 'She' just had to be Jane – and the killer had seemed so pleased to find it. Why? The more she thought about it, the more convinced Sarah became that like the photograph she had found in the utility room, Jane had put the box in here for her to find. Could it be used as evidence? The killer's fingerprints must be on it and there had been bloodstains too, Sarah was sure of it. If she was seeing flashes of the past, might the box still exist, hidden in the house – in the loft perhaps or behind the skirting somewhere? Feeling the temperature return to normal, Sarah knew the vision was over and the apparition gone. She switched off the light, went back to her bedroom and sat on the side of the bed, her mind so busy she was barely aware of whispered voices and smothered giggles on the stairs.

Jenny stumbled up the stairs and along the landing to the guest bedroom, noticing the line of light under Sarah's door. Not wanting to disturb her friend, she turned to Gary, who was right behind her, and put her finger to her lips, "Shhhh!"

Once inside their room with the door shut, Jenny moved into Gary's arms and they clung together for a few moments, savouring their first real opportunity to be alone. "I think I've had too much to drink," Jenny whispered.

"Me too," Gary murmured into her hair, "but does it matter? We have the whole night to, er... sober up," he grinned down at her making her blush. "Before I forget, I meant to ask, have your Mum and Dad seen Vinny? He hasn't been causing any more trouble has he?"

"No, I don't think so, or at least my Mum said nothing when we spoke on the phone yesterday and I think she would have mentioned if they'd seen him. He hasn't texted me since I got here. I'm hoping things will quieten down now and he'll stay away. My Dad's solicitor is going to deal with the house sale and if there is a need for me to communicate with Vinny it can be by solicitor's letter, which I think would be best in the circumstances. When I get back, I'll be busy moving. With any luck I won't have to see him again."

Gary hugged her tightly. "That's good. You seem so much more positive; far less tense. It will all work out for the best I'm sure of it. Remember, everyone's life has ups and downs. You've had a bad down, but the up is on its way, you'll see."

"I hope so," Jenny giggled and kissed him lightly and then with more passion. "I'm so very glad you opened up about your feelings for me."

"Had I suspected they were returned, I'd have said something sooner. Never mind, that's in the past; we are together now." Not taking his gaze off her, Gary took off his jacket and laid it over a chair; slowly he pulled of his tie and started to unbutton his shirt, hesitated, "Are you sure about this? I could sleep in the-"

Jenny stopped his mouth with her fingers, "I've never been surer of anything in my life."

Gary laughed exultantly, peeled off his shirt and dropped it where he stood. It was the moment Jenny had been waiting for. In a fever of impatience, she wriggled out of her dress and in no time at all her clothes had followed Gary's shirt to the floor.

"Are you asleep Sarah?" She was not; she had been thinking about the wooden box, the same questions going round and round in her head. What was in it? Was it Jane's way of telling her there might be some hard evidence? She had a photo, the picture the killer might have painted of his victim – and where *was* that? She had forgotten to ask Adam – and now the box. Was it still in the house somewhere? Aware her husband was waiting for a response she opened one eye and said, "Not quite, just trying to relax."

Adam undressed quickly and slipped into bed. "It was good tonight. The meal was excellent and I really like Gary, he seems a decent guy. He made a real effort. It can't have been easy for him coming up here knowing we'd be checking him out. He has a wicked sense of humour too. To be honest, I never really got to know Vinny that well, but Gary seems good for Jenny. She was lit up like a Christmas tree did you notice? I hope it works out for them."

Sarah knew she should be more enthusiastic and was probably being unfair to Gary; judging him without really knowing him. Adam obviously liked him and her husband did not make friends easily. She pushed herself up onto her elbow. "I hope so too. What are we all doing tomorrow? We could take them to Sherwood Forest if the weather holds; they ought to do the whole Robin Hood thing while they're here don't you think?"

"They might want some time on their own. They haven't been going out long remember. We can give them directions and let them decide. Tell you what, let's do a barby tomorrow night and invite a few people over; make it a bit of a party."

Sarah snuggled into the crook of her husband's arm, determined to remain positive and not allow her preoccupation with Jane Moore to take her over. "That's a great idea, Ad. We've got a make the most of the sunshine while it lasts; it's so lovely this year. I'll clean up the barbecue tomorrow and keep my fingers crossed that it doesn't rain."

"You know that when we go to Aussie it will be the start of their summer? We'll get more sun than we can handle then. I can't wait. I just wish we could get someone to housesit for us; keep an eye on everything. I can't help thinking it's asking for trouble leaving it unoccupied for a whole month."

"I know, I've been racking my brains, but it's not a good time of year for anyone. Don't worry, Ad, like I said before, the neighbours will keep an eye out for us and we can tell the local police."

Adam nodded, but Sarah could see his brow was furrowed. She was just dropping off to sleep when she heard him say: "I've got an idea. Leave it with me. I'll sort something out that will give us both peace of mind."

"Ok darling. By the way, where have you put that painting – you know; the one you found in the shed? I wanted to show Jenny what the garden looked like before all the shrubs had grown up."

"I haven't put it anywhere," Adam said. "In fact I haven't seen it since the day I found it. I assumed you'd given it to the Palmers."

"Oh yes, silly me, I had forgotten." But she had not given it to the Palmers, she had left it on the bookcase – and it had gone.

CHAPTER THIRTY SIX

Jenny was pleased to see the sun was shining as she drew the blinds. "Oh look, darling, it's going to be another lovely day." She turned back to Gary and blew him a kiss. They had woken early, made love again and then lain contentedly in each other's arms. "I can't believe how lucky I am to be here with you," she smiled, returning to the bed. "A few months ago it was just an impossible fantasy – and now here you are." She reached out to pinch his arm, "You are real aren't you? I'm not still fantasising."

Gary laughed, "That was some fantasy! I'm real alright. Come here and I'll prove it to you." He pulled her towards him and nuzzled her neck.

"Stop, that tickles!" Jenny pushed him away, laughing. "Seriously, though, it's made me realise how unhappy I was with Vinny. For years he and I were just drifting along, there was never any...," she flushed, "well, you know..."

"Passion?" Gary smiled.

"Yes, exactly that - oh, Gary, I know I sound like a child in a chocolate factory, but I've never felt anything like I did with you last night - and now it's morning and we're together and the sun is shining and I feel as if the worst part of my break-up with Vinny is over and I can start living my life again. I'm so happy I could burst."

"Heavens, don't do that, you'll mess up the sheets."

Giggling, Jenny fell back against him.

"I'm glad for you," he put his arms around her, linking his hands beneath her breasts, "not to mention relieved. I was afraid you were heading for a breakdown last week – and now look at you! Long may it continue – did I mention that I kill for chocolate?" He messed up her hair, planted a kiss on her nose and murmured, "And by the way, it was good for me too."

Jenny grinned, "What, chocolate?"

"You know very well I don't mean chocolate," he chuckled, frowned, "I'll be glad when you've moved though, Jen. I don't suppose you've had time to find anywhere to live yet, but the sooner you're out of harm's way the better I'll be pleased."

"As it happens, Mum and Dad have already found somewhere for me. It's a house-share with a woman who works at my new branch and wants help with the mortgage. It will do as a stopgap until I can find a place of my own and she – her name's Deirdre, evidently, sounds really nice. Dad says he's already paid a month's rent in advance and I can move in as soon as I get back, so you can stop worrying."

"That was quick, good on Mum and Dad, eh? That's great news."

"Dad's like that; he knows so many people in his line of work and he always makes things happen. I'm very lucky to have such supportive parents."

"You are indeed."

"Anyway, that'll give me Tuesday to move in and unpack everything and I can start work on Wednesday. I suppose I should call my new boss and confirm that after the weekend."

"Don't mention after the weekend," Gary rolled over and put a tentative toe to the floor, "it's going quickly enough as it is. So Miss Peters, what are we going to do today, apart from lie here - which I don't mind by the way..."

"There are quite a few places of interest to see around here. Sarah's already said if we want to spend the day on our own they won't take offence."

"If it's what you want then we will, of course, but I'm quite happy to make it a foursome. I thought I could treat us all to lunch somewhere as a thank you for putting me up at such short notice."

"Oh yes, let's, it'll be fun."

"I'd quite like to see Sherwood Forest," Gary said, "find Robin Hood and all that. I've read up on it. Will he be hiding in the Major Oak ready to jump out on us and steal our wallets do you think?"

Jenny grinned, "I don't think that's very likely – and he'd be in pretty poor condition given he's a few hundred years old; probably wouldn't have the strength even to lift *your* wallet!" She leapt out of bed and ran to the en suite. "Beat you to the shower," she said, laughing out loud as he jumped after her and made a grab, catching her round the waist and holding her against him.

"Gotcha! Is it big enough for two do you think?"

Adam drove them to Edwinstowe. It was a hot, sultry day with not even a slight breeze and Sarah was glad of the air conditioning. Looking up at the trees she noticed the leaves were just beginning to turn. "I don't want you two lovebirds in the back to be disappointed," she said over her shoulder, "I have to warn you that Sherwood Forest isn't as dense as it was in good old Robin's time."

"That's a bit of an overstatement," Adam chipped in. "Robin would have a hard time trying to hide from anyone with the few trees they have left. It's a good place to visit though. There are a lot of trails to follow and an excellent visitors' centre. The restaurant there does some decent grub too. Gary, if you're up for it we can even hire some bows and arrows and green felt hats - just to get into the spirit of things."

Gary laughed. "That's fine by me. I've got to warn you, though; my shots might be a bit off. Forgot to bring my specs, but hey, if people choose not to look where they're going, what can we do?"

Relaxing, Sarah smiled. She would put her reservations about Gary on hold if it meant Adam was going to enjoy himself. They clearly shared a similar sense of humour. "You won't do much damage," she said, "they have rubber tips, but I think they're actually intended for children to play with, not fully grown men."

"You wouldn't understand, dear: bows and arrows is a man thing," Adam grinned.

After spending several hours walking in the forest, they had a late lunch at the visitors' centre, returning to Bluebell Close around tea time. Sarah and Jenny then drove to the shops to pick up food for the barbecue, leaving Adam and Gary in charge of setting it up.

Sarah found herself dashing around the local superstore at a trot, filling the trolley with burgers, sausages and chicken drumsticks. "I forgot, I told the neighbours to come round at six. The day's simply flown."

"I know," Jenny flung a pack of beef tomatoes and some lettuces into the trolley as they passed by the vegetable section. "But there was quite a lot to do at the visitors' centre and we did choose the longest trail to walk. Don't get me wrong - I really enjoyed it. Weren't we lucky with the weather? It was great just to be out in the fresh air with the sun on our backs - so relaxing. Adam and Gary seem to get on well don't they? They talked even more than we did, which is a feat in itself." Jenny put her hand on the trolley, forcing Sarah to stop for a moment. She looked quizzically at her friend, "What do you think of him, Sarah?"

"It's what you think of him that matters, Jen. He seems very attentive and obviously cares about you."

"He does, doesn't he?" Jenny smiled, apparently not noticing her friend had avoided answering the question.

The barbecue proved a great success, Adam wearing his chef's pinny and revelling in the cooking; Gary and Jenny socialising with the neighbours, most of whom were under thirty, had come equipped with bottles of wine and obviously enjoyed partying. Mid-way though the evening, when the sun had set and the bats were flitting over the house, most people had wandered through the patio doors into the lounge, but Sarah strolled down the garden to sit on the bench. She wanted a moment's peace and quiet. The thump-thump of the stereo was muted down here and she sat back enjoying the scent of roses on the night air. "Are you here, Jane?" she whispered. "I haven't forgotten you."

It was two in the morning before the last couple went home having stayed on to help clear away. Sarah was asleep almost before her head touched the pillow.

They all had a late start next morning, but although it was nearly lunchtime before they had breakfast, and despite looking somewhat hung over, Adam and Gary were determined to go for a game of squash at the leisure centre.

Jenny rolled her eyes at Sarah, "Shall we admit defeat and go with them? Perhaps we could have a swim."

"Good idea and then we can have a go in the sauna; it's supposed to be good for a hangover!"

Maybe because it was Sunday lunchtime, the sauna was deserted. Sarah took the opportunity to tell her friend about the wooden box.

Jenny's eyes lit up. "If only we could find it. This could be the evidence you need to get your policeman friend to take you seriously. Like you say, there could be fingerprints and if we're lucky they might be able to trace the DNA and tie Bob the Builder to his victim."

"Not unless he's got a criminal record."

"Don't be so negative, Sarah. My gut instinct says you're right. It could still be in the little room. We've got to look under the floor boards. It seems a likely hiding place if any. Have you got a crowbar?"

"I'm sure Adam will have one, he's got a whole collection of tools in the garage. I seem to remember he bought one when we needed to replace some slabs on the patio."

"Great. We'll have a look tomorrow after Adam's gone to work. Gary has to leave early, but I don't need to go until after lunch."

"I hear what you say about being negative," Sarah sighed, picking up a towel and mopping the sweat from her brow, "but I can't help fearing it's a wild goose chase. Goodness, I could use a drink, let's go and get some fruit juice."

Later, having eaten a Sunday roast, which Adam insisted on cooking while Sarah pottered in the garden, they all retired to the lounge. Adam soon dropped off, snoring gently behind the newspaper. Gary, who appeared to be very much at home, had a snooze with Jenny leaning her head on his shoulder. Sarah too was very sleepy; the late night and swim had tired her out. It had been a good weekend, she reflected and certainly Adam seemed to have enjoyed Gary's company.

The sound of Gary's mobile woke them all up. He pulled it out of his pocket, grimaced, "Damn, I'd best take it, it's my boss."

"On a Sunday?" Jenny grumbled as he got up from the sofa and went out into the hall, quipping over his shoulder, "No rest for the wicked!"

Moments later he was back, looking somewhat crestfallen. "I'm so sorry; my morning's leave has been cancelled. One of the projects has gone belly up." He looked over at Jenny and grimaced. "Can't be helped I'm afraid. I'll have to leave shortly, get organised for the morning."

"That's a shame," Adam said. "I was hoping we might have a go on Playstation later. Sarah refuses to indulge me in that department."

"Another time, perhaps," Gary smiled sympathetically.

Jenny followed him upstairs, her eyes glistening with unshed tears, but trying to put on a brave face. "The weekend has just flown by," she said, sadly.

Gary took her in his arms. "I really don't want to go home. I wish I could stay, spend another night with you. I want you again right now - so very much. Can we see each other next weekend?"

"Yes please!" She smiled up at him, raising her mouth for his kiss, murmured, "I miss you already."

Profusely thanking Sarah and Adam for their hospitality, Gary left at six o'clock. When he'd gone, Adam disappeared upstairs for a shower, leaving Jenny and Sarah alone together.

"So, what do you think of him?" Jenny asked tentatively. "You avoided the question yesterday. Is it that you don't like him?"

Sarah chose her words carefully, anxious not to upset her friend. "You know me, Jen, it always takes me a while to get to know people, but Gary seems a real nice guy and Adam clearly likes him a lot. More importantly he totally adores you."

"So you don't like him."

"I didn't say that."

"You don't need to. You're my best friend, Sarah; I know when you're hedging." Jenny shrugged, "Ah well, as you say, it's what I think of him that matters. I wish you liked him, but I'm not going to fall out with you because you don't and I can only thank you for giving me this opportunity to be with him. It has been so good having him here. Gary is completely opposite to Vinny: he's got drive, is caring, intelligent and funny, and as you say, very attentive," she shrugged, "in short, I guess he's as close as I can get to my ideal man. Anyway, I'm sorry to go on about him – but at least it gives me the chance to pay you back for years of bending my ear about Adam," she grinned. "Anyway, how are you feeling? Have you had any more thoughts about Bob the Builder's box?"

Sarah could not help but smile at the distasteful ambiguity, relieved that Jenny was trying to lighten the tension between them. "Ugh, what a foul thought!" She grimaced, shook her head, "No, only that if we can't find it I don't know what to do next. Jane's murderer has clearly been clever in covering his tracks. I find it hard to believe he would have left any potential evidence lying around. Perhaps he burned it as he tried to do with the photograph."

"Not if he thought no one would ever find it and that even if they did they wouldn't think anything of it; just some old box the previous occupants left behind that would be thrown in the bin. He would never have imagined that his victim's ghost would try to bring him to justice! There was never going to be a link between Jane's murder and this house so why should he not leave things here? Whatever is inside the box – or even the box itself – might be some sort of trophy to remind him how clever he's been. I'd bet my life it belonged to Jane. We'll find out tomorrow."

"I wish I had your faith, Jen," Sarah smiled. "Yes, we'll look for it tomorrow."

CHAPTER THIRTY SEVEN

The next morning it was raining heavily. As usual on a Monday, Adam was up early and anxious to get to work in time for his regular team meeting. Sarah, keeping out of his way, but too apprehensive about finding the box to stay in bed for long, watched him getting ready.

"As the barbeque went so well on Saturday," he said, pulling on a clean shirt, "I was thinking I might do another one next week and invite some people from work. Top of the list has to be Toby. He has really helped me out. I feel much better about going on holiday with him around. I can trust him to get things done."

"That would be nice. Best invite his girlfriend too – I assume he has one?"

"Actually, he's engaged to be married; popped the question last week, evidently. In fact he invited us to the party this weekend, but obviously we couldn't have gone with Jenny and Gary here."

"Really? That must be disappointing for your female colleagues!"

Adam laughed, "You're right there. He's quite a shy chap, you know, finds all the adoration hard to handle."

"That's surprising. The few times I've spoken to him on the phone he sounded so confident."

"It's an act; he puts on a telephone voice. I suppose we all do really."

Sarah nodded; her mind already on the day ahead. "Right then, I'll make sure I stock up the freezer before the weekend. Are you not stopping for breakfast?"

"I won't, thanks, darling. It's someone's birthday today so we'll be getting bacon cobs later on and I can have coffee when I get there. I'd better go. Say goodbye to Jenny for me." Adam shrugged on his jacket, leaned over to kiss Sarah's head then bounded down the stairs. She heard him unlock the front door and go out as she was getting in the shower.

Quickly throwing on a pair of jeans and a T-shirt, Sarah pulled up the bed covers, picked up Adam's discarded clothes from the chair and threw them into the dirty linen basket, then went down to the kitchen. Her hands were shaking as she switched on the kettle and filled the toaster. 'Calm down, Sarah', she muttered to herself. But she could not stop seeing images of the dark-haired man and his satisfied smile as he had picked up the box. What did it contain? Would they find it today? She jumped as Jenny breezed into the kitchen.

"Sorry, did I startle you? You seem nervy today; not had another vision I hope?"

"No, it's just I can't stop thinking about that damned box!"

"Right, let's do this. No time like the present. I'll get the crowbar from the garage."

Sarah winced, "I'm not sure about this, Jen. Maybe we should forget the idea. It's probably nothing..."

"Stop worrying; there's no harm in looking. Adam will never know we've been under the floorboards - I'm not a DIY freak for nothing," Jenny chuckled, but her voice was unnaturally high. "Have you got a torch? And also we need some gloves – preferably plastic ones."

"What do you think this is; a forensic laboratory!" Sarah grinned, handing Jenny a torch from the kitchen drawer.

"It's ok; I've got some in the car. I always pinch a few from the garage when I fill up with diesel. They're so useful. Hang on; I'll be back in a tick."

Moments later, carrying crowbar, torch and plastic gloves, they went up to the smallest bedroom. Sarah, hardly able to speak, indicated the spot by the window where she thought she had seen the box. Jenny rolled back the carpet and prised up a floorboard. It seemed to come up quite easily. They both peered into the gap; there appeared to be nothing but dust. She prised up another.

For a few moments, Sarah held onto the torch and prayed they would find something; anything at all. For a split second she became aware that it was suddenly vitally important to her that they did. This was the moment of truth; it might prove once and for all that she was not losing her sanity. Sarah took a few deep breaths and tried to shrug off the feeling that it mattered even more to Jane than it did to her. Was she here? Watching?

Almost as soon as Sarah knelt to shine the torch into the gap Jenny had made, she saw something under the floorboards. It looked like a small cloth sack. "Could you take the torch, Jen, I think there's something there."

"Wow, really?" Jenny's face flushed with excitement. "No spiders I hope!"

Sarah leaned over the gap and pushed her arm underneath the floorboards, shuddering as she felt the cloth brush against her finger tips. It was just within her reach. She pulled the bag up out of the darkness. It was covered in dust; clearly had been there for some time. Sarah sneezed. They both sat looking at it for a few moments, unsure what to do; almost afraid to open it.

"Put these on, just in case it is the box inside," Jenny held out a pair of gloves.

"Just as well you read so many crime novels," Sarah tried to laugh. "It would never have occurred to me." She put the gloves on and picked up the sack, carefully easing back the cloth.

And there it was – exactly as she had seen it in her vision: the carved wooden box. "It's a casket," Sarah whispered. Almost mesmerised she tried to open it, her hands inside the gloves sticky with sweat, slipping and sliding uselessly as if they did not belong to her. Breathing deeply, she regained control and opened the lid.

"Oh, Jen, look, it's Jane's dolphin necklace." Lying in the box was the gold pendant and chain, some earrings and other small items of jewellery. Neither woman spoke, both aghast at what they had found. For Sarah, it was vindication; a moment of utter relief. The doubts she had tried to suppress that she had been losing her mind suddenly fell away.

Jenny too was speechless. She had never doubted Sarah was telling the truth about what she had seen, but somehow it had all been unreal. Finding the box – the proof - sent a shiver down her spine. The murderer had been here; had actually handled this casket. All the atrocities Sarah had described had actually happened. Jenny looked at her friend, her face grim. "Are you alright?"

"Yes, I'm ok. In one way I'm relieved to find this and know I'm not going mad, but in another it's so horrible knowing what took place in our home." She put the box down and looked up at her friend, tears glistening on her lashes. "These dark stains on the lid are blood, I'm sure of it."

Jenny nodded, "There is a speck or two on the pendant too, see?"

"Oh God, Jen, it's so awful."

"It's ok," Jenny wrapped her arms around Sarah and gave her a hug. "Hang on in there. I know it's worse than awful, but this can be used as evidence. You have to take the box to your policeman friend. He may be able to have it analysed. They must have a forensics team. You were meant to find this, Sarah. Jane has made it happen, led you to this moment. You must see that."

"I know. I'll try to see Simon today. Like you say, we could get lucky. Even if it's not enough for DNA, there might be some of the murderer's fingerprints still on the box.

"Let's hope so."

They put the floorboards in position and rolled back the carpet. No one would ever guess what they had been up to, Sarah thought. Leaving Jenny to replace the crowbar, she took the box in its sack into her bedroom and locked it away in the wardrobe. Pulling off the gloves and dropping them into the wastepaper basket, she went into the bathroom, buried the lower half of her face in a soft cotton bath towel and stared at herself in the mirror over the washbasin. 'You are not mad', she told herself. But no matter how much she tried, she was unable to take in the reality of what she had found; the awesome fact that the visions were telling a story of what had actually taken place in their home. She really had been seeing ghosts; they were not a figment of her imagination.

Overcome with mixed emotions of relief and fear, Sarah splashed water over her face and went to sit on the side of the bed. In all those years, no one had known what had happened here, right up until she and Adam had moved in. She was hopeful, almost convinced, that the box could be used as evidence and that the dark-haired man had made one critical mistake; had not, after all, committed the perfect crime. There were two huge problems: how could he be tied to the murder when she did not know his identity? And even if she did, how could she explain rationally how she had come to know he was involved?

Thoughtfully, Sarah got up from the bed. What had happened to turn the killer into the vile fiend he so obviously was? Was he Paul Morgan's son? The builder had sounded so caring and pleasant on the phone, going out of his way to help her; surely he could not have raised his son to be such a vicious brute? Had the child been bullied or abused? What had happened to him that he could murder a young woman so horrifically? To Sarah, what was even worse was that he appeared to have enjoyed making his victim suffer and had got some kind of insane satisfaction from covering all traces of his crime. In a single act of unspeakable rage, Jane Moore's life had been tragically snuffed out and yet her killer had shown no remorse; had been utterly impassive as he cleared away the evidence.

Maybe her hunch was wrong, Sarah thought, maybe the killer was not Paul Morgan's son at all, but someone else entirely. In which case, where did they go from here? It was like being in a maze, and she was wandering around in the middle of it unable to find her way out. Was the dark-haired man even the murderer? She had not actually witnessed the killing after all: undoubtedly he was involved, but could he be covering for someone else? Clearing up behind their crime?

Sarah gasped as Adam's face popped into her head, the way he had looked in Derby: mottled red, suffused with rage; the way he had suddenly become a frightening stranger capable of extreme violence. Absently she rubbed her wrist where he had grabbed her. Almost overwhelmed by a wave of nausea, she remembered how insistent he had been that they come here to live; buy this particular house. Why this one; why not another? Oh God, no! Surely not!

Shaking, Sarah tried to dispel the thought; it was ridiculous, she was being foolish. He was her husband and he loved her as she loved him. She rushed into the en suite and gulped mouthfuls of cold water straight from the tap. 'Get a grip, girl,' she muttered, drying her hands and making her way slowly, shakily downstairs.

Jenny was sitting in the living room, her hands covering her face. She looked up as Sarah came in. "I feel like some fresh air. Fancy a walk?"

Sarah too felt the need to get out of the house – anything to shake away the dreadful sense of foreboding that had lodged in her mind and was rapidly turning into a thumping headache. "Yes, let's; it's been a hell of a shock. I think I need to clear my head."

The rain had stopped; they walked through the fields behind Sarah's house, pushing through the long, wet grass. A few dun-coloured cows were dotted about on the other side of the hedge, and in the field beyond, a dog walker was negotiating a stile. Aside from that and the distant hum of a tractor, they might have been completely alone in the world.

"It's a lovely spot here," Jenny said, "really peaceful. You are fortunate to have these open areas so close by – despite the distinctly rural smell!"

Sarah smiled, aware that her friend was making a valiant attempt to return to normality. "I know; it's a bit pervasive at this time of year isn't it." She wrinkled her nose and inhaled deeply, beginning to feel more in control of her emotions. "But I've got used to it now. This is a nature conservation area, you know. There's a lot of greenbelt land around the town."

They walked on in silence for a while. Sarah stopped when they reached the stile, said, "Shall we go back now? I could use a coffee – and we've neither of us had breakfast. I might give Simon a ring; see if he can meet up at some point today."

"Good idea; no point in putting it off. I hope he can help. I was planning to set off around midday, but I don't want to leave you on your own, not now. Perhaps I'll go later when Adam gets home."

Sarah turned to her friend, hugged her tightly. "I'll be fine. It's funny, but I don't feel afraid any more. I just want to put poor Jane's soul to rest as soon as I can. You should go, you've got a busy few days coming up; new place, new job. I'll let you know what happens and we can keep in touch by text."

"Well if you're sure."

"I'm sure; don't worry."

After they'd had coffee and a bite to eat - and a giggle over the bouquet of flowers, which they had both forgotten and was now lying dried to a crsip on the back seat of Jenny's car –Jenny had driven away. Sorry to see her friend go, but determined to put a brave face on it, Sarah waved a cheery goodbye. As soon as she could no longer see the car, she went into the living room and dialled Simon's number.

He seemed surprised to hear from her. "None of my business, but I got the feeling Adam was mad at you for talking to me when we saw each other the other day. I rather thought you might have decided to cool it."

"He didn't know it was you," Sarah said hastily. "And yes, I had decided not to get back in touch. It's silly, I know, and I have never given him cause, but Adam is a bit insecure and I think he had some kind of a fit that day. He was probably wound up by the heat and he was tired – he's been flat out at work lately and when he saw me apparently chatting up a stranger he-" Wondering exactly what Simon had seen, Sarah heard herself making excuses for Adam's behaviour and stopped speaking abruptly.

"Like I said, none of my business, so long as you're alright?"

Sarah forced a laugh. "Yes, it was nothing - soon forgotten."

There was a slight pause. "So what can I do for you?"

"I'd rather not talk on the phone, Simon. Could we meet some time today? It's quite urgent." Sarah knew she sounded desperate, but could not help it. Talking to her old friend had brought her close to tears.

Thankfully, Simon asked no questions. "Of course; I've got a cancelled appointment at four. I'll meet you at the small bar in Market Street, you know it?"

"Yes, thank you, Simon. See you at four."

CHAPTER THIRTY EIGHT

Stopping just outside Nottingham to fill up with diesel, Jenny phoned Deirdre, her new landlady, asked for directions and arranged to meet her at the house. Preoccupied with anxiety about Sarah and this morning's find under the floorboards, Jenny was scarcely aware of the journey and it seemed to fly by.

She and Deirdre took to each other straight away and in no time at all they were chatting like old friends. Jenny liked the house; it was a brick-built semi, set back off the road in a small, tree-lined cul-de-sac. She liked her bedroom too; it looked out over a well-tended back garden and was simply but tastefully furnished. There was no en suite, but there was a wash basin in the corner and a pleasantly decorated bathroom adjacent; everywhere looked clean and comfortable. Satisfied that it would suit her very well meantime, Jenny unpacked her case. Deirdre had placed a welcoming vase of carnations on the chest of drawers and there was a 'New Home' card propped against it; it was from her Mum and Dad. Pushing her empty case on top of the wardrobe, Jenny sat on her bed and phoned home.

"How are you Mum? Thanks for the card; the house is great. Deirdre seems really friendly and I'm sure we'll get on. It's such a relief; I can't thank you and Dad enough."

"Well that's good news," Mrs Peters said brightly, "and I've got some more for you. Just as we suspected, your ex-boyfriend has had a nervous breakdown. His elder brother came round earlier to tell us that Vinny has finally agreed to receive treatment and is now on medication. Evidently his doctor has referred him to a psychotherapist and signed him off work until he recovers. I also gather that he's agreed to sell the house and has moved back in with his parents, which is probably the best place for him just now."

Jenny felt her tension draining away. Her relief at learning Vinny was being properly looked after almost brought her to tears.

"Oh, Mum, I'm so relieved. I have been very concerned about him. That's great news – and about the house too. I seriously doubted he would ever agree to sell it after all the hard work we put in."

"I thought you'd be pleased. Dad wondered if you'd like us to sound out a few estate agents and arrange for valuations prior to sale. I'll nip round and make sure the place is clean and tidy first and Vinny's brother said he'll cut the grass. Such a nice boy; he even apologised for all the trouble his brother caused us, but like I said to him, Vinny couldn't help being ill; I just hope he recovers fully and is able to move on. Anyway, love; did you have a good time with Sarah and Adam?"

"Lovely, thanks; I feel tons better – especially now. Yes please, if you're sure you don't mind dealing with the agents, that'd be such a boon. While you're at the house, could you pick up my overnight bag? I left it in the hall – I'd guess it is still there. Only I'm running a bit short of essentials. I'll come over for them at the weekend and bring you back your suitcase."

"Of course we don't mind – and while I'm about it I'll pack up your clothes, shoes, books and things and take them home with me. Dad and I will help you move them into your new place on Sunday. You need to have your own things around you. Good luck for tomorrow, darling."

Oh Mum – what would I do without you? Thank you so much for all your help and support. You and Dad have been great."

Jenny switched off her mobile and lay back on the bed. Suddenly, everything seemed to be going well: she no longer had to worry about Vinny; soon the house would be sold and she would have enough money to get a mortgage on a place of her own. Her relationship with Gary was even better than she had imagined, and the niggling anxiety that she was the person close to Sarah, whom Lola had foreseen was in danger, was no longer valid. And yet, Jenny could not help feeling a wave of sadness as she thought about Vinny. Their relationship had not all been bad and despite everything that had happened, she knew she would miss his friendship. But it was no good dwelling on the past; now she could look forward to the future – and to being with Gary.

Drifting into a light doze, Jenny wondered how Sarah was getting on and whether Simon would be able to identify and trace Jane Moore's killer.

When Sarah walked into the bar, Simon was waiting for her, perched on a stool, a glass of coke in his hand and another at his elbow. Relieved that the pub was all but deserted, Sarah smiled a greeting, "Thank you so much for meeting me at such short notice. I really do appreciate it; I know you must be busy." She knew she sounded formal, but she was too uptight to care. She clung to the carrier bag that held the wooden box, still wrapped in its original cloth sack, and leaned against the bar.

"Not a problem," he said. "I got you a diet coke, is that ok?"

"Yes, lovely, thanks."

"You said it was urgent. What have you been up to?" Eyeing the carrier, Simon grinned, lifted his eyebrow, "What have you got in there – the Crown Jewels?"

Speechless, Sarah shook her head, unable to respond to Simon's quip, which had so nearly hit the mark. She pulled herself together and launched into her story. She had rehearsed what she was going to say: they'd had a radiator leak in one of their bedrooms, taken up the floorboards and found the box. It had obviously been hidden there and contained valuable jewellery. There was a gold dolphin pendant, that appeared to be stained with spots of dried blood. It was a complete mystery how it came to be there, but remembering what the neighbour had said about seeing Jane Moore in their house, she was concerned that this might be something to do with her murder and would like the police to take a look.

Simon listened to her story with an impassive look on his face, his eyebrow shooting even higher, but he made no comment.

"I know this all sounds rather silly, but it really scared me," Sarah finished, wishing she could tell him the truth, but knowing it would do no good even to try.

"Your neighbour's story really got you didn't it. It's all a bit unlikely don't you think?" Simon smiled reassuringly, "And anyway, as I told you, the murderer was convicted and is still serving time. But I can see you're worried about it. Tell you what, I'll check to see if any jewellery has been reported stolen."

"It's not the jewellery I'm concerned about," Sarah snapped, her tension getting the better of her. "It's the blood."

"Ah." Simon nodded. "Why are you so sure it's blood? It's more likely to be paint or nail varnish or something. Maybe it's the previous owner's trinket box and they forgot all about it – or their daughter's – gifts from an unsuitable boyfriend that she didn't want her parents to know about. Is there a brooch in there? She could easily have pricked her finger."

Sarah knew he was trying to be kind. She wondered what she could say to make him take this more seriously. In the end, she elected for honesty. "Look, Simon, I know you must think this is trivial and that I'm being a nuisance, but you know me well enough to realise that I'm not given to flights of fancy. As a favour to me, please, will you just have the pendant checked out – see if it is blood, and if so, whether there is enough for a DNA test to see if it is Jane's? Believe me, I wouldn't ask, but I am really troubled about this. Something about it feels wrong: call it woman's intuition."

"Well, since it's you," Simon smiled, "I'll see what I can do to set your mind at rest – and no, I don't think you're a nuisance, but I do think you are worrying about nothing. Never mind; who am I – a mere man - to question woman's intuition, eh? I'll get it checked out for you. It may take a few days, but I should be able to get back to you by the end of the week."

"Thank you." Relieved, Sarah grasped his elbow. "One more thing; I have not handled the box, I used gloves – just in case there were any fingerprints." As soon as the words were out of her mouth, Sarah knew she had said the wrong thing.

"What extraordinary foresight," Simon said dryly, pursing his lips and looking hard into her eyes. "Almost as if you expected to find something incriminating. Is there something you're not telling me?"

Sarah held his gaze, flushed; tried to retrieve the situation. "That's not what I meant; I had been gardening and happened to still have my gloves on," she lied. "It was only after I saw the blood that I realised how fortuitous it was that I had not handled the box."

Simon looked unconvinced, but shrugged, "If you say so." He drained his glass and held out his hand for the carrier. "I assume it's in there?"

She handed it over, "Yes – still wrapped in its original bag. It's a bit dusty."

Taking it, he looked briefly inside the carrier, nodded and holding it carefully in one hand, drained his glass and eased himself off his stool. "I'm on a tight schedule and really ought to go, but maybe we could...?" for a moment he hesitated, gazed into her eyes, his lips curving in a half smile.

Sarah shook her head, aware of what he was not saying. She could tell from his wistful expression that he did not want to leave, but she was determined to do nothing to encourage him to stay. Since the scene with Adam in Derby, she had successfully expunged her feelings towards Simon: he was her old friend from Uni, nothing more, nothing less; attractive, certainly, but no longer did she view him as a potential threat to her marriage. Whatever it was that had caused her emotional response to him before had gone.

"I can't tell you how much this means to me, Simon," she smiled. "I'm really grateful, but I don't want to take you any longer from your work and in any event, I am keen to get back to my husband."

His rueful smile told her that he understood her unspoken message. He nodded, leaned forward and gave her a chaste peck on the cheek. "Take care then. I'll be in touch about the box soon."

Sarah had been home an hour when she heard Adam coming through the front door. "Hi darling," he said, striding into the kitchen. "What a gorgeous smell; are you cooking?"

"Not personally," she grinned up at him, "though it's true I am a bit hot! I've made shepherd's pie for your supper and your favourite chocolate cake."

Adam laughed and hugged her tightly, eyeing the fruits of her labour. "You sure know how to spoil a man. What have I done to deserve this? It looks great and I'm starving," he reached out to dip a finger in the chocolate topping and Sarah playfully slapped it away.

"Hands off, you can have a slice when you've eaten your pie. I've been busy today. The freezer is stocked up with burgers, sausages and spare ribs ready for the barbecue. You just need to pick up some more beer before the weekend."

"Will do – Carl and Chris said they'll come with their current partners; I'm not sure we've met either of them. Those two lads seem to have had as many girlfriends as I've had hot dinners, the dogs."

"Jealous, darling?"

"Hardly - why should I be jealous when the best girl in town belongs to me?" He bent to kiss her: "You're mine; all mine!"

Sarah smiled, not sure she quite liked the implication that she was a possession, but not wanting to destroy his light hearted mood, she let it pass.

"By the way," Adam said, "hope you don't mind, I've invited Toby and his girlfriend."

"Why should I mind? I'm looking forward to meeting this paragon of yours." Sarah took the pie out of the oven, served a big helping for Adam and sprinkled it with grated cheese, sticking it under the grill for a moment. "You'd better get in a few extra crates of beer if Chris and Carl are coming. I seem to remember they drank us dry last time."

"Good point; I'll do that," Adam laughed. "Who else is coming?"

"Not sure. I expect Gary – the other Gary! - and Rachael will come, and I've pushed an invitation through most of the neighbours' doors, but so far only Sophie opposite has responded; they'd love to come, she said. She seems like a real party girl that one. I have the feeling we'll be in for another late night – or should I say early morning?"

"No worries; we can sleep as long as we want on Sunday." Adam picked up an oven glove and carried his plate into the dining area, sitting himself down at the table. The patio doors were open and a cool breeze wafted in laden with the scent of late honeysuckle.

"I was thinking, Ad," Sarah followed him through. "It will be a good opportunity to sound out our neighbours about keeping an eye on the place while we're in Australia. I'm so looking forward to it – it's getting really close now."

"Me too," Adam said, filling his fork, "and I know I keep saying it, but it'll be the holiday of a lifetime and we've got to push the boat out, we may not get another opportunity." He paused, looked down at his plate, said with studied casualness, "I was wondering if maybe we should think about starting a family when we get back."

Dumbfounded, Sarah wondered if she could have misheard. She gazed at her husband to see if he was serious. He met her look and smiled. "I know I wasn't too keen before, but I think we're about ready now we've got our dream home sorted out, don't you? You can always put your career on hold for a while can't you?"

She nodded wordlessly, barely able take in what Adam was saying, but suddenly aware that she wanted it more than anything.

As if unaware that he had dropped a bombshell, Adam took another mouthful of food, "Mm, this is great; the cheese makes it." Still chewing, he waved his fork at Sarah and smiled, "Actually, darling, I think I might have solved the problem of leaving the house empty."

Lost in thought, she barely heard him. Lola had foretold they would have two children: a boy and a girl. Sarah conjured up images of their faces; the boy a smaller version of Adam and the girl a bit like her Mum. Which one would come first? What names would they choose....?

"Hello, is there anybody there?" Adam teased.

"What? Oh, sorry. The house – yes - how?"

"I think I've talked Toby into house-sitting for us. He said it's fine by him so long as we don't object if his girlfriend comes too; he needs to speak to her before he finally commits himself, but he doesn't think it'll be a problem."

"What a relief," Sarah smiled. "That's really good of him. He's obviously as cute as he looks."

Adam looked down his nose, "Don't say that to his face; I don't think he'd appreciate being called cute, it's a bit insulting for us chaps, you know. Anyway, he seems happy to help out and I trust him; that's the main thing."

"Well I'm glad that's sorted," Sarah tucked into her shepherd's pie. "Now we can really look forward to going away," she said, not voicing the thought that chimed a peal of excitement in her head: *except that now I am looking forward to coming home again!*

Sarah found her work schedule hectic when she returned to the office the following day. There were so many meetings to attend and projects to finish. She barely gave any more thought to Simon or to Jane's murder until late in the afternoon, when it dawned on her that since finding the box there had been no more visions. Did that mean something? Was Jane's spirit secure in the knowledge that at last she was close to getting justice? Tempted to ring Simon, Sarah reached for the phone, thought better of it. What was the point? If he had found something important he would let her know. There might be no prints on the box; the red spots may not have been blood after all. There were so many ifs and buts. Putting it firmly from her mind, she buried herself in her work until her boss, passing her door and noticing Sarah was still at her desk, popped in and said with a smile, "It's half-past-six on a Friday, Sarah. Haven't you got a home to go to?"

Making a quick, apologetic call to Adam to say she was on her way, Sarah shut down her computer, grabbed her things and with a swift glance around the office, hurried down to the car park.

Driving into Bluebell Close, she felt mentally drained. She was ready for a holiday - that was for sure. It was only three weeks away now. At least, she reflected, she had completed all her immediate tasks and the projects were off her desk; she would have a relatively easy time at work next week and would be able to start thinking about what to pack for Australia – just as soon as she had heard back from Simon....

Adam was studying a handful of menus as she entered the kitchen. "I thought we'd have a takeaway tonight since you're so late. What do you fancy - Chinese, Indian, pizza or fish and chips?"

Sarah did not much fancy any of them, but she made an effort, "Let's have Chinese for a change." Adam smiled, whistling to himself. Sarah could sense his excitement; knew he was thinking about Australia.

"Great. I'll call them; I know what you like. You can go and grab a shower if you want and I'll open a bottle of wine. I've been thinking about the holiday today – I can't wait!"

"You don't say," she laughed, kissed him lightly on the lips and went upstairs, checking her mobile for texts yet again and unable to quell her disappointment that Simon had neither called nor left a message. It seemed as if finding the wooden box was going to come to nothing after all. Sarah felt as if she was right back where she had started: Jane's murder no closer to being solved.

The shower helped to lighten her mood; slowly she soaped herself all over, standing under the spray for several minutes and letting the hot water ease her tense shoulders, forcing her to relax. All she now wanted to do was go to bed, but she did not want to disappoint Adam. Slipping into her jeans and a comfortable shirt, Sarah began to feel a little better; she even felt hungry enough to enjoy a Chinese. She was running a brush through her hair when she heard laughter in the hall. Someone was speaking to Adam, but she could not identify the voice. Sarah's heart sank; the last thing she wanted was to be sociable to unexpected visitors: 'Whoever you are, please go away,' she murmured. Checking her face in the mirror, she went downstairs and into the kitchen. A slim woman with long, straight, dark hair stood with her back to Sarah. Damn; it was Sophie; they'd never get rid of her.

"Hi, Sophie," Sarah forced a smile.

The young woman swung round.

Sarah gasped, felt herself falling backwards. As she descended into blackness she heard herself scream.

She came to drenched in sweat and lying on her bed, Adam leaning over her. Raising her arms, she clung to him, trembling. Why had the vision affected her like this; surely she was used to it by now?

"Sarah, are you alright? You fainted; gave us a real fright. Charlotte said you looked as if you'd seen a ghost!"

"Charlotte?" Sarah said weakly, utterly confused. Her heart was beating wildly; her mind grappling with what was happening and not coming up with any sense. Had Adam seen the ghost this time?

Her husband eased her arms away from his neck and dabbed her brow with a cold flannel. "Yes, Toby's girlfriend. They called round to drop off some beer for tomorrow - wanted to help; it's very generous of them."

"Yes, very." Sarah frowned, "I'm sorry, I had a bit of a shock seeing Charlotte standing there. I thought it was Sophie. But I know her Ad – Charlotte, I mean - or at least, I've seen her before, I'm sure of it. I must go and apologise for frightening everyone. Are they still here?" Dazed, she sat up.

"They're in the living room; I've just made them a coffee." Adam's face creased in puzzlement. "I don't know how you could possibly know Charlotte. She's not been around here long. Maybe she just looks like someone else you know – and anyway, why was it such a shock? You've been working too hard, my girl. The sooner we get you away on holiday, the better."

"Yes, sorry," Sarah pushed herself up from the bed and hanging onto Adam's hand, got tentatively to her feet; her knees were wobbling. "Thanks, Ad. Like you say – I'm a bit overtired and I haven't eaten since breakfast."

"Daft girl," he hugged her. "How many times have I told you not to miss lunch?"

"It's ok, I feel much better now." Sarah gave him a weak smile and broke away, almost running down the stairs to the living room. Filled with nervous apprehension, she could not wait to see the young woman again, hoping against hope that she had made a mistake; so afraid that her nightmares and visions were coming to life.

She rushed to the living room doorway, stopped dead in her tracks, unable to move; unable to breath. There, facing her, his face stamped with a sardonic smile, was the dark-haired man.

In a daze, Sarah glanced around the room. It looked perfectly normal; felt warm; there had been no shift in time; nothing to indicate she was not in the present. The man was calmly sipping a cup of coffee. The woman – Charlotte – was beside him on the sofa. She got to her feet as she saw Sarah, her expression filled with concern. The man looked up, said, "Hello, I hope you're feeling better?"

Sarah felt Adam's hand on her shoulder; he pushed the door wide open and directed her carefully to the armchair. Like an automaton she sat down, unable to take in what she was seeing; her mind grappling with the enormity of the evidence before her eyes: this was no vision. These people were real; flesh and blood.

"Sarah, this is Toby and Charlotte," Adam said gently.

She gasped, shrieked, "Toby? No, it's not; this isn't Toby; it can't be."

The dark-haired man laughed sending a chill up Sarah's spine; the last time she had heard that laugh, he had been holding a knife.

"I'm definitely Toby," he smiled, "and this is definitely my girlfriend, Charlotte."

"You will have to excuse my wife," Adam's face had turned crimson. He looked across at his colleague and gave an apologetic smile. "She's not been well lately; been knocking herself out at work and I think her blood sugar levels are down around zero!"

Sarah heard her husband's embarrassed explanation; knew how silly she must sound. Obviously the person she had glimpsed at her husband's workplace was another of his colleagues; not this one. As she stared at the murderer's face, all the images came flooding back. She was aware that her hands were shaking and tried to still them.

"Are you feeling better now?" Charlotte asked softly. "Can I get you anything – a glass of water?"

Tearing her mesmerized gaze away from Toby, Sarah faced his girlfriend. While the dark-haired man had changed slightly - as handsome as before, but older; his hair now very short with telltale strands of grey and around his eyes a web of fine lines - Charlotte looked exactly the same as when, lit up by a flash of lightening, she had sat on the floor in front of the patio doors. The same as she had that night when the taxi had almost run her over. The significance hit Sarah with the force of a sledgehammer.

"No, thanks," Sarah heard herself say. "I'm feeling much better, thank you. Forgive me, I don't mean to be rude, but as Adam says, I've not been very well lately; had a few fainting spells. The doctor says it is stress and nothing to worry about. I don't know what came over me back then. I'm so sorry."

Sarah heard the words coming out of her mouth and could not believe how calm she sounded. Her brain had gone into overdrive, putting all the pieces together and generating a lot more questions. Was this man Paul Morgan's son? Was it just pure coincidence that he was working for her husband or had he engineered it? The image of Charlotte being attacked during the thunderstorm stayed at the forefront of her mind.

Suddenly the puzzle clicked into place and Sarah knew, as though Lola was there in the room speaking into her ear, that Charlotte was indeed the person close to her who needed her help: close to her physically; just across the room. The vision of Charlotte had been of the future, not of the past. If these two people were to stay here house-sitting, this young woman would be in mortal peril. This was what Jane's spirit had been warning her about: Jane, who knew only too well just how violent this man could be and had somehow known that by some bizarre twist of fate, history was about to repeat itself and only she, Sarah, had the power to change it.

Smiling sympathetically, Charlotte sat on the sofa and turned her attention to the two men, who were standing by the patio doors chatting about Australia. Covertly watching Toby, Sarah could see how charming he appeared. She found his magnetic sexuality oppressive, yet could clearly understand why women - especially young women like Jane and Charlotte - were inexorably drawn to him. She suppressed a shudder: drawn into a spider's web by a husk of a man whom she knew to be devoid of any shred of human kindness. Yet to look at him, no one would ever imagine he was capable of committing brutal, vicious murder. Even her husband, usually such a good judge of character, had been completely taken in by him, and Charlotte, whom Sarah guessed was not much older than twenty-one, was clearly besotted.

Sarah sat back in the chair and moulded her face into an expression of polite attentiveness, but inside she was seething with anger. How dared this vile beast scheme to get into her home, hoodwinking her husband in order to revisit the scene of his crime: the place where he had so pitilessly killed Jane Moore. As she studied him, he glanced across at her; it was a look of such venom that Sarah gasped, terrified. Surely he could not know that she knew? Dropping her gaze, she concentrated on overcoming her fear; knew she was close to tears. She sent out an unspoken plea: *I need help; somebody please help me!*

In that moment Sarah felt the now familiar prickling on her skin as it sprang into goose bumps. Had Jane responded to her plea, was her spirit here now, watching? Out of the corner of her eye, Sarah caught a movement on the opposite wall. Glancing quickly across the room she saw a formless, misty shadow. Before her eyes it wavered, grew stronger, seemed to materialise into the figure of an old man; a corpulent old man with a long white beard who looked like Father Christmas. Transfixed, Sarah gazed at him as he came into focus. He smiled at her; a wide, warming smile then, in the blink of an eye he was gone.

Sarah swallowed hard, stared at the wall. Had it been her imagination? A shadow cast by the trees dancing in the breeze beyond the patio. She looked down at her hands; they had stopped trembling. Suddenly she no longer felt afraid, it was as though someone had hugged her; given her the strength she needed. Sarah knew beyond the shadow of a doubt that her grandfather's spirit was with her; he had been here with her all along, helping her – just as Lola had said he would – as she, in turn must help Charlotte; save her life. The only thing she could do was to try to expose the dark-haired monster for what he really was.

With newfound resolve, Sarah waited for a gap in the conversation and smiled across at Toby. She knew the smile did not reach her eyes, but she kept her voice calm and pleasant. "So, Toby, Adam tells me you've only recently qualified as an accountant. Did you change career?"

His eyebrow shot up in surprise, "Yes, I've tried a few things."

"Oh? What?"

"This and that; I started off as a quantity surveyor, but decided it wasn't for me."

"Oh, where was that?"

"In Yorkshire," he said shortly.

"Really? I had the feeling it was around here."

Toby looked slightly discomfited, his laughter false, "Don't know what gave you that idea. I'm new to this area; a Yorkshire man through and through."

"Must have lost your accent along the way, then," Sarah gave a cold smile. "So where did you live in Yorkshire?"

"Leeds," he said, sounding slightly nettled.

"Leeds? And your family - they come from there?"

He nodded.

"Why surveying? Is your father in the building trade?"

"Yes, he was hoping I'd join the family firm, but I wanted to get away."

"That must have a disappointment for him. So what made you decide to become an accountant in Nottingham? Rather an unusual step for a quantity surveyor to take I would have thought. Was it that you didn't make the grade?"

Adam grunted, broke in. "That's enough, Sarah! What's with the inquisition? You're making our guests feel uncomfortable."

"Just trying to make polite conversation, darling," Sarah smiled. Her palms were sweating and she knew she had blushed under her husband's stern gaze.

Toby shook his head and smiled at Adam, "I really don't mind, but I'm afraid we'll have to carry on this conversation tomorrow evening – that is, if we're still invited? Anyway, Charlie and I have to get going now. We're meeting friends later." He moved towards Sarah and held out his hand, "Nice to meet you at last."

Sarah pretended not to see it; there was no way she could bring herself to touch this vile man, never mind shake him by the hand. With his back towards Adam he was looking down at her coldly, his eyes like chips of ice, hard and challenging. She felt hypnotised, like a rabbit caught in the headlights, unable to break free of his gaze. She shivered and knew from the way his lips lifted in a slight sneer that he was aware of it. She felt her heart start to bang in her chest; the bile welling in her throat.

With a shrug Toby turned back to Adam, "I think your wife should be in bed, Adam; she really doesn't look at all well. Maybe you should postpone the barbecue?"

"No way," Adam said, giving Sarah a hard stare. "Once again, you will have to excuse my wife. She isn't herself for some reason. I daresay hot food and a good night's sleep will sort her out. Thank you both for coming round, it was really kind of you to bring the beer. I'll show you out." As he spoke, Adam ushered the couple towards the door.

Watching them go Sarah noticed Charlotte looking back over her shoulder with a questioning glance. For a brief moment the two women held each other's gaze, then Charlotte, giving a small shrug, followed Adam and Toby into the hall.

CHAPTER THIRTY NINE

Intending to call Jenny, Sarah went immediately upstairs. She knew Adam would be up in a minute to read her the riot act for being so rude, but she could hear him still talking to Toby on the front step. She retrieved her mobile and saw there was a missed call: it was Simon's number. He had left a voice message asking her to ring him as soon as possible.

Sarah heard a car drive away and moments later Adam's heavy tread on the stairs. Calls to both Simon and Jenny would have to wait, she thought, reluctantly putting away her mobile and resigning herself to face up to her husband's anger.

To her amazement, Adam came forward and drew her to him, hugging her tightly. "My poor darling; that was so unlike you; you must be feeling rotten. Toby and Charlotte understand, knew you didn't mean to be so rude. They are both concerned about you. Do you want to go straight to bed or could you manage some food? I think you should if you can. I've ordered the Chinese. They said it will be ready in about half an hour." He held her away from him, smoothed a strand of hair back from her face. "Actually, you're looking a bit better than you did. How do you feel now? I'm so worried about you."

"Don't be; I feel heaps better. I'm sorry if I upset your colleague. I'm sure Toby is great to have around the office, Ad, but there's something about him that seems kind of false. I can't explain it, but he made my skin crawl and I would prefer it if he didn't come here again."

Adam was clearly astounded. He shook his head, "You can't mean that. There's nothing about him to dislike. I think your judgement is a bit distorted darling. You've been working too hard and not eating enough - you are getting to feel like a bag of bones. You're not bulimic are you? I know you've been sick a few times lately. You really must look after yourself more. You're knocking yourself out and I think you should give up work when we get home, especially if... well, you know..." He sighed, scratched his head, "I so wanted you and Toby – and Charlotte too, of course – to get on. Maybe when you get to know him a bit better? I can't possibly stop him from coming to the barbecue, not now."

Adam's disappointment was more than Sarah could bear. In an effort to placate him, she forced herself to lie. "I expect you're right. Don't take any notice of me. He's probably very nice, and I really liked Charlotte. Even so, I'm not sure I want them looking after our home while we're away. I don't know him at all – and nor do you outside of work. It will be like having strangers sleeping in our bed and I'm really not happy with that, Ad. The neighbours can have the keys. They will look after things for us I'm sure. If you'll agree to that, I promise I'll behave myself tomorrow and make an effort to be nice to your precious Toby," she forced a smile.

To her relief, Adam nodded. "That's a fair point – I can understand your not wanting strangers in our bed if that's how you feel. Ok, I'll go and make us some drinks: hot milk for you tonight, my girl."

"Not sure it goes with noodles and I'd really rather have some wine. By the way, what's Toby's surname? You've never mentioned and I forgot to ask." Sarah knew what he would say; indeed, she wondered briefly why she had bothered to ask the question at all.

"Morgan; Toby Morgan."

As soon as her husband had gone to fetch the takeaway, Sarah, with a sigh of relief, called Simon's mobile.

He answered right away. "Hi. You must be psychic; I was just about to call you again."

"Sorry, I've been a bit tied up. Is it about the box?"

"Yes. It's a good job I'm owed a few favours and was able to pull some strings. Forensics are up to their eyeballs in work and it could have taken weeks. As it is I got the results back from the lab today. Are you ready for this? Or should I say, are you sitting comfortably?" he chuckled.

"More than ready. For goodness sake, tell me." Sarah tried to keep the irritation out of her voice.

"Ok then: you were right. The red spots on the necklace were blood. Through DNA profiling we were able to confirm it actually belonged to Jane Moore, the murder victim – you were right again, though goodness knows how you knew. I could use a piece of that woman's intuition I can tell you! It seems as if your neighbour might have been right too."

Sarah gasped, shut her eyes.

There was a pause. "You ok Sarah?"

"Yes, sorry. I was just trying to take it all in. It's scary. I'm amazed the lab managed to get any results on such a small – not to mention old - sample."

"It amazes me too, but technology has advanced no end. They said the blood had been well protected by the box or it might have deteriorated too far. Even more interesting, the guys also managed to lift some fingerprints off both the box and the pendant. Most were Jane's, but there were others. We checked the database and found a match: they belong to a man named Toby Morgan. He has a police record. He was involved in a couple of cases of domestic violence a few years ago. Presumably this is the man your neighbour saw. It begins to look as though Jane's boyfriend was wrongly convicted. We are opening up the case again. Would your neighbour be willing to come forward?"

Momentarily overwhelmed by Simon's news, Sarah realised what he had asked and panicked. "I really don't think she would want to do that. She is very shy and introvert – almost a recluse. Could she be left out of it?"

"She didn't seem like that before; didn't you say she went to the police ten years ago? I thought she wanted her moment of glory. Odd thing, though, that nobody took a statement from her. There's nothing on the case file about her at all. What is her name?"

"Look, Simon, could you just take my word for the fact that she would not be a reliable witness? Besides which, I don't think you will need her. I forgot to mention that I have unearthed a photo of Jane and a man whom I know to be this Toby Morgan. They seem totally at ease together and were obviously in a relationship. It looks as though somebody once tried to destroy it."

"They would be very useful to have. Could you bring it in? But tell me, how in the hell do you know it's Morgan?"

Sarah ignored the question. "Have you got enough evidence to arrest him?"

"Enough to bring him in for questioning, certainly – but like I said before, Sarah, what aren't you telling me? What's going on?"

"You wouldn't believe me if I told you. Maybe one day – but for now, you'll just have to trust me."

"I suppose I will, but only for now. There are a lot of questions I would love to have answered, but time is of the essence. Obviously it goes without saying that this is all highly confidential. Please don't speak to anyone about it. Nobody at all; is that understood?"

"Ok."

"I'll get back in touch as soon as I can. Sorry this had to happen and that you have somehow got caught up in it. Speaking as a friend, don't let it spoil your joy in your new home, Sarah. It was all a long time ago. I just wish you'd be straight with me. I'm so afraid you're involved in some kind of trouble."

"Still speaking as a friend – or as a policeman?"

"I told you – a friend. I'm worried about you."

Hearing his anxiety, Sarah relented. "Look, if it will stop you worrying, I can tell you that something awesomely surreal has happened to me. I have met someone called Toby Morgan – he was here in my house - today. He is a colleague of Adam's. You might think it's some sort of bizarre coincidence, but I disliked him intensely. More importantly, the photo I just mentioned of Jane with a man? I recognised him immediately. The Toby Morgan I met today was the man in the photo. I'm convinced he murdered Jane Moore and has deliberately engineered his way here to revisit the scene of his horrific crime. Don't ask me how I know that, but I'm willing to stake my life on it."

"Awesome indeed, but as it happens, I don't believe in coincidences." Simon chuckled, "Surreal you say? I begin to think I was right about you being psychic; I could almost think it was supernatural, except that I don't believe in all that nonsense either! You'd best give me the name and address of your husband's place of work. I'll check it out. And Sarah – if you're right about this, be careful. Whatever you do, don't let this Morgan chap know what you've told me and call me if you're worried about anything - anything at all."

After Simon had rung off, Sarah sat on the side of the bed, biting her nails. *I hope you're hearing this Jane!* What if the police demanded to talk to her fictitious neighbour? How could she say the old woman did not exist, but was a figment of her imagination? Worse, how could she say she had actually seen detailed visions of the murderer and was being helped by a ghost and the spirit of her grandfather? Simon clearly did not believe in the supernatural; he had said so. Sarah so wanted to call Jenny, but she knew she would not be able to resist sharing the news with her best friend and Simon had been serious when he told her not to tell anybody, so she switched off her mobile, put it away and made her way downstairs. Deep in thought, not watching where she was going, mid-way down, she slipped.

With a scream, she fell to the bottom of the stairs, her leg twisting beneath her, the pain indescribable as she hit her head on the newel post and passed out.

Sarah came to in a hospital bed. Her leg was in plaster, strapped up to a pulley. Adam was sitting at the bedside, his face stained with tears.

"Adam," she whispered.

"Oh, my poor baby; thank God. I thought you'd never come back to me."

"What happened?"

"You must have tripped on the stairs and landed awkwardly. You've fractured your ankle and torn a ligament, and you've had a nasty bump on the head."

"How stupid - I feel so tired," Sarah gave her husband a wan smile. "I guess I've scuppered the barbecue. I'm sorry, Ad."

"The barbecue is not important," he smiled, "but hey - I would have told Toby not to come if I'd known you felt *this* strongly; you didn't have to go to these lengths you know."

Speechless, Sarah could not respond to her husband's weak attempt at a joke. She caught hold of his hand, said, "Don't trust him, Adam, he's evil. Don't let him bring Charlotte into our house. Please, please..."

"Hush, my love, don't try to talk. You don't know what you're saying. They've put you on strong painkillers; you can't think straight. Get some sleep now. You will probably be able to come home in a day or two, but they want to do a few tests to make sure your head is ok first."

"Will you stay with me?"

"Of course."

She was allowed home on Sunday evening. Still not used to crutches, she waited for Adam to help her into the house. He had been uncharacteristically quiet; preoccupied though gentle and attentive. He was clearly worried about something as he eased her down onto the sofa and tucked a rug over her.

"What is it, Ad? Don't tell me I've ruined our holiday too. I couldn't bear it."

"No, you should have this cast off before then. The Doc said they have a new kind of cast now, made of plastic, which you can clip on and off. It's lightweight and means you can take it off to have a bath and for sleeping. He said that as long as you don't plan to go trekking and are content to lie around on the beach, it should be fine. I told him I thought you'd probably be prepared to make the sacrifice," he grinned. "So if it seems to be healing well in a couple of weeks, they'll cut this one off and fit you up with a plastic one. The Doc seemed pretty optimistic. Don't worry."

"That's a relief. So what is worrying you? I know you are upset about something. You might as well tell me what it is."

"I didn't want to trouble you with it."

"With what? Adam, please!"

"It's Toby."

"What about him?"

"Well, I can hardly believe it and I'm sure there must be some mistake, but he's been arrested. I can't find out why. I can't imagine what he's supposed to have done, but the police are being very close-mouthed. Ah well," he shrugged. "I suppose I'll find out soon enough. Like I say, it's bound to be some mistake. If you're ok, I think I'll go up and have a shower. Before I forget, here's your bag." He put Sarah's bag on the floor where she could reach it, bent to kiss her and went upstairs.

Adam was still in the shower when Simon contacted Sarah on her mobile.

Before he could speak, she said, "Simon, hi, I gather you've arrested Toby Morgan?"

"Yes, thanks to you – and what is more, he has confessed to the murder of Jane Moore. He's mentally unstable; looked as if he was going to pass out when we said we'd found the wooden box of jewellery with his prints and Jane's blood all over it. Then apparently he started leaping about like a madman, clapping his hands, shrieking about how clever the police are. He thought he'd committed the perfect crime, boasted about how he'd cut up Jane's body and hidden all the evidence. They'll lock him up in some institution for sure; the shrink says he would almost certainly have murdered again, if indeed he hasn't already done so. There was no hint of remorse. The guy is pure evil. By the way, that photo - you didn't bring it, but we hardly need it now. You'll be pleased to know that Robert Taylor has been released and will doubtless receive hefty compensation."

"That's good news. Thank goodness I found that box."

"Indeed – and we have to thank your neighbour too, don't we," Simon chuckled. "Tell you what, let's meet up for a drink tomorrow and you can tell me all about her and how you were so certain Robert Taylor was innocent. Did she tell you that too, eh? She's an amazing woman this neighbour of yours. I can't wait to meet her!"

Sarah knew when she was being teased; Simon had somehow guessed that she had not been straight with him and knew the neighbour did not exist, but it did not matter any more, and she had the perfect excuse not to meet him without hurting his feelings. So she told him about her fall and that she was confined to the house until they left for Australia. Cutting across his regretful concern, she thanked him profusely for all his help, wished him well and ended the call.

For the first time in weeks, Sarah glowed with an inner sense of wellbeing. It was all over. Finally, Jane Moore's spirit could rest in peace and Charlotte, distressed though she must be about Toby, was no longer in danger of her life. Sarah shifted to a more comfortable position and drew the rug down to cover her cold toes peeping out from the cast. She thought suddenly of Lola: the medium deserved to know that every single one of her predictions had come true; she would send her a card. And she wanted to call Jenny, but first she must tell Adam - everything. He deserved to know what had really been happening to his wife recently, the truth about Toby; the fact that their perfect home was not so perfect after all. After all this they would probably have to move. There were far too many bad memories here; it was no longer the house where she wanted to bring up their children.

Sarah heard Adam's footsteps on the stairs and looked up with a smile as he came into the living room. She would never be able explain why this had happened to her. She was Sarah Miller: an ordinary person. Unlike Lola, she was not psychic – it was just that somehow she had struck a chord with the lost spirit that had haunted this place.

"You look happy." Returning her smile, Adam dropped to the floor beside the sofa, his long legs drawn up beneath him, his hand resting over hers. "Oh, by the way, I meant to mention and forgot. That painting you were asking about. I found it at the bottom of the garden under a shrub, but it's in rather a bad state I'm afraid. Someone has broken the frame and gouged a hole in the woman's face. I can't imagine how it happened. Such a shame; I suppose it must have been vandals, but how they got into the house without us knowing and why they only took that one painting and nothing else is a complete mystery. It doesn't make any sense at all and I wonder if-"

Sarah reached to press her fingers against his lips. "Hush, Ad, my darling husband, and I'll tell you."

She smiled sadly – it was just so hard knowing where to begin.